A DAVINA RAVINE PSYCHIC CRIME THRILLER

SIX WAYS

A DEADLY MAZE

KAYLIE HUNTER

Cover design by Deranged Doctor Design,
www.derangeddoctordesign.com

Editing service by:
Sheryl Lee, Books Go Social

My amazing beta reader team:
Judy Gonzales and Kathie Ziegler

BOOKS BY KAYLIE

KELSEY'S BURDEN SERIES
Living a life of lies, ex-cop Kelsey Harrison is on the hunt for her enemies—the people responsible for taking her son. A crime thriller series layered in lies, love, friendship, and revenge.

SLIGHTLY OFF BALANCE
When small-town baker Deanna Sullivan finds herself in danger, Reel Thurman returns home, vowing to protect her.

DIAMOND'S EDGE
Raised on the wrong side of the law, Diamond Campbell knows how to navigate within the criminal world. And when someone targets her in a deadly game of cat and mouse, they'll get what's coming to them.

DAVINA RAVINE PSYCHIC CRIME SERIES
Amateur psychic Davina Ravine is in over her head, stumbling her way from one mystery to the next, while unraveling dark family secrets.

BOOKSBYKAYLIE.COM

To ensure you never miss a new release, register for Kaylie's newsletter. Just scroll to bottom of our website and enter your email address

Chapter One

"GET ON WITH IT," I told myself, moving my hand to the van's door. I stalled again, my fingers refusing to pull the lever.

Sighing, I leaned my head against the head rest and snuggled into the bucket seat. At least the van, though older and a beast on gas, was more comfortable than my truck. And seatless in the back, it had ample space to haul things from point A to point B.

Bernadette had gifted me the van after the feds impounded my truck as evidence in a murder case. Since then, they'd released the truck back to me but I sold it to Noah. He unbolted the back seat, threw it in the fire pit, and declared the truck good as new. I still cringed when I saw it, remembering the dead woman in the back, but to each their own.

A knock on the window startled me. Breydon stood on the other side of the glass giving me a look—one I'd seen him direct at his sons often but had never been on the receiving end of.

"Come on," Breydon said, opening my door. "Everyone's waiting."

I reluctantly slid out, my feet hitting the pavement as my shoulders sagged. "Can't this wait until next week?"

"Nope." Breydon shut my door and guided me with a firm hand on my elbow around the front of the van into the dewy grass. "It's time. We need you to decide what to do next."

"But I don't want to," I whined, mimicking Olivia's pouty tone.

Breydon grinned. "Have you seen it yet? The damage?"

I nodded, glancing up at the two-story building. One end of the building, the end closest to Edgar Park, looked like a charred marshmallow—courtesy of the angry mob who'd lit it on fire. "I came out last night after you called me."

"You should've told me. I would've met you out here."

"Which would've defeated the point of coming out alone. I didn't want anyone to see me cry." I gave Breydon a sad smile.

I'd successfully avoided the construction site for three weeks, not wanting to face it. But last night, as expected, when I walked around the building I'd bawled my eyes out, filling my pockets with snotty tissues.

"Davina!" a male voice shouted from behind us.

I turned, seeing Lance in his old farm truck. He poked his head out his window, shouting to me, "Thought we were meeting at your house this morning?"

"We are, but I have to do this first. Come join us."

Lance looked around before swerving his truck across the street, parking it facing the wrong way in front of my van. He hopped out, jogging over to us. "What's going on here?"

"Whiskey and Breydon want to discuss next steps."

"Ah," Lance said.

"Morning," Virgil, Whiskey's second in command, hollered from the front sidewalk.

Whiskey stood beside Virgil and gave me his usual nod of greeting.

"Morning," I said.

"Thanks for meeting us," Whiskey said. "I know you wanted to put construction on hold until the insurance claim was settled, but we've got some concerns."

"Concerns like the gaping holes in the walls and roof?" I asked, smirking.

"Pretty much," Virgil said, wearing a big grin. I'd only met Virgil a few times, but I liked him. He was quick to laugh, and from what I'd seen, he was a hard worker. "Let's head inside the first unit."

Everyone followed Virgil through the front door of the first-floor apartment. On both ends of the building were one-bedroom apartments, one on the first floor and one above it on the second floor. Between the apartment end units were four townhomes that had common living areas on the first floor and bedrooms on the second floor.

I gasped, seeing the blackened hole in the ceiling of the first-floor apartment. Moving under it, I could see all the way up through the roof to the morning sky. "This looks worse inside than outside."

"The insurance claim is in motion," Breydon said. "But you know the drill. It could take months before the claim is paid."

"You mean, *if it's paid*," I said, moving to the back wall to take a closer look at the charred stud wall. Before the fire, the contractors had just begun to hang the drywall. "I wouldn't be surprised if the insurance company tries to wiggle out of paying since the police couldn't pin down who actually threw the flaming liquor bottle."

"That section of the roof above you isn't stable," Whiskey said, guiding me back toward the apartment's dining room.

I took another step back, just to be safe. "Good to know."

"What happened to all the people who were arrested?" Virgil asked.

Breydon scowled. "Everyone who took part in the mob got a slap on the wrist—community service and fines." Breydon was still angry they'd gotten off so easy, which I thought was a little funny since he was a defense attorney.

"I understand why the prosecutor made the deals," I said. "It's not like anyone who was arrested was a career criminal. They were, for the most part, good people who did something dumb because they were scared and angry."

"You give those hooligans too much credit," Lance said. "But I sure am glad the charges against everyone else were dropped."

Friends, local business owners, and a few of the guys from Silver Aces Security were also arrested that night. They'd used their fists to push back the mob, making room for the fire department to reach the building. Lance's son Eric, the town's go-to mechanic, was part of that second group.

"Me too," I said, shifting my attention to Whiskey. "Okay, let's get this over with. How'd the inspection for the foundation go?"

"Good. We didn't find any heat or water damage. As you can see, the fire had just reached this first-floor unit, so it didn't get to the basement. The apartment above us is mostly gone." Whiskey turned and pointed to the long interior wall, the one bordering the next unit which was one of the two-bedroom townhomes. "Upstairs, the townhome next door got a little crispy and most of its roof is gone and part of the walls. We'll need to tear out these two apartments and the second floor of the townhome."

Virgil lifted a thumb over his shoulder, pointing it away from Edgar Park. "The other three townhomes and the apartments at the far end of the building just have smoke damage, but we'll need to hire a certified smoke restoration company to clean them."

"Just so happens that I'm certified," I said, wrapping the sides of my zip-up hoodie tighter around me to block out the cold draft from all the open windows. "It's a lot of work, though."

"Since when are you afraid of a little work?" Lance asked, nudging me.

"I'm not afraid of it. I'm just not sure I want to invest my time."

"Are you changing your mind about keeping the building?" Whiskey asked.

Was I? I wondered. I'd told myself at least a hundred times that it was *only a building*, but it felt like a lie. The construction site had become a symbol of the new life I'd planned for myself. A life with financial freedom and respect in a community where I'd always felt shunned. But it was difficult to ignore the fact that an angry mob had set out to destroy that future.

"You all right?" Lance asked, putting a hand on my shoulder.

I nodded before looking back at Whiskey. "Honestly, part of me wants to sell. Part of me wants to run away and hide from this mess. But the rest of me is still angry— angry because people I've known my whole life did this.

Destroyed what I was trying to build." I waved a hand at the blackened wall.

"Not destroyed, kiddo," Lance said, squeezing my shoulder. "Just a little scorched on one end is all."

"Use that anger," Whiskey said, shrugging. "Let it fuel you to do the restoration work."

"Sounds good on paper, but I'm not sure I've got enough anger to last the hundreds of hours it'll take to clean this mess."

"That's fair," Virgil said. "But whether you sell or not, we still need to decide what to do about the roof. Winter's coming."

He was right. Letting the building fill up with snow wouldn't exactly help me get top dollar if I listed the building for sale. At best, the building would have more water damage than what the hoses from the fire trucks caused. At worst, come spring, mold could take over.

"Let's head back outside," Whiskey said, nodding toward the door.

We all shuffled back out the door into the yard and looked up at the building.

I'd come too far to just let the building rot. "How much money are we talking to button up the walls and roof before winter?"

Virgil handed me a clipboard. "We wrote up two quotes. One is to tack up enough lumber to nail tarps to, and the other is to reframe the roof and exterior walls, add decking boards, and tarp over everything."

Lance leaned over my shoulder looking at the quotes while I read them. I liked the price on the first one, but one good snowstorm could rip the tarps off, leaving the roof and walls exposed again. It was risky.

The second quote, the one to reframe and board up the building was more expensive, but not as expensive as I thought it would be. I could afford it, thanks to the payouts on my father's life insurance and the insurance claim for the housefire that destroyed my childhood home, but I'd earmarked that money to buy a small house in case I decided to move out of the Zenner house. And since I'd closed my cleaning business, I was also leaning on my savings to buy groceries and pay the electric bill.

"Look at it this way," Lance said, moving the second bid on top of the cheaper one. "If you decide to sell the building, you should recoup most of your money."

"True," I said, nodding. "Okay, fine."

Lance pulled a pen from his shirt pocket. I took it and signed off, approving the work. "Give me a minute to transfer funds so I can write a check."

"I'm not worried about the check," Whiskey said, taking the clipboard. "We can settle up later."

"I'll call the lumberyard and order the materials," Virgil said. "With a little luck, we can get it delivered by tomorrow morning."

"Sounds good," I said. "Meet at my place next?"

"We'll be right behind you," Whiskey said as he and Virgil shifted back toward the street.

"I'm heading back to my office," Breydon said, shifting toward Edgar Park.

"Do you need a ride?"

"No thanks," Breydon called out. "Nice morning for a walk."

Lance and I moved back toward our vehicles.

"What's on the agenda at the Zenner house?" Lance asked.

"Whiskey and Virgil are meeting us to go over the work I need to contract out, and I wanted you around in case they had questions about our remodeling plan." I peeked over at Lance, grinning. "I also need you to look at the wall I built. I'm not sure how to fix it."

"What's wrong with it?"

"You'll see." I laughed, pivoting toward my van.

Chapter Two

I EYED STONE'S TRUCK PARKED along the front curb, driving past it to pull into my driveway. Stone strolled into view, waiting for me in the patch of grass between the garage and the house. I hopped out of the van, moving toward him. "It's not even eight in the morning. What brings you here so early?"

Stone held up a file. "Wanted to run something by you, but I see you're in the middle of things." He nodded toward Lance, Whiskey, and Virgil who were crossing the front yard.

"Is it something quick?" I asked.

"It'll only take five minutes, but it can wait," Stone said.

"How come you never park in the garage?" Lance asked.

"Because of this." I walked over to one of the garage overhead doors and raised it before stepping back. Half the garage was jam packed with wooden furniture, some of which was stacked on top of each other.

Stone, Lance, Virgil, and Whiskey all moved into the garage, looking around.

"What is all this?" Stone asked.

"I went yard sale shopping last weekend," I said with a dramatic sigh. "My plan was to restock my limited wardrobe, but I kept finding ridiculous deals on real-wood furniture. People were practically giving it away. Apparently, no one refinishes furniture anymore."

"It's a lot of work," Whiskey said, walking over to inspect a table. "But it's worth it. Can't buy furniture like this anymore. Everything nowadays is made with particle board."

Lance pulled out an old rocking chair, moving it to the empty side of the garage. Turning, he sat in the chair, testing it out. "How much for this chair?"

"I paid eight dollars, but if you like it, let me know what color stain you want, and you can have the chair after I re-stain it."

Lance ran a hand over the chair's arm. "It'd be nice if it was refinished in maybe a dark brown, but I'll pay you for your time."

"Walnut, chestnut, or espresso?" I asked.

Lance gave me a look like I was asking a dumb question.

"Okay then, I'll figure out the color, but you're not paying me—unless of course you're changing your mind and agree to *me paying you* for teaching me all this remodeling stuff."

Lance grumbled, but then rocked again before smiling.

"I might be interested in that table," Whiskey said, pointing. "I just need to get my better-half's approval first."

"Smart man," Lance said, standing. "Well, fellas," he said, nodding toward the house. "What do you say, I take you boys inside while Davina talks to Stone?"

"I'll only be a few minutes," I said.

"Take your time," Whiskey said with another glance at the furniture. "I have a feeling when we're done, we'll be back out here to look around some more."

"Works for me," I said.

"I've got dibs on that desk," Virgil said, pointing at said desk before following behind Lance toward the house.

"Dang it. I'd hoped you hadn't seen that," Whiskey said, chuckling. After another glance around the garage, he moved toward the house, hurrying his steps to catch up.

I looked back at Stone, but he was leaning inside the garage, his eyes scanning the furniture. "Not you too?"

"Can't help it. You've got some nice stuff in there. Did you really only pay eight bucks for that rocking chair?"

"Yes, sir. Everything except for a couple of dressers was ten dollars or less."

Stone shook his head, smiling. "Mrs. Paulson taught you well."

I laughed, leaning against the outside wall of the garage. "That she did. Since I'm currently jobless, I figured, what the heck. At least I'll make a little side money." I raised my hand to shield my eyes from the morning sun. "So? What's up? What can I help you with?"

Stone looked down at the file folder he was holding, hesitating a moment before passing it to me. "I've got a runaway case I need your opinion on."

I opened the file, seeing a school photo of a teenage girl clipped inside. "Who is she? I don't recognize her."

"Addison Randall, but she goes by Addy. She ran away sometime after school yesterday. I spent half the night tracking down teachers and classmates, but nobody has seen her since school let out."

"It's barely morning. Isn't it a little soon to worry?" I pointed to the girl's picture. "She's what? Fifteen? Sixteen?"

"Sixteen, but every case is different. Addy's never run away before and I still need to rule out the possibility of an abduction."

"But you don't think that's what happened?"

"It's unlikely, but who knows."

If she ran away, she'd likely return home in a day or two, but I could understand Stone's reluctance to think like that. If someone took her, he'd lose precious time finding her if he made that assumption. "Does she go to school in Daybreak Falls?"

"No. She lives on the dividing line between Daybreak Falls and the city, so she goes to school in the city."

I frowned at Stone. "You make it sound like the choice is obvious—that everyone would pick the city schools."

"Sorry," Stone said, raising both hands with his palms facing me. "My city-boy mentality hasn't completely washed off yet."

My attention returned to the girl's picture. Unlike most students posing for their school photo, Addy didn't smile. In fact, the pinched look on her face made me think she wanted to flip off the photographer.

She was pretty, with long black hair worn pinned back from her face in sections by small clips. Behind bold, red-framed glasses, dark eyeliner and eyeshadow accented her wide brown eyes. Her clothes, what I could see of them in the photo, were all black. With her sitting at an angle, I could only see one ear, but it had a half dozen piercings running up and around it.

I grinned at the photo. Her goth girl meets nerd persona was a bold but fun statement that took a lot of self-confidence to pull off.

I flipped the picture up, reading the page under it. "Did she go home after school?" I asked while skim reading her school transcript which detailed that except for gym, she was a straight A student.

"Her workaholic father doesn't know. He didn't get home until after ten. She wasn't home when he got there, which leaves a lot of hours unaccounted for."

"And her friends don't know where she is?"

Stone shook his head. "From what I can tell, she doesn't have any. She goes to school in the city, but she moved from Wisconsin to Michigan over the summer. She's only been at the school a few weeks."

"Could she have gone back to Wisconsin? Maybe she missed her friends back home. Maybe she was lonely."

"Unless she hitchhiked, I don't think so. She doesn't have a car and I already checked with the airlines and bus station." Stone ran a hand across his forehead, looking exhausted. "I woke the principal at her old school about two this morning. She emailed me Addy's records and promised to talk to Addy's former teachers to try to patch together a list of friends. Hopefully, I'll have something on that front soon."

My stomach knotted at the thought of the girl hitchhiking. "How can I help?"

"I don't know that you can." Stone scowled at the ground. "I was hoping you'd have some kind of girly insight that would trigger a new avenue for me to follow. I'm out of ideas."

"I wasn't your typical teenage girl. I was too worried about paying the bills. Olivia was my only real friend, and she wasn't exactly typical either. Do you know anything about Addy's personality?"

"Not much. The kids I spoke with said she was friendly enough, but no one hung out with her outside of school—at least no one I was able to track down. But again, since it's only early October..."

I nodded, understanding. "At her age, it takes a while to find your clique. Poor girl. That must suck."

"Yeah, only, I don't think that's the whole story."

"What do you mean?"

"Several kids said they'd invited her to join them for various things, but Addy always shied away, turning down their invites. Even a few boys asked her out, but she always answered with a firm *not interested*. Unless it was school related, she kept to herself."

"Shy?" I asked, studying the picture again. "She doesn't look shy. She looks defiant. Rebellious even."

"Agreed, but there's a note in her old school's records." Stone moved to stand beside me, flipping the pages in the file until he found the page he wanted. "Someone added these notes to her file, saying they were trying to contact her father. Whoever this teacher or counselor is, he or she was concerned about Addy's lack of social involvement."

"*Tried* to call her father?"

"Yeah, *tried*. He never returned their calls."

"What father wouldn't return the school's call?"

Stone raised his hands in an *I-don't-know* gesture. "Apparently, the workaholic kind."

"What about her mother?"

"Took off years ago. No contact. Parents are divorced."

"Could one of Addy's parents have done something to her?"

"Now you're thinking like a cop," Stone said, smirking. "I'm still checking out the parents, but the insight I need from you is how teenage girls think—where someone like Addy might've gone."

I tried to put myself in Addy's shoes. No friends. No active parents in her life. Where would she go? I shook my head. "I'm not sure. She's a different breed. The fact that she keeps to herself is throwing me for a loop. Can I think about it? Maybe call you if I come up with any ideas?"

"Yeah, sure." Stone pointed to the file. "Keep that. It's a copy." Stone glanced toward the house. "Contractors huh? Have you decided whether you're keeping or selling the house then?"

"No idea. I think the house is great but it's too big for just me, and truth be told, I'm a little afraid of how bad the heating bills will be this winter, even with the wood burning furnace."

"You could rent out the upstairs bedrooms," Stone said. "Britt and I would consider moving over here."

I shook my head. "I prefer living alone. Besides, Britt's been standoffish ever since the whole *Raina-tried-to-kidnap-her* thing."

"She hasn't said anything to me," Stone said, seeming surprised. "You think she blames you for Raina trying to kidnap her?"

"No. I think she's still mad that Noah forgot she was sleeping in his mother's basement when he ran over here to rescue me off the roof."

Stone tried to hold back his smile but failed. "That's between her and Noah, but I'm sorry to hear she's dragging you into their mess." Stone glanced toward the still open garage. "I'd better get back to the precinct—*before I make you an offer on that coffee table.*"

I laughed. "You know where to find me if you change your mind."

We exchanged waves as we went our separate ways, me toward the house and Stone toward his truck parked along the street.

Chapter Three

I found Whiskey, Virgil, and Lance waiting for me in the downstairs middle bedroom, staring at the wonky wall I'd built the day before. The new wall ran from the center of the room to the back wall. I'd intended to build a second perpendicular wall, dissecting the room in the other direction, but once I saw how crooked the first one was I decided to hold off until I had proper supervision.

"Well," Lance said, scratching the back of his head, "at least you can now say you've built a wall."

"Not a *good* wall," Virgil teased, winking at me. "But it's a wall."

"Ever hear of a level?" Whiskey asked, wearing a smirk.

I crossed the room, picking up my level. "I used a level."

Lance barked a laugh. "That's not the right kind of level." He shook his head. "You needed a framing level."

"And a square," Virgil added, skimming his eyes over my limited supply of tools. "What did you use to cut the lumber with?"

"This thing," I said, crossing to a box where I'd set the circular saw inside so its jagged teeth wouldn't scratch the hardwood floor. It took both hands to lift the saw to show it to them.

Whiskey took the saw from me, lifting it up and down like a dumbbell. "This is old and heavy. Where'd you get it?"

"Mrs. Paulson's garage. She let me borrow it."

"Let me guess," Lance said, studying the wall, "you also nailed the boards together with a hammer?"

"Uhm, yes." I frowned. "Was that wrong too?"

"Not wrong," Virgil said, shaking his head. "Just slow." He moved to the new wall, pressing his hands against it, testing its sturdiness. "It's a shame it's so crooked. You framed it right, and the wall is solid."

"Is there a way to fix it?" I asked.

Whiskey shook his head. "It needs to be ripped out, but the lumber can be reused."

"I'm also thinking we need to tear this plaster out," Lance said, pointing up at the ceiling. "I know you didn't want to have to gut the room, but Whiskey's crew will need to open most of the ceiling to run everything upstairs."

My eyes landed on the long crack in the plaster that had formed when I'd nailed my wall up. "I'm okay with ripping out most of the walls and ceiling, but can we keep the back wall intact? It has blown in insulation. I'd hate to replace it. And if possible, I want to keep the plaster in the hallway too."

Lance bobbed his head, studying the back wall. "I reckon we can do that."

"No promises out here, but I see what you're saying," Virgil said, glancing both ways down the hallway. "We'll do our best, how's that?"

"That's all I ask," I said, smiling.

"Lance gave us a quick walk through, but just to confirm," Whiskey said. "You want this room turned into three closets—walk in closets for the adjacent bedrooms and a third closet with bifold doors off the hallway—right?"

"Yes, and between the walls, you should have plenty of room to run plumbing and forced-air vents upstairs." I pointed to the ceiling. "In the bedroom above us, I want the room converted into two smaller closets for the adjacent bedrooms and a bathroom accessible from the hallway."

I tipped my head, motioning for them to follow me.

Exiting the bedroom, I crossed to the library and opened the hidden room that was tucked behind one of the built-in bookcases. I stepped inside, grabbing a file from the shelf before stepping back out to pass it to Virgil. "Here are my sketches. The other quote I need is to convert the two master bedrooms upstairs into one huge suite with a sitting area, two big closets, and private bathroom."

Whiskey poked his head inside the hidden room. "And for this end of the house, we'll run the plumbing and heat vents upstairs through this room?"

"Exactly," Lance said. "Davina's come up with a good plan."

"Are you worried about losing so many bedrooms?" Whiskey asked me.

"No. I ran my ideas past our local realtor, Jackie Jones. Right now, the house would be a tough sell with eight bedrooms, zero closets, no forced air upstairs, and no second-floor bathrooms. She assured me the resale value would jump considerably if I made the changes. She also suggested I convert the old playroom above the kitchen into a home office. I'll start working on that next week."

"After all this," Virgil held up the sketches, "the house will have five bedrooms, three and a half bathrooms, and a home office?"

"Yup."

Virgil nodded, looking around. "I've gotta admit, sounds about perfect. Kind of makes me want to buy the place."

Whiskey raised an eyebrow at Virgil. "You just moved into a new house six months ago. Your wife would divorce you if you made her move again."

"Don't I know it," Virgil said, laughing.

Whiskey shook his head while glancing at the ceiling again. "I still can't believe no one added forced-air vents to the second floor."

"The previous owners closed off the second floor for decades, so it didn't surprise me," I said before I looked behind me at Lance. "What about the wall I built? Are you going to take pity on me and help fix it?"

"Sure. I've got time yet this morning, but I'll need to run home for the proper tools."

"What walls are you building, and what walls are we building?" Whiskey asked.

"I'm building only the two walls for the bedroom closets downstairs, but I'd prefer if you guys cut open the closet doorways inside the adjacent bedrooms and add whatever header support is needed so the upstairs doesn't fall into the downstairs."

"Got it," Whiskey said, grinning.

"And the upstairs walls?" Virgil asked.

"Upstairs, you guys build the walls. I'll do the finishing work, though, like mud the drywall, add trim wood, paint, etc. Any idea when you'd be able to start?"

Whiskey shrugged. "If you were ready, we'd probably be able to start here sometime late next week, but I'm concerned about the new bathroom fixtures. If you're bargain shopping, you might end up buying something in a different size than you'd planned. It could throw off our wall dimensions."

"I hadn't thought of that, but it makes sense. I'll start shopping to buy all the big stuff like tubs, showers, and sinks. Can you still write up the quotes for everything else?"

"You got it," Whiskey said with a nod.

"Davina's a natural at most of this remodeling stuff," Lance said, waving for us to follow him. He moseyed down the back hallway, stopping outside the bathroom. Reaching inside the room, he flipped on the light and showed Whiskey and Virgil the remodeled bathroom which now sported new tiles surrounding the shower, re-stained cabinets, and all new light and plumbing fixtures.

Lance continued down the hall, entering the kitchen to show them the refinished toffee-colored cabinets and the thick floating shelves I'd hung between the stove and refrigerator to replace the outdated pots and pans rack.

"That spot for a dishwasher?" Virgil asked, nodding to the open space where I'd removed a lower cabinet.

I nodded. "If I ever get around to shopping for the new appliances, yes, that's where the dishwasher will go."

"You do nice work," Whiskey said, running a hand across a cabinet door. "This finishing stuff—along with picking out what'll look nice—ain't easy."

"Thanks," I said, smiling as I looked around. Not only had I enjoyed the work, but it was fun seeing the old house come alive with all the changes.

Hearing a vehicle outside, I shifted toward the dining room and looked over the tops of the privacy curtains that covered the bottom half of the windows. A freight truck parked at the end of my driveway.

I crossed the room, exiting out the kitchen side door. Walking toward the freight truck, I lifted a hand to shield my eyes from the morning sun. When I stopped to wait, Whiskey, Virgil and Lance shifted from behind me to flank me.

A guy in the passenger side of the truck jumped out, heading toward us. "Davina Ravine?"

"That's me, but I wasn't expecting anything."

"I've got three pallets of metal roof sheeting to drop off," the guy said, holding up an electronic tablet. "Where would you like them?"

When Bernadette told me she'd bought the Zenner house for me to live in, she'd also told me that she'd hired contractors to replace the aging roof. I'd called the company she'd hired a few times, trying to get information on the roofing material, but no one had called me back.

"Can I see the roofing sheets before you unload?" I asked.

"I guess," the guy said, shrugging as he moved to the back of the freight truck where another guy stood.

"Problem?" Lance asked in a hushed tone.

"I don't trust the roofers Bernadette hired," I whispered back. "They haven't returned any of my phone calls."

"Not a good sign," Whiskey murmured. "Did she pay them already?"

"She gave them a downpayment for the materials."

Stepping around the back of the truck, I waited as a pallet was lowered on the hydraulic tailgate. *Green. Bright... glossy... tractor green.*

I glanced back at the house, shaking my head. It would never work. The Tudor-styled house had buttery cream siding with dark brown trim and matching brown shutters.

"Even I know that'll look bad," Lance grumbled.

I waved at the pallet, frustrated. "I can't use these. I'd have to replace all the siding and trim for the whole house."

"This shipment is paid in full," the delivery guy said, frowning. "What do you want me to do?"

Before I could answer, two pickup trucks pulled up, parking behind the freight truck along the street. Painted on the side of one of the trucks read: *Brollstone Roofing*.

"Now it makes sense," Virgil said, shaking his head.

"You know them?" I asked as the contractors got out of their trucks.

"Tommy, one of our crewmembers, is cousins with this twit," Virgil said with a nod toward the contractor who was heading our way.

"Why aren't you unloading?" the contractor asked, scowling at the delivery drivers.

"Because I asked them not to," I said. "I'm sorry, but these need to go back."

"I've already paid for the materials," the contractor said, hiking a fisted hand to his hip.

"Then maybe you should've returned my phone calls. If you had, we could've discussed the materials I wanted."

"I ain't got time to hold hands with bored housewives while they *hmm-and-haw* over colors. I'm a busy guy."

His tone sent my temper skyrocketing. "Well, it's your lucky day. Now that you're *fired*, you'll be less busy."

One of the delivery guys snorted, turning away to hide his grin.

"You can't fire me. I was hired by a," he paused to pull a slip of paper from his pocket, reading the name, "Bernadette Quade. She's the only one who can fire me."

"Bernadette is my grandmother, but if you need to hear it from her, so be it." I pulled my phone, calling Bernadette and putting the call on speaker.

"What?" Bernadette snapped into the phone. "I'm out in the barn working on the Dodge Charger."

"I have the roofer you hired standing here. I just fired him, but he says I don't have the authority."

"Am I on speaker?" Bernadette asked, now fully alert.

"You are."

Bernadette let out a string of shouted curses that weaved in and around the words *you're fired* while threatening legal action if he didn't refund her money and get his lazy backside off my property. At the end of her tirade, she hung up without bothering with a goodbye.

I pocketed my phone, happy that for once I hadn't been on the receiving end of her vicious tongue lashing. "My grandmother wasn't kidding about taking legal action," I told the roofer. "Should I call her attorney? He's on retainer."

The contractor's face shifted into a snarl aimed at me.

Whiskey, Virgil, and Lance shifted forward, protectively.

The contractor hesitated a few long silent seconds before he turned his back to us and stomped back toward his truck. "We're leaving!"

The four other men who'd been watching and listening, climbed back into their trucks. We watched as they drove to the end of the street and turned the corner.

Virgil chuckled, crossing his arms over his chest. Looking at the delivery guys, he asked, "You boys got a catalog handy? Maybe we can get a credit on these pallets to apply against something Davina likes."

"Sure thing," one of the guys said, jogging toward the cab of the truck.

Whiskey rocked back and forth on his heels, giving me a sideways look. "You need us to bid on installing the new roof?"

"Yes, please," I said, smiling.

CHAPTER FOUR

WHISKEY AND VIRGIL LEFT, PROMISING to drop off the quotes to me in a day or two, and while Lance drove home for the tools we needed, I tore out the additional sections of plaster inside the middle bedroom.

I was just moving my ladder back into place beside my wonky wall when Lance returned and pulled a saw from an overly large tool bag. "This here," Lance said, holding up a long saw, "is what most folks call a Sawzall, but that's a brand name, like people call bandages Band-Aids or tissues Kleenex. Its actual name is a reciprocating saw."

The long skinny saw had a blade poking out one end with sharp jagged teeth. "Looks dangerous."

"All power saws are dangerous if you don't use them right. For this one, it's important to hold it with a tight grip and keep the blade pointed away from your body."

"Okay." I took the saw, holding it to get used to its weight. It wasn't nearly as heavy as the circular saw I'd borrowed from Mrs. Paulson, but the out-jutted blade made me nervous.

"Safety goggles."

I slid the goggles that were on top of my head down.

"Get in position."

Careful to keep the blade pointed away, I climbed the ladder until I could comfortably reach the top of the wonky wall. I glanced down, seeing Lance had braced his hand on my ladder.

"Now, it'll be loud, but wedge that blade between the ceiling and the wall to cut off the nails holding the wall in place. We need to take the wall down before we can fix it."

"Got it." I leaned forward against the ladder, spreading my feet apart for extra stability. Staring at my target, I waited.

"Okay, here we go," Lance said. "I'm plugging in the power cord. Ready when you are."

I lifted the saw, shoving the blade alongside the edge where the wall met the ceiling. I pulled the saw's trigger.

The saw jerked back and forth in my hands, startling me. Tightening my grip, I tried to shove the blade into the crack but it bucked, kicking back toward me.

As it jumped free from my grip, I shoved its handle, pushing the saw away from me.

Lance grabbed the back of my jeans, jerking me backward off the ladder. I hit the floor and the ladder was thrown forward, sending with it the still-running saw. The saw launched between the stud boards, spearing the outer wall with its pointy blade. It ripped a jagged line down the plaster as it fell to the floor.

I rolled sideways, extending my hand toward the power cord to yank it from the outlet.

The saw stopped buzzing and the room went silent.

I stared at the saw for a long moment before glancing up at Lance. "Question... I know I'm new at all this, but shouldn't the saw have stopped when I released the trigger?"

"Yeah," Lance said, scratching his neck. "The trigger sometimes sticks. I've been meaning to fix it." He glanced down at me, smirking.

I laughed, climbing up from the floor before exiting the room and entering my bedroom. Plaster dust still hung in the air, drifting down to coat everything. I crossed to where a jagged line ran halfway down the plaster. The saw had cut into the side of one of the many boxes I'd left stacked alongside the wall.

"Oops," Lance said.

"I'm not worried about that junk," I said, waving at the boxes. "Those papers and pictures are a few centuries old. Stuff I found in the attic that belonged to Archer Hudson." I sighed, studying the jagged cut in the plaster. "But I'd planned on remodeling the other bedroom first, the one closest to the library, then flipflopping my bedroom to that room before working on this one."

"See'n how it's my fault your plans changed, I'll give you a hand moving your bedroom furniture."

"Let's move my bedroom temporarily into the library." I crossed to my bed and bundled my bedcovers. "I don't want to wash my bedding every day."

After I started the washer, Lance helped me shift my living room furniture to one side of the library and we set up my bed, dresser, and bedside table on the other side. I preferred sleeping in a room with a locked door, but I could make do for a few weeks.

Returning to the bedroom, I stared down at the stack of boxes filled with Archer Hudson's papers, wondering where to put them. I'd been putting off going through them for weeks, but I still had no urge to tackle them.

"Where to?" Lance said, picking up the top box.

"No idea." I looked across the bedroom. "Why don't we just move them to the other side of the room out of the way. They're already coated in plaster dust."

"You sure?"

I nodded, picking up one of the boxes and moving it to the opposite corner. "Someday I'll go through them, but I'm in no rush."

When we were done, we moved back to the library.

"What's the story with Mrs. Paulson's stuff?" Lance asked, tipping his head toward the front living room which still held tables full of antiques.

"She's thinking about throwing another open house in December, but when the contractors start work on the house I'll smush the tables and everything to the outer wall."

"Kind of a pain, but I get it. What about the bookcases? Seems odd seeing most of them empty like that."

I glanced up at the bookcases, once full of leather-bound novels. After Bernadette bought the house, I shipped the books per her instructions to an auction house. Now the shelves sat empty.

"I don't have anything to put on the shelves."

"You know, I've been thinking about your housefire and how you lost everything. When I get some time, I'll dig through my boxes of old pictures. I'm sure I've got some of you and your dad. You can put some up along the shelves."

"That'd be great. Thanks."

Lance blushed as he turned his face away. "All right, it's time to take down that wall."

"Fine, but you're running the saw. I'm never touching that thing again."

CHAPTER FIVE

BETWEEN LANCE'S CONSTRUCTION EXPERIENCE AND his handy tools—like his nail gun which shot nails through the boards with a touch of a button—it only took us two hours to rebuild my wonky wall and to build the second wall which divided the room in the other direction.

Lance called it a day, packing up and driving home. I finished tearing out the rest of the plaster and trim boards where the new closet doorways would go before cleaning up my mess and showering.

While contemplating which project to tackle next, I puttered around the house, moving my bedding from the washer to the dryer and mopping the floors in the first-floor bedrooms. When the dryer buzzed that my bedding was done, I hauled the bundle to the library to make my bed.

Tucking the tail of the top sheet under the mattress, I heard my phone ring in the kitchen and ran to answer it. Reaching for it on the kitchen counter, I hesitated, seeing Bernadette's name on the screen.

Get it over with, I thought, picking it up and tapping the button. "Hey."

"Meet me in twenty minutes." Bernadette rattled off an address so quickly, I barely had time to scribble it onto a nearby piece of junk mail before she hung up.

I moved my phone away from my ear, glaring at it. The address was local, just south of Daybreak Falls out near Lance's place. It wouldn't take long to drive over, and I didn't have anything else scheduled until later in the evening, but that wasn't the point.

I stabbed the green phone icon with my finger, calling Bernadette back.

"What?" she answered.

"You can't just call me and order me to drop whatever I'm doing to meet you."

"Why not? It's not like you have a job or a social calendar to manage."

"That's not the point. It's rude."

"It's not rude, it's business. We need to discuss the next investment for the Quade trust." Bernadette hung up again.

I set my phone on the counter, my temper flaring. I was itching to blow her off, leave her waiting for me and not show, but the stupid trust account had bailed me out of a few money jams recently, and if our meeting involved the trust, I should go.

Picking my phone back up, I dropped it inside my purse, leaving out the kitchen side door.

Twenty minutes later, I turned into a gravel driveway and followed it for a stretch until it curved around a bend. Pulling into a weedy patch, I held my foot on the brake. A weather-worn clapboard house with only a few speckles of once-white paint stood half-buried behind overgrown trees, vines, and three-foot tall weeds.

I put the van in park and rechecked the address I'd written down. *Yup, this was it.* According to the address on the tipsy mailbox out by the road, this was where Bernadette had ordered me to meet her.

I climbed out and circled my van, stopping to look at the ramshackle house. The rotted front porch had scrub trees growing up between broken boards. The house's roof wore a layer of moss so thick I couldn't see any of the shingles. The overgrown trees, too close to the house, shadowed the structure, preventing sunshine from reaching it.

But as dilapidated as the house was, it was sort of cute. Design-wise, it was a bungalow-styled cottage. The upstairs likely had either one large bedroom or two small ones. The first floor was large for a bungalow, probably also having a bedroom or two.

Behind a layer of vines climbing the front siding, I spotted a wide picture window. The rest of the windows looked standard sized with white muntin bars, and most had broken glass.

Hearing a vehicle, I walked to the rear of my van. Bernadette drove her Nova around the bend and parked. A man I didn't recognize sat in the passenger seat, waving at me with the enthusiasm of a toddler.

I waved back, but with a lot less enthusiasm.

"Stay in the car," Bernadette snapped at him as she got out. "This doesn't concern you."

I couldn't hear his response, but he wore a happy smile, seemingly unconcerned with her abrasive tone.

"Who's that?" I asked after she'd closed her driver's door.

"Nobody," Bernadette snapped, walking toward me. "Well? What do you think?"

"What do I think of what? Why am I here?"

"I bought this place. Only, I'm not sure what to do with it."

Both my eyebrows shot up. I looked back at the house then at Bernadette. "Why would you buy this place?"

"Land. It's a twenty-acre lot. The question is, can the house be saved? I had an inspector come out, but he refused to venture inside until it was safe."

"You had an inspector refuse to go inside, yet you still bought the house?"

Bernadette rolled her eyes. "You're not listening. The house might be a loss, but I bought it for the *land.* I plan on divvying up the acreage and leaving only five acres with this lot to resell."

"So why am I here?"

"To decide if I need to hire a bulldozer or if the house can be saved. Why else would I ask you to be here?"

"Is this payback for that bachelor auction? For helping Mrs. Paulson win the bid for a date with Mr. Corrigan?"

"Don't be daft. That was weeks ago," Bernadette said, waving off my comment. "This is business. As a benefactor of the family's trust, it's time you start pulling your weight with the investment process. Time to step up, as the kids say."

I didn't know any kids who used that phrase and was about to tell her that but bit my tongue, deciding it was better not to poke the bear.

Looking back at the house, I had to admit I was curious about the inside. I started toward the house, eyeing the unsafe porch boards to strategize the best path to reach the door without falling through and breaking a leg.

The first three boards were meant to serve as steps, but they sat crooked and loose. I kicked them aside and climbed the riser to the top before following a row of nails, hoping the underside framing wasn't as rotted as the top boards.

When the front door was withing reach, I tugged at a layer of vines that had grown over the entrance. The vines, along with the rickety screen door, toppled to the porch.

I stared at the screen door, shaking my head. "Needs a new door," I hollered sarcastically.

"Funny," Bernadette snapped. "Hurry up. I don't have all day."

I looked up at the doorframe, seeing the screen door had been attached to nothing more than a narrow piece of trim. I tugged at the trim which broke off easily, but the wood underneath it appeared solid.

Turning the doorknob on the interior door, I pushed it open but stayed on the porch while I peeked inside. With all the trees hovering around the house, the inside was layered in shadows. I reached around the corner, feeling for a light switch. The first one didn't do anything. The second one turned on a six-bulb chandelier with only one working light bulb.

I looked down at the floor while stepping inside. The carpet was blackish with stains, littered with glass, trash, and what looked like dried vomit in the far corner. The drywall had graffiti and a fist-sized hole above where a broken liquor bottle was shattered.

The room itself was plenty big enough for a family living room and had a stretch of windows along the side of the house. I moved to my right, peeking inside an average sized bedroom before passing the doorway and following the wall to look around the next corner. On the back side of the bedroom was a bathroom that had seen better days. The tub in the far corner was starting to sink into the basement and the bathroom cabinet leaned heavily toward the toilet. On the floor, mixed in with crushed beer cans, were bloody bandages. Likely a kid cut themselves on one of the many broken windows.

Across from the bathroom door was a stairway to the second floor. I moved up the stairs. At the top was an open landing with a wood railing bordering the stairway and three doors off the hallway. Two of the doors were for bedrooms, both having slanted ceilings along the outside walls, but the larger of the two bedrooms took up the entire front of the house and had a row of windows overlooking the front yard. It also had giant brown water stains on the ceiling, but without a ladder, I couldn't poke my head up into the attic to see what the underside of the roof looked like.

The third door, situated between the two bedrooms, was to a half bathroom with a bone-dry toilet bowl coated in brownish orange rust. I moved back toward the stairway, checking the walls and ceilings. Unlike the first floor, the second floor still had plaster walls. Some of the sections were so cracked that plaster had fallen to the floor, exposing the lathe boards underneath.

Back downstairs, I passed the built-in cabinets under the stairs but stopped at the tallest section where a door was set a few inches into the wall. I opened it, reaching around inside for a light switch and flipping it on. A bulb at the bottom of the basement stairs lit.

After testing my weight on the landing and finding it solid, I descended into the basement. While dirty and filled with cobwebs, the basement was dry. I did a quick check of the mechanical equipment, seeing that the furnace was newer but that the water heater was shot.

I hurried back up the stairs, eager to distance myself from the cobwebs and the eight-legged insects that had made them. Just past the basement door was a doorless entryway into the back of the house. To my right was a kitchen nook with windows along both walls. The benches below the windows looked unsafe to sit on and the table was long gone, but it was a cute feature.

In the other direction was a long galley kitchen with crooked, doorless cabinets that ended at partition walls. Just past them was a mudroom area, which likely had a back door.

Since the kitchen floor in front of the sink bowed from water damage, I turned the opposite direction, crossing the house and exiting out the front door to circle it to the back yard.

The back door to the house had a deep crack down the center like someone had kicked it open, and the yard was a jungle of overgrown weeds, vines, and bushes. I had no idea how to set it right again. I nudged the ground with the toe of my shoe, confirming the patio underneath was a patchwork of broken concrete.

Continuing toward the driveway, I spotted a detached one-car garage, nearly hidden by thick bushes. After peeking inside to confirm it was empty, I moved further down the driveway, turning to see the garage from a distance. It leaned heavily to one side, ready to topple over, but the pull-open wooden doors could be repurposed into something cool.

As my brain started cycling through ideas, I stopped myself, deciding it was time to talk to Bernadette before I got carried away.

CHAPTER SIX

CROSSING BACK TO THE FRONT YARD where Bernadette stood impatiently scowling, I called out, "I think the house has potential, but what does the budget look like?"

"The property was bank owned and priced to sell. If you can keep expenses under fifty thousand to make the house livable, we'll break even selling the house with a profit on dividing the land into smaller lots."

"How many lots?"

"Maybe three or four, including this house. I'll take care of that side of things, order perc tests and such."

Since I didn't know what a perc test was, leaving it for Bernadette to handle sounded like a good idea. I turned back to study the house again. The new roof would eat a good-sized chunk of the budget. As for the rest of the house, the real question was how far to take the remodeling to turn a profit.

"Send me what you have on the house, and I'll tally some numbers. I want to make sure everything adds up before you sink any money into it. I might also ask Jackie to send me some figures so I can get a better sense of resale values."

"*We*," Bernadette said. "Before *we* sink money into it. We'll partner on this investment. Between my skills of buying and selling properties, and your knack to fix up old houses, we could make a pretty penny."

She'd tricked me. She asked me to look at the house, but she'd planned all along to sucker me into doing the repairs. I thought about calling her out on it, but truthfully, it sounded like fun. "Split the profit fifty-fifty and I'm in."

"Sixty-forty."

I shook my head. "Fifty-fifty—*and* I want the same cut for the Zenner house. Both houses will keep me busy for months, eating up my time. If it's not profitable for me, I'm out. I'll go find a real job."

"And what if I don't agree to an even split?" Bernadette asked, squaring her shoulders and raising an eyebrow.

I shrugged. "Then I'll halt work on the Zenner house, but you should know that I ran my plans past Jackie and she said the changes will raise the resale price considerably. We'd *both* make money."

Bernadette's scowl shifted into a smirk before she glanced away. I knew I had her. The only thing Bernadette liked more than a good investment was her muscle cars. I also suspected that on some level she respected me more for holding my ground for what I considered a fair share of the profits.

"*Fine*," Bernadette snapped before stomping over to her Nova, returning with a file folder and a large manilla envelope.

The older man sitting in the passenger seat waved again, wearing an overly enthusiastic smile.

"Are we going to talk about your gentleman friend?" I asked, waving back at him.

"No," Bernadette said, thrusting the folder and envelope at me. "Inside the folder is the information I have on the house and property, along with a copy of the real estate closing documents."

"It'll take me a few days to unbury enough of the house to figure this all out. Can we afford to hire the Donaldson boys for a day or two?"

Bernadette waved off my concern. "Do whatever you think best." She pointed to the envelope. "I opened a business account in both our names and deposited funds. It's all in the envelope, along with the checkbook and debit card."

I peeked inside the envelope but didn't take anything out. "What about the Zenner house? Can I take money out of the same account to pay the contractors?"

"Yes. Just track the expenses for the two houses separately so we can keep the profits for each house straight."

"Sounds simple enough. Do I need to run everything by you before buying things?"

"Goodness sakes, no. I don't have time to babysit you. Whatever you need done, take care of it. If you need more money deposited into the account, let me know, but you should have enough to do a dozen houses." Bernadette started back toward her Nova. "Figure it out."

"What about keys?" I said, shaking the manilla envelope and not hearing any keys rattle in the bottom.

"The bank didn't have keys, so you'll need to call a locksmith." She opened her driver's door, glancing at me. "Also, don't forget to call the power company to change over the utilities." She threw herself inside the Nova and slammed her door shut.

Mentally, I thought of a good five smart-ass replies but simply lifted my hand in a weak wave goodbye. Bernadette backed her Nova down the driveway, not bothering to wave back.

"Davina, what did you get yourself into this time?" I muttered to myself, crossing to the passenger door of my van. Opening it, I dug my phone out of my purse, scrolling through my contact list to select Lance's name.

"Hello," Lance answered.

"Hey, Lance. I'm up the road at a property Bernadette bought. It's on the west side, probably three mailboxes down from your place. House number 2233. Any chance you could come over to recommend a plan to tackle the yard? I have no idea where to start. It's a mess."

"The old Hollander place?" Lance asked.

"No idea."

Lance chuckled. "A rotted out two-story house with beer cans everywhere?"

"Bingo. That's the one."

"And you're there right now?" Lance asked, sounding curious.

"I am. Bernadette just left."

"I'm in the middle of something right now, but I could be there in maybe about an hour or so. Does that work?"

"That's fine. I need supplies, so I'll run home and load up. Come over when it suits you."

"Mind if I bring my tractor and invite a few friends?"

His question surprised me and took me a minute to respond. "I didn't mean for you to clear the yard yourself. I just hoped you could point me in the right direction."

"It's been a while since the boys and I got to play with our toys. My neighbor Pete bought a new bobcat not too long ago. It sure would be fun to take it for a spin out there."

I laughed. "Have at it then. Just don't knock the garage over until I return with some tools to take the doors off. I want to keep them."

"Well..." Lance chuckled. "I suppose if I get to knock over a garage, the least I could do is remove the doors for you. We'll set them along the back side of the house."

"Works for me. See you later." I hung up, shaking my head.

Circling my van, I stopped to send a text message to Davey. After tapping out the text, asking if he and his brother Griffin would be interested in working this Saturday, I snapped a pic of the front yard and attached it to the message.

Three days a week Davey took college courses at the community college, but to save money he was still living with his parents. Since it was Thursday, I knew he'd be home today.

Davey replied with a thumbs up and said he'd stop by my house tonight with Griffin for more details.

Climbing inside the van, I spotted the envelope and file Bernadette had given me. Before I got too carried away, it made sense to check the documents.

I flipped through the file first, skimming the purchase agreement. I was surprised when my eyes landed on the purchase price. Bernadette had bought the land and house for a heck of a lot less than I would've guessed.

Setting the file folder aside, I checked the manilla envelope, pulling out the checkbook and debit card. I flipped the checkbook open, glancing at the deposit slip tucked inside. My eyes bugged out seeing all the zeros. There was way more money than what I'd need.

Using my thumb, I parted the checks, reading the printed business name: *Quade and Ravine Investments.* Under the company name was my name.

Bernadette hadn't just opened this account. It took time to print and ship checks. My guess was that she'd ordered the checks a week or two ago. She'd tricked me, all right.

I looked out the passenger side window at the house, smiling.

Well played, Bernadette.

CHAPTER SEVEN

AT HOME, I REVERSED INTO the driveway and hopped out. After opening the van's back doors, I moved to the garage, raising one of the overhead bay doors. Skirting around the yard-sale furniture, I crossed to the back and pulled out my A-frame ladder, carrying it outside.

Davey jogged across the street, taking the ladder from me. "I've got my homework done already. Do you need help this afternoon?"

"I could use a hand, but are you sure you're caught up on your college stuff? I don't want to be blamed for messing up your education."

"All good." Davey bounced his head in his easy-going way. "My assignments are done, and I've studied my little brain cells off for my accounting test tomorrow, so yup, I'm good. Promise."

"In that case, load the wheelbarrow, both weed whips, a pile of work gloves, and see if you can hunt down my crowbars. I'm not sure where I put them."

While Davey loaded the stuff needed for the yard and porch, I loaded trash bags, a stack of five-gallon buckets, mops, brooms, flashlights, and everything else sitting on the garage shelves that caught my attention. When we were done, I smiled at how much we'd crammed into the back.

"What's the deal with this house you're working on?" Davey asked, adding three crowbars to the back before closing the doors.

"Bernadette bought it. She's splitting the profit with me if I fix it up. Lance is already out there. Apparently, knocking stuff over in the yard with your tractor is fun for men his age."

"I don't think that's an old man thing," Davey said, jogging to the passenger door. He waited until we were both inside before asking, "Think Lance will let me knock something over?"

"You'll have to ask him, but I wouldn't get your hopes up. His tractor is his baby." I pulled my seatbelt on. "But fear not, I have a long list of stuff that needs demolishing." I looked between us, my hand on my keys with the key already in the ignition. "Are we forgetting anything?"

Davey's face shifted into deep thinking. "Maybe." He threw his door open, jogging across the street back to his house.

I started the van and pulled out to park along the street in front of his house. A few minutes later he jogged back down his driveway, hopping into the passenger seat and resting the head-end of a sledgehammer between his feet. "Now we're ready." He pulled his seatbelt across him.

I laughed, driving toward town. En route, I called Jackie, asking her to print out a list of similar homes in various conditions so I could get a feel for resale prices. She offered to bring them by tomorrow.

I thanked her, disconnecting. My next call was to Ed Mason, scheduling a meeting with him to come out and quote fixing the windows, and the call after that was to the local locksmith.

Making a right turn onto a country road, I decided to hold off on the rest of the calls until I got back to the cottage.

I glanced at Davey. "Don't tell Bernadette, but this house stuff is kind of fun."

Davey grinned. "I'll keep your secret."

~*~*~

SLOWING AS I APPROACHED THE tipsy mailbox, I eyed a truck and an empty trailer parked alongside the road's shoulder before I made the turn into the driveway. I didn't recognize the truck, but that didn't mean anything. Looking up, I jammed both feet on the brake pedal, hard stopping my van.

An old guy zipped across the driveway in a bobcat within a few feet of my bumper.

Davey laughed, watching the guy ram his bobcat into a scraggly bush, uprooting it. "That's so cool."

I shook my head, continuing down the drive and parking in front of the house. We got out and stopped to watch Lance in his tractor uproot another overgrown bush growing in front of the garage. The swing-out doors to the garage had already been removed and two guys I recognized as Lance's friends stood alongside the house, drinking beer.

Davey pulled his phone, taking a video.

Lance reversed his tractor, stopping to change gears. "Ready?" he called out to the other guys.

"You got this," one of the guys cheered.

Lance drove his tractor forward while raising the front plow blade. When the blade hit the corner of the garage, making a thunderous crunching noise, the whole thing toppled over, falling like a house of cards.

"Awesome," Davey said from beside me.

The two guys lifted their beers, hooting and hollering.

"I'm sending my dad the video," Davey said. "He'll be jealous."

I had to admit it was fun to watch, but it wasn't getting my work done.

"Before you get sucked into the testosterone," I pointed toward the front porch, "I loaded hammers and nails in the back of the van. I'm hoping you can piece together something that'll be safe enough to walk across."

"Yeah, yeah," Davey said, nodding. "If I don't have enough lumber, I'll steal some wood siding from that old garage."

"Sounds good. After that, you can start weed whipping down the yard around the house while I work inside. Until I know the house isn't infested with anything like mold or roaches, keep yourself busy outside. But be sure to track your hours so we can settle your pay later this weekend."

"Gotcha," Davey said, opening the back of the van and pulling out a crowbar.

Davey got to work on the porch, and I hauled the trash bags, gloves, two flashlights, and my six-foot ladder inside the house. After adjusting a face mask to fit my nose and pulling on gloves, I dug in, bagging trash and anything else I came across that wasn't attached to the house. Every so often I'd stop to listen to Lance and his buddies whooping it up in the yard, usually just after something made a crashing noise. They were definitely having more fun than I was, but I was okay with that.

After clearing the trash, I swept up the broken glass in each room before knocking down the cobwebs in the basement. In the kitchen and each bathroom, I checked the faucets, confirming the water to the house was turned off, which was probably a good thing.

Returning to the living room, I grimaced at the blackish carpeting. I might as well tear it out now since I was already filthy. Moving to the far corner, I tugged until the carpet pulled away from the tack strip bordering the wall. Leaning back, I walked backward, pulling the carpet with me.

Davey entered the house and jogged over to lend a hand, helping me split the carpet along the seam in the center of the room before rolling the first chunk.

"This carpet is nasty," Davey said, tossing the trash bag I'd left by the door outside.

"Agreed." I dragged the roll of carpet closer to the door before dropping it. "I thought I told you to work outside."

"Oh, yeah, sorry. Lance asked me to poke my head inside and ask if they could start burning the old boards."

I shook my head. "The water to the house is off. I don't want to set anything on fire until we have water to put it out. I'm not sure there's even insurance on this place yet."

Davey bobbed his head, glancing between the roll of carpet and the front door. "So, do you want help hauling this carpet outside or should I follow orders and exit the house immediately?"

"Help, please," I said, chuckling. "I haven't spotted any health hazards. Just be careful around the kitchen and bathroom floors. They both have water damage."

"Right on," Davey said, lifting one end of the rolled carpet and dragging it out the door before I had time to pick up the other end.

Deciding he didn't need my help, I attacked the other half of the carpet, rolling it up. When Davey returned, Lance and two other guys followed him inside. Davey moved toward the next roll of carpet, but Lance and the others crossed the room, disappearing down the basement stairs.

A few minutes later they reappeared, splitting off in different directions before regrouping and walking back outside, all while chatting a mile a minute to each other.

"What was that about?" I asked Davey.

"I'm guessing it was about the water being turned off," Davey said with a shrug. "They looked bummed when I told them no fires until there was water."

I laughed, pointing to the carpet. "While you haul this one out, I'll pull the carpet in the bedroom. The rest of the house has wood or vinyl flooring."

"Got it," Davey said, disappearing through the front door, dragging the carpet with him.

CHAPTER EIGHT

AFTER RIPPING THE BEDROOM CARPET out, I gathered a notepad, a flashlight, a measuring tape, and my ladder, taking them upstairs. Forcing myself up onto the ladder, I looked inside the attic, searching it with the flashlight from one end to the other. Two of the OSB boards were darkened with rot, but the rafters looked good, and the attic was insulated. *Bonus.*

Climbing back down, I scribbled a few notes on my notepad before flipping to a new page. I sketched out the bedroom, adding measurements for the walls, windows, and doorway. Off to the side of the page, I added a note to build a closet and install a ceiling fan light.

When I was done, I moved to the next room, then the next, continuing through the house. Ending in the basement, after measuring the water heater I returned upstairs and sat on the living room floor. On a fresh page, I made a list of priorities to focus on. The house would take months to remodel, but some things, like the roof, windows, and plumbing, would need to be dealt with before winter.

I called Whiskey about the roof, asking if we could meet sometime next week, but he surprised me by agreeing to stop out midmorning the next day. After that, I called the power company to switch the utility bill over. Climbing up from the floor, I pocketed my phone and looked up when the door opened.

Jared poked his head inside and entered, followed by Griffin. "Hey," Jared said, wearing a grin.

"Hey yourself," I said, glancing at my Fitbit. It was only three-thirty. "Shouldn't you still be at work?"

Jared shrugged. "I left early. Lance sent me a message asking me to pick up plumbing shutoff valves." Jared held up a handful of valves. "You at a good stopping point?"

"Sure. What do you need?"

Jared turned to Griffin. "You run upstairs. Lance said there's a bathroom up there."

"Got it," Griffin said, jogging across the room and up the stairs.

"Davey," Jared hollered out the front door. "Come give us a hand."

"What are we doing?" I asked, confused.

"I'm going to turn the water on, so you guys can tell me what gets wet," Jared said with a big goofy smile.

Remembering how bad the bathrooms were, I thought, *Why not? The bathrooms can't get much worse.* "Works for me."

Five minutes later, I stood in the middle of the first-floor bathroom, waiting. Griffin was still upstairs, and Davey had been assigned to watch the kitchen.

"Get ready," I heard Jared yell from the basement. "Three, two, one."

Water shot out from the back of the sink faucet, ricocheting off the ceiling to shower down on me. I squatted to open the lower cabinet, mentally kicking myself for not having it already open. A spray of water smacked me in the face, blinding me.

I jerked backward, but slipped on the wet floor, landing on my rump. Wiping the water from my eyes with my sleeve, I noticed the water level in the toilet rising. I scrambled up from the floor, backing out of the room. *"Shut if off! Shut it off!"*

The water spraying from the sink petered out and the water in the toilet stopped a half-inch under the rim.

I sighed, shaking my hands to shed the excess water. Turning, I stepped out of the bathroom.

Davey exited the kitchen. From his shoulders upward to the top of his head and from his ankles down, he was soaked, but his middle parts were dry.

Griffin walked down the stairs, one step at a time. He was wet from the chest down to his knees.

Jared jogged up the steps, completely dry, grinning when he saw us. "Just a few leaks, I'd say."

I looked at Davey. "Can you dig around in the back of my van for the terrycloth towels?"

"I can do that," Davey said, sloshing his way across the room to the front door.

"Want the good news or the bad?" Griffin asked me.

"Bad."

"Everything in the upstairs bathroom leaks."

"What's the good news?"

Griffin's face lit with mischief. "Since it's a total tear-out, you don't have to clean anything."

Jared and I laughed.

Jared tousled Griffin's hair, saying, "That's my boy. Always looking on the bright side."

"Mind running upstairs for the plunger I saw up there?" I asked Griffin.

"Sure thing." Griffin ran up the stairs two at a time.

"Now what?" I asked Jared. "Should I start calling plumbers?"

"Nope. Won't take long to get the new shutoff valves installed. Lance and his buddies said they'd help." Jared started into the kitchen as Griffin returned downstairs. I took the plunger and turned into the bathroom.

When my arms wouldn't take any more, I gave up and left the plunger in the toilet. Wandering around I found Lance in the kitchen, wielding a pipe wrench under the kitchen sink. "Who should I call about a plugged toilet?"

"Randy Ikers," a guy said, walking into the kitchen from behind me and crossing the kitchen to pass Lance a pair of pliers. "Want me to call him? He's a buddy of mine."

"Yes, please. I don't have any cash on me right now, but I can write him a check."

"I've got enough cash," Lance said, shifting to poke his head out. "You can pay me back whenever." He looked at the other guy. "Pete, let Randy know we'll need the septic tank emptied too. It's probably been a good dozen years since anyone opened it."

"You got it. I'll call him on my way over to your place to pick up more beer and the garden hoses."

Lance disappeared back under the sink while Pete circled around me, back toward the front of the house.

I shrugged and walked back to the living room. I stared down at my list, trying to decide what to do next. If I tried to help with the plumbing, I'd only be in the way. I glanced up at the ceiling, remembering the tall trim boards in both upstairs bedrooms. If I had the boys tear into the walls this weekend, I wanted to make sure the trim boards were set aside so I could reuse them.

Decision made, I picked up my list, carrying it out to the van so I wouldn't forget it later, and grabbed a hammer and a crowbar to tackle my next project.

CHAPTER NINE

BY THE TIME I POPPED the last trim board free from the wall in the master bedroom, my arms and shoulders ached. The boards had proven more difficult than I'd planned. Every few inches they were attached to the wall with long square-spiked nails, and in the room's corners they were fitted one into the next, making it challenging to detach them without splitting the wood.

I'd finally won the battle, but I wasn't sure I'd be able to lift my arms tomorrow.

I rolled my shoulders before checking the time, seeing it was already after five. If I wanted to shower before I met up with Olivia later, I'd need to call it a day.

Making my way downstairs, I discovered the house was empty and the plunger I'd used earlier was sitting in the bathtub. The water in the toilet sat at a normal level.

I flushed the toilet, seeing it was working. Deciding to clean it, I grabbed my cleaning tote and pulled on rubber gloves, giving the bathroom a quick scrub. Afterward, I carried my cleaning tote outside to load back inside my van.

I smiled as I looked around. Davey and Griffin were running the weed whips, knocking down the weeds and tall grass around the house and piling anything they unearthed into one pile off to the side. In just a few short hours, the yard looked twice as big.

Hearing laughter, I walked over to look alongside the house. The menfolk were on the other side of the drive, gathered around a bonfire, drinking beer. A chunk of siding from the old garage crackled in the flames. I looked around, worried about the fire spreading, but saw the ground was scraped down to the dirt around the fire pit.

"Quit worrying," Lance said, chuckling. "We're keeping an eye on it." He pointed to one of his buddies who sat in a fold-out lawn chair, holding a garden hose nozzle.

"How long do you figure the fire will burn? I was going to leave soon."

"If you don't mind us staying, I'll take care of it," Lance said.

"I don't mind, but will you make sure nobody gets drunk enough to do anything crazy?"

Lance's smile widened. "Nope. But if we break something, we'll fix it."

"Good enough for me."

Lance nodded to the guy standing next to him. "This is Randy Ikers. He snaked the septic line, but he'll stop out sometime tomorrow to empty the septic tank. We already uncapped it for him."

"Sounds good. Thanks for coming out," I said to Randy. "How much do I owe you?"

"We can settle up tomorrow for pumping the tank," Randy said, waving off my concern. "As for clearing the drain line, I was bribed by the offer of free beer to take care of it." He held up his beer before taking a drink.

Lance threw me a wink, pulling a beer from a nearby cooler and offering it to me.

"No thanks."

He cracked the beer open. "Anything else on your priority list?"

"Just the roof, doors, locks, and windows, but I made calls about most of it. Any idea how much it'll cost to have some of these trees cut down?"

"Let me handle that. I know a timberman who might be interested in buying some of them."

"Buying them?"

Lance nodded. "You've got some nice mature hardwoods back here." Lance pointed to a large oak tree. "You won't get rich off them, but a little pocket money never hurts."

"I'm good with that as long as the house keeps that woodsy feel."

"I've got your number," Lance said. "I'll make sure it's still hidden from the road." Lance nodded toward the house. "Want me to lock up when we leave?"

I shook my head. "I won't have keys for the house until tomorrow morning."

"Mom's here," Davey called out to Griffin.

They both shut off their weed whips, leaning them against the front porch.

"I can't wait to get out of these wet shoes," Davey said.

"At least your underwear is dry," Griffin said, tugging at the back of his jeans.

I smiled, crossing to Noelle's car. Mrs. Paulson climbed out of the passenger side.

The boys grabbed the bag of clothes and shoes from Noelle, and Davey sat in the yard, peeling his wet shoes and socks off. Griffin carried the bag toward the house.

"Watch out for the floor in the bathroom," I called out to Griffin. "It's not safe near the tub."

"Got it," Griffin said.

I held my arm out for Mrs. Paulson.

She looped her arm through mine, leaning in close and wearing a sly grin. "The town is buzzing about the house. Davey posted a video of Lance knocking down the old garage. Everyone wants to know what's going on."

"Bernadette's paying me to fix it up to resell."

"It's in a great location," Noelle said, shielding her eyes from the afternoon sun.

"Come on in," I said. "Davey rigged together a few porch boards but watch where you step."

Helping Mrs. Paulson up the porch, I led them through the first-floor rooms, giving them the tour. Mrs. Paulson passed on going upstairs, but Noelle ran up to have a quick look around.

While we were alone, I told Mrs. Paulson my plan to move her tables of antiques to one side of the living room at the Zenner house so nothing would be damaged during the remodeling. She was fine with it, but asked if I was interested in refinishing a large desk she had at the store.

"Sure," I said. "I'm gearing up to do some refinishing on the other furniture I bought. Have Noah move the desk to my garage. It might be a few weeks before I get to it, but it'll be easier for me to work on there."

"Thank you," Mrs. Paulson said, patting my arm. "I'll keep looking for a more permanent solution for the rest of the inventory. I've talked to Jackie, but unfortunately there are no other storefronts coming on the market."

"I'd hate to see you move locations. You're in the perfect spot."

"I know. But what can I do? There's just not enough room."

"Have you talked to Olivia? Maybe she can get rid of my desk and shift hers further back."

Mrs. Paulson shook her head. "It's her lease, her suite rental. I don't want to be a bother."

"Can I at least broach the subject with her? Ask what she thinks about it?"

"I suppose that'll be fine, but don't make a fuss about it."

I smirked, turning my attention to Noelle as she descended the stairs.

"This house needs a lot of work," Noelle said, "but I like it."

"It's got that cottage vibe," I said, leading them back outside. "I still need to tally the numbers to figure out the budget, but I think it'll be super cute when I get it done."

"Hey, Davina," Davey called out as he, Griffin, and Jared crossed to meet up with us in the yard. "Any chance you have something ready for me to demolish?"

"Me too," Griffin said.

"Me three," Jared said, wrapping an arm around Noelle's waist. "My wife gave me permission to stay."

"I need to leave, but, Jared, if you want to stay and supervise them, the tub and kitchen cabinets all need to be knocked out."

"Sweet," Davey said, jogging over to where he'd left the sledgehammer. "I get the tub."

Jared and Griffin ran to the back of my van, loading up on hammers and crowbars. All three of them started for the front porch.

"Hold it," I called out.

All three stopped and looked back at me.

"Goggles and gloves."

They shared a look, grinning, before Griffin jogged back to the van for the safety gear.

"I'm so glad they listen to you," Noelle said, chuckling. "You've probably saved us a fortune over the years in emergency room visits."

Chapter Ten

It took another fifteen minutes before I managed to sneak away. Pulling out of the driveway onto the road, I cringed when I saw two old timers unloading extension pole chainsaws. Beer and chainsaws sounded like a bad idea.

I kept going, but picked up my phone, calling Bernadette.

"What?" Bernadette barked, answering.

"Do you have insurance on that house in case anyone gets hurt on the property?"

"Not yet. I was going to call today but didn't get around to it."

"Well, after all the recent fires I doubt my insurance company will write me another policy, and Lance's buddies are drinking beer while cutting down tree limbs and manning a bonfire."

There was a long pause before Bernadette spoke. "I have my agent's cellphone number. I'll get a policy started tonight." Bernadette hung up.

I smiled and cranked the volume up on my stereo, heading back to town.

When I reached the city limits, I was about to turn onto a side road but changed my mind. Driving straight instead, I circled behind main street, parking in the back lot of the hardware store.

I climbed out, entering through the back door, and crept toward the front of the store, keeping an eye out for other customers.

"You're safe," Isaac said, grinning. "It's just us in here." Isaac pointed between himself and Jeff Timber, the owner.

"Thank goodness," I said, crossing to where they stood by the checkout counter. "I'm too exhausted to deal with the general public."

"Heard you bought a fixer upper," Jeff said, smiling at me.

"Bernadette bought it. I'm just the hired help." I pulled out the new debit card from my wallet, waving it around. "Thought I'd take this new piece of plastic for a spin."

"Well, now, there's an idea I can get behind," Jeff said, checking the time on his watch. "And it's close enough to closing time that it won't hurt any for me to flip the sign so you can shop in peace."

"Even better," I said before glancing at Isaac. "Want to help?"

"Sure," Isaac said, shrugging. "What are we shopping for?"

I bounced my eyebrows playfully. "Power tools."

"Oh, I'm in," Isaac said, chuckling as he set his shopping bag with whatever he'd purchased back on the counter.

IT TOOK ALMOST AN HOUR to get through the entire store. I loaded up on wrenches, two sledgehammers, framing squares, a long framing level, a laser level that was on sale, two prying bars that were a cross between a crowbar and a flat-head screwdriver, a palm sander, an electric staple gun, and a pile of denim women's work bibs that I found on a clearance rack.

I also eyed the nail guns, but decided they were too expensive. Shopping for power saws was fun though, especially when Jeff and Isaac got into a heated debate over which brands and styles were the best. I ended up picking out a chop saw that would sit on a table or the floor and work well to cut big boards, and for quick cutting jobs I bought both a one-handed reciprocating saw and a four-and-half inch circular saw that was super lightweight. As a gift for Lance, I also bought a full-sized reciprocating saw to replace his sticky-triggered psycho saw.

"Anything else?" Jeff asked, ringing up the last item.

"Not today, but I'm sure I'll be back after I work out my shopping list for the cottage."

"The cottage, huh?" Isaac said, picking up the box with my new chop saw. "Sounds fancy."

"Not even close, but when I get done with it, it'll be spectacular," I said, smiling.

"By chance, does the house need a water heater?" Jeff asked. "I've got two that have been sitting in the back room for ages. I'll make you a good deal on one of them."

"Now, wait a minute," Isaac said, giving Jeff a warning look. "You know it ain't that simple. Don't try to trick her. If the water heater isn't the same height, she'll waste money changing out plumbing parts."

I frowned at Isaac, thumbing toward the back entrance. "Appreciate you protecting me from bad decision making, but I wrote down the measurements for the water heater. They're in the van."

"Oh, well then," Isaac sputtered, picking up the box for the chop saw. "Let's go have a look." He started toward the back door.

Jeff chuckled, carrying one of the boxes he'd filled with tools.

I grabbed several plastic bags before following them. After loading everything into the back of the van, I retrieved my notepad. Sure enough, one of the water heaters in the back room was the perfect size. Jeff, eager to sell it, made me an offer I couldn't refuse and helped me load it into my van.

After paying, Isaac helped me carry the last load of bags out. "That was fun. Thanks for letting me participate."

"Are you kidding? If it weren't for you, I'd still be back there reading the boxes on all those saws, trying to figure out which one to buy."

Isaac grinned, setting his bags in the back of the van. "Are you running this stuff out to the cottage yet tonight?"

"No, I'm not brave enough to go back out there tonight."

"Why's that?"

"Lance and his buddies are out there. Beer, plus bonfire, plus tractors and a bobcat, plus chainsaws."

A slow smile lit Isaac's face. "Alice has book club tonight. Maybe I'll swing out that way to check on things."

I reached inside my purse, pulling my wallet. "If you're heading that way, here." I pulled out some cash, handing it to him. "I'm sure the beer is running low."

Isaac took the cash, tucking it into his shirt pocket before hurrying across the parking lot.

CHAPTER ELEVEN

IT WAS A FEW MINUTES PAST eight when I heard Olivia's station wagon rumble down my street. I got up from the table where I'd been reading Stone's case file for the missing teenage girl. After tossing the paper plate from my cold sandwich dinner into the trash can, I gathered my stuff from the end counter and exited out the side door.

Jogging down the driveway, I waited for Olivia to coast her beast of a car to a stop at the end of my driveway before hopping into the passenger seat. I set my purse on the floor, and everything else in my lap before pulling my seatbelt on. "Before I forget, I need to talk to you about the Nightshade Treasures office space."

Olivia cringed, steering her car back into the street. "You heard?"

Confused, I looked at her. "Heard what?"

"That I haven't paid the rent yet."

"No. Is the payment late?"

"It's due tomorrow, but I usually pay it on the first of the month."

I ran the calendar through my head, landing on today being the fourth of October.

"If I can close tonight's case, get a check from the client first thing tomorrow, and run it to the bank right away, then I can drop off the rent check to the landlord by tomorrow afternoon."

"I'm missing something. Your business just had a spike of cases after the media coverage of Raina's arrest. What happened?"

"The spike of cases only lasted a week. Now business is dead again."

"But what happened to the extra revenue? Didn't you set some of the money aside?"

"No. My income is whatever's left over after I pay the bills. That's how I get paid."

I opened my mouth but closed it again. Now might not be the best time to get into a deep accounting discussion. Staying on task, I said, "Mrs. Paulson needs more space. She's trying to find another storefront suitable for her antique store."

"No way," Olivia whined. "I can't afford my share as it is. What am I going to do?"

"What if you get rid of my desk and move yours into the back room?"

Olivia wrinkled her nose. "What about the conference room table?"

"You mean your dining room table?"

"Good point."

"Look, it's not forever, but it would give you a lower share of the rent and Mrs. Paulson more space so she doesn't have to change locations. Just think about it."

"I will," Olivia said on a long sigh. "It just sucks."

"That's life. I had to move my bedroom into the library today. I'm not happy about it, but sometimes we need to suck it up and do what needs to be done."

"Hey..." Olivia said with a flash of excitement. "What about your house? I could move my office to your living room and Mrs. Paulson could move the excess inventory from your house to the store. It's a win-win."

"Uhm..."

"We'd get to hang out all the time, and since you have a kitchen, I'd save money not eating out every day for lunch."

"Well..."

"How fun would that be, right?" Olivia bounced in her seat as she drove. "Not to mention, the Zenner house has that old, hard-boiled, detective vibe with its high ceilings and thick wood trim. Clients would love it."

"Hold it," I said, raising a hand to stop her. "It won't work. I hired the construction crew to start the remodeling next week. They'll be sawing and hammering lumber from dawn to dark. Sawdust everywhere."

Olivia slouched in her seat. "Bummer."

"Yeah, bummer," I said, glancing out my side window so she wouldn't read the relief on my face. I loved Olivia to pieces, but she was a walking disaster. I had enough on my plate. If I came home every night to dirty dishes and trash scattered around my house, I'd lose my mind.

"Well, I suppose moving into the back room at Nightshade Treasures makes sense for now," Olivia said, pouting. "I'll talk to Mrs. Paulson about it tomorrow."

"Good. I know she's just as worried about inventory space as you are about paying rent."

"I suppose." Olivia turned onto a well-traveled road that led to the highway. "So? What did you do today?"

I filled Olivia in on my day, starting with the meeting at the construction site and ending with leaving the cottage in the hands of a group of semi-intoxicated farmers.

Olivia was quiet while I filled her in, but she kept glancing over at me as she drove. "All *that* in one day? *Geesh.* You make the rest of us look bad."

"It was a long, long day—even for me. What did you do today?"

"I took the boys to school, ran background reports for a few hours, then went home to take a nap."

"Oh." I giggled. "Not exactly a high-performance day."

"Exactly. Now I feel guilty," Olivia said, giggling. "I'd told myself the nap was justified because we were working tonight. But you didn't take a nap."

I smiled at her, turning my body toward her. "Is it really work though? It's not like we do anything on our Thursday night excursions."

We'd fallen into a pattern a few weeks back of hanging out together on Thursday nights for what I referred to as girl's night. But instead of going to the bar like normal women, we sat in Olivia's station wagon, ate piles of junk food, talked nonstop about whatever was happening in our lives, all while staring at whatever motel or hotel she was staking out for one of her infidelity cases.

"Believe me, it's work." Olivia checked her side mirror, merging onto the interstate. "Which reminds me, what will we do next Thursday if I don't pick up another case?"

"I have a garage full of furniture that needs to be stripped and sanded. I sold a handful of pieces this morning, plus Mrs. Paulson asked me to refinish a desk for her."

Olivia lifted her fingers from the steering wheel, studying her nails. "I guess I'd better cancel my nail appointment for Monday. No point in wasting a fresh manicure sanding furniture."

"Just think of the money you'll save," I said, laughing.

Olivia rolled her eyes. "Whatever."

~*~*~

"ABOUT EIGHT HUNDRED FOR A basic white refrigerator and two to three thousand for one of the fancy stainless-steel models with the built in water dispenser," Olivia said, glancing up from her phone to check the dark parking lot again. "If you want a commercial refrigerator though, we're talking five figures."

I took her phone to see the screen. "That's just crazy. A few years ago, I bought a new refrigerator for my dad's house for four hundred."

"Inflation's a bitch," Olivia said, taking her phone back.

I wrote the figures on my notepad, adding the basic white refrigerator price to the cottage column and the more expensive stainless-steel price under the Zenner house column.

An idea sparked, and I added an asterisk next to the cottage's price. "You know, if I buy a nice refrigerator for the Zenner house, I could move the one that's there to the cottage."

"Sure. It's not like there's anything wrong with it. It's just not fancy enough for the Zenner house."

"Exactly. But no one buying the cottage will care. Especially since I'll be painting most of the walls white and cream colors to keep everything bright."

"Already picking out paint colors?" Olivia asked, shaking her head. "You're hooked."

"I admit, I'm enjoying the remodeling gig."

"Makes sense. You always liked taking something messy and turning it into something pretty. It's what drove you to clean houses."

"That, and I needed money." I lifted my notepad, smiling. "Thanks for helping with this. Whiskey told me I needed to get a jump on the shopping."

"No sweat. What's next?"

"I need prices on showers and tubs. Standard sizes."

"Watch the parking lot," Olivia said, nodding toward the dark and mostly empty parking lot as she tapped her thumbs on her phone's keyboard. "Okay, here we go. The shower base is around five hundred, the glass doors will run another five to six hundred, but if you buy a tub unit with the walls and glass doors included, I'm seeing sale packages in the six to seven hundred range. Does that make sense?"

"Not really, but I just need ballpark prices for the budget. I'll figure the rest out when I go shopping." I scribbled the amounts down, adding the tub unit price to the cottage bathroom and writing both options down for the Zenner house—already thinking the tub unit would work best in the hallway bathroom upstairs and the shower unit for the master bath. "Toilets?"

"Way ahead of you. A hundred bucks for a cheap one. Five hundred and up for anything that sprays your backside clean."

"Basic is good." I scribbled the price before leaning my head back against the headrest. "I need a break. Not only am I getting a kink in my neck, but I need to pee."

"Can you hold it?" Olivia asked, picking up her fancy new digital camera. "My guy just showed."

I looked to where she was pointing her camera. A medium-sized guy with a thick head of hair, bushy eyebrows, and way-too-long sideburns slid out of an expensive sedan and after glancing around suspiciously, he hurried to the side door of the hotel where a feminine hand pushed the door open to let him inside.

After taking a series of pictures, Olivia lowered her camera to her lap.

"Is that it? Are we done for the night?" I asked.

"Afraid not. Most clients are satisfied with meet up photos, but this guy's wife is paying extra for the in-the-act kind. She said he's the king of lying and can spin a tale to make just about anything sound innocent."

I made an icky face. "You were hired to take porn pictures?"

"It doesn't have to be *the* deed, but it needs to be at least tongue-down-throat level." Olivia reached into the back seat. "The good news is, it will take the lovebirds a few minutes to, uhm, *warm up* for their nightly activities, which gives you time to use the restroom and change." She handed me a paper tote bag.

I peeked inside the bag. "No..." I whined. "Olivia, we've talked about this. I don't like the disguise gigs."

"It's all good. I have a plan."

Oh, boy, I thought, pushing my car door open.

Chapter Twelve

I OPENED THE BATHROOM STALL and tugged the short skirt down for the umpteenth time. *The things we do for best friends*, I thought as I looked up at the long mirror above the sinks. I was hoping the skirt wasn't as short as it felt but, for better or worse, the mirror only reflected me from the waist up. I tucked the cash I'd pulled from my wallet into my bra since my outfit offered zero pockets.

"Are we ready?" Olivia asked, bouncing out of the other stall.

I scanned her outfit. Unlike the one she'd suckered me into wearing, Olivia's covered every inch of her. Dressed in a maintenance uniform onesie, she pulled a hat on top of her head, tucking her hair under it. Not only did she look comfortable in her getup, but she obviously wasn't feeling the vent directing cold air up her backside.

"This is a terrible plan. You know that, right?" I asked.

"It's a great plan. Besides, you won't be anywhere near the action. I just need you to warn me if someone's coming." With a bounce to her step, she exited the bathroom.

I tugged my skirt down again before following her out. "Let's get this over with."

It turned out that the guy Olivia was stalking tonight was a creature of habit. Twice a week he met up with his sidepiece at this hotel, always booking the same room on the third floor at the end of the hallway. I was only half listening to Olivia rattle while we climbed the stairs to the third floor.

Her plan was simple enough, at least my part of it. I was to stay near the elevator, pretending to clean, while she hooked a magnetic camera to the door's peephole to record whatever was going on inside the room. I didn't want to know where she got the spy device, and only hoped she hadn't practiced using it at my house.

Exiting into the hallway, I carried the cleaning tote that held only a bottle of glass cleaner and a roll of paper towel over to a decorative table that sat across from the elevator. "Where'd you get the tools," I asked, pointing to the handyman toolkit full of household tools that she was carrying.

"Borrowed them from the garage. Breydon won't notice them missing. I'll put them back tomorrow."

"Uh-huh," I said, pulling out the glass cleaner and spraying down the frameless mirror above the table.

I glanced sideways, watching Olivia creep down the hallway like a kid playing a game. I rolled my eyes, tearing off a section of paper towel to polish the mirror.

For several long minutes it was quiet, and I was on my third round of spraying and wiping the mirror when a real housekeeper for the hotel pushed a cart around the corner, stopping to look at me.

We both silently eyed each other from head to toe, her raising an eyebrow at my overly short skirt, me frowning at her black cotton pants.

The housekeeper shook her head and continued down the hall. Working in a hotel, she probably saw more than her share of crazy stuff, and learned long ago it was best not to ask questions.

Lifting the spray bottle, about to spray the mirror again, I heard Olivia screech.

I tossed the glass cleaner toward the tote and took off running in that direction.

"What the hell?" a man shouted.

"I'll get her," a familiar woman's voice called out.

Shelly Bright, I thought as I skidded around the corner.

"Get off me," Olivia yelled, twisting away from Shelly who was trying to get her hands on the electronic recording device.

Running toward the end of the hall, I watched Shelly trying to pry the spy camera from Olivia's fingers. Olivia twisted away again, and Shelly bent over, moving with her. I was rewarded with a full view of Shelly's G-string undies.

Only a few feet away from them, Shelly snagged the camera and tossed it to the man who was fleeing the hotel room. Somehow, he caught the device, despite his hands being busy buttoning buttons and zipping zippers. Pocketing it, he hurried down the hall, running past me toward the elevators.

I stopped, hesitating over whether to go after him or help Olivia. Shelly took advantage of the indecision and dove into the hotel room, slamming the door shut.

Dang it, I thought, glaring at the door. I glanced over at Olivia. "Are you okay?"

"Yeah," Olivia said, rubbing a red mark on her wrist.

"What happened?"

"Shelly happened," Olivia said, leaning over to pick up her toolbox. "Come on. Let's get out of here."

As we made our way back down the hall and into the stairway, me picking up the cleaning tote along the way, Olivia explained how all was going as planned until she recognized the voice inside the room. Wanting to confirm her suspicions that Shelly was the one she was hearing, she tried to wiggle a listening device under the door. The door opened and all hell broke loose.

Olivia looked downright downtrodden, exiting the stairwell with sunken shoulders. She turned, heading for the side door exit.

"I'll catch up with you," I said, handing her the cleaning tote.

"You need to pee again? How much coffee did you drink earlier?"

"Not nearly enough," I said before pivoting in the opposite direction.

Despite my ridiculous outfit, I crossed to the front desk and asked the justifiably surprised clerk if I could speak to the security officer. She picked up the phone, turning her head away as she whispered into it. I stepped back from the desk, waiting.

A man in the usual uniform came out of a back room a few minutes later. He smiled a knowing smile, his eyes scanning down my exposed legs before he nodded for me to follow him.

When we were out of earshot of the clerk, I asked, "How much?"

"Forty for the hallway video outside their room and another twenty if you want me to add the elevator footage where they were groping each other."

"I'll take both," I said, digging the cash out of my bra.

Chapter Thirteen

I WOKE CONFUSED, UNABLE TO figure out why the morning sunlight was facing the wrong way. It took me a minute to remember my bed was now in the library. Tossing the blanket off, I rubbed my hands up and down my face, trying to get my brain to kickstart. It was Friday. Two days ago, my schedule had been wide open, free to do as I pleased. Now I had to get up and get moving, or I'd be late for the appointments I'd scheduled at the cottage.

Less than an hour later, I pulled into the front yard at the cottage wearing my comfortable new denim bibs, a long-sleeved t-shirt, and my hair worn up in a messy bun. I moved the cooler from the passenger seat to the floor behind it before picking up my notepad and tucking it under one arm. Pushing my door open, I grabbed my travel cup of coffee and hopped out, using my foot to shut the door.

Rounding my van, I spotted Lance's tractor and Pete's bobcat still parked in the driveway where the garage had been. I smiled, suspecting both men were nursing hangovers this morning.

I set my coffee and notepad down in the yard and dug around in the back of my van for a tape measure. After measuring the front porch, I sat down in the weeds to scribble out my idea to screen the porch off, even adding a few bushes and flowerpots to my drawing.

I wasn't much of an artist, but the sketch was good enough to show someone my rough idea, including mimicking the angles of the house roof. I smiled down at my drawing, liking the idea more and more. With the porch sitting off center of the rest of the house, it added a layered look while making the house seem bigger.

Hearing a vehicle, I looked over my shoulder. Jackie Jones drove around the bend and parked behind my van. I smiled, climbing up from the ground. "Morning," I called out when she was within earshot.

"Morning." Jackie looked around. "By golly, this place is already looking better."

"I wish it were that easy." After brushing the backside of my pants clean, I clipped my tape measurer to my bib's pocket. "Want some coffee? I brought four travel mugs. If I drink them all, I'll float away."

"No, thanks. I have an appointment to get to, but I wanted to drop off the market comps you asked for." Jackie handed me a file folder. "When you're going through them, pay attention to the date of when the property sold. Around here, early spring is usually the best time to sell and people seldom buy fixer uppers in the middle of winter."

"Good to know," I said, flipping through some of the printouts. "Geesh. These resale prices are all over the place."

"It all depends on the condition of the house and the size of the land. Is Bernadette dividing the property like she normally does?"

"Yeah. Five acres will stay with the house."

"That's good. It'll sell faster."

I picked up my notepad, turning it to show Jackie my sketch. "What do you think about adding a screened porch along the front side of the house after the trees are all cut back?"

Jackie took the notepad and looked between the sketch and the house. "I like it, but maybe move the screen door to the driveway side. That way you won't have to create a fancy walkway in the front yard."

I took the notepad back and scribbled a note to myself. "Do you have time to go inside so I can run another idea past you?"

Jackie grimaced, glancing up at the house. "Yes, but is the house safe to enter yet?"

"Most of the rooms are." I led the way up the porch. "The floors in the kitchen and downstairs bathroom are unsafe, but what I want to show you is in the upstairs small bedroom."

Jackie followed me into the house and up to the second floor, commenting on things as we went. I entered the smaller of the two bedrooms, stopping in the center of the room and turning to gauge her expression.

"Good sized bedroom," Jackie said, scrunching her nose.

"You don't have to sugar-coat it. This room is a mess. The natural light is horrible, and the sloped ceiling makes the room feel more like a closet than a bedroom."

Jackie grinned. "Will it make you feel better if I tell you I've seen worse?"

"Maybe, but the idea I'm brewing up is to add square skylights along the sloped ceiling and beneath them, building shelves and drawers for storage." I moved to the outer wall where the ceiling was the lowest and raised a hand to about the six-foot mark. "If I bring the new built-in storage to about here for depth, the room will be narrower, but the space will be fully functional."

"Might make the room feel less like it's about to eat its occupants," Jackie said, smiling as she eyed the space. "I like it, but won't it be expensive?"

"I don't think so. I accidentally accumulated a pile of furniture to re-stain and resell. I can repurpose some of the pieces for this project." I pulled out my phone, scrolling through pictures until I found the pair of short dressers I was looking for. I turned the screen to show Jackie. "I can paint the storage pieces white, and the walls a light accent color."

"I don't know how to build something like that, but if you build it—I can sell it." Jackie snagged the file she'd given me and flipped it open. Pulling out three listings, she turned them to show me. "Look here. These three houses are similar in size, but the first one is on ten acres and the house needs a lot of work." She pointed to the price. "The second has two acres but the house has been completely remodeled."

The price was fifty thousand higher.

"But this one," Jackie flipped to the third house, "has only one acre of land but the house is loaded with personal touches like what you're describing. Nothing too fancy, but when you walk in, it feels homey."

I looked at the price, pulling the sheet from her hands. "Holy shamoley, that much more money?"

"Yes, ma'am. Build the features to make the house stand out, and you'll make *a lot* more money."

"Thanks. That's exactly what I needed." I grinned at the far wall, imagining the built-in storage.

"I have another meeting to get to," Jackie said, checking her phone. "Anything else before I take off?"

"No, I'm good. Appreciate the advice."

"I'll see myself out. Just remember that early spring is the best time to sell. The clock is ticking." Jackie crossed to the bedroom door.

"I won't forget." I followed her into the upstairs landing but stopped to gather an armload of trim boards I'd left stacked along the floor.

CHAPTER FOURTEEN

BETWEEN CONTRACTORS POPPING IN TO replace door locks and measure windows, and Randy Ikers stopping by to pump the septic tank, I plugged away at small projects around the cottage and added more notes to my notepad.

In the mudroom off the back corner of the house, I studied the space opposite the back door. A four-foot wide wall separated the kitchen from the mudroom, leaving a bare section of space on the mudroom side. I'd hoped to repurpose the space for a laundry hookup, but after measuring, I discovered it wasn't wide enough. The current laundry hookups were in the basement, which wasn't ideal.

Feeling a breeze, I looked behind me, noticing the door wasn't shut completely. I pulled it open, poking my head outside. *Did the wind blow the door open?* I shut the door, tugging on it, but the latch held. If jerking on the door handle didn't open it, the wind certainly hadn't blown it open.

Turning the knob again, I stepped outside onto the crumbling concrete patio. The boys had weed whipped in the back yard, clearing a good ten-foot radius around the house. Near the door, I spotted a half dozen cigarette butts stubbed out on a chunk of concrete. The butts were fresh, not weathered like they'd been there for a long time.

The cigarette butts could've been left by one of Lance's friends, and because the front porch was a mess, after it got dark last night everyone likely used the back door for any bathroom breaks. I stepped back inside and closed the door, refocusing on the opposite wall. I remeasured the width, but the length from one wall to the other hadn't grown since I'd last measured it.

"Davina?" Whiskey called out.

"In here!" I called back. I waited until Whiskey and Virgil appeared around the corner. "Careful." I pointed at the bowed flooring. "Watch your step."

"Looks a little warped," Virgil said, chuckling.

"Just a little." I looked back at the wall. "Any ideas here? I want to move the laundry hookups upstairs, but the only place that makes sense is here and it's not wide enough."

"How many bedrooms?" Virgil asked, looking up at the ceiling.

"Three."

"That rules out a stackable unit," Whiskey said.

"You know," Virgil said, rubbing his chin. "I hear the all-in-one washer and dryers are all the rage these days. Got no idea how pricey they are, though."

"I can look into it," I said, scribbling a note. "But this a low budget job."

Whiskey skirted around the bowed floor and pointed to the wall separating the kitchen and mudroom. "If we need to, we could build a header through here to open the room into the kitchen." Whiskey slapped a hand against the dividing wall. It made a sharp cracking noise.

Whiskey threw a protective arm in front of me, backing us both up a few feet toward the back door. The dividing wall swooped down, crashing onto the kitchen floor. The window behind me rattled and the floor beneath my feet vibrated.

"Oh, shit," Whiskey mumbled. "If I'd have known…"

I stared at the wall for a long moment before glancing up. The drywall along the ceiling had one dark smudge like a rub mark, but not a single hole where a nail or screw should've been. I looked between Whiskey who stood next to me and Virgil who'd backpedaled into the doorway across the room. "Well... I guess that answers my next question."

"What was your question?" Virgil asked, staring at the wall lying on the floor.

"I wanted to know how hard it would be to take out that wall."

"Not hard at all, apparently," Virgil said, chuckling.

Whiskey barked a laugh, running his fingers through his hair. "If you want the wall back up—"

"I don't," I said, holding my hand up. "Really, I don't." I looked at the ceiling again before scribbling a note on my notepad. "Next on my list... Push against each wall to make sure they're nailed down."

They laughed. Whiskey stepped back, relaxing against the back door. When the door creaked, he jumped forward, spinning around to look at it.

Virgil laughed again, shaking his head. "Are you try'n to destroy her new house?"

"It's not Whiskey's fault," I said, pulling my tape measure and measuring the width of the door. "This door is on my replace list. Not only is it hollow, but someone kicked it in at some point."

"Who installs a hollow-core door for an exterior entrance?" Whiskey asked, rapping his knuckles against it.

"I'm guessing it was the same dumbass who forgot to nail up the wall," Virgil said, turning out of the room. "Come on. Let's go check out the attic before you knock the house over."

Whiskey followed, stepping around the wall and bowed flooring. "You want me to haul this out?" He pointed to the wall.

"Nah. I might repurpose it elsewhere. It can stay where it is for now."

Whiskey nodded, but leaned over and tipped the wall up on its side to clear the walkway before walking out. I heard their footsteps climbing the stairs.

"Can't believe you broke her wall," Virgil said, chuckling.

"Damn thing just fell over. You ever seen that before? Because I sure as hell haven't."

Virgil chuckled again.

As their voices trailed off, I grinned, remeasuring the space at the back of the mudroom down the length of the kitchen to the doorway, scribbling the measurement down before exiting the kitchen.

Upstairs, I found Whiskey in the larger bedroom, looking out the windows into the front yard. He glanced over his shoulder at me, hearing me enter. "A balcony off this front bedroom would be cool."

"Something to consider, but I have a different idea to run past you. I want to screen off the front porch." I moved to stand beside him, flipping my notebook to the page I'd sketched out. "Can you give me a quote for the rough framing? I can make the insert panels for the screens and do the finish work myself."

Whiskey studied the sketch before glancing down at the half-rotted porch below. "How solid is the underside frame of that porch?"

"I think it's good," I said, leaning forward to look down. "But maybe you should push on it and see if it falls over."

Whiskey chuckled, nodding. "I'll give it a good heave ho before I leave." He tapped my drawing. "You want the roof lines to have the same angle?"

"Yes. And if the porch has to wait until spring, I'm okay with that. I know I'm throwing a lot at you guys right now."

"Might not be an issue," Virgil said, climbing down the ladder from the attic. "The roof replacement won't take much. Half the cost will be in the tear off."

"Those decking boards and rafters are good?" Whiskey asked, raising an eyebrow. "Under all that moss?" He pointed at the brown water stains on the ceiling.

"Rafters look good and only two decking boards need replacing. But if the roof isn't dealt with before winter, then come spring, the house could suffer a lot more damage."

"What do you guys think about me doing the tear-off? Think it's something I could handle?"

Whiskey nodded. "Sure, as long as you use safety ropes and have someone here to babysit you."

"It's a messy job, and wears on your muscles, but it's simple enough to do," Virgil agreed. "Plus, if you do the tear off, we can buzz over and knock out the roof and the porch after we get your construction site buttoned up. I figure we'll need one, maybe two days, to do both."

"That'd be cool," I said, nodding. "Can I bounce another question off you guys?"

Both men shrugged.

I led the way down the hall into the smaller bedroom. "I have a few ideas how to make this room look less claustrophobic, but one of my ideas is to add skylights to this section of the roof that slopes low. Anything I should know before I start shopping for windows?"

"Two things," Whiskey said, pointing at the sloped ceiling. "One, make sure the windows you buy will fit between the rafters. If not, you'll have to reframe part of the roof to make them fit."

"Your rafters are spaced sixteen inches apart," Virgil said.

I scribbled down the measurement. "And the other thing?"

"Buy and install the windows *before* we show up to slap on the new roof."

"I can do that."

"Hello?" a voice called out from downstairs. "Anyone here?"

"Upstairs!" I called out, moving into the hall to glance down the stairs.

Austin stepped into the opening, looking up. His dimple appeared when his eyes met mine. "Well, hello gorgeous," he said, jogging up the steps. "I heard you picked yourself up a new project."

"I did. I'm trying to get everything buttoned up before winter." I checked my Fitbit for the time. "Why aren't you at work? It's only mid-morning."

"Playing hooky." Austin rounded the corner of the railing, slowing his steps as he sauntered toward me. "I was hoping you'd play hooky with me."

"Can't." I held up my notepad, grinning at him before nodding across the hall.

Austin glanced over, seeing Whiskey and Virgil standing there watching us. Austin straightened, shifting away from me. "Sorry. Didn't realize you were in the middle of something."

I crossed back into the bedroom, Austin following behind me.

"We're just about done," Whiskey said, holding out a hand to shake Austin's. "Good to see you again."

Austin exchanged handshakes and Whiskey introduced Virgil. As they chit-chatted about things, I rechecked my to do list. I put checkmarks next to the roof, the locksmith, and the broken windows. Ed Mason had arrived right after the locksmith left this morning, and after measuring the windows, he'd agreed to start replacing the panes as early as tomorrow morning.

The next item on my priority list was a new back door for the cottage and to shop for the bathroom fixtures for the Zenner house.

"Davina?" Austin said, grinning while waving a hand in front of me to get my attention.

"What? Sorry. My brain won't sit still."

Whiskey chuckled. "I was telling Austin about how you planned to do the roof tear off yourself and he offered to loan you his safety ropes along with free labor tomorrow."

"All we need is an extension ladder," Austin added.

"I've got an extension ladder in my garage," I said, glancing toward the stairs, hearing someone's footsteps. When Lance rounded the corner, heading our way, I looked back at Austin. "I appreciate the offer to help, but I'm not sure tomorrow will work for me. I really need to get some of the shopping done to find deals on the stuff I need." I held up my notepad.

"Like what?" Austin asked.

"Doors, showers, kitchen cabinets, skylights," I said, waving a hand toward the bedroom's slanted ceiling. "I have a two-page list of things to buy for here, plus another list for the Zenner house."

"If you're trying to save money," Austin said, smiling. "I know a guy who sells leftover construction stuff. Doors, faucets, sinks, cabinets—"

"Bathtubs?" I asked, interrupting.

"Probably."

"I'm interested, all right. I pieced together a budget last night, so I'm ready to shop."

"Is that so?" Lance said, leaning against the door jamb. "Got all your measurements?"

I flipped my notepad to the shopping list page before handing it over.

Lance skimmed down the list, nodding. "Looks good. Why'd you cross out the water heater?"

"Bought one last night off Jeff Timber. It was priced to move." I thumbed over my shoulder. "Before everyone skedaddles, I sure could use a hand hauling it down to the basement."

Whiskey raised a hand. "Since I still feel guilty about knocking over that wall, I'd be happy to move the water heater."

Lance's eyes swiveled between Whiskey and me. "Do I even want to know?"

I shook my head, laughing, but pointed to the notepad. "See anything I missed?"

"Nope. Looks thorough." Lance handed the notepad back to me.

"I won't be buying everything today. Without a garage, I don't have enough space to store everything."

"I live just down the road," Lance said, thumbing over his shoulder. "We can store stuff in my barn."

"Are you sure?" I asked.

"Wouldn't have suggested it if I wasn't," Lance said, raising an eyebrow. Lance turned to Austin. "This place you're recommending, they got fair prices?"

"Yes, but if you're into haggling, you can save even more. Plus, his inventory is top of the line."

"And you've got cash?" Lance asked me.

"Not yet, but I can pull money from the new account. Any idea how much I'd need?"

"Couple grand I'd say, for cabinets, sinks and such," Austin said.

Whiskey took my list from me, wobbling his head while skim reading it. "Buying for both houses... bathrooms, doors, kitchen cabinets... I'd say five grand is a good start, but if you can afford it, I always carry double the cash I think I'll need, just in case I happen upon the deal of the century." He handed my notepad back.

"You run to the bank," Lance said with a nod. "I'll pop into town and see if Mrs. Paulson will go with us. Her talent for negotiating might come in handy."

"Agreed." I looked at Austin. "Are you shopping with us or fleeing the scene?"

"Are you kidding? I'm in," Austin said. "Sounds fun. It's about a thirty-minute drive south of here. Lance, maybe you should follow us over with your truck and trailer?"

Lance crossed his arms, nodding. "I can do that."

"Are you talking about Walter Young's place?" Virgil asked Austin.

"Yeah, that's the guy," Austin said. "I was out there a few months ago. He's got three big barns, plus behind the barns he's got another half dozen lean-to buildings."

Virgil glanced at Whiskey. "I haven't been over t in years. Back then, he had only one barn. Might be wo n the drive."

Whiskey shrugged. "Why not."

Austin gave them directions, while I ran downstairs to empty the back of my van.

CHAPTER FIFTEEN

AFTER MOVING THE WATER HEATER to the basement, everyone helped to unload the bags and boxes from the back of my van into the living room.

"You went power tool shopping without me?" Lance asked, scowling at the boxes of saws.

"I did, but before you grumble, Isaac was with me. He helped me pick out saws that would be easier for me to handle."

"You did good," Virgil said, holding up the four-and-a-half-inch circular saw. "I bought one of these for each of my brothers last year for Christmas. Handy little saw for small projects."

Lance eyed the saw with more interest.

"And it doesn't weigh thirty pounds," I said. I set the boxes down, pulling out the full-sized reciprocating saw to hold out for Lance. "I bought this for you. I think it's time for you to retire your old one before someone gets hurt."

"For me?" Lance said, taking the box.

"Yup. Just a small thank you for all the help on the houses."

Lance blushed, muttering his thanks. He unpackaged the saw, admiring it with a grin and holding it up. "It's a knock off brand, but I like the looks of it."

"I like the knockoff brands," Whiskey said, reappearing from the basement. "If you drop them off a roof, it doesn't hurt your wallet nearly as much to buy a new one."

"Good point," Lance said, chuckling.

After finishing up inside, the men walked off toward their trucks and Austin climbed into the passenger side of my van, planning to ride with me. Turning onto the road with my windows down, I inhaled a lungful of crisp fall air.

"This is kind of fun," Austin said. "I'm usually not the 'hey, let's go shopping' type."

"Me either, but buying stuff for the houses sounds fun." I picked up my phone and called Mr. Henry, the bank manager. After putting the call on speaker mode, I turned left onto the next road.

When I asked Mr. Henry to prepare a ten thousand dollar withdraw from the new business account, he sounded somewhat distressed. After I explained I was going shopping, he assured me he'd have it ready for me. I hit the disconnect button, glancing at Austin. "Why are you playing hooky today?"

"It was too nice a day to sit in my office." Austin turned on the radio, adjusting the volume down to a fraction of my usual setting. "My grand plan when I'd stopped by was to invite you to lunch."

At the mention of food my stomach rumbled. "My cooler is behind your seat. Grab us some sandwiches, will you? Refueling before shopping might be a good idea."

Austin twisted sideways, leaning around his seat to reach the cooler. After unwrapping one of the sandwiches, he passed it to me. "It's been ages since I've had PB&Js."

"Lucky you. It's my go-to menu when I'm working crazy hours."

"Technically," Austin held up his sandwich, "this counts as a date. About time, considering how many times we rescheduled."

"I'm not the only one who keeps rescheduling. Some of the canceled dates were your fault."

Austin chuckled as he chewed and swallowed. "Sorry. Work has been crazy. But the last canceled date was you, not me. I still can't believe Breydon called at the last minute for a babysitter."

"I can. After spending three days with two sick boys, he wasn't equipped to handle Olivia getting sick too. She's the queen of whining when she doesn't feel good."

"But why would Breydon expect you to deal with it?"

"It wasn't like that. We negotiated a deal. In exchange for me taking over his household for the twenty-four hours, Breydon wiped the slate clean on all the favors I owed him for legal work, including handling three insurance claims for me. We're back to even-Steven. Besides, I already owed him two nights of babysitting anyway."

"Bartering with your friends. I like it. So, what do I get for helping with the roof?"

"I'd ask what you want, but I'm afraid of your answer," I said, grinning at him.

Austin's dimple popped out.

I rolled my eyes. "How about a home cooked meal some random night in the near future?"

"Make it two homecooked meals and I'm in."

"Deal. But fair warning, Noah can smell my cooking from across town. He usually walks in and helps himself."

"How's Britt feel about that?"

"Not good. I've become a sore subject in their relationship."

"She doesn't trust that you're just friends?"

"That's the problem, we're not just friends. Noah's more like a brother, you know? We're close, but not in that boy-girl kind of way."

My phone rang. Glancing down, I saw it was Olivia. I waited until I parked behind the bank before answering. "Olivia, hang on a second." I set the phone in my lap.

Mr. Henry rushed over from the employee's entrance to my driver's window, passing me a withdrawal slip. I signed the slip, passing it back and taking the envelope full of cash.

Saying our goodbyes, I stuffed the envelope inside my purse.

"What was that?" Austin asked, looking between my window and the back door to the bank.

"That's how outcasts like me do their banking," I said, picking the phone back up and holding it to my ear. "Okay, I'm back. What's up?"

"I heard you, Lance, and Mrs. Paulson are meeting to go shopping. What's the deal? Why didn't you invite me?"

"We're buying things like toilets and sinks. Not exactly your style."

"Sounds more fun than running background checks," Olivia said in a pouty voice.

"When I get to the girly stuff, I promise I'll take you with me. Deal?"

"Fine. But tomorrow I'm driving out to see this house Bernadette bought. It sounds horrible."

"It's a fixer upper for sure. It's somewhere between my old house and that abandoned house that Collin owned. You know, the one where the stairway to the basement fell out from under you?"

"Don't remind me."

"No new cases to solve?"

"Not yet, but I scheduled a meeting with a potential new client for tomorrow morning. Fingers crossed that it'll be something fun and not another infidelity case."

"Good luck. I'll see you tomorrow, but wear grubby clothes, not one of your pastel frilly outfits, okay?"

"We'll see," Olivia said, disconnecting the call.

I dropped the phone into the cupholder and reversed the van. "Where to?" I asked Austin.

"Head toward the city, but we'll circle around to the southern end of the county."

"Out near the county fairgrounds?"

"Yup. It's about two miles further south."

"Got it."

I turned onto the street, and at the next intersection I turned again to drive through the center of town. Two blocks up I spotted Isaac, leaning against the hood of his car, wearing a big ole grin.

Pulling up alongside his cruiser, I leaned toward Austin's window and shouted to Isaac, "Working hard?"

Isaac dipped his head in the direction of the other side of the street. "Just watching the show."

I looked that way, seeing a man standing outside a clothing shop holding a giant bouquet of flowers. I smiled. "Aw, that's sweet."

"*Wait for it...*" Isaac said.

Bernadette came out of the store and was startled when she came face to face with him. He lifted the bouquet in front of her, offering her the flowers.

Bernadette grabbed the flowers, and after looking both directions down the sidewalk, she beat the bouquet against his shoulder. Flower petals flew everywhere.

When he ducked, I caught his profile, seeing it was the same man who'd ridden shotgun with her to the cottage the day before.

Isaac laughed as Bernadette tossed the flowers down and stomped off. Her mystery man picked up a handful of the discarded flowers and chased after her, not deterred.

"If anyone asks, I'm not related to her," I said.

"I hear that," Isaac said, chuckling. He moved toward his driver's door. "Later."

"Later," I called out before continuing down the street.

CHAPTER SIXTEEN

BY THE TIME WE REACHED our destination, Lance and Mrs. Paulson were already deep inside the first barn and Whiskey and Virgil were out back somewhere, rummaging through the lean-to buildings. Austin and I jumped right in, with him marking off things on my notepad and checking measurements for me, Mrs. Paulson negotiating prices with Walter, the owner, and Lance shifting the things I wanted to buy out into the main walkway, so when we were done we could easily come back to load everything.

I'd not only saved a ton of money, but by the time we exited the last barn I'd ticked off a page and a half between both my shopping lists. The only thing I still needed for the bathrooms at the Zenner house were a set of towel racks and one light fixture.

Handing the cash envelope to Mrs. Paulson, she walked away to settle both invoices, somehow managing to keep the two houses on separate tabs. I helped Lance and Austin haul everything to the front parking lot to take back to Daybreak Falls.

"Davina," Whiskey called out, crossing through the last barn to the front parking lot, "how certain are you about building that screened porch at the cottage?"

"Pretty certain as long as we can keep the costs reasonable. Why? What's up?"

Whiskey turned his phone, showing me a picture of a pre-framed roof. "It's about a foot shorter than what you need, but I'm thinking we could get a good price. There's also shingles back there, in all kinds of colors."

Mrs. Paulson was returning with my receipts for my purchases, handing them and my cash envelope over to me. I took the receipts but nodded to the envelope. "Hang on to that a second." I looked back at Whiskey. "Mrs. Paulson is the queen of negotiating, but she'll need you to tell her how much this stuff normally costs."

Whiskey showed Mrs. Paulson the picture of the roof, explaining what it was for, and how much it typically would cost to build. Her eyes lit up before she settled into her poker face. She glanced at me, looping her arm through mine. "I'm ready."

We followed Whiskey through the barn to where the lean-to buildings were.

Not having much to contribute, I hung back while Mrs. Paulson negotiated the roof frame down to pennies on the dollar. Walter seemed happy to get whatever he could for it, but insisted Whiskey had to pick it up no later than the next day. They moved over to shingles, and I picked out the charcoal ones I liked. The price dickering restarted. Mrs. Paulson seemed less excited by the price they settled on, but I understood Walter's reluctance to go lower. It wasn't like charcoal shingles would go out of style anytime soon.

About to head back toward the front lot, I spotted a building off to the side. "What's in there?"

"Ah," Walter said, leading the way. "I can't believe I didn't show you. This is where I keep the more expensive appliances. The ones I don't want to chance getting dinged and damaged in the main barns."

Walter unlatched the door, opening it and letting me enter first. I made it only a half-dozen feet into the building before I stopped to stare.

"Give us a minute," Mrs. Paulson said to Walter, reading my face.

"Sure," Walter said, snickering as he exited back outside.

"You know better," Mrs. Paulson scolded in a whisper. "Wipe that grin off your face."

I pursed my lips, trying not to smile. "I want it. I really, really, want it."

"Just the refrigerator?"

"I love the refrigerator, but I need the matching stove and dishwasher too if the price is right."

"Any idea how much this stuff is worth in the store?"

"Fifteen hundred on the refrigerator, minimum. I'd guess six or seven on the gas stove, maybe more. No clue on the dishwasher."

"If I can get the price to two grand, you'd be happy?"

"Yes, but I'll have to cross something off my list. I was looking at the lower end refrigerators."

"Got it." A mischievous grin crossed her face. "Doesn't fit your budget," she said, nodding. "I can work with that. Now skedaddle. If Walter catches you still grinning like a fool, you'll be paying retail prices."

I hurried from the building, scowling at the ground as I zipped past Walter. I glanced up, winked at Whiskey, but kept going.

Chapter Seventeen

Mrs. Paulson negotiated a deal so good I couldn't stop smiling the whole drive back to Daybreak Falls. She'd closed at a price of seventeen hundred for all three appliances. The stove was wider than the stove that was already there, but I could move the end cabinet and countertop over, so I wasn't worried.

Turning into Lance's driveway, I saw that Jared, his boys, and Noah were already waiting to help us unload. I'd called them before we'd left the city, asking them to meet us. Shopping had eaten most of the day and it was already after five, but it had been worth it.

After unloading the big stuff for the cottage, we all moved to the Zenner house to unload there. The bathroom fixtures were carried upstairs to store in one of the bedrooms while I emptied the old refrigerator into a cooler. After that, the old appliances were hauled outside and the new ones inside.

I was a little disappointed when Lance told me I had to wait twenty-four hours to plug in my new refrigerator—something to do with the refrigerant gas settling after being jostled around—but waiting one day wouldn't kill me. Besides, the stove couldn't be installed until the end cabinet was moved anyway.

Mrs. Paulson walked from the Zenner house to her house, and the rest of us climbed back into our vehicles to drive once again across town. At the cottage, we hauled everything else inside, packing it inside the living room.

I dug around, climbing over boxes, until I unearthed the tools needed to move the cabinet at the Zenner house.

I carried them outside, setting them in the back of my van. I turned to head back inside when Noah walked past, heading down the driveway. "Taking off?" I called out.

"Yeah. I promised Britt we'd meet up later. I'll catch up with you sometime this weekend." Noah didn't wait for me to comment, crossing the driveway and disappearing around the bend, walking back toward the road where he'd parked. He looked tired and frustrated, and I felt bad for the minefield he was trying to navigate.

Returning inside, I followed the sound of voices into the kitchen, seeing Austin and the Donaldson boys staring down at the fallen divider wall.

I was about to ask Austin a question when I was distracted by a whiff of cigarette smoke. I stepped closer to Griffin, sniffing him before shifting to Davey to sniff him too.

"Uh, Davina..." Griffin said. "Everything okay?"

"Have either of you been smoking?" I asked, taking a second sniff of Davey.

Both boys leaned away, raising their hands, and adamantly shook their heads.

"You're joking, right?" Austin said, chuckling. "Noelle would hang them by their toes and beat them senseless if she caught them smoking."

I crossed to the back door, opening it. The cigarette butts were still on the back patio, but now there were more of them. I stepped out, looking around.

"Problem?" Lance asked from where he stood near his tractor in the back of the driveway talking to Jared.

"Someone's been out here smoking." I pointed to the cigarette butts.

Both men walked over and looked down at the cigarette butts. Lance leaned over, scooping them up.

"One of the guys here last night smokes, but he pockets his. Doesn't leave them lying around like this."

"Teenagers?" Austin asked, standing behind me next to the Donaldson boys.

"I doubt it," Griffin said. "I put the word out at school that whoever's been partying out here, better knock it off."

I grinned at Griffin. "I knew I liked you," I said, wrapping an arm around him and giving him I sideways hug.

"Yeah, same goes for kids my age," Davey said, nodding. "Most of them are away at college, but I posted on my social sites with a headline saying *party's over.*" Davey held out his arms, waiting for his hug.

I obliged, giving him a good squeeze.

"Probably just a contractor," Lance said. "Someone who dropped by, trying to catch you earlier."

"You're right," I said. "But that reminds me... I have the new housekeys." I re-entered the house and moved back into the living room, climbing around stuff to get to the windowsill where I'd left the keys.

I picked up three keys and was about to turn when I noticed only two remained. *I'd asked for six keys.* I looked at the floor and around the windowsill but didn't see another key. There were only five.

I thought back to when the locksmith had been here, replaying our conversation in my head. I'd had a million things going on and after he'd handed me the keys, I set them in the windowsill—*without counting them.*

I relaxed my shoulders and picked up the remaining two keys. Making my way to the front door where I'd left my purse, I dug out my keyring, adding a key to it, and tucked the fifth key in the outside pocket of my purse.

Returning to the kitchen, I handed out the other three keys: one to Davey, one to Griffin, and one to Lance.

"I don't get one?" Jared asked.

"Sorry. You'll have to borrow one of the boys' keys if you need one. I only have one key left and Whiskey will need it."

Jared chuckled. "I'm just teasing. Besides, most of the windows are smashed out. If I want inside, it'd be easy to get in."

"Which reminds me." I looked back at Davey and Griffin. "I'm supposed to meet Ed Mason tomorrow morning. Can I trust you boys to start work without me?"

"Sure," Davey said. "What do you want us to work on?"

"Have you ever torn out plaster walls?" I asked.

Both boys grinned, shaking their heads.

I waved for them to follow me into the living room. After a considerable amount of time spent digging around, I found gloves, full-face safety masks with special air filters, three crowbars, and both of my new sledgehammers. Davey and Griffin took everything from me, and on my way to the stairway I grabbed a box of trash bags.

Upstairs, I entered the smaller bedroom and tossed the trash bags to the floor before taking one of the sledgehammers. "First, only hit the wall with enough force to break the plaster." I gave the wall a slight whack before setting the sledgehammer down and using my hand to tug the loose plaster and lathe boards from the wall. "If you hit the wall too hard, you'll break the exterior wood siding." I pointed to the clapboard siding which had only a thin layer of black tarpaper covering it.

Both boys stepped closer, looking inside the hole.

"That would be bad, right?" Davey said, grinning.

"Yes, very bad." I turned, pointing toward the windows. "As you work, bag up the mess and toss the bags out the window, but don't overfill them. Plaster can be heavy."

"Got it," Griffin said, throwing a sly grin toward Davey. "This will be fun. More demolition."

I took the masks from Griffin, holding them up. "Wear these masks, not the cheap ones. The dust will get thick."

Both boys nodded.

"And most important—"

"*Don't do anything stupid*," they answered at the same time.

I laughed. "Exactly. I should be here by nine at the latest."

"Can we start as early as we want?" Griffin asked.

"As long as the sun is up, yes, but no working before or after dark. Got it?"

They bobbed their heads.

"Boys," Jared called up the stairway. "We need to get home. Your mom texted that dinner was almost done."

"Cool. I'm starving," Griffin said, moving toward the door.

"You ate a whole frozen pizza like an hour ago," Davey teased, shoving Griffin.

"I'm a growing boy," Griffin said, rubbing his stomach.

CHAPTER EIGHTEEN

EVERYONE EXCEPT AUSTIN WENT HOME. I was about to pick up a box of electrical outlets when Austin snagged an arm around my waist, turning me to face him. "I had fun today," he said with a teasing smile. His eyes lowered to my lips.

"Me too." I relaxed against him, liking the feel of his hands on my hips. "But as you can see, I've got a mess to deal with."

"Are you sure you want to keep working?" he asked in a whisper before placing a feather light kiss on my lips. "I was thinking we could find a quiet restaurant, eat a nice meal..." he brushed his lips against mine, "enjoy each other's company..."

"Tempting." I looked at the mounds of boxes surrounding us and sighed.

Austin chuckled, leaning his forehead against my shoulder. "You're killing me, woman. I'm pulling out my best moves and you're still thinking about work."

I giggled. "Everything's a mess. If I don't clean this up, it'll haunt my dreams."

Austin sighed, stepping back and moving his hands to his own hips as he looked around. "Want help?"

"No, get out of here. Go enjoy your night."

"Fine." Austin raised his hands in surrender. "I'll leave you be." He turned toward the front door, one hand reaching out to the knob. "Do you still want to strip the roof tomorrow?"

"Yes, please. I'll haul my ladder over in the morning. I should be here by nine. Does that work?"

"Nine works." Austin opened the door. "I'll bring donuts."

When the door shut behind him, I turned and scanned the room from one end to the other. I wasn't a fan of disorganization. I'd always believed time spent searching for things was time wasted.

Starting where I stood, I slid boxes around, sorting the bigger items first: a pile for the upstairs bathroom, another for the downstairs bathroom, and yet another grouping formed along the back wall for everything meant for the kitchen, including the stove and refrigerator which took some effort to move.

When I came across the five-gallon buckets I'd brought over the day before, I separated them before filling them with hand tools. Each bucket was designated a purpose: electrical, plumbing, drywall, and a fourth bucket for general tools since I didn't own a toolbox. As I emptied bags and boxes, I added smaller supplies to each bucket like wire nuts and plumbers' tape. Empty boxes were tossed outside, and empty shopping bags were stuffed into a nearby trash bag.

Unearthing a set of sawhorses and random-sized boards, I moved them into the front bedroom, forming a workshop area for any cutting needs. I added the new power saws, unboxing them, and placed the new levels and squares in the corner where they'd be safe from being stepped on or tripped over.

By the time the room met my organizational standards, my back ached from bending over. I stretched to one side and then the other before moving to the door to pick up the nearly full trash bag. Under it sat a crumpled cigarette pack. I set the trash bag aside, picking up the cigarette box. Tugging the flap open, I looked inside and confirmed it was empty.

I looked toward the kitchen, thinking about the boys. When they'd said they didn't smoke, I'd believed them. I'd also never smelled cigarette smoke on either of them.

My mind raced through everyone who'd been inside the house, but to my knowledge, none of them smoked.

"Probably teenagers," I said aloud. I tossed the empty pack into the trash bag before tying the bag shut and carrying it out to the burn pit.

When I returned inside, I checked the time. It was almost eight, but for the first time today I could work without being interrupted every ten minutes. I grabbed a hammer and crowbar from the general tools bucket and headed for the bathroom, determined to uproot the rotted subfloor where the tub used to be.

I MENTALLY KICKED MYSELF FOR forgetting to replace the burned-out light bulbs throughout the house. Holding my hands out in front of me, I navigated across the dark kitchen, staying close to the wall to avoid the bowed flooring. Reaching the back door, I pushed it closed and locked it before retracing my steps, hoping not to trip over anything.

I'd worked later than I'd planned, and it was now approaching midnight. Every muscle in my back and shoulders hurt, but I'd finished tearing out the rotten subfloor in the downstairs bathroom where the tub once sat.

Entering the living room, I lowered my hands. The single bulb in the old chandelier lit the room enough to see. I crossed to the door, stopping to gather my purse and keys, and exited onto the porch. Reaching inside, I shut the light off and closed the door, locking it. Once again surrounded by darkness, I slid one foot in front of the other to cross the porch, hoping I didn't step too far off to either side.

When I stepped off the last step into the grass, I looked around. My white van was easy enough to see but the ground wasn't. With half steps, I moved forward, stumbling over something after only a handful of steps.

I tapped my foot against the object, identifying it as my overturned wheelbarrow. I made a mental note to move it in the morning.

I continued forward until my hand touched the hood of my van. Circling it, I climbed inside and tossed my purse into the passenger seat. With one hand, I pulled the seatbelt across me while turning the key in the ignition with my other hand. The van's headlights lit up the trees on the other side of the yard. Movement caught my attention just inside the woods a few feet into the tree line.

I flicked the lever to change the headlights to their brightest setting.

Scanning the woods, I waited, but didn't see anything. I shook my head, changing the lights back to normal. "It was just an animal, dummy."

I wasn't very outdoorsy, but even I knew that around these parts the woods were full of deer, coyotes, and wild turkeys.

I reversed my van up the driveway, toward where the garage had been, before driving forward to the road. Turning left, I pointed my van toward home, kicking up the speed.

While driving, my mind kept wandering back to the movement I'd seen in the woods. I didn't think it was a deer. It didn't move like a deer. And whatever was out there was three times the size of a coyote or a turkey.

By the time I spotted the speed limit sign marking the edge of town, I was still second-guessing myself. Pulling alongside the shoulder of the road, I made a U-turn, driving back to the cottage, muttering complaints to myself about how silly I was being. But for whatever reason, I couldn't let the mystery go.

I slowed at the tipsy mailbox, turning into the driveway and following it to the end of the drive. Cranking the wheel to park in my usual spot, I hit the brakes, staring at the house.

The living room light was on.

Inside the house, a dark figure moved past the picture window. The light snapped off.

My pulse raced. I sat with my van idling and both feet pressed against the brake pedal.

"Did that just happen?" I asked myself aloud.

I shifted my van into reverse but kept my foot on the brake. No way was I going inside, especially not alone. I briefly considered calling Lance since he lived just down the road, but if whoever was in there was up to no good, I didn't want to put him in danger.

I picked up my phone, calling Stone.

"Do you know what time it is?" Stone answered, groaning a chuckle.

I glanced at the glowing clock on the dash. "Sorry. I should've called 911."

"What's wrong?" Stone asked, suddenly alert.

"Bernadette bought a house and hired me to fix it up."

"Yeah, yeah, I heard. It's out by Lance's place."

"Right, but when I left the cottage, I thought I saw someone in the woods. It was bothering me, so I drove back to look around." I paused, fiddling with the driver's door to click the door-lock button, ensuring it was still locked.

"And?" Stone asked, impatient to hear the rest of my story.

"And I'm here, but someone's inside the house. When I pulled down the driveway, someone shut off the living room light. I'm not making this up. Someone's in there."

"Calm down. Are you still there?"

"Yes, but I'm inside my van."

"Okay, get out of there. I'll have Robert pick me up and we'll drive out to look around. If you go now, we have a better chance of surprising whoever's inside. I'll call you and let you know what we find." Stone disconnected.

I tossed my phone into the cupholder and reversed down the long drive.

Chapter Nineteen

I DROVE HOME WITH THE VAN'S heater cranked to the highest setting, trying to shake off the icy chill coating my skin. Parking in front of the garage, I climbed out and hurried inside, walking through the house and checking each door and window on the first floor.

Not seeing anything out of place, I decided the best course of action was to distract myself while I waited for Stone to call me back. Grabbing my laptop, I placed it on the dining room table, powering it up, before turning into the kitchen to make myself a cup of cocoa.

Forty minutes later, I snatched my phone off the table when it rang. "Anything?" I asked, answering.

"Nothing," Stone said. "When we got there, the lights were off and the doors were locked. Robert wiggled one of the broken windows open to get inside. We walked around, but no one was there."

I scraped my lower lip between my teeth, thinking.

"Robert wants to know if the person you saw could've been a teenager. He says he's caught kids partying out there a few times."

"Maybe. Davey and Griffin put the word out that it was no longer a party house, but with teenagers..."

"Yeah. They don't exactly use all their brain cells. Anyway... I'm heading your way."

"Okay..." I said, confused. *Why did he want to stop out?* I checked my Fitbit. It was almost one in the morning. "Should I make coffee?"

"Heck no. I plan on sleeping at some point, and Robert can't join us. A nuisance call just came in, so it'll be just me."

"Okay, no coffee. I'll make you a cup of cocoa."

"Sounds good. Be there in five."

I got up and pulled another mug from the cupboard, fixing his cocoa. After hitting the start button on the microwave, I walked over and unlocked the side door, turning on the outside light before crossing back to the table.

I tapped my pen against my notepad as my mind bounced like a ping-pong ball between whoever had been at the cottage tonight and why Stone wanted to pop in for a visit.

Lost in thought, I jumped when Stone entered through the kitchen side door.

Laughing at myself, I got up to retrieve his cocoa from the microwave. "All right, what's up? Why didn't you go home and go back to bed?"

Stone grinned, crossing to the table, holding up a white bag. "I figured if you'd worked this late out at that house, you probably haven't eaten today. I called the bar and picked up a to-go order on my way through town."

"I ate today," I said, carrying a pile of napkins and his cocoa over to the table.

Stone raised an eyebrow, not saying anything.

"Okay, fine. I ate a sandwich like twelve hours ago. I'm starving. Are you happy?" I tugged at the bag, opening it. "What'd you get us?"

"BLTs, onion rings, and side salads, just in case you were worried about your cholesterol."

"I'll save my salad for tomorrow. The grease sounds perfect." I doled out the food, two sandwiches for him, one for me.

Stone got up, carrying the salad containers to the refrigerator. He opened the door and glanced back at me. "The new refrigerator looks nice, but it isn't working." He set the salads inside, closing the door.

I smirked, crossing the room to plug it in. "All fixed, but don't tell Lance I plugged it in early. He said I had to wait twenty-four hours." I crossed to the cooler and pulled the ketchup, offering it to Stone.

"I won't tattle," Stone said, taking the ketchup bottle. "Why were you out at the house so late?"

I followed him back to the table, sitting across from him. "Oh, I don't know. I suppose it was just nice to have a little peace and quiet. The last few days have been hectic."

"You work too much," Stone said before taking a bite of his BLT.

"You're one to talk," I said before diving into my own sandwich.

We ate in comfortable silence, both of us practically inhaling our food.

When Stone finished both of his sandwiches, he wadded the wax paper wrappers, tossing them inside the bag before pointing at the case file still sitting on the table. "Any new thoughts about Addy Randall?"

"No. Anything on your end?"

Stone shook his head, frowning. "I don't like it. Usually by now we're getting a call from the parents saying they tracked down their kid, but her dad hasn't seen or heard from her."

I studied Stone's expression, seeing something off about it. "Why are you so worried? I know you want to find the girl, but I thought you didn't suspect foul play?"

Stone leaned back in his chair, staring at the table. "I'm not thinking she was abducted, but I'm also not sure she simply ran away. Something's off. When I was at her house to take the official missing person's report, I checked her room. Everything was still there. Laptop, clothes, everything. I didn't see anything missing."

"What do you think happened then?"

Stone's worried eyes met mine. "If she had an accident... If she got lost or hurt..."

I nodded, raising a hand to stop him. "If the worst happened, for whatever reason, then her body is out there somewhere."

"Exactly," Stone said, exhaling heavily.

We both stared off into space until Stone's eyes caught on my laptop's screen. He turned the laptop, angling it to face him. "I can't believe it. You, Davina Ravine, have a social media account? Is the sky falling? Is it the end of the world?"

"I couldn't help it," I said, shaking my head while getting up to toss our trash into the wastebasket. "I was Googling cottages for design ideas and got sucked into that Pinterest site." I grabbed a hand towel off the counter and carried it over to the cooler, tucking it under one end and picking up the other to slide the cooler over to the refrigerator.

Stone grinned, swiveling the laptop back to how he'd found it before carrying the ketchup bottle over to place it inside the refrigerator.

I emptied the cooler, not worrying where I placed things since it was mostly condiments.

Stone took our cocoa mugs to the sink, dumping them before dabbing some soap on them to wash them. "When I leave, do you want me to take the cooler out to the garage?"

"Nah," I said, sliding the cooler back toward the laundry-pantry room. "The garage is a bit of an obstacle course right now. I'll haul it out in the morning." I pulled the towel from under it, tossing it on top of the washer before crossing back into the kitchen to pull a clean dishtowel from the drawer. I took the first mug, drying it.

Stone dried his hands on his jeans, moving toward the door. "If I don't have any leads on Addy's case this weekend, want some help on that house you're fixing up?"

"Cottage. I'm calling it the cottage." I shook my head. "Thanks for the offer, but I don't think your help this weekend is a good idea."

Stone snorted. "Austin?"

I shrugged, placing the dried mugs in the cupboard. "He's helping me tear off the roof, and since the two of you don't get along..."

"Yeah, yeah, I get it. You have enough broken windows to deal with." Stone opened the door. "Which reminds me—"

"I'm already on it," I said, cutting him off. "Ed Mason is replacing most of the broken glass tomorrow, and he'll fix the rest early next week."

Stone nodded, stepping through the doorway. "Goodnight, Davina."

"Night." I turned to look across the room. I should wipe down the counters and table, but I was too tired.

Hearing Stone's truck engine start, I relocked the door and shut off lights as I made my way to the library. Turning off the last light, I crossed the library in the dark, kicked off my shoes, shimmied out of the denim bibs, and threw myself onto my bed. Drifting off to sleep, I wondered what had happened to Addy Randall.

CHAPTER TWENTY

I WOKE WITH A START, overwhelmed with a sense of panic, but as my foggy brain cleared I realized my panic was from a lingering dream. In it, I'd been running around the cottage like a madwoman, carrying on about none of the kitchen cabinets fitting. All my friends were there too, staring at me like I'd lost my mind.

I laughed, throwing my blanket off as I sat upright. I looked across the library toward the patio doors, seeing the sun was up, but barely. No matter how early or late I went to bed, I was a *wake-at-dawn* kind of girl.

Remembering I had places to be this morning I crossed to my dresser, pulling a clean set of clothes before moving down the hallway toward the bathroom, picking up my discarded clothes from the night before along the way.

Fifteen minutes later I re-emerged, entering the kitchen freshly showered and dressed. I was midway to the coffee pot when I noticed both Lance and Isaac sitting at my dining room table.

"Morning," Isaac said with a smile. He lifted his coffee cup and took a sip.

"When did you guys get here?" I asked, pouring coffee into the empty mug one of them had left out for me.

"About twenty minutes ago," Lance said, setting his cup down and pointing to a box of donuts. "Breakfast?"

"Yes, please." I took my cup and a stack of napkins to the table, sitting next to Isaac. Flipping the lid up on the box, I pulled out a giant apple fritter. "Mrs. Denning?"

"Yup," Lance said.

"Yum." I tore the fritter into pieces, popping one piece into my mouth.

"Figured you could use a little sugar this morning." Lance picked up the picture of the missing teenage girl that I'd left sitting out on the table. "Who's this?"

"Addy Randall. She's missing. Stone's looking for her, but so far, he hasn't figured out where she ran off to."

"He mentioned the case, but I don't know much," Isaac said, taking the picture from Lance. "She looks like a fireball. Full of piss and vinegar."

"I thought so too," I said with a sad smile. "Spunky." I grabbed the file from under my laptop, sliding it to Isaac. "Stone gave me a copy of the file. If he's desperate enough to ask me to think on it, I'm sure he'd appreciate your insight too."

Isaac nodded, flipping it open. "Kids run off all the time. They turn up eventually."

"Maybe, but Stone's worried the girl might be injured or something."

Isaac's eyes narrowed at the file. "Is that so..." he said more to himself than to me.

"Talk to him. Maybe you can help him get the word out in the community. If something happened to her close to Daybreak Falls, maybe the townspeople can help find her."

"Agreed," Isaac said, with a nod. "We've been working opposite shifts this week which is why I forgot he had this case. I'll get with him yet this morning."

I ate another bite of my fritter, wondering again where Addy could be. When no new ideas popped into my head, I turned my attention to Lance and Isaac. "Why are you boys here so early?"

Lance's expression lit with a mischievous grin. "I know you've got some errands to run this morning, and if you don't mind, I thought I'd tag along."

I nodded, sucking the sugared glaze off my thumb. "You know I don't mind. I'm heading to Ed's place first to look through his storage barn for suitable skylight windows. After that, I'm popping in for a few things I forgot to buy at the hardware store."

"You bought a pile of stuff already," Isaac said. "What'd you forget?"

"I need an exterior light for the front porch, shovels or scrapers of some kind to tear off the roof, and there was something else, but I haven't had enough coffee to remember what it is."

Lance slid the notepad from the table over to him, flipping to a blank page where he started a list. "Mind if I add a couple utility knives and blades?"

"Nope. Can you also add a scoop shovel?" I asked. "With the upstairs tear out starting today, I'm guessing we'll need one."

"Got it," Lance said. "If they're too pricy, you can borrow one from my place."

"Sounds good. Does Jeff sell OSB board? I tore out the rotted subfloor in the bathroom last night."

"He does, but it's a good bit more expensive than what you'd pay in the city."

"One board should be enough to fix the bathroom and the kitchen. The way I see it, it makes sense to pay a few extra dollars if it means fixing the floors before someone falls through to the basement."

"Good point," Lance said, chuckling. "Did you happen to measure the board that's there?"

"It's three-quarter inch," I said.

Lance smiled proudly, adding the OSB board to the list. "I sorted my tools and set aside some for you. Just odds and ends I had lying around. Stuff like wire cutters, needle nose pliers, more screwdrivers and hammers." Lance tapped the notepad. "Do you have sawhorses?"

"Yup. They're already at the cottage in the front bedroom. Everything is set up and ready for use."

"Is that it then?" Lance asked.

"Yes, except that I could use some help loading my extension ladder on top of my van." I stuck out my lower lip and batted my eyelashes.

They both laughed.

"What kind of porch light do you want?" Lance said, pointing to the list.

"Actually, I want two lights. One regular one for outside the front door and another one on the front corner of the house that turns on when it detects motion. I was out there last night and nearly broke my neck on the wheelbarrow left in the yard."

"If the price is right, we'll pick up a couple of motion detecting ones. They even have cheap solar ones nowadays."

"Works for me." I lifted my cup, taking a big sip.

Lance scribbled some more items onto the list.

I glanced at Isaac. "What's your excuse for being here so early?"

Isaac grinned. "I spotted Lance leaving the inn with a box of donuts. I followed him so I could mooch breakfast before my shift starts."

I grinned at Isaac, sipping my coffee.

Lance, still focused on work, scowled. "If you're tearing out the upstairs walls already, we should pick up insulation. Winter will be here before you know it."

"I'll buy insulation in the city either tomorrow or early next week. I need groceries anyway."

Isaac shook his head. "Still not grocery shopping in town?"

"Not yet." I looked down at my coffee, avoiding his eyes. My most recent round of humiliation at the local grocery store ended with Isaac telling me I needed to learn how to stand up for myself. I was working on it, but I still had a long road ahead of me.

"Anything else?" Lance asked, gaining my attention.

"Not that I can think of, but knowing Jeff, he'll try to sell us half his inventory."

Lance grinned while flipping through the other pages, stopping at a rough sketch for a garage. He whistled, pointing to the price I'd scribbled at the top of the page.

"Yeah, building a garage isn't in the budget. Whoever buys the house will need to build one or go without."

"What about a carport?" Isaac suggested with a devious grin directed at Lance.

"That might work," Lance said, blushing. "Could always add a shed behind the carport to store stuff."

The two of them were acting funny, like Isaac was teasing Lance. "Wouldn't a carport look too commercial?"

"Yeah, Lance," Isaac said. "Wouldn't a carport look out of place?"

Lance threw Isaac a glare before swiveling his eyes to mine. His cheeks reddened. "I have to confess something."

"Okay." I looked between them, dumbfounded. "You've got my attention. Spill."

"When we got here, you were still asleep. Your laptop was out, so I thought, why not check the score for the ballgame last night..."

My face lifted into a smile when I figured out why he was squirming. He'd been snooping on my laptop.

"Well, see, when I opened the laptop," Lance peeked up at me, "this funny looking website came up. It had all these pictures of cottages and such."

"Pinterest," I said, sliding my laptop toward me and opening it. "Last night I got sucked into looking at the pictures."

Isaac chuckled. "Lance got sucked in, too. That is, until he heard you rustling around in the other room. Closed the laptop so fast I had to check to make sure he hadn't cracked the screen."

Lance rolled his eyes but shifted into the chair next to mine. "Check this out." Leaning across me, he clicked on a browser tab along the top. "Look at this picture with the carport."

I clicked the image, making it larger. The carport resembled a pergola, built with landscape timbers. It was wide enough for two cars and the roof was covered with see-through plexiglass, letting the sunlight stream through.

"It fits, don't you think?" Lance asked. "Fits with that cottage look you're going for?"

"Yes, it does. If I added vinyl lattice to the far side, it would help cut down on snow in the winter too." I nodded. "I love the idea, but how much will it cost?"

"Well now," Lance slid the laptop closer to him, clicking on another browser window. "They sell these package deals for us do-it-yourselfer types. Everything's all bundled together."

My eyes swept the page, toggling between the pictures and the prices as Lance scrolled downward.

Building the carport would cost a tenth of what building a garage would.

"What do you think?" Lance asked.

"I think it's worth the money. I'm in."

Lance smiled proudly. "Thought you'd like it."

Isaac got up and crossed the kitchen, dumping his coffee in the sink. "I better get going. My shift starts soon."

I got up, planning to rinse my cup but noticed the new stove was now sitting tucked against the back wall. "Did you guys move the counter?"

"Yup," Lance said, carrying his cup over to the sink. "We moved it while you were showering. The wall needs some touch up paint."

I wasn't worried about the touch up paint. I turned the stove's burner on, listening to the click-click-click before the blue flame popped to life. "Sweet."

Isaac chuckled. "See you later." He left out the kitchen door.

"I'm heading out to the garage," Lance said. "I want to load a few things like your ShopVac."

"I'll be out in a minute. I just need to gather my stuff," I said, turning off the stove burner.

"Take your time," Lance said, opening the door. "But don't think I didn't notice that you plugged that refrigerator in before the twenty-four hours was up."

I ducked my head, hiding my smile.

Chapter Twenty-One

After washing the coffee cups, I gathered my stuff and went outside to help Lance load the extension ladder on top of my van. He looped bungee cords around the rungs, fastening the ladder tight against the cargo rack.

Hearing a vehicle, we looked over as Whiskey parked along the street curb. Lance and I crossed to the center of the front yard, exchanging good mornings with Whiskey and Virgil.

"Just dropping off the bids," Whiskey said, passing me a clipboard. "I meant to give you some of them yesterday, but the whole shopping thing sidetracked me."

"Yeah, I got a little sidetracked too," I said, taking the clipboard. I skim read the quotes before glancing at Lance, holding out my hand.

Lance pulled a pen from his shirt pocket, passing it to me.

Signing off on each bid, I passed them back to Whiskey and he separated the carbon copy, passing each pink page to Lance. All the quotes were less than the amounts I'd budgeted, though my eyebrows jumped at the price of the plumbing pipes for the new bathrooms. When I was done, I handed the clipboard back and took the pink copies from Lance. "Everything looked good. I'm hoping to have the cottage roof torn off this weekend, but I have tarps to cover it."

"Sounds good. Hope you don't mind, but I parked my trailer with that porch roof at your cottage. It's off to the far side of the yard though, out of the way."

"I don't mind, but..." I glanced at Lance. "What about the trees?"

Lance shrugged, letting me know he didn't know the answer.

"Problem?" Virgil asked.

"We've got tree cutters coming out sometime next week," Lance said. "I don't know what day, but I'd hate for them to drop a tree on top of your trailer."

"Me too," Whiskey said, chuckling. "We'll move it to the construction site."

"Nah," Lance said. "Park it beside my barn. I'm just down the road and that way you don't have to worry about someone stealing it."

"It won't be in your way?" Whiskey asked.

"Nope. Plenty of space. Besides, it's not like it'll sit there forever."

"Unlike that ancient bulldozer you bought a good ten years ago?" I teased.

Lance chuckled. "Been meaning to fix that. It'll be worth a pretty penny if I ever get it running."

Lance was never going to get around to fixing the dozer, but I didn't comment. Instead, I turned my attention back to Virgil and Whiskey. "The bathroom fixtures are upstairs in the master bedroom if you want to see what I bought."

"You bought everything already?" Whiskey asked.

"Everything except the towel racks," I said with a nod. "I owe Mrs. Paulson a steak dinner."

"More like several steak dinners," Whiskey said, chuckling. "What about the skylights for the cottage? Any luck finding what you want?"

"Not yet, but my next stop is Ed Mason's pole barn. Hopefully I'll find the windows I need, but if I don't, I'll shop in the city tomorrow."

Whiskey nodded. "Late next week we might move a few guys to the cottage to start on that roof."

"Let me get you keys then," I crossed to my van and dug keys out of my purse. "Here you go, one for each house. I'll be bouncing back and forth for the next couple of weeks, so come and go as you please." I held the keys out to Whiskey, but Virgil snagged them first.

"I'll take these. Whiskey tends to misplace keys."

"*Once!*" Whiskey said, shifting his hands to his hips. "I lost the keys, *once and only once*. You ever going to let that go?"

Virgil grinned, pocketing the keys. "Nope."

Whiskey shook his head but let Virgil keep the keys.

My old truck pulled up and parked at the end of the driveway. Noah climbed out and hollered at us. "Hey, D, any chance you can clear the driveway? I've got that desk Mom wants moved to your garage, and I'm supposed to haul some of the antiques from your living room into town."

"I was just getting ready to leave," I called back. "Give me a minute." I looked back at Whiskey. "Did you need anything else signed?"

"Nope. We're all set."

"What do you think about me showing these guys our carport idea?" Lance asked. "Don't hurt none to have them give you a bid."

"I'm good with that, but I'm running late."

"You take off," Lance said, nodding to the street. "If I don't catch up with you in town, I'll see you at the cottage."

"Deal," I said, shoving the passenger side door closed. "If anyone needs me, just give me a call." I jogged around my van.

Reversing into the street, I lifted my hand to wave at Noah. He halfheartedly waved back before climbing inside his truck. He looked downright miserable.

Britt, I thought, shaking my head.

CHAPTER TWENTY-TWO

PARKING IN THE BACK LOT near Ed's storage barn, I climbed out and waved to Ed who was loading glass into the back of one of his service trucks.

"Morning," Ed called out. "I got your message about needing skylights. I pulled a few misordered windows I had in the barn for you to look through. I'll make you a good deal if you find something you like, and if'n you don't, I've got a catalog you can order from." Ed slapped a hand against the side of his truck. "After you're done looking around, I'm driving out to get started replacing some of that broken glass."

"Sounds good." I held up my notepad. "Also... Do you have any exterior doors in stock? The back door needs to be replaced, and so far, I haven't found a good deal on a new one."

"I've got a few," Ed said, leading the way. "You got dimensions?"

I flipped to the page listing the dimensions, rattling them off. Ed nodded, taking me to a row of doors. I picked out a basic metal door that had a top window with white muntin bars.

Next, Ed led me over to some windows. I looked through the stacks, finding four matching square skylight windows that were perfect for the slanted roof in the smaller upstairs bedroom. After I paid from the envelope of cash, Ed insisted he'd bring the door and windows out, delivering them for free. I thanked him and went on my way.

Driving to the hardware store, I parked next to Lance's idling truck and got out, waiting for him behind my van. "I didn't expect you to be here already."

"Yeah, well, Noah didn't want my help loading and unloading, and it only took a few minutes to show Virgil and Whiskey our carport idea."

I frowned. "Noah's acting strange with you too? I was hoping it was just me."

"He's just unhappy right now, and since he's usually such a jolly fellow, it stands out on him more than it would on others."

"I suppose, but if I hear he's behaving like that with his mom, we're going to have words."

Lance chuckled, nodding. "Hear, hear."

We crossed the parking lot, aiming for the front door.

"Did you get your windows?" Lance asked.

"I did. I also bought a new door for the mudroom."

"Good price?"

"Of course."

A car horn tooted, and we turned to look. Isaac pulled up alongside us in his police cruiser, lowering his window. "You know you're supposed to have red flags on the end of that ladder, right?"

I glance at my van and the ladder perched on top. The end of the ladder hung past the bumper by a good five feet. Pulling a pen from my purse, I scribbled red flags onto my notepad before holding the page up to show Isaac. "Red flags are now on the list."

Isaac smirked, driving away.

Just inside the hardware store, Lance and I stopped to share a grin.

Jeff Timber had been expecting us. A new display table was set up a few feet from the door with a sign advertising a sale on home improvement oddities. The table was overflowing with things like outlet covers, light switches, plain light fixtures, door stoppers, and everything else you could think of.

Lance chuckled. "I'll keep Jeff busy helping me load the OSB while you fill a cart."

I laughed. "Good idea. Can you also find the red flags I need for the ladder?"

"I'm on it." Lance started toward the counter, steering Jeff away from me toward the back room. I grabbed a cart and started filling it with the odds and ends I still needed.

Twenty minutes later, I walked out wearing a smile. Not only had I crossed off a bunch more stuff from my shopping list, but I'd found three more pairs of denim bibs in my size on the clearance rack. I practically had a new wardrobe. I glanced down at my outfit. Olivia would hate my new look, but I liked it. The bibs were comfortable and cheap.

Following Lance's truck, I drove south out of town, heading toward the cottage. Halfway there, I noticed a police cruiser following me. I turned on my blinker, slowing my van while veering onto the shoulder of the road.

Putting my van in park, I hopped out and ran to the back doors, rifling around inside until I found the red stretchy plastic flags. I climbed up on the van's bumper and tied two on before hopping down to turn and look at Isaac.

He chuckled, gave me a thumbs up, and whipped a U-turn, pointing his car back toward town.

I closed the back door and returned to the driver's seat, but waited for a line of trucks and trailers to pass, all loaded down with stacks of hay, before I pulled back onto the road.

CHAPTER TWENTY-THREE

AS SOON AS I PUT MY van in park, Austin and Lance were climbing up on the tires to unhook the extension ladder. Rather than standing around watching them, I went inside to check on the Donaldson boys.

Upstairs, I frowned at the still packaged masks lying on the floor outside the bedroom doorway. I peeked inside the room. Davey was using the sledgehammer to chop against the plaster while Griffin followed behind him with the crowbar. Beneath their feet was a good foot-deep pile of lathe board and plaster. The hardwood floor bowed and bounced as they moved.

"*Hey!*" I called out while leaning over to turn off the blaring radio.

Both boys turned to look at me. They were at least wearing goggles and the paper-thin, cheap face masks.

I raised a hand and curled a finger for them to step out of the room.

"What's up?" Davey asked, taking his mask off as they stepped into the hallway.

"First," I took his mask from him, holding it up, "are you trying to shorten your life? Do you like the idea of carting an oxygen tank around with you when you get older?"

Griffin groaned. "Those other masks are ugly."

"Ugly or not, I spent good money on them because they'll protect your lungs. Wear them or go home."

"Okay," Davey said, grabbing the full-face masks with the air filters. He passed one to Griffin. "We'll behave."

"Yeah," Griffin said, taking his. "Sorry. You won't have to tell us again."

"Good. Now, the second thing." I pointed inside the room. "Any idea how much more weight that floor is going to hold before it caves in?"

Their heads swiveled toward the bedroom, their eyes widening. Neither of them said anything.

"There's a new scoop shovel in the back of my van. Go get it and bag all this before you break the cottage."

Both boys nodded, looking a little freaked out.

"One more thing," I said, holding a straight face for as long as I could before cracking a smile. "How early did you guys start? I expected this room to take most of the day to tear out."

Both boys exhaled, relaxing their shoulders when they realized I wasn't going to chew them out for something else.

"We're on a mission," Griffin said, adjusting the head strap for his face mask. "Davey has a date tonight. We're trying to get both rooms done before he needs to leave."

"It's not a date," Davey said, blushing. "We're just meeting to study."

Griffin gave Davey a playful shove. "On a Saturday night? Dude, it's a date."

"Jealous?" Davey teased, shoving Griffin back.

"Okay, stop messing around before one of you gets hurt," I said, laughing. "Scoop all this up, but no matter how far you both get with the walls, leave when you need to leave. I'll be on the roof. Holler if you need me."

Griffin followed me outside to the van where I handed over the new scoop shovel. While he jogged back inside, I emptied my keys and phone onto the passenger seat through the open window before digging work gloves and the roof scrapers out of the back of the van, carrying them over to where Lance and Austin stood talking in the driveway.

"I brought donuts this morning," Austin said, nodding to his Jeep parked along the shoulder of the driveway a few feet away. "But I'm not sure there's any left. The boys scarfed down a pile of them."

"It's all good. Lance brought me apple fritters this morning."

"Mrs. Denning's?" Austin asked, looking jealous.

"Yup," Lance said, picking up a harness belt from the ground and studying it.

Hearing a vehicle, I looked up. Ed drove down the drive but slowed when he saw all the vehicles.

I walked over, motioning for him to park in the yard next to my van. I waited for him to get out before hollering over to him, "The Donaldson boys are chucking bags of plaster out the upstairs window out back. Might be safer to work on the front windows for a while."

Ed gave me the contractor nod to let me know he'd heard.

I took a step back toward the side of the house but stopped, hearing another truck.

Whiskey pulled his truck around the bend, stopping behind my van. I looked behind me, spotting their trailer tucked close to a row of trees on the other side of the yard.

I walked over to the passenger side window where Virgil sat. "Feel free to move my van. The keys are on the seat."

Virgil opened his door. "I can do that."

"I'll help to hitch the trailer," Lance said, striding past us across the yard.

"Busy place today," Ed called out, unloading a window. "Where do you want the skylight windows and new door?"

Virgil did a one-eighty, moving toward Ed. "Got the skylight windows, aye?"

I glanced at Whiskey, smirking. He sighed, putting his truck in park.

After Virgil inspected the new windows—nodding to me I'd done well—he pivoted toward my van.

Ed looked back at me with a raised eyebrow, still waiting to hear where I wanted everything.

"The only safe place inside is the downstairs bedroom, but set everything along the front wall. I put my saws on the other side of the room to make a cutting area."

Ed gave me a nod, carrying two of the skylight windows toward the house.

Before anyone could corner me again, I crossed to where Austin was untangling a set of black ropes.

I tipped my head back, looking upward. The roof was higher up than I remembered. I wasn't afraid of heights, but I wasn't a fan of falling, either. "Are we really going to do this?"

"If I ever get these ropes untangled, we will," Austin said, grinning over at me.

I picked up the other rope set, wrapping one end around my arm while shaking the other end loose and looping it from hand to elbow.

"You hear about Dr. Gilmore?" Austin asked, setting his now untangled rope down before tying a knot in one end.

"No, what's up?"

Austin shrugged. "Word is he's selling his lake house and has movers coming today to move him to a new condo in the city."

I'd known Steven Gilmore my whole life, yet I couldn't muster one nice word to say about the man. *Good riddance*. The town was better off without him. "I won't miss him, that's for sure. What about his seat on the town council?"

"It'll be filled with an interim council member until the next town election," Austin said, taking the rope I'd unwound. "Ready for the bad news?" He set the rope down to pull his phone, handing it to me.

"What am I looking at?" I asked as Lance returned to stand next to us.

Austin nodded toward his phone. "Someone created a poll on the town's Facebook page for candidates to fill the open spot. Unfortunately, my mother's name is on it."

"Great," Lance muttered. "Just what we need."

Looking at the poll, I read through the three listed names. I didn't know two of them, but Belinda Vanderson was the first name displayed on the poll, leading the votes. Unlike Austin, his mother treated people like they were *less than*—which made her the last person Daybreak Falls needed as a council member.

Tapping the screen, trying to scroll to the comments, a window popped up asking me to enter the name of the person I wanted to add to the poll. I grinned, typing in Mrs. Paulson's name. After hitting enter, her name appeared in the poll at the bottom with zero votes.

"Why are you wearing one of Olivia's devious smiles?" Austin asked, his dimple popping out.

I handed him his phone back so he could see for himself.

His eyes widened, staring down at the screen. "Oh, crap."

"What?" I asked. "You don't think Mrs. Paulson would make a good council member?"

"It's not that," Austin said, glancing up at me. "You posted it on *my* phone. Which means my mother will think *I added* Mrs. Paulson's name."

I lifted a hand to my mouth. "Austin, I'm so sorry. The window just popped up... I typed in her name without thinking."

"It's fine," Austin said, though the grimace he wore told me otherwise. "I'll call Mom later and explain." A slight smile touched his lips. "On the bright side, Mrs. Paulson has five votes already. Oh, wait, make that six."

"That was me," Lance said, grinning as he tucked his phone back into his shirt pocket.

Still feeling bad about messing up, I tried to hold back my grin, but it was hard. *Really hard.*

Austin's phone rang and after checking the screen he visibly paled. "I need a minute," he said, walking away and answering the call. "Good morning, Mother."

Lance and I exchanged looks, cringing.

"I feel awful," I whispered.

"You didn't intentionally throw him under the bus," Lance said, chuckling. "But oh man, he's going to get an earful."

"Not only for the poll, but she'll know he's with me. She hates the idea of the two of us dating."

"I didn't know you two were a thing," Lance said, surprised.

"We're not. We've set up several dates but keep having to reschedule."

"Ah," Lance said, glancing down the driveway at Austin who abruptly ended his call and walked back toward us.

Deciding not to ask about the call, I picked up one of the scrapers. "Are you sure you want to help me? This could get messy."

"Sure. Why not." Austin picked up a harness belt, buckling it around me.

"You kids have fun." Lance started toward the front porch. "I need to take a look at a few things inside and check on the boys."

"Do me a favor and see if they're still wearing the *good* face masks. If they took them off, tell them they're fired."

"Will do," Lance said without looking back.

"You ready?" Austin asked, his dimple popping out as he buckled his own belt around his waist.

I looked up, not sure. "What if we fall?"

"If you feel like you're going to fall, throw yourself flat toward the center of the roof."

"What if I fall off the side?"

"Stay away from the sides." Austin looped his rope into a metal toggle.

"That's not an answer."

Austin lifted his face to meet my eyes. "I think you already know what happens if you fall off the side, but I've also got these." He picked up something that looked like a large door hinge.

I took it from him, turning it over. It had metal spikes on the other side. "What is this?"

"A roof anchor. I'll nail two of them to the roof once we're up there. We'll loop our ropes through them as a precaution."

"And that'll keep us from falling?"

"Maybe."

"Why maybe?"

Austin glanced up. "All depends on how solid the roof is."

"Ah, I see," I said, following his gaze to the roof. "If the boards are mush, the anchors won't hold."

Austin picked up the other rope, wiggling one end through the metal loop on my belt. "As I said, it's best if you stay away from the sides."

Chapter Twenty-Four

"Stripping shingles sucks," I muttered to myself, jabbing my shovel-like scraper under a patch of shingles to pry them up. After three more jabs, the shingles slid off the roof.

I straightened, wiping the sweat off my face with my arm. After looking around, I made my way to the center of the roof where Austin sat perched on the roof's peak, taking a break.

Next time I'm hiring contractors to do this part, I thought while sitting beside him.

"Well, we're half done," Austin said, glancing at the side we'd just finished.

"I feel like crying," I said, dropping my head between my shoulders. "I didn't know roofing could hurt this much."

"This is the easy part," Austin said, flashing his dimple. "Try hauling bags of shingles and decking boards up extension ladders."

"No, thank you."

Hearing a vehicle, we both looked toward the driveway. Olivia's black station wagon appeared from under the thick tree limbs, parking behind Austin's Jeep.

I shook my head, seeing the hot pink magnetic sign advertising Nightshade Treasures stuck to the side of her driver's door.

"I swear, Olivia gets kookier by the day," Austin said.

"Probably."

Olivia hopped out and looked around before heading toward the porch.

I cupped my hands, shouting down to her, "I thought I told you to wear something less girly if you stopped out?"

Olivia's head snapped skyward. Using her hand to shield her eyes and taking a half dozen steps backward into the center of the yard, she stared up at us, grinning. "How'd you get up there?"

"I jumped," I hollered down to her. "I have longer legs than you."

Austin laughed, placing a hand on the roof to steady himself.

"Funny girl," Olivia said. "Can I come up?"

"*No!*" we both shouted.

"Then you need to come down. I need to talk to you."

Austin shifted his feet under him and stood. "We both need to rehydrate anyway." He started down the now shingle-less side of the roof toward the ladder. "Are you coming?"

"Yeah." I stood, adding tension to my safety line like he'd taught me.

"*Ahh-cheww.*"

"Bless you," I said, focusing on walking sideways down the incline.

"What?" Austin called back, already at the ladder.

I looked up then behind me, half expecting to see someone else on the roof, but no one was there. Was it Olivia who sneezed? Or maybe one of the boys in the upstairs bedrooms? Sound must carry funny up here. "Nothing. Never mind."

While crossing to the ladder I briefly wondered if I was losing my mind. Peeking over, I saw Austin was already on the ground, bracing the ladder and waiting for me. I gripped the top rung and stepped around to the other side before detaching my safety rope.

"Did you bring any sandwiches today?" Austin called up to me.

"No, sorry." I moved down the rungs. "I was running late this morning."

Austin waited until I reached the bottom before stepping back.

Hopping off, I felt relieved to be back on solid ground. I checked my Fitbit, seeing it was almost one. "The Donaldson boys are probably starving. I can order pizzas, but I'm not sure who delivers out this way."

"I'll ask Lance and place an order." Austin tipped his head toward the front yard. "Go see what Olivia wants."

"Thanks. The envelope of cash is still in my purse. Take whatever you need, but can you make sure to get a receipt? I can write off our lunch as a business expense." I started across the yard toward Olivia.

"Look at you," Austin said behind me. "Thinking like a businesswoman already."

I could hear the smile in his voice but kept walking without looking back. His comment annoyed me. I'd been running my own business since high school, but I guess when you grow up with full-time housekeepers, you don't think of house cleaning as a business.

"Why are you wearing that face?" Olivia asked.

"What face?" I asked.

"Your *I'm annoyed with everyone* face." Olivia pinched my cheeks, tugging them upward. "Smile. I promise it won't hurt."

I laughed, swatting her hands away. "Stop it." Crossing to a cooler sitting in the yard beside my van, I pulled out a water bottle, uncapping it. "So? What's up? Why'd you make me come all the way down here?"

"I need your help with a case. It's a good one." Olivia was doing her bouncy thing.

Mentally, I rolled my eyes, but on the outside, I waited patiently.

"See, there's this girl, and a few days ago, she ran away, but—"

"Wait. Are you talking about Addy?"

Olivia's eyebrows launched upward. "Uhm, I'm not sure. Addison Randall?"

"Yeah, yeah. Stone's working the case."

"Well, crap. I didn't know the police were involved."

"Does it matter?"

"It might. The client—Addison's aunt—didn't want me to involve the police. She's afraid the girl could've been up to no good."

Stone hadn't mentioned an aunt, nor had he mentioned any kind of legal trouble the girl might be in. "She's only sixteen. What could she possibly be up to that would be that bad?"

Olivia raised her hands in an I-don't-know gesture. "Beats me, but the aunt said Addison was last seen in a sketchy area out near where Jamie Brent lived. Remember him? The bouncer at Kami's bar? The neighborhood where we saw the bikers shoot at the corner house?"

"Oh, I remember. I remember Jamie and I remember the neighborhood. That's Bleeding Souls territory. The cops call that stretch of housing Felony Row." I took another swig of my water before asking, "Why would Addy be out there?"

"Again, no idea, but her aunt figures she had to have been up to something illegal. She can't think of any other reason for Addison to be in that neighborhood."

Felony Row was a country strip of redneck houses where couches were considered common to use as outdoor patio furniture. Maybe the aunt was right. Maybe Addy was up to no good, but even if she was, so what? If she were my niece, my first priority would be to find her and make sure she was safe. "Where does the aunt think Addy ran off to?"

"The aunt doesn't know. She doesn't even know how Addison got to Felony Row in the first place since she doesn't own a car."

"When was this?"

"Wednesday night."

That fit. Stone said no one had seen Addy since school let out on Wednesday. But if Stone didn't know Addy went to Felony Row, how did the aunt know? I shook my head, confused. "None of this makes sense. I'm not sure I buy the aunt's story. Did you look into her? Run her through your computer programs?"

"No." Olivia seemed surprised by my question. "She's the one paying me. Why would I investigate my own client?"

"Because her story has holes, big ones. How did this woman know Addy was seen in Felony Row? Stone doesn't know, nor did he mention the girl had any concerned relatives other than her father."

"So what?" Olivia asked, throwing her hands into the air in frustration. "Maybe it was the aunt who was up to no good and dragged the girl into it. Does it matter? The girl still needs to be found, and if I find her before the cops, the aunt will pay me handsomely—enough to keep my business afloat for another two months."

"I don't like this, Olivia. What kind of aunt would be more concerned about the police finding the girl first? Addy's been missing for four days. She could be hurt, waiting to be rescued, but the aunt doesn't want you working with the police to find her?"

Olivia fisted her hands on top of her hips. "The aunt's reasons don't matter. She hired me, not you, and if I want to get paid—which I absolutely want—then I need to follow my client's instructions."

I studied my best friend, seeing her defensive stance. I wasn't trying to get under her skin, but I had a bad feeling about the missing girl and suspected something fishy with this so called aunt. "Olivia, this isn't you. You don't put money before people. If you continue down this road, you could be putting the girl in further danger."

Olivia jabbed a pointy finger at me. "I'm not a monster."

I looked down at her pointy finger, surprised by the level of her anger. "I'm sorry. I'm not saying you're a monster. I'm trying to get through to you that this girl could be in serious trouble, and whatever's going on, your client might be a part of it. Is making a buck worth risking the girl's safety?" I cringed as the last comment slipped out, wishing I could take it back. I'd gone too far.

"Oh, I see." Olivia's eyes narrowed to slits. "Now that you discovered your grandmother has money, you can afford to get all sanctimonious, huh?" She pointed her finger again, coming closer and closer to poking me with it.

"Is that what you really think?" I asked, shifting to anger. "You think *I'm the one* behaving poorly because of money? Really, Olivia?"

"Woah, whoa, whoa," Lance said, jogging across the yard to step between us. "I'm not sure why you girls are all riled up, but maybe it's time to give each other some space."

"Space?" Olivia snapped, stomping back toward the station wagon. "No problem!"

Olivia threw her driver's door open and flopped down into the seat, slamming the door closed. The wagon's engine roared to life and a split second later, dust and stones kicked up under its tires. Olivia came close to sideswiping a tree, reversing at full speed back to the road.

Lance and I just stood there, staring down the driveway.

"What in Sam-hill was that about?" Lance asked.

"I'm not sure. We've had fights before, but never like that."

"Well, I'm sure the two of you will get it sorted," Lance said. "Give her some time to cool off."

Would we sort it? I wasn't so sure this time. We'd been best friends since middle school, and over the years our friendship had survived plenty of squabbles, but this felt different.

"You're right, she just needs time to cool off," I said, hoping it was true.

I took another drink from my water bottle, looking around the yard. "Okay, what was I doing before all the drama?"

Lance pointed at the roof, smirking.

"Right," I said, my shoulders deflating.

CHAPTER TWENTY-FIVE

WITH NOODLE-NUMB ARMS, I LIFTED the roof scraper high enough to fling the last shingle over the side. Looking behind me, I checked to make sure Austin's side was done. It was. Glancing down into the yard below, I confirmed no one was there before tossing the shovel-like scraper over the edge, hoping it would break when it hit the ground.

"That's cheating," Austin said, chuckling. He sat on the roof's peak, wiping sweat off his face with a rag. His skin glistened under the sun and his shirt was soaked through.

I looked down at myself, seeing very unladylike wet circles around my armpits. *Lovely.* For October, the weather was warmer than usual. I had a new appreciation for people who did this kind of work in the height of summer.

I adjusted my rope, adding only enough slack to the line to turn the other direction before starting up the roof. "Is it really over?"

Austin nodded while chugging water. He held out his half empty water bottle, offering it to me. "We just need to nail down the tarps."

I angled toward him, raising my hand to take the bottle when the board beneath me cracked and buckled inward.

I stared into Austin's widened eyes as I plunged feet first through the roof.

"*Davina!*" Austin shouted.

My body dropped hard and fast. My left foot hit something solid, and my knees and hips folded like an accordion before I bounced sideways between two rafters. The ceiling below me cracked and crumbled, sucking me through.

A hard yank from my harness belt flipped my body before I jiggled and bounced on the end of the safety line.

I waited a long moment, expecting to drop again, but nothing happened. I peeled one eye open, then the other. I was dangling sideways, facing the wall. Less than three feet below me was the hardwood floor. I looked up and around, seeing I was dangling inside the front bedroom on the second floor. I glanced at my harness belt and saw the knot Austin had tied was snug against the metal loop on the belt.

"Davina!" Austin shouted from above. "Can you hear me?"

I looked up and around the room again, this time noticing Davey and Griffin who were standing pressed against the wall, clutching each other. Both were wearing their alien-like face masks.

"*Help*," I squeaked.

Davey darted forward, placing his hands on my shoulders to lift me upright so I could maneuver my feet under me. "Are you okay?"

"I'm not sure," I answered, wincing when I put weight on my ankle. "Everything hurts."

Davey unbuckled my harness, freeing me from the rope.

Feeling wobbly, I sat on the floor, not caring when chunks of plaster poked my butt cheeks.

Austin and Lance ran into the room, Austin diving knees first across the floor to grab me, scattering chunks of plaster past me. "Davina, do you need an ambulance? Did you break any bones?"

"I'll live," I said with a groan. Reaching down, I pulled up my pant leg to inspect a cut. I must've snagged my skin on a nail or a chunk of wood. It wasn't deep, but I'd need to clean it. I lifted my leg and rotated my ankle. It throbbed but wasn't broken.

Austin moved his hand to my ankle.

"*Ow*. Don't touch it," I whined. "Next time, I'm paying the contractors to do the tear-off."

Austin raised his hands, removing them from me. A hint of a smirk touched his lips.

I leaned back, lying flat on the debris covered floor. The ceiling above me had a Davina-sized hole in it. I looked around the room, seeing the boys were almost done knocking down the plaster and lathe boards along the walls. "See," I said, pointing at the ceiling. "I helped."

"Yeah, you helped, all right," Griffin said. "But I think our way is safer."

"You know," Davey said. "Davina's way has potential. If we knock the rest of the ceiling down from the attic—you know, like kick it in—we won't have it falling in our faces."

Lance picked up a long chunk of insulation that had fallen with my descent. "This insulation looks to be in pretty good shape. You boys need to roll it up before you knock down the rest of the ceiling."

I sat upright. "They could get hurt."

"Nah," Lance said, waving off my concern. "If'n they stay on the rafters—sit on them while kicking out the ceiling—they'll be fine."

Davey looked at Griffin, still wearing his alien mask. "Think we can get it done before six?"

Griffin pulled his phone, checking the time. "If we hurry."

Davey shifted the ladder under the attic access.

"Davina, are we working tomorrow?" Griffin asked.

Lance reached down, offering me a hand up.

"Not tomorrow," I answered, groaning while standing. "If I can still move my limbs tomorrow morning, I might work for a few hours, but I won't need you guys again until maybe next weekend. Write down your hours before you leave today, and I'll drop off your pay tomorrow."

"Rats," Griffin said to Davey before starting up the ladder. "Means Mom will drag us to church tomorrow."

Not wanting to be in the room when they started kicking down the ceiling, I followed Lance through the door, limping.

"Need me to carry you?" Austin asked, following behind me.

"No. It's just bruised. I whacked it on my way down."

"You should ice it," Lance said, walking sideways down the stairs with his arm out to make sure he was there to catch me if I fell.

"I think the ice in the cooler melted hours ago. I'll ice my ankle when I get home tonight."

"I'm at a good stopping point in the first-floor bathroom," Lance said. "I'll make a run to my place for an icepack."

"You've been working on the bathroom?" I asked, stepping off the last step.

"Yup. The boys would've had the upstairs done by now, but I borrowed them to help move the shower."

Limping to the bathroom doorway, I peeked inside. "You did all this in one afternoon?"

Not only was the subfloor fixed, but the new vinyl flooring was laid. Along the back wall of the bathroom was the new shower unit, the base and walls installed with the pipes sticking through the end panel. I crossed to the bathroom cabinet and turned the new bronze faucet handle. Water flowed out.

Turning the handle off, I glanced over my shoulder at Lance. "I'm impressed. This is great."

"I took your new power saws for a spin," Lance said, thumbing toward the kitchen. "Virgil was right about the smaller circular saw. It zips right through small projects."

I followed Lance into the kitchen, seeing he'd cut out the bowed flooring and patched in a rectangular shaped piece of new OSB.

"Is this the saw?" Austin asked, picking up the hand-held saw and turning it over.

"Yup," Lance said. "Handy little sucker. I might have to steal it." Lance threw me a wink, smiling.

I laughed, glancing around at all the progress made on the house. At this rate, we'd have the cottage buttoned up for the winter season by the end of next week, far sooner than I'd thought possible. "This is all great. I can't believe how fast everything is coming together." I limped out of the room, crossing into the living room.

Noticing the new ceiling fan was installed, I moved to the front door and flipped on the switch, but nothing happened.

"I'll fix that," Lance said, chuckling while scratching the back of his head. "I must've mixed up the wires when I hooked it up."

I was about to say something when a thunderous noise crashed above our heads. We ducked, glancing at each other while we listened.

The boys' laughter drifted down the stairway.

"That was a good one," Griffin called out. "Took out half the ceiling."

"Let's see if we can knock out the other side," Davey hollered.

I glanced at Lance, straightening. "You're really not worried they'll fall?"

Lance shrugged. "Boys will be boys. If'n they fall, they'll just race each other back up to do it again."

Austin picked up an empty five-gallon bucket, carrying it toward me and flipping it upside down. "Sit. Rest that ankle. I'll tarp off the roof."

I let him nudge me to sit, all while planning to get up as soon as he walked outside.

Lance, chuckling when he read my face, started for the door. "Austin, I'm heading home for icepacks, but when I get back, I'll help with the tarps."

I watched them walk out and waited until they'd cleared the porch before I stood.

Grabbing a rusty putty knife and a hammer, I limped toward the kitchen. My ankle might need a break, but there was no reason I couldn't scooch across the floor on my butt while scraping up the old, cracked vinyl flooring.

CHAPTER TWENTY-SIX

AT SIX, GRIFFIN AND Davey left, and I finished sweeping up the plaster dust upstairs. By the time I returned downstairs, my ankle was throbbing again.

"Thought I told you to take it easy," Lance said with a scowl. He crossed to the back wall in the living room, opening the old refrigerator to retrieve an ice pack out of the freezer. He must've plugged it in earlier in the day.

When he tossed the pack to me I used both hands to catch it. Limping to my overturned bucket, I sat, placing the pack against my ankle's hot skin.

"Well?" Austin asked. "Are we going to install the new back door?"

"No," I answered before Lance could speak. "It's been a long day. You guys have done way more work than I'd planned to get done today."

"But we moved all those bags of plaster out back so we could install the new door," Austin said, glancing over at Lance.

Lance hesitated, reading my face. "She's right. It can wait. Davina can help me put the door in next week."

"Exactly," I said. "You two should take off. Enjoy your night."

"Well, all right then," Lance said. "But are you sure you're not working tomorrow either?"

"If I stop here tomorrow, it'll be for only an hour or two. Besides, Sundays are the day of rest, remember?"

Lance snorted. "I reckon." Lance wasn't the sit still type either, no matter what day of the week it was, but without further complaint, he moseyed out the door.

Austin looked back at me, hesitating, but ended up following Lance out. I wasn't sure what he'd been thinking, but I was happy he hadn't tried to guilt me into leaving just yet.

When I heard their vehicles leave, I got up and tossed the ice pack back inside the freezer. Moving room to room, I picked up trash, returned tools to their proper place, and tossed empty boxes off the front porch into the yard. When everything was somewhat organized again, I retrieved my cleaning tote from the van and cleaned the bathroom, polishing the new fixtures and shower surround and scrubbing the dirt smudges off the new floor. With my ankle acting up, the cleaning took a good hour to finish.

Exiting the bathroom, I realized the night sky had swooped in, sending the living room into darkness. The air drifting through the still open front door was a good ten degrees colder.

Not wanting to trip and fall, I crossed a few feet along the back wall and opened the refrigerator, letting the tiny bulb inside light my path. Now able to see the boxes, I started toward the front wall where my work lights sat.

A dark figure moved into the front doorway.

I stopped, waiting for the figure to speak, but he didn't. He took a step inside, and two more men moved through the doorway behind him.

I turned, planning to flee through the kitchen, but three more shadowy figures entered through the narrow entrance. I was trapped.

Panicking, I bolted toward the bedroom.

A set of strong hands latched onto me, one at my shoulder, gripping it hard enough to pinch a nerve, and the other wrapping its fingers in my hair.

I screamed.

The man behind me chuckled, dragging me back to the center of the room while keeping my back pinned tight against his chest. "Looks like we got ourselves a scared li'l rabbit," the man behind me laughed. "Maybe we should skin it."

Behind us, I heard the distinct clicks of someone flipping the light switches, but since Lance had replaced the old chandelier with the new ceiling fan light that wasn't working, nothing happened. A second or two later, a work light was turned on and the room lit up so bright I flinched.

Barely more than an arm's length away, a man with cold dead eyes glowered at me. I glanced down to read the patch on his leather vest. *The Bleeding Souls.*

My eyes flashed back up to meet his. "Please, don't hurt me."

Hearing movement behind me, I tried to swivel my head but the man holding me reefed on my hair, tipping my head further back. Several hairs sprung free from my scalp. I uttered a small cry, tears building behind my eyes.

"Yeah, baby, scream," the biker behind me whispered into my ear. "I like it."

I clamped my mouth shut but was unable to stop myself from whimpering. Hot tears streaked my cheeks. I'd crossed paths with the Bleeding Souls, a nefarious biker gang, earlier in the summer when working a hit and run case with Olivia. Our brief interaction had told me all I needed to know. The Bleeding Souls were ruthless. Violent. Dangerous.

To my left, a man moved into my peripheral vision. I blinked rapidly to clear my blurry eyes. It was LoJack, the biker I'd confronted a few months ago and struck a deal with to leave Olivia and me alone.

I wanted to plead with him to let me go, but he wasn't looking at me. He was watching the man who stood a few feet in front of me.

"What do you want?" I asked, hissing when the man behind me yanked at my hair again.

"*Why are you here?*" I yelled. "*What do you want?*"

LoJack's eyes narrowed at me, and with a minuscule shake of his head he ordered me to be silent.

I pursed my lips together, feeling my lower lip tremble against my upper lip.

LoJack focused on the other biker, the one in front of me, but that biker was too busy watching me to notice him.

"The girl," the other biker hissed, walking forward to stop in front of me. "Where is she?"

"What girl?" I asked, though I knew he meant Addy.

"Don't play games," a raspy voice whispered into my ear. The biker behind me jerked my hair again, moving his face beside mine. He extended his tongue, licking a tear off my cheek.

I whimpered, cringing.

"You taste good," the biker behind me said. "Boss, can I keep her? Play with her?"

"*The girl*," the biker boss shouted into my face. "Hand her over!"

"Please. I don't know where she is," I said, gulping down tears.

When the biker behind me jerked my hair hard enough to rip more strands out, I screamed, raising my hands to try wedging my fingers under his grip.

The other bikers laughed, enjoying my pain.

When his grip lessened, I sniffled, crying. "Please. I'm telling you the truth. I've never met the girl. I don't know where she is. One of the local cops told me she ran away. That's all I know."

"*Don't lie!*" the biker in front of me yelled in my face. "We know she was here."

"*Search the house!*" I yelled, praying that if for some reason Addy had been here, she was long gone. "I'm not lying. She's not here."

"*Then tell us where she is!*" the biker in front of me roared.

"*I don't know.* I haven't seen a girl or anyone else here."

The biker leaned closer, his face nearly touching mine. "I don't believe you." His breath reeked of rot and cigarettes. He panted in front of me, his rage spiraling.

I heard a snap-click and a knife's blade appeared in the biker's hand.

I cried out, trying to squirm away from the knife. My head was reefed back again, exposing my neck. I couldn't see anything but the ceiling, but I felt the metal from the blade against my skin, dragged at an angle so it wouldn't cut me.

Sandwiched between the two bikers, I stilled, afraid that if I moved my neck would be slashed open.

"Boss," LoJack said, in an even voice, "she's a friend of the Devil's Players. They'll retaliate. We'd be violating their rules. No women. No children."

"*Shut up.* This doesn't concern you," the biker in front of me snarled. "Go outside. Watch the perimeter."

"No, no, no," I whimpered, a spike of fear overwhelming me. "Please don't kill me. Please."

"Boss if we—" LoJack started to say.

"*Get outside!*" the biker in front of me yelled, cutting LoJack off. "*That's an order!*"

I heard boots move across the floor, thumping out onto the porch. Snot drip from my nose. My vision blurred, swimming in tears.

"You've got forty-eight hours," the boss biker said, running the flat side of the blade down my neck again. "Find the girl. Deliver her to us. Or the next time we meet, things are going to get bloody."

I flinched when he nicked my skin with the knife.

After a long moment of staring at me with his cold dead eyes, he stepped around me, his bootsteps vibrating the floor as he exited the house. The biker behind me tossed me forward. I landed on my hands and knees. Scurrying a few feet away, I curled my body inward, placing my face on the floor and raising my arms over my head.

I lay there, waiting for one of the bikers to hit or kick me, but heard the thud-thud of their feet move across the floor and out the door.

CHAPTER TWENTY-SEVEN

A GOOD TWENTY MINUTES LATER, I peeled myself up from the floor and stood on shaky legs. My brain swam in fear and confusion. I picked up my notepad, phone and purse and unplugged the work light. I stumbled out the front door, dragging the door closed behind me but not bothering to lock it.

Only half aware of my movements, I somehow crossed through the darkness to reach my van. I climbed inside, shutting the door and tapping the lock button on the door's interior panel.

I'm safe.

I whimpered, a wave of fear rolling over me. Draping my arms around the steering wheel, I leaned my forehead against it, trying to focus my thoughts. *How did they sneak up on me? How did they get so close? Why hadn't I sensed them? Sensed the danger I was in?*

Rolling my head to the side, I stared through the passenger window at the house. LoJack was without a doubt violent, and yet, the last time our paths had crossed I'd managed to reason with him. But his boss? His boss was on a level of evil that matched my sister's. When he'd threatened me, he'd meant it. He'd hurt me, kill me even—and enjoy it.

I dragged myself off the steering wheel, sitting upright and wiping my face with the cuff of my sleeve. I had no idea how I was going to get out of this, but even if I knew where the girl was I'd never hand her over to them—not in a million years.

Leaning back in my seat, I felt a chilled breeze brush against my face. I glanced to my right, noticing that when I'd locked the van's doors my brain had failed to process that the window was down.

I lifted my keys and turned over the engine. Pushing the button on the door panel, I watched the glass slowly creep up to close. Fiddling with the heater, I set it on the highest setting.

I should call Stone to report the bikers' threat, but what can he do? It would be their word against mine with no proof. And since they didn't hurt me...

I lifted a hand to my neck, feeling the nick on my skin. The size of a mosquito bite, the cut didn't hurt but it made the bikers' threat feel all that more real.

I glanced at the house again.

How did the bikers get into the house without me sensing them?

I thought back over the last week, not remembering a single psychic episode. Thinking back further, I realized I couldn't remember sensing much of anything after capturing Raina the month before. *But that can't be right, can it?*

I closed my eyes, focusing my thoughts while trying to relax my body. I called for my psychic doors, but they didn't appear. I tried to pull my energy forward but felt nothing.

Why? What changed?

I reached toward the passenger seat, wrapping my fingers around my phone when something behind me shifted from inside the van.

The sound should've terrified me, but it didn't. A calm washed over me and without hesitating, I put the van in reverse, backing up into the space alongside the house before driving forward toward the road.

Still unable to pull my psychic energy to the surface, my brain scrambled to understand why I wasn't afraid. How I knew it was the girl in the back, not one of the bikers.

Because the bikers said Addy had come to the cottage, I remembered.

It had been Addy who'd been in the woods last night. She was the one inside the house when I came back to check on things. She was the one who left cigarette butts on the patio.

Even now, I could smell the lingering scent of cigarette smoke clinging to her. She must've been hiding nearby when the bikers came.

At the end of the drive I looked both directions, searching for motorcycles, but the road was clear. I turned left, pointing my van toward Daybreak Falls.

I need to get Addy out of here. I need to get her somewhere safe, but where? Where can I take her?

I checked my mirrors, looking for headlights. I didn't see any, but if the bikers followed with their headlights off...

Picking up my phone, my eyes swiveled between the phone's screen and watching the road while I scrolled for Bernadette's name and tapped the call button.

"I'm busy," Bernadette snapped, answering.

"I need your help, but I can't explain. Are you at home?"

"Of course I'm at home. Where else would I be?"

I was about to list a slew of places but thought better of it. "I'm heading your way." I hung up, calling Isaac next.

"Hey, Davina," Isaac answered.

"Are you at home?"

"Sure am. Need something?"

"I'll be driving by in about five minutes. Can you watch out your front window and make sure no one is following me?"

"Why?"

"Please, Isaac. It's important."

"Fine. I'll play along. But don't think I won't be asking questions next time I see you."

"I get it." I hung up, setting my phone in the cupholder.

Isaac lived on the southwest corner of town, so at the next cross street I hung a left turn. A few minutes later I passed his house without slowing. A mile down the road, I turned right, heading north just as my phone rang.

"Anyone?" I asked, answering.

"You're clear," Isaac said. "No vehicles drove by after your van."

"Thanks. I'll explain later." I disconnected before Isaac started his cop thing, nudging me to explain.

After turning onto the road that led out to Bernadette's place, I glanced in the rearview mirror, trying to see into the back. "Addy, I'm pretty sure that's you back there. You're safe. I won't turn you over to those bikers."

She was quiet, not saying anything.

"It's okay. I know you don't know me, don't trust me, but I'm taking you somewhere safe. They won't find you."

"Give me one good reason to trust you," a voice whispered from the back of the van.

"Because you don't have a choice. I don't know what you did to those bikers, but they're out for blood. If you stay at the cottage, they'll find you."

Addy remained silent for a good mile stretch before she spoke again. "Who'd you call? The cops?"

"No. I called Bernadette."

"Who's that?"

"My grandmother."

"Why?" Her voice was elevated, full of surprise.

"I trust Bernadette to keep you safe."

"You think a little old lady can protect me from those guys? Are you nuts?"

"Bernadette's not your typical grandmother. She knows her way around a shotgun, has a secluded house with the freakiest of security systems, and she'll sense if the bikers get too close. She'll protect you." I waited a beat before saying, "Why don't you move up here. No one is following us."

"Fine," Addy muttered defiantly.

I heard stuff in the back being knocked around. Her leg appeared between the bucket seats, followed by the rest of her.

"Something was poking me in the back anyway." Addy picked up the pizza box from the passenger seat before throwing herself down, placing the box on her lap. "Mind if I eat this? I'm starving."

"Help yourself, but fair warning, it's been sitting in the van for hours."

She opened the box, pulling out a slice of pizza. "I'm too hungry to care." She bit into the slice, chewing as she watched the road. "Who are you anyway? I heard the teenage boys call you Davina, but are you like their aunt or something?"

"Davey and Griffin? No, I'm their neighbor. They live across the street from me."

"The older one is kind of hot. Is he fake like the younger one?"

"Fake? You think Griffin's fake?"

"I know he is," Addy said with a snarl to her voice.

Her comment was puzzling, but we were only ten minutes away from Bernadette's. "I'm not sure what you're insinuating, but I'm more interested in the bikers. What happened? Why are they after you?"

Addy snorted, lifting her foot to the dash. "Like I'm going to spill my secrets to *you*, a stranger? I don't think so." She tore the crust off her pizza. "A goody-two-shoes like you would call the cops. And if'n the cops find out what happened, I'm dead. It's that simple." She pointed at the road. "Just drop me off along the shoulder. I can take care of myself."

"Kid, I'm not letting you fend for yourself against a gang of thugs. If you don't trust me with your story, fine. But you climbed into *my* van. You hid on *my* property. You're my problem now whether you like it or not, so I'm taking you somewhere safe." I pointed to her foot. "Now get your foot off my dash. Feet belong on the floor, young lady."

Addy lowered her foot, but slouched low in her seat like she was sulking. After finishing off her pizza, she peeked inside the box.

"Help yourself to the last slice."

She swooped it up, tossing the empty box behind her into the back.

"Before we get to Bernadette's, I need to know if you have a phone or any other electronic device that someone could use to track you."

"I'm not an idiot. I turned off my phone and pulled the battery first chance I got."

"Good. That's good." Hoping to keep her talking, I asked, "Were you hiding inside the house this whole time?"

"Mostly." Addy spoke between bites of food. "I hid in the attic until this afternoon. By the way, you scared the crap out of me when you fell through the roof."

"I bet, but if you were in the attic why didn't the boys see you when they went up there?"

"After everyone ran into the big bedroom to check on you, I lowered myself through the ceiling in the other bedroom and snuck downstairs. I hung out in the woods, waiting for everyone to leave."

She'd been at the cottage the whole time. I ran a hand through my hair. My psychic abilities were really gone. "You sneezed!" I said a little too loudly. I glanced sideways at her. "Earlier today, when you were in the attic, you sneezed."

Addy giggled. "Yeah, that was me. That plaster dust did a number on my sinuses." She nibbled on her pizza.

"You disappeared Wednesday night, miles away. How'd you get all the way out to the cottage?"

Addy snorted. "That's what you're calling that dump? The cottage?"

I pursed my lips and gave her a disapproving look. "Don't be rude."

Addy scowled, swiveling her head toward her window.

I focused on the road ahead, keeping my eyes peeled for deer along the shoulder.

"I have a moped," Addy whispered. "I knew about," she paused briefly, "*the cottage* because the kids at school sometimes party there. It wasn't safe to go home, so I drove there instead and hid my moped in the woods. But when I heard the motorcycles tonight, I didn't have time to get to my moped, so I hid in your van. After they left, I was too scared to get out."

"A moped, huh?" I said, sparing her a glance. "I take it this moped of yours isn't registered?"

Addy's head swiveled my way, her eyes wide. "How'd you know that?" Her hand rose to the door handle.

"Olivia, my best friend, was hired to find you."

"Olivia..." Addy let the name drift off into silence. "Isn't that the name of the woman you were arguing with this morning in the front yard? She's looking for me too?" Addy's grip on the door handle tightened as she leaned toward it.

I was pretty sure the door wouldn't open while the van was moving, but since it was an older model, I wasn't positive. Afraid she'd try to jump out, I grabbed her jacket sleeve. "It's fine. I won't tell Olivia anything. And yes, I'm surprised you heard us from the attic, but our argument was about her taking on your case."

Addy settled back into her seat.

I let go of her but kept my hand ready to grab her again. "Addy, Olivia's my friend, but I won't tell her where you are."

"If she's your friend, of course you'll tell her where I am."

"No, I won't. I was trying to get her to stop searching for you."

"Why?"

"Because the story her client gave her sounded bogus."

"Who hired her? Who's her client?"

"Your aunt."

"I don't have an aunt. It's just me and my dad." She shifted her body, slumping and about to raise her foot to the dash but after catching me watching, she planted it back on the floor. "I doubt my dad has even noticed I'm missing."

"He's noticed." I moved my right hand back to the steering wheel, slowing the van for the upcoming turn onto Cicadas Lane. "Your dad was the one who filed the missing person report."

"Wow. That's almost... surprising. I don't think we've spoken a single word to each other in years."

"Why? Is he not a good dad?"

Addy sighed, fiddling with the window to raise and lower it. "He doesn't beat me or anything. He's not mean like that. He just doesn't like being around me." She pulled her hand back, fiddling with the multiple rings on her fingers instead. "It's complicated."

Deciding to change tactics, I asked, "If Olivia's client isn't your aunt, who is she?"

"No idea, but she's gotta be someone working with the bikers."

"Great," I mumbled, turning onto Bernadette's private road.

Addy sat upright, looking through the windshield. "This place is even more boondocks than your house."

"The cottage isn't my house. I'm just fixing it up to sell it."

"Makes sense." Addy pulled a pack of cigarettes from her jacket pocket. "Mind if I smoke?"

"I don't allow anyone to smoke in my van, especially underage kids not old enough to buy cigarettes." I pointed to the end of the drive. "Besides, we're here." Passing the open gate, I drove up to the house.

Another vehicle, one I didn't recognize, was parked next to Bernadette's Nova. "Get down."

"What?"

"Get down on the floor. Someone's here." I turned off the van, pocketing the keys. "I'll run inside to get rid of whoever it is. Stay out of sight until after they leave. I don't want anyone knowing you're here."

Addy giggled, rolling over so her stomach was lying on the seat and her feet and knees were on the floor. "Your grandma's having a sleepover. Good for her. A healthy sex life is important at all ages."

"*Ew*. Don't say things like that." I reached up to click off the van's ceiling light before opening my door. "Just give me two minutes."

Staying low, Addy wiggled between the bucket seats, disappearing into the back. "Ow," she said as something fell. "You need to empty this thing."

"Just stay out of sight." I got out, shutting the door. Reaching my hand into my pocket, I thumbed the key fob, locking the van's doors while making my way up the porch steps.

Chapter Twenty-Eight

When Bernadette didn't appear on the front porch in her typical shotgun greeting, I entered the house, crossing to the panel door that separated the façade side from the real side.

Unless her abilities as well as her security system were on the fritz, she knew I was here. I slid the panel door open and entered the main room, spotting Bernadette between the kitchen and dining table. My mouth dropped open before I snapped it shut.

Bernadette was dressed in an orange quilted house robe and her hair was up in rollers. A good ten layers of makeup caked her face, her muddy lipstick cementing an unlit cigarette to her lower lip.

I crossed the room, shaking off my stupor. "I don't even want to know why you look like that." I nodded to the guy sitting at the table. "Who's this?"

"That's Darrel." The cigarette bobbed up and down when she spoke. "Darrel, this is my granddaughter."

Darrel stood, keeping Bernadette's evil cat Satan tucked against his chest. He reached out with his free hand, offering to shake mine. "Nice to meet you."

I started to reach out, but Satan hissed, swiping his claws at me.

"Now, now, kitty," Darrel said, petting the cat.

Satan purred, nuzzling into the crook of Darrel's arm.

"Darrel, it's nice to meet you, but I need you to leave." I moved to his side, staying out of Satan's reach while guiding Darrel toward the panel door. I need to talk to Bernadette alone. I'm sorry, but it's a family matter."

"But Sammy here," Darrel looked down at the cat, "will be upset if I leave."

"Take him with you," Bernadette said, moving behind Darrel to nudge him at a faster pace toward the door. "He likes you better than me anyway. You two are made for each other."

Darrel tried to turn sideways and wiggle free, but I tightened both my hands around his elbow and dragged him with me.

By the time we got him outside onto the porch, he was bordering panic, trying to figure out how to get back inside. "But, but, but—"

I kept going, pulling him down the porch steps. "Sorry to be rude, but it's an emergency." Reaching his car, I opened the driver's door. "Maybe you can visit again next week."

"*No!*" Bernadette yelled from the porch. "Don't come back. Forget where I live. Forget we ever met."

"But, snookums," Darrel started to say.

"Don't you *snookums* me," Bernadette yelled. "I've been trying to get rid of you for days."

With a hand on his shoulder, I shoved Darrel down into the driver's seat, accidentally causing him to whack his head on the side of the car. He raised one hand to rub his head, still holding the cat with his other arm. Taking advantage of his confused state, I picked up one leg then the other, and tucked them inside.

"Okay..." I said, trying not to laugh. "Enjoy the cat." I shut the door and wiggled my fingers in a wave. "Bye-bye, Darrel. It was nice to meet you."

Darrel sat there a long moment, looking between me and Bernadette who still had the unlit cigarette dangling from her lower lip.

I pointed toward the road, giving him my best *don't-even-think-about-arguing-with-me* look, usually reserved for Olivia's boys. "Go on. Time to leave."

He started the car's engine, reversing into the open drive to turn around.

I stepped back toward my van and watched him turn onto the gravel road.

"About time," Bernadette said. "I thought I'd never get rid of him."

"Why didn't you just tell him to leave?"

"I did! Believe me, I tried everything. Every time I demanded that he leave, he'd start bawling like a baby, saying how we were soulmates." Bernadette pointed toward the road. "Like that sniveling fool would be a match for me!" Bernadette turned, waddling back toward the door. "I'm going to close the gates, so he can't come back."

"Good idea." After glancing once more toward the driveway and not seeing or hearing anything, I clicked the key fob in my pocket, unlocking the van. "You can come out now."

The van's side door slid open, and Addy stuck her head out. "Are you sure?"

"I'm sure. But let's hurry inside just in case."

Addy jumped out, accidentally kicking a roll of duct tape out of the back. Bending over, she picked the roll up and tossed it back inside.

I glanced into the back, seeing several boxes were crushed and lying on their side, spilling supplies everywhere. *I'll deal with it later*, I thought before sliding the door closed.

Halfway up the porch steps, Addy stopped to stare at the house. "I think I like the cottage better."

"This side of the house purposely looks haunted," I said, passing her to lead the way. "Bernadette is, uhm, *unusual*. You two will probably hit it off. Come on, the other side is nicer."

Addy followed me inside, staying close behind me until we crossed through the panel opening. "Oh, wow. Cool." She jogged across the room to look beyond the wall of glass.

Bernadette was behind her desk. The glare of the computer cast a blue glow across her face.

I walked over, tugging the cigarette free from her lip, and crossed to the kitchen. "What's with the cigarette? You don't smoke."

"I was trying to look less sexy. I thought if I looked cheap and unsophisticated, Darrel might give up his pursuit of winning my affections."

I tossed the cigarette into the trashcan. "I take it your plan failed?"

"I guess I'm just too sexy, no matter what I wear," Bernadette said.

"Yeah, that's it," I mumbled, opening the refrigerator to look for something to drink. "Addy's going to stay here for a few days. Can you show her the security system?"

"I'm not running a hotel. Besides, I just finally got rid of Darrel. Why would I want someone else in my house?"

"Because Addy needs a place to hide, and we both know your house makes the perfect safehouse."

Bernadette's head snapped up, glancing between me and Addy, who stood motionless facing the windows as she listened to us. "Who's she hiding from?"

"A gang of dangerous bikers," I answered.

"Really?" Bernadette said, her voice full of curiosity. "Why?"

Addy moved to stand beside Bernadette, glancing at her computer while trying to pull off a look of nonchalance. "They're trying to kill me," she said, shrugging.

"*Really...*" Bernadette said, sounding even more intrigued. "Well, that's impressive."

I eavesdropped as they chatted.

Addy explained the bare bones of the situation, not revealing anything I didn't already know. Bernadette didn't ask any questions, but I was relieved when she showed Addy the security system, explaining how it worked. She'd only take the time to do that if she'd decided to let Addy stay.

When a shotgun blasted from outside the house, despite knowing it was only the security system's sound effects, I jumped, nearly dropping the carton of orange juice I'd pulled from the refrigerator.

I directed a dirty look toward Bernadette and set the carton on the nearby countertop.

Bernadette snickered, pointing out something else on the computer to Addy.

After pulling glasses from the cupboard, I filled them halfway before placing the orange juice back inside the refrigerator. Grabbing a carton of eggs, I opened it to see that all but two of the slots were full. "Who wants hard-fried egg sandwiches?" I asked, grabbing a stick of butter.

"Me," they both said.

I got out the frypan and a loaf of bread, knowing where everything was.

"How long are you staying here?" Bernadette asked Addy.

"Not sure. I need to lay low until everyone gets bored trying to find me. Then I can sneak home and get my stuff before I take off for good."

"But where will you go?" Bernadette asked.

Addy shrugged. "Anywhere I want, I guess."

"You're sixteen," I reminded her, cracking eggs into the pan. "How long do you think you could *lay low* from a gang of bikers?"

"I'm smart. I'll figure it out."

"Oh, yeah? How?"

"I have a fake ID and enough money for motels. I'll get by. I've got skills to earn money."

"Skills, huh?" I asked. "You mean illegal skills?"

Addy stomped across the room, stopping near the kitchen counter. "I'm not a criminal."

"Are you sure about that?" I asked, glancing sideways at her.

Her scowl shifted into a frown while scrunching her nose. "Okay, maybe some of the things I do are sketchy, but I don't steal if that's what you're insinuating." She walked over to the table and sat.

"You don't steal," I repeated, bobbing my head while breaking the egg yolks. "Okay, Miss Law Abiding Citizen.... I had six keys made for the cottage, but hours later when I went to get them, one was gone. Any idea who took it?"

Addy defiantly swung her head to face the wall of windows, crossing her arms over her chest.

"It sure would be a shame if I had to pay the locksmith to come out and change the locks again," I said, setting my spatula down long enough to load the toaster. "All that money wasted."

Addy's shoulders slumped and her arms fell from her chest. One of her hands slid into her front jeans pocket. "I didn't steal the key. I was only *borrowing* it until I didn't need it anymore." She pulled the key from her pocket, tossing it onto the table.

I flipped the eggs. "What about your unregistered moped? If you didn't steal it, why is it unregistered?"

"A kid at school owed me money. He gave me the moped as payment. I have the ownership papers, but I purposely didn't register it so no one could trace it back to me."

"A getaway car," Bernadette said, crossing the room and taking two of the juice glasses to the table. "I like it. Every good criminal needs an unregistered vehicle." She sat across from Addy.

"Bernadette," I said in a warning voice.

"What? I watch TV," Bernadette said.

"You're not helping," I said, flipping the eggs again. I peeked over at Addy. "Explain how one teenager ends up owing another teenager a moped's worth of money."

"I'm resourceful," Addy said, smirking. "I discovered an untapped market to swindling jerk-faced kids out of their allowance."

"You con them?" Bernadette asked.

"No. I'm more of a *truth enforcer*."

"Blackmail," Bernadette said, nodding. "I like it."

"It's illegal and immoral," I said, scowling at Bernadette.

"Is she always this judgmental?" Addy asked Bernadette.

"Unfortunately, yes," Bernadette said, getting up and moving to the stairway. "I'm heading downstairs to wash this makeup off my face. Follow me, Addy. I'll show you Davina's room where you'll be sleeping."

"Lead the way, Grandma," Addy said.

Bernadette stopped and glared at Addy. "You can call me Bernie, but if you mock me again, in my own home, I'll toss your skinny butt out the door. Do we understand each other?"

"Got it." Addy ducked her head to hide her grin.

They disappeared down the stairway.

CHAPTER TWENTY-NINE

SITTING TO EAT NEXT TO Addy, I watched her unzip her hoodie and slip her arms free. The black t-shirt underneath looked stained. I leaned closer, tugging the hem toward me and saw a rip in the side and the fabric coated in dried blood. "You're hurt." I lifted her shirt a few inches, seeing a bloody scorch mark along the side of her ribs. "What happened?"

"It's nothing," Addy said, looking down at her wound. "It's just a graze."

"*From a bullet?*" Bernadette asked, hurrying out of her chair and around the table. "I've never seen a bullet wound before." Bernadette leaned over and poked the skin below the wound. "There's no hole."

Addy winced, leaning away. "Like I said, it was just a *graze.*" Addy tugged her shirt back down before picking up her egg sandwich to take a bite.

I watched her. She was trying to act tough, but I suspected the wound stung. "What happened?"

Addy shrugged. "I was hiding behind a tree when the bikers started shooting at me. One of the bullets peeled the bark off the tree before nicking me in the side. It's fine. Barely hurts."

"It looks infected," I said, getting up to cross to the kitchen where I'd left my phone. "Did you wash it out? Put anything on it?"

"Hello? I was kind of busy running for my life and all." She rolled her eyes and lifted the heel of her foot to the front edge of her chair. Resting her chin on top of her knee, she said, "By the time I got to the cottage, it had stopped bleeding. I patched it up with some stuff I keep in my moped seat, bandages I'd packed in case I wiped out, but with no water, I couldn't clean it."

"Not good," I said, scrolling through my phone for Noah's number.

"Yeah, well, I was low on options. By the way, thanks for getting a toilet running. I was tired of going outside in the middle of the night to pee." She chomped down on her sandwich.

Checking the time, seeing it was after ten, I hesitated. It was late, but Addy's wound looked infected. I didn't dare wait for morning. I hit the call button.

Noah answered on the third ring. "Yeah, D, what's up?" he asked with a sigh.

"I need you to drive out to Bernadette's house, but you can't tell anyone where you're going."

"Uh, that could be a problem," Noah said.

"Please, Noah. No one can know. And bring a med kit."

"Are you hurt?"

"Not me, but I can't explain anything over the phone."

There was a long pause before Noah said, "Yeah, yeah. Be there in a few." Noah hung up.

"Who did you call?" Addy asked, watching me, looking ready to bolt.

"It's fine," Bernadette said. "Noah won't tell anyone you're here."

Addy set the other half of her sandwich down, no longer eating.

"When you're done eating," I said, walking back to the table to sit. "You can shower downstairs. Clean the wound as best you can. Noah's a paramedic. He'll know what to do from there." Picking up my sandwich, I kept one eye on Addy, waiting to see what she'd do.

She was quiet for a long time, still not eating, but eventually frowned down at her shirt. "I guess taking a shower's not such a bad idea. It's been a few days. I'm starting to smell." She glanced sideways at me. "Got any clothes I can borrow?"

"Help yourself to anything you find. The clothes inside the closet are outdated and ugly, but they're clean."

Addy picked up her sandwich as she stood. "Thanks for the food." She circled the table, disappearing down the stairs, taking her sandwich with her.

"Think she'll bolt?" Bernadette asked.

"I have no idea, but I hope not."

Bernadette studied me, wearing a quizzical expression.

"You sense it, don't you?"

"Sense what?"

"That my abilities are gone."

Bernadette's eyes widened. "I couldn't put my finger on what was different, but yes, now that you mention it, what the heck happened?"

"I don't know. I didn't even notice they weren't working until a gang of bikers surprised me tonight."

"No warning at all?"

I shook my head.

"How long has it been since you've had a vision?"

"I don't know. The best I can recollect, I haven't sensed anything since Raina was arrested."

"That was weeks ago."

"I know."

"And since then, *nothing?* Are you sure?" Bernadette asked, setting her sandwich down.

"I think so."

"Well," Bernadette said, glancing toward the wall of windows, "Raina being captured could explain the change, I suppose."

"What does one have to do with the other?"

Bernadette shrugged. "I always suspected you manifested your abilities at a younger age because you knew you were in danger. Following that logic, years later when Raina was no longer a threat..."

"Just like that? Raina getting locked up and *poof*—my abilities are gone?"

"I doubt it's that simple, but maybe. I grew up psychic and liked being different. But you've always bucked against having your abilities. Subconsciously, you probably blocked them out when you no longer felt threatened."

"How do I unlock them again?"

Bernadette snorted, getting up and clearing her and Addy's plates. "Years of therapy I suppose."

"That's not funny." I turned in my chair to watch her.

"It's kind of funny." Bernadette set the plates next to the sink before glancing toward the front of the house. "Noah's here already. He must've been at his fishing cabin."

Just as she said the words, the driveway alarm on her computer dinged. She waddled across the room, fiddling with it to open the gate.

I got up and walked out to the front porch.

Parking his truck next to my van, Noah climbed out, carrying a medical bag. "You owe me. *Big time*. When I wouldn't tell Britt where I was going, she stormed out, cursing both our names."

"I'm sorry," I said, opening the door and leading him to the other side. "I know she's hung up on you and me being unnaturally close."

"Mom keeps telling me it's her problem, not mine, but Britt has a point, you know?" Noah slid the panel door closed behind him and followed me to the dining table. "You call, and I stop whatever I'm doing to come help you."

"I promise, this time, it couldn't be helped."

Noah looked around, not seeing anyone but me. "Where's the patient?"

I walked over and looked over the rail to the basement. Bernadette was downstairs, arguing in a whispered voice with Addy, encouraging her to come upstairs.

"It's okay, Addy," I called down the stairway. "Noah won't call the cops."

"Call the cops?" Noah asked from behind me. He looked over the rail. "She's just a kid."

"I know. But she was grazed by a bullet and she's running for her life. We can't call the cops. You can't tell anyone she's here. You could get us killed."

Noah studied Addy, switching to his soothing voice. "You can trust me. Come on up here, and I'll get you patched up."

Bernadette nudged Addy up the first step. When I saw Addy continue up on her own, I moved away from the stairway, locking eyes with Noah.

He was mad. Like fuming, mad. When I'd called him, I'd known him treating an underage patient with a bullet wound would be an issue. If anyone found out, he could lose his job.

"I'm sorry," I whispered.

"We'll discuss this later," Noah said, moving his bag to the table and opening it.

Addy reached the top of the stairs and Noah pulled out the end chair. "Have a seat, kiddo. You'll be feeling better in a jiffy."

Addy spared me a nervous glance but sat. Noah did his good-ole-boy smile thing, winning her over by talking non-stop to put her at ease.

Five minutes later, I followed Noah outside, whispering, "You can't tell Britt about this."

"You think I don't know that?" Noah asked, swiveling around to face me. "If I mention any of this to Britt, she'll report me. I'd lose my EMT certification."

"I know," I said, looking down at my hands.

Noah released a frustrated sigh, crossing to his truck and throwing the door open. After tossing his medical bag inside, he stood there looking off toward the woods. "It's late. I'm going home."

"Noah..."

Noah glanced back at me, one hand resting on the top of his door, lips pursed, silently waiting.

"You have every right to be mad," I said. "But you'll forgive me, right? Eventually?"

His shoulders deflated a fraction. "Yeah, I'll forgive you." He climbed into his truck. "But it won't be tonight." He kept the door open for another second, glancing up at me. "You know, I think I'd forgive you faster if you baked me something."

My lips twitched but I forced myself not to smile. "I was thinking if I had time tomorrow, maybe I'd bake you an apple pie."

"That's a start." Noah shut his door, turning over the engine.

CHAPTER THIRTY

I'D BARELY SLEPT, SITTING UPRIGHT in bed every time the old house creaked or groaned, which was a lot. Climbing out of bed as the sky outside started to brighten, I pulled on a pair of sweatpants and grabbed my phone.

Making my way to the kitchen, my thoughts returned to Addy and the bikers. I had to figure out what was going on.

I tapped out a message to Stone, asking him to call me, but before I set my phone down, it rang. "That was quick," I said, answering.

"I'm already at work. I came in early to take another look at Addy Randall's file."

"About that... I was wondering if you could take me to her dad's house? Maybe if I looked around, saw her room, it would knock loose an idea of where she would've gone."

"This isn't a psychic thing, is it?"

"Since my abilities are on the fritz, no. I just want to help find her." I tugged on my lower lip, feeling a twinge of guilt for lying. I knew Stone was worried about Addy, yet I'd promised to keep her secret.

"I guess it won't hurt," Stone said. "Nothing else is working. I'll call her father and set it up. Pick you up at eight?"

I checked the time on my Fitbit. It was nearing seven. "Sure. See you soon."

After disconnecting, I called Olivia. When the phone rang a half-dozen times, I suspected she was either still sleeping, working, or avoiding my call.

Deciding to leave her a message, I waited for the customary beep before saying, "I know you're mad at me, but you can't stay mad at me forever. Isn't that what you always tell me?" I sighed, wishing she'd answered. "There's something else. Addy Randall doesn't have an aunt and your client might be associated with the Bleeding Souls. Olivia, I know you're worried about your business, but this girl is in real danger. You've got too big of a heart not to see it. Call me. Please."

I hung up, crossing my fingers that she'd listen to the message. Carrying my phone with me, I walked over to fix a pot of coffee. After getting it ready, I pressed the brew button just as my phone rang. Olivia's name flashed across the screen.

"You called me back," I said, answering.

"I'm still mad at you."

"I figured as much when you ignored my call." My nature had me wanting to apologize, but I didn't want to chance starting another argument.

"I'll check into the fake aunt, but now I'm worried."

"Why?" I asked as the hairs on my arms stood upright.

"Because the fake aunt asked me for daily updates. Before I left the office yesterday, I emailed her a handful of pictures I found of Addy online."

"What kind of pictures?"

"Pictures of her at some party. The place looked like a dump. Beer cans everywhere and writing on the walls. No furniture. A bunch of drunk kids."

"Well, that explains it."

"Explains what?"

"How the bikers landed on my doorstep at the cottage last night. Until recently, the cottage was where the local kids met up to party."

"*The bikers were at the cottage?*" Olivia screeched three octaves higher than her normal voice. "Are you okay? What happened?"

"I'm okay, but they gave me forty-eight hours to find Addy and hand her over."

"*What?*"

"Relax. I'm fine. I'll figure it out."

"But..." Her words trailed off.

"I know. It's bad. Stone is picking me up later this morning and taking me to Addy's house. I'm hoping I'll find something in her bedroom that'll explain whatever's going on."

"I'll go too. Maybe I can create a distraction to give you more snooping time."

"No, thanks," I said a little too quick, shuddering at the thought of one of Olivia's distractions. "Figure out who the woman is instead. Maybe the information will help. Also, keep sending her updates and play along like nothing's changed. We don't want to tip her off that you know anything."

"What about the girl? We need to find her. We need to move her somewhere safe."

Guilt rolled through me, wanting to tell Olivia that Addy was already safe. "Let's focus on figuring out what's going on with the bikers first. The girl obviously has a talent for hiding."

"Okay. Let me know if you unearth anything at her house and watch your back."

"Same to you." After disconnecting, I set my phone down and pulled a coffee mug from the cupboard, nearly dropping it when someone knocked on the kitchen door.

I crossed to the door and pushed the curtain aside. Lance and Isaac stood with their arms crossed and wearing scowls.

Unlocking and opening the door, I returned to the cupboard, pulling two more cups and filling them. "Morning."

"Morning," Lance grumbled, taking a coffee cup from me before stomping over to the table.

"Is that donuts I'm smelling?" I asked, handing Isaac his cup before following him to the table.

Lance scowled at the table, shoving the bag of donuts toward the center. "Cinnamon and sugar twists."

"Smells good," I said, sliding the napkins from the end of the table over.

Lance held up my notepad. "I got into your van for the list. It's a mess in there."

"I know. I'll clean it out later." I set a donut on each napkin, sliding one in front of each of them. "So what's up?"

Isaac raised an eyebrow. "That's what I want to know. Mind explaining that call last night? Why you had me watching out my window to see if you were being followed?"

I'd forgotten about calling him. I scrambled to come up with a good lie but couldn't think of one. I decided to be truthful instead. "I can't tell you. I wish I could, but I can't."

They exchanged looks.

Lance leaned back in his chair, crossing his arms over his chest again. "Does this have anything to do with the motorcycles racing down my road last night?"

"Motorcycles? I didn't hear any motorcycles?" I lied.

Isaac shook his head, picking up his cup. "You're the worst liar ever."

I sighed. "Look, I'm okay. I know both of you worry, and I appreciate it, but the more people who know what's going on, the more danger I'll be in."

"You can trust us," Lance said.

"I know I can, but Lance, you can be a bit overprotective. The last thing I need is for you to start waving around your shotgun."

Lance smirked.

"And you..." I said, turning to face Isaac. "You wear a badge. If I shared what I know, you'd have to do your cop thing which could put me and others in harm's way." I looked between them. "Just give me time to figure this out on my own."

"How much time?" Isaac asked.

"Forty-eight hours. That's all I need." Since my deadline with them would be a good twelve hours *after* my deadline with the bikers, my problem would already be resolved, one way or another, by then.

"Two days, huh?" Isaac asked, exchanging glances with Lance. "What do you think?"

Lance let his folded arms slide off his chest. "I think she's got a good head on her shoulders and if she wants us to butt out, we need to butt out. But I'm not happy."

"Noted," I said, trying to hold back my smile. "Can I eat my donut now?"

"Smartass," Lance mumbled, picking up his own donut. "How's that ankle of yours doing this morning?"

I lifted my foot to the empty chair beside me and pulled up the leg of my sweatpants. From my shin to the top of my foot the skin was a blackish shade of purple.

Lance whistled. "You did a number on it, that's for sure. No wonder the swelling was so bad yesterday."

"How'd you hurt yourself?" Isaac asked, standing to lean over the table to see my ankle.

"Fell through the roof," I said, laughing.

After explaining to Isaac my fall, we chatted about my plans for the cottage while we ate. A half hour later, Lance and Isaac left so I could get dressed, brush my teeth, and wrangle my hair into a high ponytail.

When Stone pulled into my driveway a few minutes before eight, I carried two travel mugs and the bag with the last donut out of the house.

CHAPTER THIRTY-ONE

STONE DROVE US IN HIS personal truck instead of his Chief of Police SUV. Nearing the southern outskirts of the town's border, he steered the truck into a tidy subdivision.

"Shouldn't this area be covered by the County Sheriff's department?"

"It could've gone to either, but I took the initial 911 call," Stone answered.

Parking in the third driveway, Stone got out and I followed him to the door of a ranch-style house. The lawn was well kept, but unlike the neighboring yards, this one had no shrubbery or flowerpots, only grass. The low maintenance house didn't jive with Addy's bold personality. I'd expected something livelier, like her.

"Are you okay?" Stone asked, raising an eyebrow at me.

Before I could answer, a man with dark circles under his eyes opened the door. He stared at Stone for a long moment before stepping back to wave us inside. "Good morning. Please, come in. I don't have any coffee or tea, but could I offer either of you a glass of water?"

"We're good," Stone said, crossing the small living room to sit on the couch. "This is Davina Ravine. She's assisting me with the search for your daughter."

The man looked confused but reached his hand toward me. "Trent Randall."

"Nice to meet you," I said, returning his handshake before sitting beside Stone on the couch.

I fidgeted, annoyed that I hadn't picked up any psychic images. Only a month ago, a simple handshake would've sparked a wealth of information, but I'd sensed nothing.

Stone gave me a confused look, trying to decipher my expression.

I focused on Trent. "Can you tell me a little about your daughter? How she spends her time? Who her friends are?"

Trent glanced away while taking a seat in the upholstered chair across from us. He kept his body on the frontmost edge and one knee bounced with nervous energy. "Unfortunately, I work a lot, even on the weekends. Every Monday morning, I leave two hundred dollars on the table and by Friday there's a hundred dollars worth of grocery receipts waiting for me. I don't even know how Addy spends the other hundred, not that it matters. She's pretty self-sufficient."

"When was the last time you saw her?" Stone asked, flipping open his pocket notebook and readying his pen.

"You asked me that already." Trent tensed his jaw. "I told you that when I got home Tuesday night, I heard her in her room. Wednesday morning, I left before dawn, so I believe she was in there, but I don't know for sure. I only know she wasn't home Wednesday night."

"You *heard* her Tuesday night?" I asked, trying to keep my face blank. "When was the last time you *saw* her?"

Trent dragged a hand through his hair, studying his shoes. "I don't know."

"You don't see her, do you?" I asked. "That's what you're struggling to say. You stay away from the house until you know she'll be in her room, and you leave before she gets up in the morning."

Stone looked between us with one eyebrow arched.

Trent sighed. "It's easier that way. I can't explain it, but we keep to different schedules."

Stone's posture stiffened. "Mr. Randall, if your daughter has an issue I don't know about—" Stone started to say.

"It's not like that," I said, placing a hand on his arm. "He's just keeping his distance from her."

"Why?" Stone asked.

Trent leaned forward, his elbows on his knees, and rubbed his hands up and down his face. "Her mother has treatment-resistant schizophrenia. She didn't have any symptoms until her mid-twenties when Addy was just a baby."

Stone flipped his notebook back a few pages, reading his notes. "You told me your wife took off years ago, abandoning her family. Where is she really?"

"She's in a mental hospital in Wisconsin," Trent admitted.

"I'll need the phone number to confirm she's still there," Stone said.

Trent stood with slumped shoulders and crossed to the kitchen table, checking his phone before scribbling on a piece of paper. Setting his phone down, he tore the page off the pad and brought it back to Stone. "I already called the hospital. Janelle's there. Over the years, she's tried living outside the facility, but it never stuck for long."

"Could your daughter have gone back to Wisconsin?" Stone asked. "Would she go back to visit her mother or a friend?"

"Not to visit her mother," Trent said, shaking his head. "A few years back, Addy weaseled her way into the hospital. It was the first time since she was a toddler that she'd seen her mother, and it was altogether horrible timing. The doctors were switching Janelle's meds, trying to take her off one pill to test another. Janelle was manic that day, saying all kinds of crazy stuff. By the time I got there, Addy was trembling. For months afterward, she slept with her bedroom light on."

"That must've been scary for her," I said. "Did you talk to her about it?"

Trent avoided making eye contact as he sat back in his chair. "No."

"Is that why you avoid Addy?" I asked. "Do you think she'll become schizophrenic?"

"It's hereditary."

"So is cancer, alcoholism, and a million other things." Anger boiled inside me. I pressed my lips together and fisted my hands, thinking how alone Addy must've felt dealing with the fear of inheriting such a mind-altering disease.

Stone reached over and rested his hand on mine but kept his eyes locked on Trent. "Schizophrenia doesn't usually manifest until adulthood. Was Addy showing early signs?"

"Not that I'm aware of," Trent said, keeping his head ducked.

"Then explain why you avoid Addy," Stone said using a firm tone.

Trent launched out of the chair, fisting his hands at his sides. "*I couldn't do it, okay?* I couldn't go through it again. I couldn't watch another person I love vanish into mental chaos." He ran both hands through his hair. "I just couldn't do it, so I just..." He lifted his shoulders in a half shrug before letting them fall.

"Stopped loving her?" I finished for him.

He lifted his head and stared at me with tears in his eyes. "No, no. I love Addy. But as she got older, she looked more and more like her mother. I was scared. I thought if I gave myself some space, prepared myself, I'd feel safer, you know?"

"And if she's dead?" I asked, standing.

Trent flinched.

"Davina," Stone whispered.

I kept my eyes on Trent. "And if the next time you see your daughter she's lying in a casket? Will the years of isolation help you to grieve?"

"Don't say that. She'll be okay. Addy will come home."

I stepped closer to him, wishing I had my abilities so I could better understand. "I hope she does come home. I hope for her sake she lives long enough to discover her father loves her. I hope she experiences what it feels *to be loved*."

"I'll do better. I promise." Trent reached a hand to my forearm. "Just bring her home. Please, you've got to bring her home."

I circled around him, tugging my arm away from him. Entering the hallway, I peeked into the room on my left, a bathroom. On my right, I opened a closed door. I recognized Addy's bold style. The walls were painted black with neon orange and green lines crisscrossing each other. Her bedspread was white, a bright contrast to the dark walls.

I knew Stone and Trent had followed me and stopped in the doorway, but I ignored them. A laptop sat on top of a small desk in the corner along with a stack of schoolbooks. Her closet door was open, filled with mostly black clothes. On top of her dresser sat a get-well-soon bear like you'd buy in a hospital gift shop. I pointed to the bear. "When did she get that?"

"I don't know. Must've been when she had her tonsils removed a few years ago. Maybe it's from one of her teachers or a neighbor or something."

Pressing my lips together, I tried to stifle my anger before I said something that got myself thrown out of Trent's house. I came here to find clues as to what Addy had been up to, clues that would explain how she crossed paths with the bikers.

I looked under her pillows, inside each dresser drawer, and checked the upper shelves inside the closet. Not finding anything, I turned back to the center of the room, trying to think like a teenage girl. *If I was Addy, where would I hide something?*

The room was carpeted, so there were no loose boards to look under. The only furnace vent I saw was a floor vent which would run straight down to the basement, so it was unlikely she hid anything behind the vent. I turned in a circle. Addy had only three pieces of furniture: a bed, a desk, and a dresser. She didn't even have a nightstand.

I looked back at her desk. Maybe I was overthinking this. Addy wasn't a typical teenager. Her father went out of his way to avoid her. She lived an isolated life. "How long has it been since you stepped inside Addy's bedroom?"

"Probably since I bought the house a few months back," Trent answered. "Why?"

Addy didn't need to hide anything. Heck, she'd probably be ecstatic if she caught her father snooping through her room—a sign, albeit a small one, that he cared.

I looked over at Stone. "You should go wander around outside. Check under bushes or something."

Stone raised an eyebrow. "Seriously?"

I shrugged. "I think it's for the best."

Stone sighed, tucking his notebook away. "I have some calls to make. I'll be in the truck." He turned out of the room, disappearing down the hallway.

I crossed to Addy's desk and pulled out the chair, sitting. After hearing the front door open and close, I opened all three desk drawers, two on the right side and one middle drawer. The middle drawer only had pens and blank notepads. I closed it.

"Why did Chief Stone leave?" Trent asked.

In the top right drawer was a square cash box. I lifted it out, setting it on top of the desk. "Because he's a cop. He's sworn to follow the law no matter where it leads him. I, on the other hand, am a civilian. If I find something illegal that's unrelated to his case, I can simply just not tell him." I opened the unlocked cash box. Inside were several folded envelopes, crammed full of cash.

"Illegal? Why would you think you'd find something illegal?"

I didn't answer him. In the same drawer, I pulled out two aged greeting cards, reading them. One was a birthday card for a little girl, signed by Addy's mother. The other was a get-well card signed by several pre-teen girls, evidenced by all the hearts dotting the I's and over the top messages of gooeyness.

I set both cards back in the drawer before sliding the drawer closed.

In the bottom right drawer, I pulled out a mini card printer and a stack of ID cards. Picking up one of the IDs, I studied the background image and the details on the card. It was a fake driver's license, only there was no photo. Other than the missing profile picture, it looked legit, including the scanner strip on the back.

"What is all this?" Trent asked, hesitantly stepping inside the room.

"Your daughter is selling fake IDs."

"But why? I leave her money every week. If she needed more, all she had to do was ask."

"That would require you speaking to her." I set the blank ID card down.

Trent picked up one of the cash envelopes. "Why would she need all this money? There's got to be a few thousand dollars here."

"I have a theory, but I'm not sure you want to hear it." I looked up at him.

"Tell me."

"I suspect she's saving money so when she graduates from high school, she can support herself. She expects that's how long she'll have before you throw her out."

"But that's ridiculous." Trent's face lit with surprise. "After high school, she'll go to college. I've been saving for her tuition for years."

"Does she know that?" I asked. "Did you ever, at any point in her life, tell her she wouldn't be homeless after high school?" I stood and moved toward the closet. "Your daughter raised herself, Mr. Randall. You only went through the motions of providing food and shelter. At her age, with her living conditions, I would've made plans to protect myself too."

I pulled out an empty gym bag I'd seen and opened it, setting it on the desk. I filled it with Addy's laptop, power cord, mini printer, and the blank IDs.

Trent watched with a stricken expression. "She's a smart kid. She has to go to college. She's only sixteen, but they moved her up a few times. This is her senior year."

I zipped the bag closed, ignoring him. "I'm taking anything incriminating with me but hide the cash in your bedroom. If the police search the house at some point, you can tell them you were squirreling money away for whatever reason."

"Can't I just leave it in her desk?"

"No. The cops will ask too many questions."

Trent stuffed the envelopes back into the cash box and tucked the tin box under his arm.

"One more thing," I said, lifting the duffle bag's strap over my shoulder. "A local private investigator was hired by a woman to find her missing niece. Any chance that this PI is looking for Addy? Does Addy have an aunt?"

"No. I'm an only child and my wife's family has never met Addy. I'm not sure they even know she exists."

I nodded, confirming what Addy had already told me. After one last glance around the room, I stepped around Trent into the hallway.

"Why are you doing this?" Trent asked in a hushed voice. "Why are you helping look for Addy?"

I stopped at the edge of the living room but didn't turn around. "Because she's a teenage girl who doesn't have anyone in her life to turn to." I crossed the room and walked out the front door, not bothering to close it.

Some people really suck, I thought as I veered toward Stone's truck.

CHAPTER THIRTY-TWO

"WHAT DID YOU FIND?" STONE asked, turning his truck out of the subdivision.

"Not much. Addy was preparing to leave eventually, but whatever happened, whatever reason she took off now instead of later, wasn't planned."

"Yeah, that's what I thought. She didn't take any clothes with her."

"Not just her clothes, but also her laptop. Kids nowadays can't live without their electronics."

"I ran a trace on her phone and got nothing. You don't think someone kidnapped her, do you?" Stone asked, his voice full of concern.

"No. I think she's hiding."

"Hiding from her father?"

"I'm not sure."

Stone's attention swiveled to the duffle bag between my feet. "What's in the bag?"

"I borrowed a few of her things. My psychic senses are on the fritz, but maybe Bernadette can get a read on the girl's whereabouts." The untruth rolled off my tongue so easily it surprised me. I'd always thought of myself as an honest person, but the lies were stacking up, weighing me down.

I forced myself to relax in my seat, trying to act casual so Stone wouldn't notice how uneasy I felt. I stared out the passenger window, barely noticing the landscape zoom past.

Entering Daybreak Falls and slowing for a four-way stop, Stone pointed to a side street.

Leaning forward, I followed his finger to where a police cruiser had pulled over a black station wagon. *Olivia*. I shook my head. "I thought she was getting better."

"She was." Stone drove through the intersection. "It's been almost two weeks since one of us pulled her over." At the next cross street, he turned right, circling around town to get back to my house.

"You guys keep track of when you pull Olivia over?" I asked, giving him a look.

"Sort of. The community service deal she made with us was working out so well that we posted a list at the precinct of things the town needed volunteer labor for." Stone grinned, flashing his perfect teeth. "Next on the list is to scrub the park's bathroom, inside and out."

The park bathroom was a painted cinder-block building that accumulated mildew. "I'll try to remember to pull a case of bleach and a scrub brush broom for her to borrow."

Stone's smile widened. Steering into my driveway, he put his truck in park. "Are you going to be around later? I was thinking about ordering lunch from the diner."

"Nope. I have errands to run, but if all goes well, I'll be home for dinner tonight. My stomach will revolt if I eat another cold sandwich, so I plan to cook an actual meal."

Stone continued smiling, staring at me.

"Yes, I'll make enough food for both of us." I pushed my door open, lifting the duffle bag off the floor. "I have no idea what I'll cook, but I'll figure out something."

"How about I grill burgers and you toss together some side fixings?"

"Sounds like you've got yourself a deal." I stepped away from his truck, threw my hand up in a wave, and shoved the door closed. While I crossed to the kitchen door, I heard Stone's truck back out of the driveway.

Unlocking the door, I entered and dropped my purse, keys and phone on the nearby counter before carrying the duffle bag over to the table. My errands could wait. The entire ride back to Daybreak Falls I'd wondered if the laptop held any clues, and now it was time to find out. I opened the duffle, pulling out the laptop and power cord. After plugging it in, I flipped it open and pressed the power button.

I sat in the end chair, sliding the laptop closer. I didn't know a lot about computers, but I knew enough. I smiled, seeing the laptop wasn't password protected.

I checked her desktop screen files first, but there were only a few icons for browser windows. I opened the laptop's document folder, finding three folders labeled: School, Personal, and Business.

The school folder had a long list of neatly labeled homework assignments going back three years. The personal file had two documents. One was a spreadsheet with two tabs, both having projections of how much money Addy would need after high school. The first tab was the amount she'd need if she went to college. The second tab was if she skipped college and got an apartment. The other document in the personal folder was labeled: Journal. After meeting her father, I suspected Addy's journal held a lot of pent-up anger. I didn't open it, deciding it was too personal.

Clicking back to the main document folders, I opened the last file folder labeled: Business.

This folder seemed to center around Addy's questionable means of earning money. Between finding the fake IDs in her bedroom and Addy herself hinting that she blackmailed classmates, I wasn't surprised to see a long list of subfolders.

Each subfolder was labeled with a name and date. After a fast scroll to the bottom of the list, I estimated there were at least fifty names. The dates started a little over a year ago.

I opened the first subfolder titled *Alex Allenton*, dated only last month. Inside were two picture files and a Word document. I opened the Word document. At the top of the page was Alex's full name, address, and date of birth. Midway down the page was a section with a different name, different address, but the same date of birth except for the year. At the end of the page, with no other callouts, Addy had typed: *DL only. $200. Close file.*

DL for driver's license, I thought, clicking on the picture files. Sure enough, one of the pictures was of a fake driver's license and the other was a posed picture of the kid who bought the ID.

Addy was a smart kid, but keeping all this information on her laptop, so easy to access, was a dumb teenage move. I was glad I hadn't told Stone about this.

Closing out Alex Allenton's folder, I scanned the list of subfolders, reading each name. My eyes landed on a name I knew well—Griffin Donaldson.

Oh, no.

I stared at the folder, not wanting to open it.

What had Addy said about Griffin? That he was fake?

Knowing it was going to haunt me if I didn't look, I opened the file. Griffin's folder held dozens of image files, a video file, and a Word document. I opened the Word document.

At the top was Griffin's full name, date of birth, home address and what I believed was his cellphone number. Further down was the information for a fake ID and near the bottom of the page where the other kid's document had only had a quick note to close the file, Griffin's had a list of dates, payment amounts, and other notes.

I read through the last column, the one with the notes. Starting at the top, it read: *DL purchased*, then *BM payment 1*, then *BM payment 2*, and last was *BM payment 3*.

I already knew DL stood for driver's license, so like the other kid, Griffin had bought a fake ID for two hundred dollars. But my gut clenched when I realized BM stood for blackmail.

"Griffin, what did you do?" I said aloud.

Each blackmail payment was for a hundred dollars, totaling three hundred in payments.

What could she have on him that was worth paying that kind of money? I shook my head, baffled. The kid I knew was sweet and courteous.

I went back to the list of images in Griffin's subfolder, noticing they were dated for three separate days last month. I picked one at random, opening it. An image of Griffin appeared, showing him tipping a clear liquid bottle straight up, like he was chugging it. I clicked the arrow for the next image. In this one, Griffin sat on the floor, leaning against the wall. He was passed out drunk and had vomit down the front of his shirt.

Taking a deep breath, I returned to the subfolder and opened the video file.

As expected, Griffin was partying with his friends, but what terrified me was seeing how intoxicated he was. He could barely stand. He slurred insults at someone and threw a liquor bottle at the wall. The shattered bottle nicked a guy standing nearby, but Griffin just laughed, pointing at the guy and calling him a loser. Griffin wasn't just drunk—he was a mean drunk.

When the video ended, I felt sick to my stomach. Sweet innocent Griffin had a dark side.

I closed the laptop, not wanting to see any more. I'd known Griffin since he was just a little guy, waddling down the driveway in his diaper. He was always so smart and funny, never mean.

Hearing a car door outside, I snapped out of my stupor, looking toward the window. From where I sat, I couldn't see anything, so I got up to see over the top of the mid-window curtain.

My heart stuttered when I saw the Donaldsons laughing as they climbed out of the car wearing their Sunday best. They seemed so happy, like everything was right with the world.

I knew I was about to blow up that happiness, but I had to. I couldn't ignore the troubling images. For Griffin's sake, I needed to speak up.

I picked up the gym bag and laptop, taking them to the other side of the house. Opening the hidden room behind the bookcase, I set the duffle bag on the floor and placed the laptop on one of the many empty shelves. Before I had time to chicken out, I crossed to the front door and walked outside.

Crossing the street, I followed the sidewalk to the Donaldsons' driveway. I was halfway up the drive when Davey and Griffin ran back outside, having already changed into jeans and sweatshirts. Davey held a basketball in his hands.

They both stopped, wearing goofy smiles, when they noticed me.

"Hey, Davina, what's up?" Griffin asked.

"Davey, I need a word with Griffin," I said, holding Griffin's stare.

"You're in *trou-ble*," Davey teased, shoving Griffin's shoulder. "What'd you do, bro?"

Griffin didn't laugh. His eyes remained locked with mine. He knew. With one look, he knew why I was here.

"Whoa, seriously, bro, what did you do?" Davey asked, tensing.

"I'll be inside in a minute," Griffin said to Davey without looking away from me.

Davey looked between us before hurrying inside. I suspected I'd only have a minute or two alone with Griffin before his parents came out.

"You know," Griffin said.

"Yes."

"How?"

"The how doesn't matter." I held out my hand. "Let's start with the fake ID."

Knowing I wasn't asking, but demanding, he pulled his wallet, handing it over.

I tucked it into my back pocket, not even sparing it a glance. "Griffin, the last thing I want is to cause problems, but I'm worried. I saw that video. I saw the pictures of you passed out drunk. I saw the binge drinking."

"It's not that bad."

"No, Griffin, it's *worse*. You were cruel to people. You were throwing things. You were downing alcohol like it was water. You could've died. Do you get that?"

"It was only that one night."

"*Don't lie to me.*" I locked my jaw, taking a moment to reel in my emotions. "Griffin, you are a good kid. I adore you, truly and wholeheartedly. You're smart and funny and kind..." I braced my hands on his shoulders, waiting until he lifted his head to meet my eyes again. "But you have a problem. And the only way you're going to get through this is by being honest with the people who love you."

His lower lip quivered as his eyes filled with tears. "I don't know how to tell them."

"You just tell them," I said, tightening my grip on his shoulders. "Griffin, you just say it. If necessary, you repeat it over and over until they understand that you're in trouble." I pulled him a fraction closer. "They love you. We all love you. You're not alone in this. Let them help you."

The house door opened and Jared walked out, but he stayed near the door, watching us.

"Griffin, you can do this," I said in a lower voice. "I know you're strong enough to do this, and it'll be a hundred times better if you're the one to tell them. But if you don't, I will, even if it means you end up hating me."

Griffin collapsed against me, crying.

I hugged him tight, swallowing my own tears.

Jared, unable to stay away, ran over, resting a hand on Griffin's shoulder. "What is it? What's wrong?"

Griffin pulled back, ducking his head. "Dad, I messed up. I did some things. Things you're not going to like."

Jared pulled Griffin into his arms, holding him against his chest. "I'm here, son. I'm right here. It's going to be okay." Jared glanced over Griffin's shoulder at me, his face full of fear.

I gave him a chin up and dried my tears with the back of my hand. Knowing Griffin needed to at least try to talk to his parents without my interference, I turned away, recrossing the street. When I glanced up, I saw Mrs. Paulson on her front porch, wringing her hands, her eyes shifting back and forth between me and the Donaldsons.

I veered her way, and without speaking she led us inside her house to the kitchen table. We sat in our usual places with me staring down at the table.

"Are you okay? Is Griffin, okay?" she asked, extending her arm across the table toward me.

"Griffin needs to face a few hard truths, but it's a family matter."

Mrs. Paulson looked toward her living room for a long moment. "You know, whatever it is, Jared and Noelle are good parents. They'll deal with it. And they're lucky to have you looking out for their boys."

"Maybe, but talking to Griffin was hard," I said, wiping away fresh tears. "It must really suck being a parent."

Mrs. Paulson chuckled. "Yes, sometimes it does, and it never ends, no matter how old your children get. I've been sitting here trying to keep myself from driving over to yell at Britt for being childish, but I don't figure Noah would be too pleased with me interfering."

"Let me guess, Britt is mad because Noah went somewhere last night but won't say where?"

"Mostly. She's figured out you're somehow involved which set her off again."

"Ugh." I ran both hands through my hair, tugging at it. "I'm sick of her nonsense."

Mrs. Paulson leaned back, wearing a surprised look. "Are you okay? You look to be at the end of your rope as they say."

"No, I'm not okay. I've got a lot going on and I don't have time for Britt's drama."

Mrs. Paulson nodded her understanding. "I can't say as I blame you for your feelings, but why did you summon Noah last night?"

I frowned. "I can't say."

She blinked a few times before saying, "Okay."

"That's it? Just, okay?"

"If you feel it's best not to share the information, I won't pry. I know whatever your reason for keeping it a secret is an honorable one."

"Well, that was about the easiest conversation I've had today."

Mrs. Paulson chuckled, pushing herself up to stand. "The next one might not be." She picked up her phone from the kitchen counter. "I was on my way over to see you when I spotted you talking to Griffin." She swiped at her phone's screen before handing it to me. "I hear I have you to blame for this little stunt."

Her voice sounded stern which had me glancing up to see her expression. She was wearing her poker face, but I caught a twinkle of humor in her eyes. I looked down at her phone and barked a laugh. On the screen was the Facebook poll for the open spot on the town council. "I totally forgot I did this."

Next to Mrs. Paulson's name showed over three thousand votes. The second name on the poll was Belinda Vanderson. She had only two hundred votes.

"Well, at least you're winning."

"Which is pretty funny since it'd never crossed my mind to become a council member." She sat in her chair, trying to give me her best motherly scowl, but she couldn't fool me.

"We need you," I said, sliding the phone across the table to her. "You know you could make a difference."

"Maybe, but I don't see how I'd have time enough to take on anything else."

"How bad can it be?" I asked. "Most council members have full-time careers. I doubt they do much except show up at the monthly meetings to vote on stuff."

"Maybe."

"You know you want to..." I teased.

"Oh, hush," she said, rolling her eyes. "I'll consider it, but I'm not committing to anything."

"Call Edith and ask her about becoming a member. She'll be honest about the time commitment."

"I'll do that," Mrs. Paulson said, but lifted her hand and wagged a finger at me. "But you owe me for this little sabotage."

"Yeah, yeah," I said, standing and pushing my chair back under the table. "I'll think of a way to make it up to you."

"Whatever you come up with, better be good," she said, grinning.

I nodded but changed the subject. "I'm making a trip into the city. While I'm there, my plan is to pick up groceries. Need anything?"

"Yes, a can of coffee. It's two dollars cheaper in the city."

"Got it. I'll drop it off later." I crossed to the front door.

Chapter Thirty-Three

After walking home, I opened the back of my van, sighing at the mess. Addy had scattered my tools and supplies everywhere. Needing the space for my trip to the city, I emptied everything just inside the garage, planning to sort and reload it later.

Tossing the empty pizza box into the trash bin on my way inside, I locked up the house, shut off the lights, and drove to the city.

En route, I called Whiskey, arranging a meeting with him at the retail store across the street from Silver Aces. When I turned into the parking lot thirty minutes later he was already there, leaning against his motorcycle, waiting.

I pulled up and parked two spots down from his bike in the empty lot, getting out. "Sorry to mess up your Sunday family time."

"All good," Whiskey said with a shrug and a smile. "Gave me an excuse to get out of grocery shopping."

"Yeah, I get that. That's on my errand list today." I looked down at my feet, trying to figure out the best way to ask him the questions I needed to ask.

"Something wrong?" Whiskey asked. "Is there a problem at the construction site?"

"No. I haven't even been back to the site since Thursday."

"Is this about one of our quotes?"

I shook my head. "It's not about any of that. It's about that leather vest you wear." My eyes lowered to the patch on his leather vest that read: *Devil's Players*. "I'm here because you're part of a motorcycle club."

"I see," Whiskey said, nodding. "Folks in Daybreak Falls giving you a hard time that your foreman is a biker?"

"The folks in Daybreak Falls are too busy judging *me* to notice you're a member of a motorcycle club." I leaned against my van. "The reason I asked you to meet me is because I need some insight on how motorcycle clubs work."

Whiskey shook his head. "Bikers don't talk club business with outsiders."

"It's not about *your* club. I'm looking for info on *another* club."

"Doesn't matter. Bikers don't talk."

"Even when a teenage girl's life is on the line?"

"What do you mean?"

"This girl knows something or saw something, but I'm not sure what. I crossed paths with the bikers last night and they gave me forty-eight hours to hand her over. The '*or else*' was implied when one of them held a knife to my throat."

Whiskey released a string of curses. "Please tell me you're not referring to the Bleeding Souls."

"I wish I could."

"Damn it." Whiskey pulled his phone, calling someone and telling them to meet him in front of the store, pronto. After he hung up, he looked back at me. "Those guys are dangerous. Do you know this girl? Do you know where she is?"

"I've met her." That's all I said. That's all I was going to say.

"And you've got no clue what she saw or heard?"

"No clue whatsoever." I looked across the lot at the cars and trucks driving past on the busy road. "I'm sorry. I'm not trying to put you in a spot here. A few months back I had a run in with this club, but I dealt with a guy named LoJack and was able to strike a deal. This time, the biker threatening me is someone LoJack refers to as his boss. And let me tell you, the bossman is scary."

"Sounds like their club president, Hurricane. Like his nickname, he leaves a path of destruction wherever he goes."

"But you can't tell me anything? You can't share anything that might help me figure out what this is all about?"

Whiskey hiked his hands on top of his hips. "I can't, but maybe they can." He nodded toward three motorcycles pulling into the parking lot.

"You called your club?" I ran a hand across my forehead. "If Bleeding Souls find out, what will they do to me?"

"They won't find out," Whiskey said. "You're standing in the middle of Devil's territory. The Souls keep their distance."

I was somewhat relieved when I saw that one of the three newly arrived bikers was Bones. I didn't know the other two bikers though. All three walked over, with the younger one hanging back and scouting the area.

"Hey, Davina," Bones said, looking between Whiskey and me. "Don't tell me your sister escaped again."

"Nope," I answered. "Raina's locked up tight."

"You know Bones already," Whiskey said. "That's Tyler," he nodded to the younger biker who hung back to keep watch, "and this is James, our president."

"Hi," I said, trying to keep the nervousness out of my voice.

James nodded but his eyes narrowed at Whiskey. "Explain why I'm here."

"Davina has a problem with the Souls," Whiskey said.

Bones stiffened. "What kind of problem?"

"They delivered a death threat," Whiskey answered. "Gave her forty-eight hours to do what they want."

"Which basically means they'll kill her even if she does what they want," James said, sounding somewhat indifferent.

"Knock it off, James," Bones said before ordering me to explain everything.

I did, mostly. I left out the part of Addy hiding in my van and taking her to Bernadette's, but I shared the rest, including the fake IDs.

When I was done explaining, the three men exchanged looks.

"Think they'd go through with it?" Bones asked James.

"Definitely," James said. "I told you months ago, they've been beefing up recruitment. While you've been off doing your bodyguard thing, they've doubled their membership."

I held my hand up, palm out to stop them. "Look, I'm not trying to drag you guys into this. In fact, the fewer people involved the better. I don't want to add any more fuel to the fire."

"What *are* you asking for?" Bones asked.

"Information. The more I know about their club, the better chance I have of figuring out what's going on."

"They're into everything," James said. "Drugs. Prostitution. Hired thugs to break kneecaps. Occasionally a dead body turns up, but so far, the bodies were all other lowlifes, so we've looked the other way."

"But that's just the stuff we know about," Whiskey said. "We've kept our distance, not wanting to start any disputes unless they push us to act."

"If they kill you, we'll *have* to act," James said, again sounding indifferent. "You're a civilian with no ties to criminal activity, so they'd be breaking the rules if they slit your throat."

Bones gave him a look.

"What?" James said. "I'm just being honest."

Despite his cavalier way of mentioning my murder, there was something about James that made me smile. With tan skin and sun-kissed wavy hair, James put out a weird surfer-meets-biker vibe.

"Anyway," Bones said, rolling his eyes. "Let me drop a call to someone I know. He might be able to shed some light on whatever's going on, but it's tricky. Might take me a few hours to make contact."

"That would be great, but don't do anything to put yourselves in danger."

"When does your clock run out?" James asked.

"Tomorrow night."

"Not much time," Whiskey said. "What's your plan if you can't solve the problem?"

I lifted my hands in an I-don't-know gesture. "Move to Mexico?"

James laughed. "I wouldn't do that. I'm pretty sure the Souls have cartel connections in Mexico." He tipped his head toward the busy street. "Head north instead. It'll be colder, but you'll live longer."

"James," Bones warned.

I grinned at James. "Canada, huh?"

"Go, Maple Leafs," James cheered with a fist in the air.

Living in a hockey friendly state, I recognized his reference to the Canadian hockey team. Still grinning, I swiveled my focus back to Whiskey. "If I flee the country, Breydon's in charge of the construction site and has access to my bank accounts."

Whiskey snorted. "Now you sound like him." He jerked his head toward James.

"Well, sitting around worrying isn't helping, so why not plan accordingly."

"Fine," Bones said. "But don't run off until you've got no other options. You never know how these things will play out."

Bones was being cryptic, so I just nodded before shifting to my van's door and opening it.

"Chin up, darlin'," James called out before moseying back to his Harley.

CHAPTER THIRTY-FOUR

MY NEXT STOP WAS TO the home improvement store where I bought six two-by-fours and a vanload of insulation. It took some time to jam the bags of insulation into the back, but with the help of two men who stopped to lend me their muscles, we managed to get the back doors shut.

After that, I drove across the street to the big chain grocery store, buying an overflowing cart of groceries that I stacked in the passenger side of the van and between the bucket seats. The drive back to Daybreak Falls felt a bit claustrophobic with the insulation behind my head and groceries stacked shoulder high beside me.

I took the first exit for Daybreak Falls and followed the roads toward the cottage. Spotting the tipsy mailbox, I slowed to a stop with my blinker on, waiting for a convoy of trucks and trailers moving in the opposite direction. Each trailer was stacked high with bales of hay.

The last truck slowed, stopping beside me. Lance stuck his head out his open window. "I thought you were taking the day off?"

"I am. But I picked up insulation in the city and want to get it unloaded."

"Need a hand hauling it inside?"

"No, I've got it." I glanced at the trailer he was hauling. "What's with all the haybales?"

"The Fall Maze."

"What maze?"

Lance grinned. "You've lived here your whole life and never been to the Fall Maze?"

"Is it dirty and muddy? Because if so, it wouldn't be somewhere Olivia would want to go, therefore it's not likely I would've gone."

Lance chuckled. "I remember you went a few times when you were just a little thing. Your dad took you." Lance pointed down the road. "It's put on every year about a mile southwest at old man Thompson's place. Proceeds from the maze go to a cancer foundation, but old man Thompson hosts it so he can sell pumpkins on the side. Some of the other farmers sell cider. Everyone donates what they can though."

I looked at his trailer again. It was stacked seven bales high. "All this hay must get expensive."

Lance shook his head. "We only loan out our hay. When it's all over, we collect the number of bales we dropped off, hauling them back to our barns."

A car behind me honked.

I checked my rearview mirror, seeing the driver behind me was being impatient. "I'd better get unloaded. I'll call you tomorrow."

"Sounds good," Lance said, thumping the side of his truck and pulling away.

I hurried to make the left turn so the driver behind me could be on his way. Once off the road, I slowed my speed, eyeing the trees on both sides, on the lookout for bikers. Parking on the front lawn, I sighed with relief, not seeing any other vehicles.

Getting out and moving to the back, I opened the doors. The bags of insulation started expanding toward me and I hopped back as one shot out, followed by several others avalanching out onto the ground. Picking two bags up, I dragged them up to the porch and inside the house.

Standing just inside the house, I looked around, trying to decide where to put them. The living room was already too full. The front bedroom was also out since I'd designated half the room for cutting lumber. The kitchen still needed too much work, so that too was out.

Deciding I might as well haul the bags upstairs, I started up the stairway, tossing the bags inside the smaller bedroom. Returning to the van, I made several trips back and forth, but by the time I hauled the last two bags inside the house, my bruised ankle was swelling.

I tossed the two bags onto the floor at the bottom of the stairs, telling myself I'd take them up tomorrow. Turning back toward the front of the house, I looked up and stumbled to a stop. LoJack stood in the doorway.

I didn't move, waiting to see what he'd do.

LoJack took two steps inside before shoving the door shut behind him.

Not good, I thought. "I have until tomorrow night. Your boss said I had forty-eight hours."

"Relax. I'm not here to kill you." LoJack moved to his right, peeking inside the first-floor bedroom. Crossing the room again, he walked toward me.

I cringed, waiting for something to happen, but he moved past me and checked the bathroom and kitchen before returning to the front of the living room, positioning himself near the picture window.

I moved a few inches toward the kitchen, planning to flee out the back door if needed.

"I got a call from an old buddy of mine. He asked me to meet you."

Bones, I thought. *They know each other? But they're rivals, right?* "Are you two *good* friends?"

LoJack shrugged. "Let's just say we know each other. But if you tell anyone, it'll be very bad for you. Hear me?"

I gulped. "Uh, sure."

His body appeared relaxed, but his eyes kept shifting in every direction, telling a different story. "Where's the girl?"

"Even if I knew, I wouldn't tell you."

LoJack snorted. "Can't say as I blame you. I'd like to talk to her, though—find out what she knows."

"Torture her for answers?"

"I don't torture kids," LoJack said, glaring. "I'd just ask her what's going on. That's it."

"What do you mean, ask her what's going on? Don't you already know?"

"I wish I did." LoJack sighed, glancing outside again. "The girl must know something big, but I don't know what it is. I only know my boss has been on a rampage trying to find her. He's always had a temper, that's nothing new, but this is different. He's losing it. He's running scared."

"But aren't you a big deal in your club? Shouldn't you know whatever's going on?"

"Doesn't work like that in our club. Hurricane keeps the club divided so that if one branch goes down, it doesn't hurt the others. He has five different vice presidents, one for each branch."

"Is that what you are? A vice president?"

"No. I'm muscle."

"Okay, so which so-called branch of the club is going after the girl? Which group is hunting her?"

"That's the thing," LoJack said, shaking his head. "None of them. All of them. Whatever's going on, Hurricane's running the show himself and only a few handpicked members seem to know anything." He glanced out the window again, scanning side to side. "But the entire club, all five branches, has been ordered to find the girl."

"None of this is helping. You must know *something*."

LoJack picked up a nearby five-gallon bucket and emptied the electrical supplies onto the floor before flipping the bucket upside down to sit. "Over the last few weeks Hurricane has been tight lipped about something he's had in play. Lots of closed-door meetings and hushed conversations, which isn't like him. He's the kind of guy who likes to brag. But whatever he's wrapped up in, it's strictly need-to-know. And I get the sense that his life depends on it."

I moved to the bucket I'd used as a chair the day before and sat. "If I don't know what this is about, what do I do?"

"Only one thing you can do. *Run*."

"And if I don't want to run?"

"Chances are good, you'll die. The only way to avoid your fate is to find the girl, figure out what she knows, and use that information to turn the tides against Hurricane and his club. But your chances of taking the entire club down are slim, and if a single member is still standing when the dust settles, that club member will be honor bound to kill you."

I felt a little lightheaded and looked down at the floor. None of what LoJack was saying was making me feel better.

"Don't forget," LoJack said, "my first suggestion was to run. If you don't heed my advice and you end up dead, it's not my fault." He stood, crossing to the door. "You never saw me, got it?"

"Yeah, yeah," I said, waving off his concern. "If I tell anyone, you'll kill me. Get in line."

LoJack opened the door and walked out.

I sat there, thinking, for several long minutes. LoJack was right about one thing: Addy had all the answers. If I was going to flee town, go on the run, I deserved to know why.

I checked my Fitbit, seeing it was almost two o'clock. If I was going to stop at the orchard to buy a bushel of apples on my way home, I'd need to get moving. Forcing Addy to answer a few questions would need to wait until later.

Decision made, I walked out, closing and locking the door behind me.

CHAPTER THIRTY-FIVE

I SPENT THE REST OF my day baking pies, making a big bowl of potato salad, and catching up on my laundry and housecleaning before going outside. After vacuuming out the insulation dust from the back of my van, I started refinishing the table Virgil bought.

By the time Stone arrived, I was almost done stripping the table's first layer of stain.

"That looks like a messy job," Stone said, setting several grocery bags and a six pack of beer down before crossing into the garage to drag my gas grill into the driveway.

"Messy, but worth it." I used my forearm to push a strand of hair out of my face. "I made potato salad, but I also have asparagus wrapped in foil ready to toss on the grill."

"Full heat or top rack?" Stone asked. "I've never cooked asparagus."

"Top rack for about fifteen minutes."

"Got it." Stone grabbed the grill lighter from the nearby shelf and lit the pilot. "Want a beer?" he asked, picking his grocery sacks back up.

"Nah. Maybe later."

He pulled one bottle, leaving it on the concrete before carrying everything else toward the house. A few minutes later he returned, setting the wrapped asparagus and a platter of burger patties on the grill's side shelf before picking up his beer bottle. "Your fancy new refrigerator is full of groceries. Does that mean you're going to start cooking meals again?"

"When I have time, but only because I owe so many people free meals." I ran my putty knife across the top of the table. "And yes, one of the pies cooling on the counter is for us to eat after dinner."

"I was hoping you'd say that. My mouth started watering when I entered the house."

"Yeah, I decided to work out here so I wouldn't cut into one of them. I was afraid I'd eat the whole thing." I flung the gooey mess off my putty knife onto a sheet of old newspaper before nodding to the platter of burger patties. "Isn't that a lot of burgers for just the two of us?"

He took a drink of his beer before saying, "Britt and Noah had another big fight today. I suspect Noah will pop over to mooch dinner."

"He might still be avoiding me. He's been keeping his distance lately, trying to appease Britt."

"That ship has sailed. Britt came home and packed a duffle bag of clothes, saying she was crashing at a friend's house in the city for a few days."

"Seriously?" I set my putty knife down. "I'm getting a little tired of her tantrums." I peeled my plastic gloves off, tossing them next to my putty knife.

"I bet," Stone said, lifting the lid on the grill. "I'm surprised to hear Noah's been avoiding you, though." He set the asparagus on the top rack before sliding the patties on the lower one.

"Noah says Britt has a point about him spending too much time with me." I moved to stand in the sun just outside the garage.

Stone closed the grill lid. "I get why Britt feels jealous, but the truth is, you outrank her."

His comment surprised me. "How do you figure?"

"You're family. You've been in Noah's life since his sandbox years. Britt can't expect to waltz in and force you out. And if Noah's going along with that nonsense, maybe you should call him out on it."

I scrunched my nose, not liking the idea of confronting Noah. "I think I'll let Noah figure it out."

Stone snorted. "Why am I not surprised?"

"Be nice," I said, swatting him.

"Davina?" Jared called out, walking toward us down my driveway. "Do you have a minute?"

I smiled, tipping my head toward the house. "Of course. Let's go inside."

Following me through the kitchen side door, Jared said, "Sorry to interrupt your date."

"It's not a date, but even if it was, Griffin is more important. How's he doing?"

Jared glanced away. "Can I be honest?"

"Absolutely."

"I don't understand why he's so upset. He's a teenager. Teenagers drink. They get into trouble and do stupid things."

"Yes, teenagers drink and do stupid things, but this is different." I motioned for Jared to follow me. "I have some pictures and a video I think you should see." Crossing down the hallway into the library, I opened the hidden room and pulled out Addy's laptop. "Whatever you do, don't tell Stone I have this. It's sort of evidence for one of his cases, but he doesn't know about it."

Jared chuckled. "Funny."

I sat on the couch, glancing up at him. "Not joking."

Jared's face froze, surprised. He glanced back down the hallway before hurrying to sit next to me. "Why are you hiding evidence?"

"It started out protecting just one teenager, but now there's a whole list of them, including Griffin." Remembering I still had Griffin's fake ID in my pocket, I pulled it out and handed it to Jared.

"Well, crap," Jared said, leaning forward and rechecking the hallway. "Stone doesn't know about this?"

"Nope." After starting up the laptop, I clicked my way to Griffin's subfolder and slid the laptop across the coffee table to Jared. "When you're done, can you put the laptop back inside the hidden room? Also, I'd appreciate it if you didn't mention the laptop to anyone."

"I can do that," Jared said, leaning forward. "What is this?"

"The blackmail files on Griffin. Prepare yourself. The video, especially, is hard to watch." I got up and returned to the kitchen, keeping an eye on Stone through the kitchen window while I washed the dishes.

Ten minutes later, Jared walked down the hall, stopping next to the refrigerator. "I'm at a loss. What I saw..."

"I know. It's like Griffin morphed into someone we don't know."

"What do I do? How do I help him?"

"Keep listening. Keep talking. And if it were me, I'd call Alice Hooper and ask her about therapists who specialize in this type of thing."

"That's a good idea. If she doesn't know what to do, Isaac will." Jared started toward the door.

"Hang on a second." I crossed to the far counter and picked up one of the apple pies. "Take this with you. It's for all the help at the cottage this week."

Jared took the pie, looking down at it. "I feel like this is backwards. Like we should be making you a pie. If it weren't for you..."

I placed a hand on his arm. "We look out for each other. We always have. It's what we do."

Jared ducked his head and moved toward the door. "Thank you, Davina," he whispered before walking out.

I turned back toward the sink, rinsing the silverware.

"Everything okay?" Stone asked, poking his head inside the door.

"It will be." I picked up a nearby towel, drying my hands. My phone rang from the countertop, flashing Olivia's name. "Hey, Olivia," I answered. "What's up?"

"Are you free tonight?"

I looked out the window at the garage. I'd wanted to finish stripping the table tonight and after that I'd planned to drive out to talk to Addy. "Depends. What time and for how long?"

"Late. Like ten o'clock."

I snorted. "Stakeout?"

"Yup. I could use some company."

Since chances were good that I'd be fleeing for Canada in another day or two, hanging out with Olivia might be nice. "Sure. Why not."

Olivia squealed her excitement. "I'll pick you up." She hung up.

I laughed, setting my phone back on the counter.

"Do I even want to know?" Stone asked, washing off the platter he'd used for the burger patties.

"Probably not." I crossed to the cupboard to get out plates.

"Knock, knock," Noah said, strolling inside. "What's for dinner? I'm starving."

I smiled, grabbing another plate.

CHAPTER THIRTY-SIX

AFTER EATING, I SPLIT THE leftovers into plastic containers, preparing a bag for both Noah and Stone. In Stone's bag, I added two slices of apple pie. In Noah's, I set an entire pie inside.

Noah took his bag and glanced down at the pie. "For the record, we're not even yet, but we're getting there."

"Yeah, yeah," I said, grinning. "I'm working on it."

"I don't even want to know," Stone said, taking his bag. "Thanks for letting me invite myself for dinner." He moved toward the side door.

"No problem. Thanks for grilling the food."

Stone winked at me before walking out. "Have a good night," he called out as he disappeared.

"I'm heading out too," Noah said. "I've got a load of laundry that I'm hoping Mom will wash for me."

"Hold up a second." I grabbed the grocery bag with Mrs. Paulson's requested can of coffee and picked up one of the apple pies. "Will you drop these at your mom's house for me?"

Noah nodded, taking both. "Sure thing. Need anything else?"

"No," I said, smiling while watching him. Noah was behaving like his old self again, which warmed my heart. I moved to the door, opening it for him. "Don't even think about mooching any pie off your mom. You have your own to eat."

Noah grinned but didn't comment, walking out the door. I jogged out to the garage, checking to make sure Stone had shut off the grill before rolling it back inside and closing the overhead door. Moving back inside, I rubbed my hands up and down my arms, trying to warm them as I used my foot to shove the door closed. Entering the laundry-pantry room, I grabbed a zip-up sweatshirt off the wall peg and pulled it on before crossing back into the kitchen to place my share of the leftovers inside the refrigerator.

When I was done cleaning up the kitchen, I looked at the clock and was reminded that my time was running out. I couldn't keep ignoring the problem. It was time to prepare myself for the worst-case scenario.

Marching down the back hallway into the library, I retrieved my three duffle bags from under my bed and started piling clothes and shoes inside two of them. I had no idea what would happen in the next twenty-four hours, but if I needed to run, at least I'd have clean underwear.

I carried the smaller duffle bag to the bathroom and filled it with spare toothbrushes, toothpaste, soap, towels, a hairbrush, an assortment of hair scrunchies, and anything else I saw that I might need. When I was done, I hauled all three duffle bags outside, loading them into the back of my van.

On my trip back inside, I gathered odds and ends like flashlights, blankets, spare pillows, and a medical emergency kit. It took a while to load everything, adding more things like non-perishable food, Addy's laptop and duffle bag, and my own laptop, but when I was done, I felt somewhat better, more in control.

I grabbed my purse and the last two pies, and after locking up, I left for Bernadette's house, hoping to convince Addy into telling me what was going on.

Twenty minutes later, I pulled off along the shoulder of the road only a dozen feet before the turn onto Cicadas Lane. I got out and walked over to Darrel's gold Camry.

"Hi, Davina," Darrel said, smiling up at me from the driver's seat.

"Hi, Darrel." I glanced around, but there was no one else in sight. "Whatcha doin?"

"Just waiting to see my sweetheart. I popped in for a visit, but she started shooting at me." He snickered. "She's such a kidder."

"Darrel, go home. Bernadette doesn't want to see you."

"She'll change her mind. She's just in a mood, is all. We're soul mates."

"Glad to hear it, but you still need to leave. If you're here when I come back, I'll call the cops to report you for stalking." I crossed back to my van, climbing inside but waiting to see what he'd do.

It took him a few minutes, but after a sad glance at me in his rearview mirror, he started his car and drove away. I pulled ahead and turned onto Cicadas Lane, following the narrow gravel road.

As I passed the gates, a shotgun blasted. I swerved, nearly hitting a tree before flooring the gas to the end of the drive and parking in front of the house.

Storming up the front porch, crossing to the other side of the house and sliding the panel door open, ready to tear Bernadette a new one, I spotted Bernadette and Addy standing behind Bernadette's desk, both looking guilty.

"It's my fault," Addy said before I could speak. "I pushed the button before I realized it was you, not Darrel. Man, that guy can't take a hint."

My anger fizzled. I'd accidentally set off the security alarm the first time I'd played with it too, freaking Stone out in the process. "Fine. But next time, *look to see who it is* before setting that stupid thing off."

"It's not stupid," Bernadette snapped.

I ignored her, glancing at Addy. "We need to talk. Let's walk down to the channel."

Addy's shoulders deflated but she led the way down the stairs, glancing nervously back at me several times. "Did the bikers come back?"

"Not yet, but I'm running out of time." I followed her out the basement patio door before walking alongside her on the two-track lane that led to the channel. "I have your laptop. I know about your little side business. But what I can't put together is how you crossed paths with the bikers."

"It wasn't planned," Addy said, keeping her eyes focused on the path ahead. "It was sort of one of those wrong-place wrong-time things. I got the directions messed up while delivering a new batch of driver's licenses."

"And?"

Addy scrunched her nose. "That's probably all I should say." She pushed her red-framed glasses back up the bridge of her nose.

"Addy, you're not the only one in danger. Those bikers will come after me too unless I get this mess sorted before tomorrow night. Canada sounds great for a vacation, but I really don't want to leave my home and move to another country."

Addy shrugged. "Doesn't sound so bad to me."

"Despite how your dad has treated you, I don't think he'd like it if you disappeared. He's worried about you."

Addy laughed. "You're lying. My dad barely knows I exist."

"Last week, maybe. But he's had to face reality this week. He's scared for you, and he knows how badly he screwed up."

Addy stumbled but recovered her balance without falling. Her face tensed and she wore a determined expression, staring straight ahead. "Too little, too late."

She had a right to her anger. If I were in her shoes, I'd be angry too. "Maybe you're right. Maybe it's too late to fix the damage between you and your dad. But you still need to tell me what happened Wednesday night. I have people I care about, people who will be upset if I disappear. If you tell me what happened, maybe I can stop all this."

"I can't." Addy stopped walking, staring down at her feet. "If I tell you, you'll tell the cops. The cops will arrest the bikers, but they'll also force me to testify against them. Those bikers will kill me. They'll kill my dad. I might not like my dad, but that doesn't mean I want to see him murdered."

I cringed. She was right. Testifying against a gang of bikers sounded... *unsafe*. For both of us. So where did that leave us?

Nowhere, that's where. I continued down the path to the water's edge.

Hearing a boat, I turned to tell Addy to hide but she was already gone. I walked out onto the dock, seeing Austin puttering down the channel in his pontoon.

"Fancy seeing you out here," Austin called out across the channel, steering his pontoon toward Bernadette's dock.

"Came out to talk to Bernadette about a few things and decided to take a walk. Were you out fishing?"

"Nope. Just taking the boat out one last time before it gets stored for the winter."

"Hard to believe we'll have snow in another month or two."

"I know," Austin said, cutting the throttle. "Want to go out on the lake? Still a good hour of daylight left."

"Sorry, can't. I have a few things to do before I meet Olivia later. But I have an apple pie in my van with your name on it. I planned on dropping it off after I left Bernadette's."

"Apple pie, huh?" Austin's dimple popped out. "Sounds just about perfect. Want me to walk back to Bernadette's with you?"

I looked back at the two-track lane and the woods surrounding it, knowing Addy was out there somewhere. "Probably not a good idea. Bernadette's in one of her shoot first and ask questions later moods."

Both Austin's eyebrows rose. "I thought I heard gunfire earlier. Was that her?"

"Yeah," I said, giggling.

"In that case, I think I'll wait for my pie. Do you know how long you'll be, though? I need to run to town to pick up a few things."

"If you're heading to town, we can meet at Nightshade Treasures. Say thirty minutes? It'll save me the hassle of driving around the lake."

"That'll work. See you in a few." Austin pushed away from the dock, waiting until his boat was clear before puttering across the channel to his own dock.

I started walking back up the path toward the house when Addy jogged out between two trees, slowing to walk beside me. "Who was that?"

"Just one of the many people I'll miss if I'm forced to leave town," I said, glancing over my shoulder back toward the dock. Austin was out of view, which meant he wouldn't be able to see her. "Addy, I'm out of patience with you. I promise I won't tell the cops anything, but you need to tell me what's going on."

"I can't. I—"

"Enough," I said, stopping to face her. "I deserve answers. You've endangered my life and everyone around me. Tell me what this is all about. I'm not asking, Addy. Not anymore."

Addy pursed her lips, getting angry. "Do you promise not to tell the cops? Like swear on your life promise?"

"Yes, I promise I won't say anything to the police." I didn't like it, but her keeping me in the dark wasn't getting me anywhere.

Addy looked toward the woods on both sides of us before whispering, "Guns. It's about guns."

I was dumbfounded. "What about guns?"

"The bikers met with two scary dudes. The scary dudes showed the bikers a bunch of automatic rifles, like the kind you see in action movies. They negotiated a deal to buy three dozen."

I felt my face pale. *"You witnessed an illegal arms deal?"*

"Yeah, sort of. But it wasn't an exchange. They were only meeting to negotiate the price."

Addy turned and continued walking back toward the house. "Like I said, I got myself lost..."

I hurried to catch up to her.

"When I realized I was in the wrong place, I started to turn back but then heard voices. I got curious. I mean, it was the middle of nowhere, just a dead patch of grass at the end of a two-track lane." She waved her hand at the two-track lane we were currently following. "There shouldn't have been anyone out there. I snuck closer to see what was going on."

I looked skyward, mentally cursing. "You *intentionally* eavesdropped on a gang of bikers?"

"You can skip the lecture," Addy said, throwing me a defiant look. "It's not like I planned to witness what I witnessed."

"What did you see? What did you hear? I need specifics."

Addy sighed a dramatic sigh. "Three bikers were standing around waiting, acting all nervous. About five minutes later, a truck pulled in with the other two guys. They got out guns from the back of the truck, showing them to the bikers. The biker in charge struck a deal to buy three dozen. That's it."

"But no cash or guns changed hands?"

"Right. The truck left, and the bikers were getting on their bikes, when I stupidly stepped back, snapping a twig. They heard it and started shooting in my direction. I ran. I got back to my moped and got the heck out of there."

"How'd they know it was you?"

A guilty look crossed her face. "Remember the IDs I said I was delivering?" She peeked over at me before quickly glancing away. "I must've dropped them. I think they tracked down one of my clients and found out who I was."

"*Addy...*" Her clients were teenagers. Hopefully the kid the bikers tracked down wasn't hurt when he or she was terrorized into answering questions.

"I know, I know," Addy said. "I messed everything up. I endangered everyone, but I didn't mean to. I was just curious."

"When's the exchange?" I asked, changing the subject as we exited the woods into Bernadette's yard.

"Wednesday night. Same place as last time."

"Wednesday," I repeated. "Two days *after* my deadline."

Addy looked away, and I caught her swiping a hand across her cheek.

Throwing an arm over her shoulder, I tugged her against my side as we walked. "It'll be okay. I'll try to figure this out, but if I don't, we'll become Canadians together."

"Really?" Addy asked, turning to face me. "You'll take me with you?"

"If we're forced to leave, yes. If that's what needs to happen to keep you safe, that's what we'll do." I started back toward the patio, tugging her with me. "I'm assuming you can make us fake IDs?" I hated asking her to commit a crime, but it sure beat the alternative of the bikers tracking us down.

"If I can get to my house for my printer and supplies, sure, no problem."

"I have everything already. Your dad let me take your stuff so the police wouldn't get their hands on it."

"Sweet. Did you grab my money too?"

"No. I had your dad hide it. But I'll borrow the money we need from Bernadette. You just stay here and keep your head down. Be ready to leave tomorrow night."

Crossing the patio, Addy reached out for the door handle, but stopped to look at me. "This is really happening, isn't it?" For the first time, she looked young, vulnerable, scared.

"I hope not, but it looks that way."

CHAPTER THIRTY-SEVEN

"OH, GOOD, YOU'RE BACK," BERNADETTE said, surprising us just inside the patio door. "I thought we'd try an experiment." Latching onto my arm, she hustled me down the hallway to my bedroom, the one Addy was using.

Inside, we both stopped to look around. The room was a mess, clothes strewn everywhere. Peeking into the closet, I saw it was empty.

"Sorry," Addy said, sliding past me to shovel clothes up from the floor, piling them on top of the bed. "I've been sorting through the clothes, trying to find something wearable." She waved a hand at the outfit she was wearing, a loose-fitting pink button-down blouse with peacock feathers printed on it and a pair of gray sweatpants. "I'm sort of glad I'm in hiding. At least no one can see me in this crap."

After losing my old wardrobe in the housefire, I'd raided the clothes here for anything somewhat okay to wear, leaving only the bottom of the barrel behind. I wasn't picky when it came to clothes, but even I wouldn't wear the shirt Addy was wearing.

I looked over at Bernadette. "Can you take her clothes shopping tomorrow morning? Some place out of the way where no one will recognize either of you?"

"Sure," Bernadette said, surprisingly agreeable. "We'll drive north and shop in Grand Rapids."

"That'll work," I said. "We'll need cash too. Enough to live off the grid for a few months."

"You're leaving?" Bernadette asked.

"Looks that way. I'll need to flee before the bikers come looking for me again, demanding I turn Addy over to them."

Bernadette frowned, appearing almost sad. "When will you go?"

"I'll pick up Addy tomorrow night around dinner time."

Bernadette was quiet a long moment, but her face gradually shifted from sad to angry before she kicked a pile of clothes off to the side. I wasn't sure why she was angry; it wasn't like she was the one forced to leave town.

"I'll handle the money and make sure the girl has clothes," Bernadette snapped. She looked at Addy. "I need a moment with my granddaughter. It has nothing to do with you."

Addy glanced at me, giving me an uneasy look before she left the room.

Bernadette snorted, glancing back toward the door.

"Is she hiding around the corner?" I whispered.

Bernadette nodded. "Worried I'll yell at you again. She feels guilty." Bernadette's eyes narrowed. "Must be strange, not sensing anything. What's it like?"

"Weird. Like a bad head cold that messes with your sense of taste and smell. Even direct contact with people, shaking hands, has no effect on me."

"Well, I have an idea." Bernadette rubbed her hands together. "I want to try something."

Oh, boy, I thought.

Bernadette flopped down to the floor, tugging me down with her. "Since you can't access your psychic world, I'll go to mine and pull you into my vision."

"What should I do?"

"Just relax that noggin of yours and be receptive when I call you."

Sounded harmless enough. I closed my eyes, relaxing my shoulders and my mind. The minutes ticked by. Starting to worry I'd be late to meet Austin in town, I cracked one eyelid open to peek at the bedside clock. Deciding I could wait a little longer, I closed it.

My thoughts wandered, wondering what Olivia had planned for our stakeout later tonight. Probably another infidelity case. I was starting to get concerned about the divorce rate in Daybreak Falls.

"*Didn't you hear me yelling?*" Bernadette snapped, causing me to jump.

I leaned away, opening my eyes to see her scowl. "No, I didn't hear anything."

"Well, it's settled. You're *normal*," she sneered. "After spending all that energy to train you—" She lifted a hand to my shoulder, using my body to help herself stand. "What a waste of time."

I made myself take a moment before speaking, trying to bank my anger. Pushing myself up from the floor, I kept my voice even. "This isn't about you. It's about me. It's about me never having visions again. It's about me not being able to protect myself or my friends."

"It's a little about me," Bernadette said, fisting her hands and narrowing her eyes. "It's my family legacy. It's about generations of psychics being born and raised. It's all over now. When I die, that's it. Our family will be forever... *Normal*." She said normal like it left a bad taste in her mouth.

"You're blaming me? After all the crap you've put me through, you're blaming me? What's next? Are you going to start pretending I don't exist again?"

"You're psychic?" Addy asked, popping her head around the corner of the doorway. "For like, real? It's a legit thing?"

"Yes, it's a legit thing," Bernadette snapped at her. "Only, she's no longer psychic." Bernadette waved a hand at me, giving me a disgusted look. "She's completely broken."

Her words stung. I was just getting used to her being in my life, and now I was useless to her. "So that's it? You're done with me? Cutting me back out of your life?

"Don't put words in my mouth!" Bernadette shouted. She inhaled sharply, almost startled by her own reaction.

I started for the door, not wanting to be here.

"I'm sorry," Bernadette called out.

I stopped but didn't turn to face her.

"I'm upset, but not at you. Psychic or not, you're family. You're my granddaughter. Nothing can change that."

My anger deflated. As cantankerous as Bernadette could be, I'd gotten used to her being part of my life. "Really?" I glanced back at her. "Do you mean that? We're still family?"

"Yes, really." Bernadette rolled her eyes before walking past me out of the room. "Don't be daft."

I smiled at the doorway. Some things never changed. Turning my attention back to Addy, I asked, "Are you good to stay here another night with that loon?" I pointed toward the hallway.

Addy grinned. "Yeah, I'm good. I think she's funny."

"Just don't let her become your role model. The world can only take one Bernadette Quade." I picked up another pile of clothes, tossing them on top of the bed. "I feel the urge to clean this up, but I'm running late." I started toward the door. "See you tomorrow night."

"Davina?" Addy called out.

I stopped, looking back at her.

Addy fidgeted, glancing away. "Thanks for giving a damn."

I nodded, not saying anything.

Chapter Thirty-Eight

Before leaving Bernadette's, I texted Olivia to let her know to pick me up at Nightshade Treasures. Twenty minutes later, I let myself inside the suite and entered the security code. Not bothering with the main lights, I crossed to my desk, stopping to look around.

Olivia's desk and her filing cabinets were gone, and in their place now sat tables full of antiques. My desk and the matching credenza were in their usual spot.

I set Austin's pie down before moving to the back hallway to peek inside the conference room, laughing at the arrangement.

Along one wall was the row of filing cabinets and on top of the cabinets was the office copier. Olivia's desk and credenza were tucked into the far corner, complete with the pair of guest chairs. But instead of Olivia's dining room table, her much-smaller kitchen table was now here. The table looked horribly out of place for an office, and I could envision Olivia throwing a fit, hating it.

Remembering I had a better table in my garage that needed refinishing, I made a mental note to offer it to Olivia. I wouldn't have time to re-stain it, but not only would it fit an office better, Olivia returning her kitchen table would likely end a new round of arguments between her and Breydon about their home furniture being repurposed as office furniture.

Moving back to my desk, I decided to empty it so Olivia could have it moved out of the suite. After turning on the undercabinet light on the credenza, I wandered around Mrs. Paulson's side of the suite, finding an empty box. Returning to my desk, I checked and emptied the drawers and cabinets, filling the box with pens, sticky notes, a stack of new file folders, pads of paper, and a random ruler I'd never seen before.

Pulling the three file folders for my construction site, I wondered if I should leave them here or take them home. If I left town, Breydon might need them. My mind wandered to the cottage and the Zenner house. Bernadette might need the paperwork on those as well.

I dug out two new file folders and emptied the wad of quotes and receipts that had accumulated inside my purse. After separating them, I slid the paperwork into the corresponding file and stacked them on top of the box. I moved the box to Olivia's new office, setting it on the floor just past the row of file cabinets. From Olivia's desk chair, she'd see the box. I trusted her to get the files to Breydon if I left town, and Breydon in return would coordinate with Bernadette.

I returned to the front room, sitting behind my now empty desk. I'd never needed a desk, but I'd gotten used to having one. I wondered if I should set up a desk at home; but if I fled town, I wouldn't even have a home, so what did it matter?

Hearing the front door, I looked up. Austin entered and strolled toward me. "Did you forget to turn the lights on?" Austin asked, looking around the dark room.

"I didn't want to advertise I was here," I said, reaching across my desk to pick up his pie and hand it to him. "And no, I haven't forgotten that I still owe you two homecooked meals, but I'm hoping the pie will tide you over until I have more time."

Austin's dimple popped out. "This buys you at least a week, maybe two. I even stopped at the store and bought vanilla ice cream to go with it."

"Well, enjoy." I sat back in my chair, leaning back. "I appreciate all your help. I wouldn't have gotten the roof stripped without you."

"Speaking of," Austin said, his eyebrows furrowing. "How's your ankle?"

"All better." I lifted my leg, rotating my ankle. "It's an ugly shade of purple but it doesn't hurt when I walk on it."

"Glad to hear." Austin stepped around the desk and leaned toward me, dropping a feather-light kiss on my lips. "I wanted to do that earlier but chickened out." He walked backward, smiling wide. "Thanks for the pie. Sweat dreams, Davina Ravine."

I laughed, watching him stride with confidence back to the door, exiting.

"Goodbye, Austin," I whispered to an empty room.

My lighthearted mood faded, replaced by dread about leaving my friends and the only town I'd ever lived in. I leaned forward, resting my forehead on top of my desk.

"Don't tell me you're feeling defeated already," Olivia's voice called out from the front of the suite. Olivia skipped across the room, full of energy. "Buck up, camper." She grinned. "We've still got twenty-four hours to fix this mess."

"I hope that means you have a plan, because I'm at a loss at what to do."

"I have a plan," Olivia said, giggling. "And disguises." She held up a paper tote bag.

"I'm not wearing a wig. My scalp itched for a solid week after the last one."

"Fine." Olivia tossed the bag on the floor beside my desk. "We'll skip the disguises, but can we take your van? We can put those magnetic signs on it, so it'll look like a contractor's van."

"Sure. Why not," I said, standing. "But before you drag me into whatever cockamamie idea you've brewed up, we need to stop by Lance's house to drop off a pie."

"Pie?" she asked with too much interest.

"Yes, but no, you can't have any. I only made pies for the people who helped on the cottage."

"Fine. I packed stakeout snacks for us anyway. And..." she bounced up and down, "I bought a stakeout toilet! It's super cute and portable. It's made for fishing boats and—"

"*No, never, and absolutely not,*" I interrupted, shaking my head. "*You're not putting any kind of toilet inside my van.*"

"But—"

"*Nope.*" I shut off the credenza light and grabbed my stuff.

Olivia followed behind me muttering, "You're no fun."

Chapter Thirty-Nine

Dropping off Lance's pie was quick and conversation free. He was so focused on the pie he barely muttered a *goodnight* before turning back inside his house.

I jogged back to the van where Olivia was slapping a magnetic sign on the passenger side. I stopped to look at it, recognizing the logo for the local power company.

"I'm not sure that's legal," I said, climbing into the passenger seat while Olivia got into the driver's side.

"As long as we don't pretend to be government employees, we're good," Olivia said, putting the van in reverse, backing up toward the barn to turn it around.

"But couldn't the power company sue us?"

"I guess they could try, but since the PI business is broke, they won't get much." Olivia giggled and after a quick glance both ways, she turned onto the road, heading south.

"About that... I saw your office was moved to the conference room. I emptied my desk so you can have it moved out of the suite, and I also have a table in my garage that'll look better than your kitchen table."

"Sweet. You wouldn't believe how mad Breydon got when he saw the kitchen table was gone. He went a little bonkers on me."

"I bet. Anyway... I think you need to have another sit down with Mrs. Paulson."

"Why?" Olivia asked, glancing at me with a confused look.

"Remember when you started this PI gig and Breydon volunteered me to be your partner?"

"Yeah, but you didn't really seem pleased about it. Are you changing your mind?"

"Nope. Still not interested in becoming a private investigator, but one of the reasons he did that was because you lack experience running your own business. He knew if he helped with the bookkeeping, it would turn into a feud between the two of you, so he volunteered me."

"Makes sense."

"Only, I don't want the job either. I don't want to jeopardize our friendship by having to teach you financial discipline."

"Financial discipline? But I've been good about keeping records and paying the bills before I pay myself."

"Yes, but not so good with projecting your income long term. To be successful, you need to plan further ahead."

"Like not treat myself to a spa day when rent will be due in another week?"

"Something like that, yeah."

Olivia smirked, sparing me another glance. "Okay. What are you suggesting?"

"For the next six months at least, I think you need to have monthly sit downs with Mrs. Paulson to go over your income and expenses. She helped me when I first started out, and I'm sure she can guide you in the right direction too."

"So, first Breydon passes me off to you, and now you're passing me off to Mrs. Paulson?"

"It's either that or one of us will need to step in and take over your accounts to put you on an allowance."

Olivia cringed, glancing at me. "Seriously?'

"I love you, but you have a lot to learn."

Olivia blew out air, exasperated. "Fine. I'll ask Mrs. Paulson if we can set up regular meetings to go over the books. She's dropped hints offering to help, so at least I know she won't pass me off to someone else."

"Thank you." I relaxed, glad to have the awkward conversation over with. "You know, if you arranged one of your meetings strategically so Breydon sees the two of you going over the books together, he might let you dip into the trust one more time."

Olivia giggled. "That's a good idea." Olivia hit the brakes, stopping in the middle of the road. She pointed out the passenger window. "What is that?"

I looked in the direction she pointed. A corn field had been harvested and the ground turned over, but now a long wall of haybales lined the field. "This must be the Fall Maze Lance told me about."

"I've heard about this, but never seen it. Couldn't they put this somewhere indoors though? Somewhere with less dirt?" She sped up again, driving away. "I mean, who wants to walk around a dirty field? Yuck."

"I'm guessing a lot of people, or they wouldn't keep putting it on every year."

"Whatever," Olivia said, rolling her eyes.

I noticed how fast she was driving. "Slow down. The sheriff's deputies are less likely to give you community service for speeding."

Olivia let up on the gas. "Speaking of—"

"Yeah, I know about you getting pulled over again," I said, giggling. "You can borrow whatever you need to clean the park bathroom, just remember to return everything when you're done."

"How'd you know?" Olivia asked with a cheeky grin.

"I was with Stone, driving through town, when you got pulled over. He said they have a list at the precinct of projects to assign you."

"Figures," Olivia said, slowing for another turn.

"Are you going to tell me where we're going?" I asked, looking around. "Seems like we're heading to the middle of nowhere."

"According to the map, we are. We're heading to the northern edge of the city, about two miles south of Kami's bar."

"What's there?"

"You're not going to like it," Olivia said, stalling.

I watched Olivia's face, seeing an edge of nervousness. Olivia was the bravest person I knew. If she was nervous, we were about to do something dangerous. "We're staking out the bikers, aren't we?"

Olivia cringed. "Maybe?"

"It's a horrible idea."

"Got a better one?" she asked.

"No." I exhaled a long breath.

"Well," she shrugged, "what've we got to lose?"

"Our lives?"

"We'll be careful. I studied the satellite images of the area and found the perfect place to keep watch from a distance."

"How do you even know where the bikers will be?"

"I poked around and found out where their clubhouse is."

"You're not serious? You want to surveil their *clubhouse? Like where all of them hang out together?*"

"I know, I know, it's dangerous. But we need to do *something*. We can't just wait for your clock to run out, and I couldn't think of anything else."

The truth was, neither could I. "I don't want to drag you into this mess."

"You're forgetting the woman who hired me already knows that we're partners. They'll come knocking on my door looking for you."

I hadn't thought of that. My stomach rolled, threatening to bring my dinner back up. "Still... At this point you can still play clueless, and they might leave you alone. But if you get into this any deeper, that might not be the case."

"I can't *not* get involved. I'm worried about the girl. She's out there somewhere scared and alone. She's in danger."

"No, she's not," I admitted, caving under the weight of my guilt. I knew I was breaking my promise to Addy, but if Olivia was going to risk her life to help, she deserved the truth. "I found the girl. She's safe. If I flee town, I'll take her with me."

Olivia's head swiveled my way, staring at me with bugged out eyes.

I grabbed the steering wheel, jerking the van back to the center of our lane.

"You've been lying to me?" Olivia asked, now looking ahead.

"I had to. I'm sorry, but I promised Addy I wouldn't tell anyone. Besides, the fewer people who know where she is, the safer she'll be."

"Dang. That's devious. I didn't know you had it in you. I'm sort of impressed."

"Impressed that I've been lying to everyone?"

"Well, yeah." A hint of a smile lit her face. "You suck at lying."

"It's not funny."

"It's sort of funny. *Little Miss Morals*—lying to people. *Ha*."

"The lies have been eating at me. I can't warn anyone that I might be skipping out of town, either. It's going to crush people."

"Look, if the worst happens—if you need to leave town—I'll make sure everyone understands. Just don't give up yet. If we can get dirt on these guys, maybe we can come up with a plan to stop them."

"But that's the problem."

"What?"

"Addy is hiding because she doesn't want to testify against the bikers. They could retaliate, send other bikers after her or her dad."

"Yeah, bikers do that kind of thing. I saw it on *Sons of Anarchy*."

"That's a television show. That's not real life."

"Are you sure? Because I get the feeling that some of that cray-cray stuff, like killing witnesses, was legit."

"Whether it's real or not, we need a plan that doesn't involve testifying."

"Right, but what?"

"I don't know."

"Well, we still have time to think of something," Olivia said, cutting the headlights and letting up on the gas. She pulled the van along the shoulder of the road.

I looked around, seeing several dark and abandoned buildings on both sides. Not a single person was in sight. "Where are we?"

Olivia pointed down the road to the right. "The clubhouse is back there. I'm hoping we can get close enough to see who's coming and going. The street entrance is on the next road over, but it was too exposed. They'd see us watching."

The fact that she was keeping us at a safe distance was way more mature than the Olivia I knew as a teenager. The reckless younger Olivia had always pushed the limits, often getting us into trouble.

"We'll have to sneak through the woods to get closer," Olivia said, passing me a dark hoodie. "We can huddle down in their parking lot."

So much for not being reckless.

CHAPTER FORTY

CROSSING THROUGH A NARROW strip of trees, we approached the clubhouse's side parking lot, wearing black hoodies, black driving gloves, and carrying mace. If it came down to it, their knives and guns beat our mace, but since we didn't have anything else, it was better than nothing.

We snuck between a pair of rusty, broken-down vehicles, keeping ourselves hunched low but leaning forward to peek across the lot.

"We should get closer," Olivia whispered.

"This is close enough," I said, grabbing her arm to make sure she stayed put.

"But we won't be able to hear anything from here."

"If we're caught, there won't be anything to hear because we'll be dead."

Olivia made a face but stayed put.

A group of bikers walked out of a building, laughing. They each lit up a cigarette, stopping just outside the door.

Olivia was right. We were too far away to hear what they said, but I was able to catch a few words as they joked amongst themselves. Their conversation either centered around a stripper with big boobs, or a tripper with big boots, but based on their hand gestures I was pretty sure it was about a woman's knockers. I didn't need, nor did I want, to hear the rest.

I glanced over my shoulder at Olivia. She was leaning against me, watching the bikers and trying her hardest to listen to their fragmented conversation. Even with the black hoodie drawn over her head, I could see her wide eyes gleaming with excitement, swiveling from one man to the next.

I couldn't help but smile—regardless of how much danger we were in by being here. Olivia, my small-town best friend, loved to ride the line of danger. If she wasn't so accident prone, she could've had a career in law enforcement.

The quieting of the men's voices pulled my attention back to them. I watched as they parted to let a tall, dark-haired woman wearing a skintight blouse and snug jeans pass them to enter the front door.

"*That's—*" Olivia started to say.

I swiveled, clamping my hand over her mouth.

She waved a pointy finger in the direction of the clubhouse, bobbing her head.

I nodded back, knowing she was trying to tell me it was the woman who hired her.

Keeping my hand firmly over her mouth, I watched the men as they began whispering to each other, throwing disgusted looks toward the door.

Whoever she was, they didn't like her. I wondered why they'd shown her the respect of stepping back. Who was she? Hurricane's girlfriend? Being the boss's woman might protect her, whether they liked her or not.

Olivia's antsy jiggling had settled so I lowered my hand, motioning with a finger to my lips for her to be quiet.

The front door opened again and LoJack walked out, lighting a cigarette.

Some of the other guys were already flinging their cigarettes to the ground, heading back inside. LoJack glanced sideways at the group before wandering away from them, halfway across the parking lot toward us.

Three more guys flung their cigarettes to the ground, returning inside. Only one man remained. He dropped his cigarette to the asphalt, toeing it out, but lit another one. Keeping his back to the building and facing the road, he kept glancing sideways at LoJack, but pretending he wasn't.

LoJack kept his back to the clubhouse, unknowingly facing us. Pinning his cigarette between his lips, he pulled his phone from his inside leather vest pocket and tapped against the screen, discreetly moving the phone to his ear while taking a few more steps in our direction.

Olivia and I pressed our backs against the rusty pickup truck behind us, trying to become invisible.

"Hey," LoJack said, barely above a whisper. "Can't talk, but something's up. I'll call back when I can."

The guy at the door moved soundlessly toward LoJack, dropping his cigarette along the way. LoJack's face tensed. He pocketed his phone before turning to face the other guy.

"Who was that? Who'd you call?" the biker asked LoJack.

LoJack moved purposefully toward the biker, squaring his shoulders. "Not that it's any of your business, but I was calling my old lady."

"Bullshit," the biker said, getting in LoJack's face. "You're a rat. I told Hurricane he couldn't trust you. I told him how you kept sneaking off." The biker pulled a gun so fast I wondered if what I was seeing was real. LoJack lunged toward him, grabbing the other guy's wrist and fighting to push the barrel of the gun downward.

A gunshot fired, ringing loud.

Olivia screamed and for a fraction of a second, the biker holding the gun looked our way. LoJack straightened, wrapped an arm around the guy's head, and spun the guy so his back was against LoJack's chest. With one hand locked under the guy's jaw, LoJack used his other to twist the biker's head.

The *crack-crunch* sound of breaking bones had me slumping downward until my butt hit the asphalt. LoJack killed him. He'd snapped his neck. *I just witnessed someone die.*

LoJack tried to step in our direction, but he stumbled, falling to one knee. One hand dropped to the asphalt with the other tucked against his side. A single streak of blood ran over the top of his hand.

He's bleeding. He was shot.

I don't know why, but in that moment, I knew I had to help him. I darted into the parking lot, pulling his arm up to drape over my shoulders. Pushing up with my legs, I managed to get his feet under him.

"Hurry," LoJack whispered. "They're coming."

"What the hell?" Olivia whispered, wearing a baffled expression.

"Get his other arm. We need to get him to the van."

"But he's one of them," she said, scurrying to his other side.

"Just help me."

Between LoJack's stumbling movements and our help, we moved past the rusty vehicles into the patch of trees.

Multiple voices started shouting in the parking lot behind us, yelling over each other. "*He's dead!*" "*Where's LoJack?*" "*Get the body inside!*"

We kept moving, exiting the trees into a vacant business parking lot. Cutting across the asphalt, I gauged the distance to the van which was parked alongside the road's shoulder. It felt impossibly far away, especially since with every step, LoJack became more sluggish. "Come on, LoJack. Help us out here. Move faster."

He put extra effort into the next two steps before stumbling sideways.

"We're not going to make it," Olivia whispered.

"We have to," I said. "We can't leave him."

"Are you sure? Because the way I see it, I'm okay with us living and him dying."

"I'm not," LoJack said through a pain-stricken expression.

"Go figure," Olivia said.

The shouting voices drew closer. Olivia was right, we weren't going to make it.

"Keep going," Olivia said before she ran back the way we'd come.

LoJack moved his blood-covered hand back to his stomach. "Is she nuts?"

"A little, yeah. I need to go after her. Can you get to the van?" I asked, pointing to the van ahead.

"No," LoJack groaned, stumbling forward again.

"Damn it," I said, glancing over my shoulder briefly before surging ahead, half dragging LoJack with me. "If anything happens to her, you'll be sorry."

LoJack fell to his knees.

Rather than trying to pick him up again, I shoved him sideways, making him fall onto his back. Moving behind him, I pulled him up into a sitting position and latched my arms under his armpits, locking my hands at his chest to drag him backward. No longer burdened with balancing his weight, the distance to the van drew smaller and smaller.

Reaching the edge of the parking lot, I ignored LoJack's groans of pain and jerked him up and over the curb before hauling him over a patch of dirt to the van's side door. I let go of him, turning to open the panel door.

Moving in front of LoJack, I hugged my arms around him, straining to lift him high enough to get his butt inside. LoJack pushed up with one leg, landing his upper body into the van.

"Either get yourself the rest of the way inside or fall out and wait for your biker buddies to finish you off." I ran around the van, stopping when I heard a man scream in the distance.

I scanned the tree line on the other side of the parking lot, searching for Olivia.

She ran out of the woods, moving at full speed. "*Start the van!*"

I climbed into the driver's seat with my hand reaching for the ignition, but the keys weren't there. I patted myself down but didn't have them. I looked up, flipping the visor down. The keys landed in my lap.

I started the engine as Olivia jumped in through the side door, pulling LoJack's legs the rest of the way inside. "*Go! Go!*" Olivia yelled.

I took off down the narrow street, squealing the tires as the side door slammed shut. Gunshots sounded. The passenger side mirror exploded.

I turned left at the next street, nearly hitting a car that was parked too close to the corner.

Driving down the center of the street, I floored the gas, doing fifty in a deserted business district. A mile or so later, I turned onto a side road, checking the van's compass. I was relieved to see I was heading north.

I sped up again, topping off at around sixty-five. If the police pulled me over, I'd happily pay the ticket. The thought of police lights and sirens sounded pretty good right about now.

Olivia wiggled between the bucket seats, throwing herself into the passenger one. She grabbed a handful of tissues from the packet I'd left in the cupholder, wiping her face.

"Are you crying? Are you hurt?" I asked.

"No, I'm not crying. Well, technically I guess I am." Olivia blew her nose. "Word to the wise, don't spray pepper spray upwind. It blows back in your face." Her eyelids were poofy, wet, and an angry red. "Sorry about your mirror, but if it helps, I don't think they got a good look at the van. The two who shot at us got a face full of pepper spray. They could barely see."

"It won't matter. They'll suspect it was us. Who else would it be?"

"Maybe not," LoJack hissed from the back. "They've got a lot of enemies."

"You hush," Olivia said, turning to look back, wagging her finger at him. "I'm mad at you for messing up a perfectly good stakeout."

"That's why you two were there?" LoJack asked, his chuckle followed by a groan.

"You need a hospital," I said, trying to see him in the rearview mirror but unable to. "What's the closest route to take?"

"No hospital."

"Look, buddy," Olivia said, "you're bleeding like a stuck pig. You need a hospital."

"Can't. They'll pull me off the case. I don't have enough evidence. I've spent years trying to get these guys. Can't throw it all away."

"What are you babbling about?" Olivia asked.

"He's a cop," I said out loud as the puzzle pieces zoomed together.

CHAPTER FORTY-ONE

SPEEDING DOWN BACK ROADS, I thought back to my prior encounters with LoJack. The first time our paths had crossed was in Kami's driveway, after the bikers followed Olivia to Kami's house, threatening to kill us. LoJack had bridged a truce to let us live. Back then, my abilities were working just fine, and though I'd sensed that LoJack was a threat, dangerous even, I'd also sensed he had an underlying goodness, similar to what I felt when I was around Bones and Ryan.

I'd also learned through Kami that LoJack was the one who arranged for her to hire a club member for the bouncer role at her bar in exchange for the Bleeding Souls to stay out of her bar. Now I knew it was to protect her.

Both LoJack's secret friendship with Bones and his mysterious phone call in the club's parking lot now made sense. He was pretending to be one of them, while secretly trying to take the club down. The only piece that didn't feel cop-like was him snapping the other biker's neck.

I shivered, remembering the sound. "You killed that biker," I said, breaking the silence.

"Self-defense," LoJack groaned. "He shot me. I didn't have time to pull my gun and knew the others would be coming." He cursed under his breath. "You wouldn't happen to have any Vicodin, would you?"

"Sorry, I'm all out." I turned at the next road, recognizing where I was. The interstate was a few miles ahead. "Have you changed your mind about going to the hospital?"

"No," LoJack said, breathing heavily. "I'm not letting them pull me off this case. I've been undercover too long. I sacrificed too much. I need to take the club down."

Music to my ears, I thought, pulling along the road's shoulder. After putting the van in park, I maneuvered between the bucket seats into the back. "Olivia, drive toward the interstate."

Running a hand across the ceiling, I felt around until my hand found the dome light, turning it on to light up the back of the van.

"Once I get to the interstate, where should I go?" Olivia asked, hopping into the driver's seat.

"I don't know. Just drive. I need to see how bad he's hurt."

"Just a graze," LoJack said between gritted teeth.

He was white as a ghost, covered in sweat, and panting as blood pulsed between his fingers. I knew it was worse than a graze even before I pulled his shirt up to look.

A jagged gash started at his lower abdomen and angled upward out through a larger gash below his last rib along his side. He'd gotten lucky the bullet hadn't blown straight through his stomach, ripping apart internal organs, but if I didn't do something to stop the bleeding, it wouldn't matter. "You need a hospital."

"Rather die," he said, panting.

"Careful what you say. That's a real possibility."

"No hospital."

"Stubborn idiot," I mumbled, digging around in the back of the van, taking inventory of everything. Since I'd packed for life on the run, luckily the van held more than the usual cleaning supplies. Sliding one of the duffle bags filled with my clothes closer, I unzipped it and pulled out a handful of shirts, pressing them against his wound.

I moved his hands on top of the clothes. "Hold that. Keep pressure on it."

Shifting closer to the back doors, I shuffled bags around, tossing a few bottles of water toward LoJack and after lifting another duffle bag, I unearthed the medical kit.

I dragged it over, glancing up at LoJack. He was slumped against the metal cabinets, barely conscious. "Wake up, you fool." I uncapped a water bottle and pulled back the clothes. When Noah had cleaned Addy's wound, he'd said the biggest worry was infection. The water wouldn't sanitize anything, but it would be better than nothing. I poured the water over the gash.

LoJack hissed.

"Like that?" I asked. "Just think, if you'd let us take you to a hospital, they'd have you too numb to feel anything."

"I can take it," LoJack groaned.

I threw another shirt on top of his wound, placing his hands on top again. "Hold this."

LoJack's movements were sluggish. He was barely applying any pressure to the gash.

"Come on, LoJack, stay with me. If you pass out, I'm taking you to the hospital."

He blinked a few times and nodded.

Opening the med kit, I was relieved to see it was one of Noah's over-the-top packs. One side was for civilians, filled with everyday bandages and antibacterial cream. The other side was packaged for Noah's use only. Digging around Noah's side, I pulled out latex gloves and a suture kit, accidentally knocking something made of hard plastic out. I picked it up, about to toss it back inside, when I realized what it was. *A suture stapler.*

"Hot diggity," I said to myself as I pulled the gloves on. "LoJack, you might actually survive the night, but fair warning, I have no idea what I'm doing."

"I'll take my chances."

Readying another pile of clean shirts, I pulled the soaked one off and pinched the two sides of his skin together enough to flip the yellowish fat back inside. Holding the skin in place with one hand, I picked up the stapler, lined up the end, and pulled the trigger.

LoJack yelped in pain, causing me to flinch.

I looked down at the staple gun and felt a wave of nausea. The sound it had made was a simple clicking noise, but hearing it, knowing it was piercing flesh, and feeling the tug of the skin in my other hand was revolting.

I gulped air, hoping I wouldn't be sick.

"Don't stop," LoJack moaned.

He was right. I had to keep going.

Pinching the next section together, I flinched again adding another staple but kept going, adding one after another across the gash, moving fast—just in case I had to stop to throw up.

Following the gash up his side toward his ribs, I paused to help LoJack roll toward me, half lying across my lap. When I set the last staple, I pushed him upright again to lean against the metal cabinets.

Backing up, I sat and raised my knees in front of me with my feet flat on the floor and my head tilted down between my knees, focusing on my breathing. The van reeked of blood, but I tried not to think about it. I used my forearm to wipe the sweat off my forehead.

"I hate you," I whispered, peeling the gloves off. "I hate you for making me do that."

LoJack made a sound somewhere between a groan and a chuckle.

I looked over at him, watching him as he slid to the side, passing out. Cursing his name, I threw the gloves at his chest before moving toward the front of the van.

"How's he doing?" Olivia asked.

"I closed the wound, but other than that, I have no idea." I moved between the bucket seats, dropping down into the passenger side.

"Well, if he dies, it's his own fault."

"Yeah," I said even though I knew if he died it would haunt me.

"I've been crisscrossing all over the place. Did you figure out where we're going?"

"Where are we?"

"I took the interstate north of Daybreak Falls, then exited to drive back south. We're about a mile north of the first city exit."

South would lead to the hospital or Silver Aces. North would lead us back to Daybreak Falls.

I glanced between the seats back at LoJack. His gash had stopped bleeding. "Take us to the cottage."

"Won't the bikers look there?"

"LoJack said the club has a lot of enemies. They might not know we were behind the chaos tonight. If they do know, chances are they'll break into the Zenner house to come looking for me, not the cottage. They know I don't live at the cottage."

"Sounds risky."

"Got a better idea?"

"Not really." Olivia exited the interstate and looped back onto the northbound ramp.

I picked up my phone, still sitting in the van's cupholder, and called Bones.

"Hey," Bones answered. "Did an associate of mine reach out to you?"

"He did. In fact, our paths crossed again tonight. He's injured. I patched him up the best I could, but he's refusing to go to the hospital."

"Where are you?" Bones asked, his voice turning deadly.

"We're about ten minutes from the cottage, but Bones, LoJack doesn't want this called in. He doesn't want the people who call the shots to pull him from the case."

Bones was silent, not saying anything.

"Yes, yes, I know he's undercover. Can we stop being cryptic now?"

Bones snorted. "Give me the address."

I gave him the cottage address and detailed the best route for him to take to get there, warning him to watch out for a pack of angry bikers.

"Got it. I'll head your way," Bones said. "Is he going to live long enough for us to get there?"

"He's out cold, but I'm not sure if it's because of blood loss or from the pain of me patching him back together without painkillers. It was a horrifying experience."

"Wuss," Bones said, disconnecting.

I wasn't sure if he was calling me a wuss or LoJack a wuss, but I didn't really care. I set my phone down and tilted my head back to lean against the headrest, trying to think about anything besides blood and staples.

CHAPTER FORTY-TWO

"ARE YOU SURE THEY WON'T look here?" Olivia asked, groaning while juggling her side of a woozy LoJack.

I waited until we had LoJack through the doorway before answering. "No. Not really." I veered us into the first-floor bedroom. "But what other options do we have? I'm sure as heck not taking him home with me, nor will I risk anyone else's safety by dragging them into this mess."

Olivia and I both turned to guide LoJack into the front bedroom, backing him up and lowering him to the floor near the front window.

Panting with my hands on my knees, I looked down at LoJack who was slumped sideways, once again passed out.

"Is he going to live?" Olivia asked.

"No idea." I walked out of the bedroom and back outside. Inside the van, I pocketed my phone, grabbed another handful of shirts and water bottles, and tucked the medical kit under one arm before returning inside.

Back in the bedroom, I uncapped a water bottle, holding it out to LoJack and using my other hand to slap lightly against his cheek to wake him. "Drink. You need to stay hydrated."

LoJack moaned but managed to get his lips on the bottle, drooling half the water down the front of him.

My phone chirped and I set the water down to read the text message from Bones. He was here and approaching the cottage on foot.

Getting up, I moved to the front door, flipping the light switch. When the light didn't come on, I looked up at the ceiling fan Lance had installed, remembering he'd had a wiring issue. I leaned over, plugging in one of the new work lights, nearly blinding myself when the bulb lit.

Ducking away, I opened the front door, hoping Bones had enough light to see the wonky porch boards.

Two manly figures jogged up the drive, both carrying duffle bags. It wasn't until the first man crossed the porch that I recognized Bones. I didn't recognize the other guy who followed him inside, but unlike Bones, this guy was shorter, stockier, and smiled warmly as he passed me to enter.

"In here," Olivia called out from the front bedroom.

I closed and locked the front door, not fooling myself that the deadbolt would stop a gang of bikers. After shutting the work light off again, I moved to the bedroom doorway.

"You look like crap," Bones said to LoJack.

One side of LoJack's mouth tipped up as he struggled to focus.

The other guy, the one I didn't recognize, cut off LoJack's blood-soaked shirt before inspecting the wound. "Was the person who stapled you drunk?" he asked LoJack, leaning to the side to check the wound along his ribs.

"Scared out of my mind and stapling in the dark, but unfortunately, I was one hundred percent sober when I did that."

"*You* stapled him?" Bones asked, wearing a hint of a smile. "I'm impressed."

"Yeah, well, when he complains about the ugly scar, do me a favor and remind him I offered to take him to the hospital."

"On the bright side," the other guy said, "you got his insides back on the inside and managed to stop the bleeding." He dug in his bag, pulling out bandages.

Bones dipped his head toward LoJack but spoke to the other man. "Is he going to live or not?"

"He'll live. But he'll be weak for a few days."

"My work here is done then," I told the guy before looking at Bones. "You guys do what you need to do, but fair warning, the house doesn't have any hot water, most of the lights don't work, and if you hear motorcycles, *run*."

Bones full out smiled at me. "I like a challenge."

I turned out of the room, walking on shaky legs. *Adrenaline crash*, I thought as I stumbled into the bathroom to wash the blood off my wrists and forearms. When I was done, I leaned forward and splashed cold water on my face, trying to cool myself.

"Here," Olivia said, walking in behind me and dropping a terrycloth towel on the countertop. "It was all I could find."

I dried my hands and patted the excess water off my face before following her into the living room where Bones was waiting for us.

"What's the deal with this place?" Bones asked.

"Bernadette bought it for me to fix up. The bikers know about it, though. If they figure out we were the ones at their clubhouse tonight, they might stop to have a look around."

Bones tensed. "Tell me everything."

I explained the events of the evening exactly how they'd played out. Bones, familiar with Olivia's shenanigans, didn't seem surprised that Olivia had convinced me to stake out the clubhouse, but he did crack a grin when I explained Olivia backtracking to mace the bikers. His grin faded when I mentioned the bikers shooting blindly at us, taking out the side mirror on my van.

"All three of you are lucky to be alive," Bones said, running a hand across the back of his neck.

"Agreed," I said, leaning against a wall. "But what happens now? Do we leave LoJack here? Do we call the cops? Do I go home? Or should I flee to Canada before the bikers catch up with me?"

Bones shook his head. "LoJack was right about the Souls having other enemies. Chances are, they'll hang low tonight to see if anything else happens. I give them a day, maybe two, before they start poking their heads out, looking for answers."

"Doesn't matter," Olivia said. "Davina's deadline is only," she checked her phone, "twenty-one hours and thirty minutes away."

"Thanks for the countdown," I said, rolling my eyes.

"I set a timer, just to be safe," Olivia said, holding her phone up to show me.

I looked back at Bones. "The only reason I listened to LoJack and didn't take him to the hospital is because he wants the same thing I want—to take down the club. But how? Even if we use the info Addy shared with me to have the bikers arrested, their illegal stuff isn't taking place for another two days. I don't have that long."

Bones looked down at the floor, laughing. "First you staple a guy's skin together, and now you're admitting you've known all along where the girl is? *Davina, Davina, Davina...*" he shook his head. "You're full of surprises tonight."

"Right?" Olivia asked, grinning. "She's rocking out her devilish side this week."

I directed a narrow-eyed glare at Olivia, and she took a step back.

"*Geesh*. You're getting cranky," she mumbled.

"I'm exhausted, half my crappy wardrobe is bloodstained, and I have a gang of bikers who want to slit my throat. I have every right to be cranky."

Bones tilted his head toward the bedroom. "One thing at a time. First, let's see if LoJack's awake yet. He knows the Bleeding Souls better than anyone. Maybe after you share what you know, he'll have an idea of how to handle this mess."

Not having a better idea, I followed Bones into the bedroom where LoJack was now upright, somewhat alert, and had a needle in his arm that was attached to an IV bag dangling from a nail in the wall above his head. He lifted a water bottle unassisted to take a drink.

After I shared the details of the arms deal going down Wednesday night, everyone, including LoJack, stared at me with their mouths gaped open.

"What?" I asked.

"You did it," LoJack said, tossing the empty plastic bottle into the corner of the room. "I've been working these guys for years, and in one week, you got the intel I needed to take the club down."

"Not the whole club," Bones said.

"The head of the snake, man." LoJack shook his head. "Unbelievable." LoJack shifted to the side, trying to stand.

The other guy pressed weight against LoJack's shoulder, shoving him down. "If you pop those staples, your insides are gonna fall out."

LoJack settled, wearing a grimace of pain as his face started to sweat again. "The guns," LoJack said, looking back at me. "Hurricane brokered the deal himself? You're sure? He set up the meet?"

"Yes, that's the story I was told."

"Who told you about this?"

"Not saying."

"The girl," LoJack guessed.

I looked up at the ceiling. "I don't know what you're talking about."

"Whatever," LoJack said. "Bones, I need to be there, but I'll need a team. If we can catch Hurricane in an arms deal..."

"Do you have enough evidence to take the other members down?" Bones asked.

"Piles of it," LoJack said, nodding. "I've been waiting to snare Hurricane. If I can net him, it's game over for the Souls."

"Then let's do it," Bones said. "Silver Aces will back the play."

"Make the call," LoJack said. "Just don't tell them where I am. I need to stay close."

"You're not safe here, bro," Bones said.

"Safe enough. I know this area."

"Kami," I whispered, seeing him flinch when I said her name. "You know this area because you keep tabs on Kami."

"She's not involved in this," LoJack snarled. "She's not to know about my involvement in any of this until it's over. Until it's safe."

I held up my hands. "Got it. She won't hear a peep from me. Besides, I'll be long gone by the time this goes down."

"If this plan works, though," Bones said, locking eyes with me, "you'll only have to leave for a few days."

A few days sounded way better than the rest of my life. I glanced at Olivia. It took her a full minute to process what Bones had said, but when she did, she squealed, launching her body at me and wrapping her arms around me as she bounced up and down.

"Settle down," I said, gently pushing her away. "There are still a lot of moving parts that have to go right for this to work in my favor."

"Yeah, but there's a chance it'll end soon. That's a better outlook than we started the night with."

"True." I swiveled my attention back to Bones. "What about him?" I asked, pointing at LoJack. "He's not exactly in good enough shape to protect himself right now, and I'm not equipped to look after him."

Bones sighed. "I'll keep tabs on him tonight. You two can take off."

"LoJack needs rest," the other guys said, stacking a pile of bandages and a bottle of painkillers beside LoJack. "The more sleep he gets, the faster he'll heal."

"Got it," Bones said. "I'll text Donovan and have him pick you up at the end of the drive." He walked alongside the guy toward the door. "Appreciate you coming out."

"Yeah, yeah," the guy said, waving a dismissive hand. "That's what you always say."

Taking advantage of Bones being outside, I hooked my arm through Olivia's and dragged her out the door, not letting her go until we crossed to the van. I wasn't about to waste the opportunity to leave while it was safe.

CHAPTER FORTY-THREE

AFTER DROPPING OLIVIA AT her station wagon in front of Nightshade Treasures, I drove home on autopilot. I walked through the house, checking to make sure the doors and windows were locked before taking a hot shower, trying to relax.

Wrapped in my towel, I entered the library and opened the top drawer of my dresser where I kept my pajamas. I hesitated, my fingers grazing the top of soft cotton pajama shorts. If the bikers came looking for me, I didn't want to be cornered in any form of undress.

Closing the drawer, I opened the bottom one, pulling out a pair of my denim work bibs and a long-sleeved t-shirt. From another drawer I pulled a sports bra, underwear, and a pair of socks before quickly dressing.

Sitting on my bed, I laced up my shoes while looking around. My bed being in the library wasn't going to work. I'd never fall asleep with a row of glass doors only a few feet away. I'd be too exposed. If the bikers came, they could force their way in through the glass doors and there'd be no escape for me.

I looked toward the hallway, considering dragging my mattress to my old bedroom. The room had a door and a lock, but it also now had a gaping hole in the wall to the adjacent room.

I could sleep at Mrs. Paulson's, but what if the bikers were already outside, waiting in the dark? And even if I made it safely inside her house, I'd be putting her in danger.

Hearing something outside at the front of the house, my pulse spiked as I crossed to the living room windows. My neighbor, Boyd Benson, was emptying suitcases from his SUV, returning from his week-long anniversary cruise with his wife.

I moved away from the window and started to pace back and forth between a set of tables. A car door shut, and I jumped, listening for motorcycles. I turned to pace the other direction, crossing into the library before looping back to the living room. On my third loop, I stopped to stare at the bookcase with the hidden room behind it.

The bikers would never find the hidden room. If not for the evil cat, I would've never known it existed, which meant it was the perfect place to hide.

I smiled, opening the bookcase door before hurrying to my bed to strip the blankets and pillows. Dumping my bedding inside the room, I made a nest for myself on the floor before walking through the house and gathering an LED lantern, my phone, my purse, and a chef's knife—just in case.

After setting my loot on one of the lower shelves, I checked the door to make sure it had a release lever on the inside of the room before I pulled the door shut, plunging myself into darkness. I wasn't a fan of dark, small spaces, but I also wasn't a fan of being murdered in my sleep. This would work.

I kneeled and felt around my makeshift bed, finding the edge of my blankets and snuggling under them, not bothering to kick off my shoes. Resting my head on my pillow, I caught the faint smell of the litter box that once occupied this space, but I didn't care. Knowing the bikers would never find me, I drifted off to sleep.

~*~*~

My phone vibrating woke me. I shifted onto my knees and felt along the shelf until my fingers identified my phone. I looked at the screen, seeing Lance's name.

"Hello?" I answered, groggy and confused.

"Uh, hey. You okay?" Lance asked.

"Yeah. Why?"

"Well, see... I'm at your house... Your van is here, but you're not."

"What time is it?"

"Almost nine."

"*Nine?*" With my free hand, I reached around in the dark, feeling the back side of the door for the latch. Finding it, I flipped it up and pushed the door open. Sure enough, the library and living room were bright with sunlight.

I heard footsteps and leaned out the doorway, looking toward the stairway. Lance stood near the newel post, staring at me while still holding his phone to his ear.

"Morning," I said, disconnecting my phone and stumbling over my bedding to stand. "Please tell me you made coffee." Still groggy, I glanced down to make sure I was fully dressed, which I was, before I moved out of the room.

Lance crossed to the hidden room and peeked inside. "Is there a reason you slept in there?"

"Yes." I rubbed the sleepy dust from my eyes while shuffling into the kitchen. The coffee pot was half empty already. Lance must've been waiting a while.

I pulled a cup from the cupboard, filling it and carrying it over to the table.

"You scared of something?" Lance asked, entering the dining room and thumbing over his shoulder toward the other side of the house.

"Sleeping in the library without a door has proven challenging for me." I yawned, raising my hand to cover my mouth. "Man, I feel so out of it. Total brain fog. I always wake to sunlight, but it was like sleeping in a cave in there."

I flipped my phone over, seeing I had six text messages. Three of them were from Lance, the first asking if I wanted to go to the city to pick up a trailer load of supplies today, the second saying he was driving over to check on me, and the third asking where I was. The other three were from Olivia, all asking me to call her. There were a lot of exclamation points in her text. "Did you call Olivia?" I asked Lance.

"Yeah. I called her about two hours ago, trying to figure out where you were. I might've called a few other people to ask them too."

A car door slammed shut outside.

Lance moved to the front window, looking out. "Uhm, Isaac was one of those calls." He chuckled, crossing to the entryway to open the front door. "False alarm!" he shouted out the doorway.

I texted Olivia, letting her know I was fine. She texted back that she'd let Mrs. Paulson know followed by three rows of smiley faces. A second text came through saying she'd be over soon to pick up the cleaning supplies she'd need to fulfill her community service.

Setting my phone down, I cupped my hands around my coffee mug, raising it to my nose. I loved the smell of coffee almost as much as I loved drinking it.

Isaac, dressed in his cop getup, entered the house and followed Lance into the living room. When they reappeared at the archway, Isaac studied me for a long minute.

I smiled a fake smile, showing all my teeth.

He rolled his eyes and moved past me to the coffee pot, starting a fresh pot after filling his cup.

Lance moved over to the table and sat but didn't say anything. Isaac joined us at the table, also not saying anything.

I drank my coffee, enjoying the peace until my thoughts wandered to LoJack. Wanting to know how things were on their end, I thumbed a text message to Bones.

Mere seconds later, Bones replied that he'd left at dawn when a crew of tree cutters showed up. LoJack was awake and alert, still hiding in the cottage.

I glanced up at Lance. "The tree guys are cutting trees today?"

"Yeah, that's why I came out this way. Mark called to let me know they were widening the main drive this morning. Hopefully, when they're done, we can get a roll off dumpster back there."

"Okay." Hopefully the tree cutters wouldn't spot LoJack wandering around inside, but if they did, it was his problem.

"You going to tell us what's going on?" Lance asked, scowling.

"I wasn't planning on it. You guys gave me until tomorrow, remember?"

"We did, but that was before you felt the need to sleep in the hidden room," Isaac said.

"And before I found bloody clothes in the back of your van," Lance said.

I cringed. "You searched my van?"

"After I saw your side mirror was blown apart, yes ma'am, I sure did." Lance leaned back, crossing his arms over his chest. "Start talking."

I took another drink of my coffee, trying to figure out how much to tell them when I heard a vehicle outside. I stood, looking over the top of the mid-height curtains.

Whiskey and Virgil climbed out of Whiskey's truck, walking toward the house. I glanced down at the table, seeing the carport quote they'd left for me. "Was this a good price?" I asked Lance.

"Yeah. About two hundred less than those kits I showed you. Virgil got a good deal on the landscape timbers."

I scribbled a signature, tearing off the top copy of the quote before jogging outside to meet Virgil and Whiskey in the driveway. "Looking for this?" I asked, passing Whiskey the signed off quote.

"No, but while I'm here, I'll take it," Whiskey said, folding the quote and tucking it into an inside pocket under his vest.

"Did you just get up?" Virgil asked, pointing to the top of my head. "You got that bed-head thing going."

"I sure did, which is weird. I never sleep this late." I ran a hand through my hair, my fingers snarling in a batch of tangles. Since I went to bed with my hair still wet, I wasn't surprised. "If that's the worst that happens today, I'll be happy."

Whiskey snorted, glancing away. "I ran into Bones this morning. Sounds like he had an eventful night too."

"Must be going around," I said.

Whiskey glanced at Virgil before looking back at me. "Virgil wants to split the crew today and pull a handful of guys to start work at the cottage, but I told him we should ask you first."

"I want to get a jump on that roof," Virgil said, smiling. "Being Michigan, you never know when the weather will turn."

"Shucks," I said, feigning disappointment. "Lance just told me the tree guys are working out there right now. Unless you want a tree falling on your heads, it would be better to wait a couple of days."

"Well, dang," Virgil said, frowning. "I was looking forward to working on that porch."

"We've got plenty of time," Whiskey said, seeming relieved. "It can wait."

"Yeah, I suppose," Virgil said. "All right then, guess we better get back to the construction site." Virgil strolled back toward the truck.

Whiskey paused, glancing behind us before whispering. "What do I need to know?"

"I doubt the Bleeding Souls will make an appearance during daylight hours at the construction site or here at the Zenner house, but I'd steer clear of the cottage for a few days. Wait until at least Thursday but check in with Bones to be sure."

"You got it. Virgil won't like it, but the cottage is out in the middle of nowhere, so it makes sense." Whiskey's worried eyes lifted to meet mine. "What about you?"

"My bags are packed. I'll be on vacation until the dust settles."

Whiskey nodded. "Stay safe. Call me if I can help with anything." Whiskey crossed the front yard, heading back to his truck.

About to head back inside, I heard the familiar rumble of Olivia's station wagon. I waited as she pulled up and parked in the driveway. Whiskey's truck pulled out and my old truck, the one Noah bought from me, drove down the street and took its place along the street curb. Noah hopped out of the driver's side, jogging around to help his mother out from the other side.

Great. They were all about to gang up on me. I glanced over at my van, seeing the passenger mirror that had been shot out. Add in the bloody clothes Lance found, and I supposed I couldn't blame them for wanting answers.

"It's going to be a long day," I said to Olivia as she skipped toward me.

She scrunched her nose, glancing behind her at Noah and Mrs. Paulson. "Sorry. I tried to tell everyone you were fine, but Lance got them all wound up."

"And you decided to come over and witness my intervention?" I asked, turning back toward the house.

"No, silly. I'm here because I'm hoping someone brought donuts." Olivia hooked her arm through mine. "What are you going to tell them?"

"What do they already know?" I asked in a low voice.

"A lot."

"Crap. I should've cleaned the van last night."

"Should've, could've, would've, but it's too late now. Time to face the firing squad."

Chapter Forty-Four

Entering the house, I refilled my coffee cup and sat in the chair closest to the window, pushing the curtain aside so I could keep an eye on the street. I didn't think the bikers would be stupid enough to come here in broad daylight, but I also didn't want to be caught off guard.

Olivia sat across from me next to Lance, Mrs. Paulson settled into the chair next to me and Noah turned the end chair around and sat backwards in it.

Lance locked his eyes with mine. "Start talking."

I glanced around the table before looking back at Lance. "Remember those bikers we ran into at Kami's place a while back?"

"Yes."

"Last week, the girl who ran away, Addy Randall, witnessed the bikers doing something illegal, and now they're after her. They've ordered me to find her and hand her over to them."

"Which you'd never do," Mrs. Paulson said.

"Right, but they sort of added *or else* and gave me a deadline of tonight to fulfill their request."

"What bikers?" Isaac asked.

"The Bleeding Souls," Olivia answered for me.

Isaac's eyes widened. "Not good."

"Exactly," I said. "They're not the most law-abiding citizens."

"You were just going to take off?" Lance asked. "Just leave us worrying about you?"

"No," Olivia said with a bite of anger. "After Davina left, it was my job to tell everyone what was going on."

"Damn, D," Noah said, shaking his head. "That's cold."

Mrs. Paulson's head swiveled to Noah while her hand moved to rest on top of mine. "It's not cold; it's brave. Davina was willing to set aside her own feelings to protect everyone. Do you think her leaving town without saying goodbye would be easy? That it wouldn't eat at her?"

Lance, Isaac, and Noah ducked their heads.

"She's right," Olivia said. "Davina's been a wreck worrying about everyone."

"What's the plan then?" Lance asked.

"The plan is for me to sneak out of town later this afternoon and hide." I raised my hand to stop him from arguing. "But with the help of a team from Silver Aces, I'm hoping I'll only be gone for a few days."

Lance crossed his arms over his chest. "And if lady luck isn't on your side?"

I looked down at my coffee. "Then I stay away until it's safe. Until Addy's safe."

"You know where the girl is?" Isaac asked, surprised.

"Yeah. I found her after the bikers delivered their threat. I'll take her with me when I leave town."

"If you leave town with the girl, especially if you cross state lines..." Noah said, letting his words trail off. "That's kidnapping."

"I know, but I don't have another option. Hopefully, her dad won't press charges when he hears the whole story, but even if he does, I won't leave her behind to fend off a gang of bikers."

"There's gotta be another way," Lance said, scowling.

"I wish there was, but if I stay, they'll come after me. They'll come after Addy. As handy as you are with a shotgun, there are too darn many bikers to take on in a fight." I looked around the table. "Even if the whole town rallied together to help me, we're no match for them."

"But Silver Aces is working on the problem?" Isaac asked.

"Along with a law enforcement agency that had a guy undercover. If the stars align and everything plays out the way we hope, the bikers will be hauled off to jail Wednesday night."

"But Davina can't stick around that long," Olivia said, holding up her phone and showing them the countdown clock. "She needs to be gone before the sun sets tonight."

"Especially now," I said, nodding toward the driveway. "The undercover cop working the case was shot last night. The bloody clothes in the back of my van were from rescuing him."

Mrs. Paulson gasped.

"He lived," I said quickly, patting her hand. "He'll be fine." I glanced over at Noah, grinning. "I used Noah's suture stapler to piece him back together."

"He's going to have the ugliest scar ever," Olivia said, giggling.

Noah shook his head. "You're just full of surprises this morning."

Isaac chuckled. "You tricked us." He pointed back and forth between himself and Lance. "You conned us into giving you two days to sort your problems, knowing you'd be gone by then."

I sheepishly grinned, but neither confirmed nor denied.

"What now?" Lance asked. "Do we just go about the day like nothing's changed?"

"For the most part, yes." I looked between Olivia and Mrs. Paulson. "But Nightshade Treasures needs to be closed for the rest of the week. The woman who hired Olivia is somehow involved in whatever's going on with the bikers. She might send bikers to the store, looking for me."

Mrs. Paulson started to say something, but I shook my head. "Please. It's not safe. Nothing inside that store is worth risking your lives for."

Her nose crinkled, but she nodded. "Fine. You're right. Noelle had to take Griffin to a doctor's appointment this morning, but I'll text her that we're closing the store for a few days."

I looked across the table at Olivia, but she only shrugged. "I've got community service hours I need to do, and the only thing going on with my PI business is the crazy biker woman and a pile of background checks which I can do from home."

I looked around the table. "None of you can repeat any of this. No one can know about the bikers, the girl, me leaving, none of it. It's not safe to talk about, especially because if word got back to the bikers, it would ruin the sting operation."

"What about Stone?" Isaac asked.

"I feel awful for not telling Stone, but..."

"But what?" Isaac asked. "He's worried. Real worried."

"I know, but Stone is a by-the-book kind of guy. He'll insist on getting a statement from Addy and involving himself in this mess. I promised Addy I wouldn't tell the police. She doesn't want to be forced to testify against the bikers."

Isaac's eyes lowered to the table. "Can't say I blame her, and you're right, Stone would insist on bringing her in."

"If everything goes well, we'll be back home this weekend. If it doesn't..."

"If it doesn't," Isaac sighed, "this is goodbye." He shook his head. "I knew you got yourself into something, but bikers?"

"Yeah," I said, frowning. "My bad luck struck again. Addy was hiding at the cottage, only when the bikers came looking for her, they found me instead."

Noah barked a laugh. "What are the odds?"

"Right?" I said, grinning.

Everyone's expressions lightened a fraction.

"Bottom line is I'll be okay. But while I'm gone, I need everyone to keep their distance from the bikers, and if they come looking for me—even if they trash the Zenner house or the cottage—I need everyone's promise not to interfere."

"I'm a cop," Isaac said. "I can't sit back and do nothing while a gang of thugs turn this town upside down."

"I get that, but after they search the houses, they'll ride off. *Let them.* Please, Isaac. Even if you arrested some of them, it could mess up the plan to take the club down later this week."

Isaac pursed his lips, but eventually dipped his head in agreement. "Are the bikers the reason you slept in the hidden room last night?"

"I figured if they couldn't find me, they couldn't kill me," I said, shrugging.

Mrs. Paulson chuckled before throwing a hand over her face. "Sorry. That's not funny."

"It's kind of funny," Noah said. "Only Davina would be so nonchalant about someone trying to kill her."

"How many times does this make?" Isaac asked with a sly grin. "First there was Collin." He ticked off a finger, counting.

"Collin doesn't count," I said. "He was only trying to scare me."

"Raina," Mrs. Paulson said. "Not once, but twice."

"Her father must've come after her a hundred times," Noah added. "Too many to count."

"Do we count the evil ghost that kept messing with her?" Isaac asked. "Or are we only counting the living?"

"If you count the ghost, you need to count that evil cat," Lance said, wearing a big ole grin.

I leaned back in my chair, somewhat appalled they were listing off all my near-death experiences.

Chapter Forty-Five

After everyone got their fill of teasing me, I walked outside with Olivia and entered through the side door of the garage to gather the cleaning supplies she needed. On the far wall, I got down the extension scrub brush, passing it to her.

"That went better than I thought it would," Olivia said, glancing back toward the house.

"Agreed." I passed her a jug of bleach and set two more on the floor next to me. Grabbing a cleaning bucket, I tossed in a smaller scrub brush, several cleaning rags, and a pair of safety goggles. "I recommend you soak the walls in bleach water before you start scrubbing them— but *wear the goggles*. Getting bleach in your eyes is no fun."

"Sounds simple enough," Olivia said.

"Do you have a garden hose?"

"Yup. I already stole the one behind your house."

I snorted, turning to look at her, and noticed her outfit. She was wearing a sleeveless lilac-colored silky blouse with tan slacks and matching lilac pumps. "Is that what you're wearing to clean?"

Olivia glanced down at herself. "What? It's supposed to be nice out. I thought I'd get a little sun on my arms."

Most of my wardrobe was still in the back of my van, coated in blood, so I didn't have anything to offer her to wear. Deciding to let it be, I crossed to the furniture. "While we're here," I said, dragging the round table out. "I wanted to show you this table. I think it will look nice in your office." I lowered one of the drop-leaf sides. "You can use the guest chairs from my desk."

"It's nice. Are you sure you don't mind? It looks expensive."

"I'm sure. I won't have time to refinish it, but it's still a hundred percent better than your kitchen table. When it's safe to go back to Nightshade Treasures, ask Lance or Noah to move it for you."

"I can do that," Olivia said, bouncing toward the side door.

I picked up the remaining two jugs of bleach and the bucket, following behind her. "As for your cleaning project, you heard the part about wearing the goggles, right?"

"Yup," Olivia said, glancing over her shoulder at me. Not paying attention, when the far end of the extension pole rammed into the doorframe, it knocked Olivia back a step and the other end of the brush slammed into her leg. "Ow, ow, ow," she whined.

I shook my head, setting the bucket of supplies down and taking the extension brush from her to carry outside and load in the back of her station wagon.

Olivia came out and added the other jug of bleach and the bucket of supplies. "Is this it?"

"Yup, you're all set." I looked skyward. "At least you're knocking this task off your list before winter."

"See? Sometimes it pays to break the law." Olivia wore a big smile, moving around the station wagon to the driver's door. "Are you going to check in before you leave town?"

"That's the plan, but if the plan changes, I'll send you a message." I pointed a finger at her. "No matter what, stay away from Nightshade Treasures. Don't make it easy for the woman who hired you to track you down."

Olivia looked past me down the street, her smile dimming. "It's only for a few days, right? You'll be back?"

"You know I don't want to leave, which means I'll be back as soon as it's safe."

She pressed her lips together in a firm line. We held each other's gaze, both of us saying everything we needed to say without speaking a word. I'd miss her. She'd miss me. I'd worry about her. She'd worry about me.

I nodded, closing the back of the wagon and moving into the grass. Olivia dropped into the driver's seat and backed her car down the driveway, intentionally keeping her eyes focused on the street ahead as she drove away.

"You okay?" Lance asked, walking over to me.

"Nope. I'm a nervous mess. I'm half tempted to just leave now. Sounds less stressful than worrying for the next eight hours."

"You'll be too busy to worry," Lance said, walking over to the side of my garage and rolling my trash bin over to my van. "Let's get the back of the van cleaned up, and afterward, we'll work on your bedroom closets."

"I should do something about the mirror too," I said, pointing at the mirror that the bikers shot out.

"Already took care of it. Eric's calling the junkyards, trying to scrounge up a replacement mirror."

I moved to the back of the van and opened both doors, stepping back when I saw all the blood. It looked way worse than I remembered. "How freaked were you when you saw this mess?"

"I thought you were dead, so I'd say I was plenty freaked." Lance picked up the suture stapler and tossed it into the trash barrel. "Most of those clothes need to be tossed."

I looked down at the denim bibs I was wearing. "Good thing these bibs are comfortable. I think they're the only clothes I've got left."

~*~*~

ISAAC LEFT TO HEAD BACK to the precinct, promising to keep Stone distracted. Mrs. Paulson— worried that the bikers would break into the house and trash the antiques still in my living room—asked Noah to help her box and move everything to her garage.

Lance and I cleaned out the back of the van, throwing away three-quarters of my already limited wardrobe before I started scrubbing the worst of the blood out and he sorted the boxes of supplies in the garage. Whiskey showed up with a few of his guys, and I found out Lance had called him over to build the headers needed for the first-floor closet doorways.

I didn't question Lance's reasoning. He'd been quiet and moody all morning, and I decided it was best to leave him be for now.

"Hey, D—" Noah said, poking his head inside my old bedroom where I was watching the construction guys set up support posts to hold the ceiling in place. "Got a minute to help me carry an old sewing table?"

"Sure," I said, following him into the front room.

The sewing table wasn't big, but it had a cast iron support under it, making it heavy for one person to maneuver without damaging it. I picked up one end, and walked backward out the front door while Noah carried the other end.

Exiting onto the porch, we turned in a circle so Noah, being taller, could go down the porch steps first. When my feet met the grass, I looked up, hearing a vehicle. Britt's sporty red car sat idling in the street with her sitting behind the wheel, staring at us like a creepy stalker.

"Shit," Noah said, also seeing her. He set his end of the table down and started across the lawn toward her, but she took off down the street. "Dang it. Just what I needed."

He returned and picked up his end of the table, but instead of lifting my end, I crossed my arms over my chest. "I've had enough. If you want to ice me out, fine. But quit being a jerk to everyone else."

"Stay out of it, D."

"No. I won't stay out of it. It's time for you to man up, Noah. I know you like Britt, maybe even love her, but she's making you miserable."

"D, she has a point—"

"Bullshit. You and I were raised together. Your mom taught us the importance of friendship and loyalty." I waved a hand at the house. "Lance, your mom, Isaac, the Donaldson family... *They are your family*. They're important, and yet you're letting Britt tear those relationships apart. You're letting her turn those lifetime connections into something ugly."

"It's not like that," Noah said.

"It *is like that*. You've been avoiding everyone, not just me. If you're happier without me in your life, I'll find a way to deal with it, but everyone else? I won't silently stand back and watch Britt turn you into *that* guy. The guy who breaks lifetime friendships because it makes his girlfriend happy."

I walked away, stomping up the porch steps and skirting around Mrs. Paulson who stood in the doorway. She followed me inside. "Good for you," she whispered.

I glanced back at the door, checking to make sure Noah hadn't entered the house. "I can't remember the last time I was this mad."

Mrs. Paulson chuckled. "You don't get mad often, but when you do, oh boy, you let it rip. It's about time someone told him how it is." She nodded toward the front windows where Griffin was now helping Noah carry the table across the yard.

"Wow," Noelle said, walking in through the front door. "Sounds like you're dropping the hammer on all the neighborhood boys this week." She wore a big smile. "We caught the tail end of you telling Noah off. Good for you."

I ducked my head, rubbing my fingers against my temples. "He'll probably never speak to me again."

"Oh, I don't know," Noelle said, walking over and slinging her arm over my shoulders. "I know my son appreciates what you did for him. Give Noah time. He'll see the light."

"How is Griffin?" I asked, looking up at her.

"Good. I'm letting him play hooky the rest of the day." She shifted her attention to Mrs. Paulson. "Got your message about closing the store. What's up?"

"I want us to focus on this stuff," Mrs. Paulson said, waving at the boxes. "The house renovations will start soon, so we're moving what's left to my garage."

"Works for me. I'll run home and change clothes." Noelle crossed back toward the door.

"Do you need help?" I asked Mrs. Paulson.

"I'm fine, dear. You go help Lance."

I crossed back to the bedrooms, but neither Lance nor the contractors were around. Seeing the closet doorway header was done, I pulled my gloves on to start nailing in the extra support boards for the closet rod and shelves.

By the time I finished, Lance returned, carrying a full sheet of drywall into the room.

"Where'd the drywall come from?" I asked, hurrying over to help him set it along the far wall.

"I bought a half dozen sheets from the hardware store." Lance glanced away, scratching his chin. "Figured if we button up the walls and install the closet door, when you come back home in a few days, you can move back into your bedroom."

I watched him fidget, and knew he was struggling with the idea of me leaving. We'd always been close, but since my father died, since learning that Lance was my biological father, we'd been spending more time together. I could see that the possibility of me leaving was eating at him.

"Okay," I said. "Let's get the drywall unloaded then."

Lance jerked his head in a nod and led the way out the door.

CHAPTER FORTY-SIX

PEOPLE CAME AND WENT, EVERYONE pitching in to help install the closet door, hang drywall inside the new walk-in closet, and to move antiques and tables to Mrs. Paulson's garage.

"Looks pretty good," Lance said, peeking inside the closet. "I'll swing by later this week to sand and slap another coat of mud on the walls."

"I'd prefer you didn't," I said, capping the bucket of drywall mud. "Best to stay away this week."

Lance waved a dismissive hand. "I'll keep my distance from the cottage, and only come over during daytime hours, but I'll feel better if me and my shotgun stuck close to Mrs. Paulson's house for the next few days. Just in case, you know."

"I know. But don't do anything stupid. This house isn't worth it."

"If you say so."

"Hey, guys," Griffin said from the doorway. "Got a minute?"

"Sure thing," Lance said, grinning like he knew a secret.

I trailed behind Lance down the hall into the library where Noelle, Jared, Noah, and Mrs. Paulson were already gathered. Everyone stared at me, smiling.

I was about to ask what was going on when I noticed the bookcase shelves.

"Lance put the word out for everyone to gather pictures," Griffin said, pointing to a photo taken a good ten years ago.

My eyes scanned all the shelves as I turned in a circle, seeing pictures of myself from when I was only a few days old to as recent as two days ago when I was on the roof with Austin at the cottage. Weaved in and around pictures of me were photos of everyone I held dear. Mrs. Paulson, Isaac, Noah, Olivia and her family, the Donaldsons... Some photos were professionally shot, but most were candid shots from different gatherings over the years, like Olivia's boys playing in the backyard plastic pool.

"We tossed in a few knickknacks too," Noah said, picking up a stuffed animal of a bullfrog from the shelf.

I smiled, remembering back to when we were teenagers and I'd won the frog after beating him at a carnival game. I'd given him the frog as a reminder of how I, a mere girl, had beaten him.

"This is amazing," I said, tearing up.

"We had lots of help," Mrs. Paulson said. "Isaac, Alice, Olivia, her parents, Mrs. Denning... Everyone contributed photos and it took Lance most of the day yesterday to round them up from everyone."

"Wasn't just me," Lance said, blushing. "Mrs. Paulson framed them all."

"I don't know what to say." I picked up a photo of Olivia and me with our faces smushed together. "Even before the fire, I never had this many photos."

"We wanted you to know how much we all care," Noah said. "Especially me. You're my sister. Hope you can forgive me for acting like a buffoon."

"Brothers are supposed to annoy their sisters, right?" I said, smiling.

He chuckled. "I suppose. But I'm a little embarrassed you had to chew me out about the Britt thing."

I searched Noah's face but he only shrugged, smiling.

"While we're all here," Griffin said, getting everyone's attention. Griffin took a deep breath before blurting out, "I'm in therapy for a drinking problem. My counselor recommended I tell people and not try to keep it a secret, so there you go. I'm a binge drinker."

Lance, Mrs. Paulson, and Noah exchanged worried looks.

Griffin nervously chuckled, glancing over at me. "Just say it, right?"

I nodded, smiling. "You did good. I'm proud of you."

"Me too," Noelle said, laughing as she wiped a tear away. "Now quit making me cry."

Mrs. Paulson smiled, walking over to Griffin to place her hands on his shoulders. "You are one impressive young man. Now, what can we do to help you?"

Griffin tipped his head toward me. "I guess just do what Davina did. If you see me doing something stupid, call me out on it."

"We can do that," Lance said, tousling Griffin's hair. "Are we done here? Cause I could use a hand packing up my tools."

Griffin nodded, starting toward the back hallway but stopped to throw his arms around me, hugging me. "Thanks," he whispered before jogging down the hall after Lance.

I blew out a long breath, trying to keep myself from crying. My eyes met Noelle's. She too was fighting off the urge.

"You did right by him," Noah said to me. "You did right by me too." He glanced between his mom and me. "I called Britt and told her it was over. I won't let her keep driving a wedge between me and the people I care about."

Mrs. Paulson pointed at a folding table. "Good. Now make yourself useful and move that table to my garage. I can't handle any more of this serious stuff today. I'm emotionally exhausted."

"Hear, hear," Noelle said.

Noah grinned his easy-going grin, dropped a quick kiss on his mom's cheek and walked over to pick up the table. Noelle followed him out with a small box.

Mrs. Paulson moved to stand in front of me and folded her hands around mine. "It's getting late, and you need to get going. I want you to be long gone before the sun sets, but know this." She pulled her shoulders back, standing proud. "If the cops don't get those bikers, we'll find another way. Never give up hope, because there's no way I'll accept not having you around. Do you hear me?"

"Yes, ma'am." I accepted her brief hug and when she released me, I hurried down the hall into the kitchen and out the side door with my purse and keys in hand.

CHAPTER FORTY-SEVEN

ON THE DRIVE INTO TOWN, I worried about the tree cutters and LoJack at the cottage. With a few more hours of daylight left, I decided to drive to the property and if needed, shoo everyone away.

Twenty minutes later, I followed the much wider, sunnier driveway to the cottage. Parking in the front yard, I felt the sun heat my skin through the windshield. Not only had the tree cutters doubled the width of the drive, but they'd opened up the front yard and cut back the heavy limbs that had been umbrellaed over the house.

I looked around while listening, but neither saw nor heard anyone. Getting out, I hurried to the front door, unlocking it and pushing it open. "It's Davina," I called out. "Anyone here?" I didn't expect an answer, but just in case someone was inside, I didn't want either of us to be startled.

I crossed the room, heading for the kitchen doorway, but stopped when I heard water running in the bathroom. I lunged to the door, throwing it open, expecting to see water gushing out of one of the faucets or pipes. Instead, I stared with my mouth gaped open across the room at a very naked LoJack who was showering in the new shower.

My brain kicked back to life, and I muttered an *oh, crap,* before backpedaling out the doorway. I swung the door closed in my own face, taking another step back.

LoJack wasn't the first man I'd seen naked, but it had been a few years, and none of the men I'd seen were built like him. Embarrassment heated my skin, climbing to the tips of my ears.

"That did not just happen," I said to myself, trying to evict the naked image from my brain.

"Hi, Davina," a female voice said.

I spun around, coming face to face with Kami Douglas. "Uhm, hi, Kami." My face heated again.

"Sorry to just walk in, but the door was open. I saw your van drive past my place, and I followed you, wanting to drop this off." She held up a basket. It was filled with hand tools, work gloves and protein bars. The basket was wrapped in cellophane with a big red bow on the handle.

I stared at the basket, confused. "I'm only fixing the house up to sell it. I'm not moving in."

"I heard," Kami said, placing the basket in my hands. "I'm just glad my days of calling the cops about kids partying out here are over."

"Yeah, I bet." I moved to the back wall and set the basket down. "Thanks for this. I like it. It's fun."

"It was fun to put together," Kami said, grinning. "I didn't know—"

I cringed, hearing the bathroom door open.

"Davina, do you have any human-sized towels?" LoJack asked, walking out of the bathroom dripping water on the floor. Around his hips he'd wrapped a black trash bag and was drying his hair with a terrycloth towel. "Kami..." he whispered, locking eyes with her.

I looked between them, seeing a myriad of emotions cross Kami's face while her eyes scanned down his wet body.

"I'm interrupting," Kami said, shifting toward the door. "So sorry. I, uh, I need to go." She pivoted out the door, practically running.

"Shit," LoJack said, punching a wall.

His trash bag started to slip from his hips and I turned my back to him, facing the front door. Just outside, Kami was hurrying across the yard toward her truck.

The bikers, I thought. Kami's house was across the street, only one mailbox north of here. She would be vulnerable if the bikers came out this way.

I ran out the door. "Kami, wait!"

Kami threw her truck door open and leapt inside, scrambling to leave.

I ran to the passenger side and opened the door, jumping up onto the running board. Kami was trying to latch her trembling hands around the keys in the ignition as tears flooded her vision.

"Kami, it's not what you think."

"It's none of my business," Kami said, not looking up. On the third try, she managed to turn the engine over.

"Maybe not," I said, climbing in so she'd have to listen to me. "But did you see the staples? The ones holding his skin together?"

Kami flinched. "Is he okay?"

"He will be, but he's only here because he needed a place to hide. He's on the outs with his club."

Kami looked out the windshield, listening.

"You saw me drive past your place only two minutes ago. You know there wasn't time for any hanky-panky." I wagged a finger at her. "Get that out of your head. We both know he's not my type."

Kami smirked, despite the tears streaming down her face. Using the back of her hand, she wiped the evidence away. "You tell anyone I cried, and I'll hunt you down."

I grinned. "You'll have to get in line, which is why I climbed into your truck like a crazy person."

"Did he get you into something?" Kami asked, pointing at the house. "Do you need help getting rid of him?"

"No. Actually, he's sort of on my side. For different reasons, we're both hiding from the Bleeding Souls, but I'm worried you'll be in danger. LoJack is the one who negotiated your deal to keep the bikers away from you and your bar. They might try to use you as leverage against him. Now might be a good time for you to take off to a beach somewhere and work on your tan."

"I can't just leave town," Kami said, shaking her head. "I have a business to run."

"I get that. But which scenario is better? One, you close the bar for a week and take a nice vacation, coming back refreshed. Or two, you stay here, and the bikers come after you, maybe even kill you. Heck, they'd probably show up at your bar, smash everything into pieces, then torch the place."

Kami grimaced. "You have a point."

"I expect the bikers to show up either later tonight or tomorrow," I said, jumping out of her truck. "Can you get out of town that quick?"

"Yeah. I keep a bag of clothes and money at the bar." Kami glanced at the dashboard clock. "It'll take me about an hour to shut down and kick everyone out, but my bouncer is a club member. I'll have to be long gone before he starts his shift at six."

"Get going then. Lance knows what's going on. Call him for an update before you come back to town."

Kami looked past me at the cottage. "Is he going to be okay?"

"Honestly, I think he was sticking close by to keep an eye on you. If you leave town, he might smarten up and hide somewhere safer."

She nodded but didn't look away from the cottage. "And the gash along his side with the staples?"

"Do you like that?" I said, grinning. "I got to staple him myself."

Kami flashed a smile, putting her truck in reverse. "Stay safe, Davina Ravine."

"Right back at you, Kami Douglas." I hopped out, shutting the door and stepping away so she could turn her truck around.

I waited until she reached the end of the drive before returning inside. LoJack exited the bathroom, now wearing sweatpants, although he was still shirtless and barefoot. He tried hooking his gun holster to his sweatpants, but gave up, setting his gun on the floor along the back wall.

Not a fan of guns, I scowled on my way past him, entering the bathroom. Scooping the wet terrycloth towels off the floor, I tucked them under one arm and dropped a handful of dry ones down to shuffle around with my foot to dry the new flooring.

"I was going to do that," LoJack said from behind me.

"Why are you showering here? We haven't even installed the glass shower doors yet." I turned toward the mirror, realizing it still had steam in the corners. "Wait, how'd you get hot water?"

"Bones helped me hook the new water heater up last night."

I walked over to the sink, turning on the hot water. Sure enough, it was running hot enough that I had to pull my hand back. "Well... thanks, I guess. But until the doors are installed, *no more showers!*"

"Whatever," LoJack said, walking off toward the kitchen. "I'm starving. Got anything to eat around here?"

"No, I don't. Look, you can't stay here. Your biker pals know about this place. My van is already stained with your blood, I don't need this house coated in it too."

"If they come, I'll hide in the woods."

I followed him as far as the kitchen doorway. He moved to the back door, opening it before lighting up a cigarette. He was tense and quiet, looking out into the back yard while wearing a worried expression.

"She's leaving," I said loud enough for him to hear.

LoJack swiveled his face my way, narrowing his eyes. "Who?"

"You know who. Kami. She agreed to leave town and take a vacation. She's driving to the bar right now to shut it down."

LoJack visibly relaxed. "You're sure?"

"I'm sure. Your biker buddies could do a lot of damage if they popped in for a visit. She knows her bar will be safer if she closes it while all this is happening."

"They're not *my* bikers, or buddies, or my club. It was all pretend, remember?" He crossed back to the front of the house, entering the front bedroom.

I followed him as far as the bedroom door.

Squatting, he tucked the cigarette between his lips and picked up his phone. He winced, moving a hand to his side.

Cigarette smoke wafted toward me. Annoyed, I crossed the room and snatched the cigarette, carrying it outside into the front yard, toeing it out.

"Do you mind?" LoJack asked from the front porch. "I was smoking that."

"Yes, I do mind. Smoking in my house isn't allowed. More importantly, you can't stay here. Kami agreed to leave town, so now it's your turn. Do you need a ride somewhere?"

"Nah. I'll be fine. Bones said he'd drop off a car for me before dark."

"Good. I'd rather the bikers didn't find you here and cause any damage to the house."

LoJack grinned. "Are you worried about me or the house?"

"The house," I answered, trying to keep a straight face.

His grin got bigger, reading the lie on my face.

"Anyway," I said, kicking at a large stone that was poking out of the grass. "What are the chances that you'll arrest these guys later this week?"

LoJack looked past me, thinking. "If they keep to their original plan *and* Hurricane shows up for the meet, chances are good."

"And if they don't stick to the plan? Or if Hurricane doesn't show?"

LoJack sighed. "We're both screwed."

I looked down at the stone, studying it just for the sake of focusing on something. Moving my foot to the other side of it, I kicked it with the heel of my shoe until it loosened and rolled free. "I hate this," I said without looking up. "My life was just starting to get good, and now this. I'm being forced to leave town and start over."

"Tell me about it," LoJack said, looking down the driveway. I was pretty sure he was thinking about Kami.

"LoJack, promise me you'll get these guys."

"It's Owen. My real name is Owen Sable, and no, I won't promise you I'll get them. I can't. I've wasted years of my life trying to take them down."

"At least you chose this life. The club never gave me a choice. They just showed up and threatened me."

LoJack's eyes lit with humor. He tilted his head. "Are you always this grumpy?"

"When I'm being forced to do things I don't want to do, yes!"

"Maybe this will help." He stepped back inside, grabbing a notepad and tearing a sheet off. He walked to the end of the porch, holding it out to me.

I walked up two porch steps and took it, reading it. It was an address with directions. Below the directions was a list of reminders like ditch my phone, no credit cards, no debit cards, and don't log into any websites using my real name.

My stomach hardened into a rock with each bullet point on the list. I didn't have to just leave town, I had to cut off all contact.

"Whose address is this?" I asked, holding up the piece of paper.

"Mine, but it's in my cousin's name. Nobody knows about it. You'll be safe there."

"How will I know when this is all over if I can't reach out?"

"I'll either drive up to let you know, or I'll call the retired neighbor up the road to have him deliver a message."

I folded the piece of paper and stuffed it into my bib's pocket. "Thanks, but if I don't hear anything by Friday morning, I'm moving to my next destination."

"Don't blame you. Safer that way."

I turned to cross the yard, circling the front of my van. "Leave the doors unlocked when you leave. I don't need the bikers kicking them in to search an empty house."

CHAPTER FORTY-EIGHT

BACK IN TOWN, I DROVE to the west side, slowing at Edgar Park. Not only was Olivia still washing the park's bathroom, but Mike Napier, one of the deputies, was filming her with his phone.

I smiled, passing the park, planning to make a U-turn at the other end. Waiting for an approaching car to pass, I realized it was Britt's sporty red car. Without thinking, I hit the gas and cut the steering wheel, blocking the street.

Throwing the gearshift into park, I got out and ran around to the other side. Britt opened her door, pointing at me as she got out. "Move your van!"

"I will—when I'm done saying what I need to say."

Britt's eyes narrowed to mere slits. "I've got nothing to say to you."

"Good, because I don't have much time and I've got zero patience left to listen to the crap you're selling."

"How dare you speak to me like that."

"How dare I? How dare you!" I said, pointing back at her. "You are making everyone miserable. Do you see that? Do you see the wedge you're driving between Noah and everyone else? Do you see how unhappy he is? From day one we took you in, included you in our circle, and you betrayed us. You practically spit in our faces, especially Noah's."

"He's the one who's ruining everything!"

I was about to yell something else when I suddenly saw the bigger picture. "This isn't about Noah..." I said more to myself than to her. "This isn't about any of us."

"It's about all of you!" Britt snapped.

"No, Britt, this is about Raina. This is about Raina drugging you and trying to kidnap you." I moved closer to her as the last of my anger fizzled. I studied the dark circles under her eyes, seeing the evidence that I was right. She wasn't sleeping. She was probably losing weight. She was lashing out because she'd been through a trauma.

Left alone, sleeping in Mrs. Paulson's basement bedroom, Britt had been drugged and dragged to within a few feet of Raina's getaway car. If the guys hadn't been there to save her, Britt would've been tortured and killed. It was the stuff of nightmares.

Britt's glare slipped from her face and her shoulders deflated. She looked ready to break down into tears.

"Britt, I'm so sorry." I reached out, pulling her toward me. "I'm sorry my sister did that. I'm sorry Noah was at my house when it happened, but he *did save you*. He rescued you before it was too late. He was devastated that he nearly lost you. He cares about you."

"Not enough," she cried, leaning her head against my shoulder. "He should've been there for me!"

"He was, Britt. He was right there. He carried you to safety." I waited for her breathing to even out before shifting her back so I could see her face. "You need to talk to someone. Someone who specializes in trauma. You can't keep going the way you're going."

"I'm a paramedic—"

"Yes, which provides you training to deal with someone else's trauma, but this is different. You're the victim. You need someone to help you process what happened."

Britt tugged a wadded tissue from her pocket, wiping her face.

A car honked on the other side of my van, but I ignored it. A minute later a truck pulled around my van's back bumper, squeezing past.

I kept my eyes on Britt. Her lower lip trembled, but she was crying less than before.

"I keep thinking," Britt whispered, peeking up at me, "that you've been through worse. If you got through it, why can't I? Then I just get so angry. Angry at you. Angry at Noah."

"Well," I said, grinning, "a good shrink would probably tell you that comparing yourself to me is a bad idea. I grew up surviving one trauma after another. I got used to my life being threatened. Nowadays, my brain automatically resets after an adrenaline crash, but I'm not sure that's a good thing."

Britt nodded but stared down at the asphalt. "I always thought of myself as brave..."

"You are brave. Remember when we first met? Remember running through the woods with me, trying to catch whoever was out there? That's the real you, Britt. What's happening now has nothing to do with whether you're brave. It's about healing."

Britt didn't say anything, wiping away fresh tears.

"Talk to Noah. Tell him what's really going on. He'll help you. He cares about you."

Without saying anything, she nodded and moved back to her car, climbing inside.

I walked back to my van, hoping she'd talk to Noah. I finished the U-turn and pulled up to park behind Mike's police car. Britt's car continued down the street.

I leaned forward, resting my head on the steering wheel. *Poor Britt.* If I hadn't lost my psychic abilities, I would've seen what was going on. She wouldn't have felt so alone in all this.

~*~*~

EVENTUALLY I GOT OUT OF my van, walking toward Mike while watching Olivia across the park. Olivia was attacking the cinderblock wall with the scrub brush, drenched from the top of her head to her lilac pumps. Setting the brush down, she picked up the hose to rinse the wall, but standing too close, most of the water ricocheted right back at her.

At least she's wearing the safety goggles. I glanced at Mike. "How long has she been here?"

"Maybe six hours. When she first started, she kept squealing every time she accidentally sprayed herself, but as you can see, she's given in to the inevitable."

"How many videos have you posted on the town's Facebook page?"

Mike grinned over at me, lowering his phone. "This'll be my fifth."

I shook my head, laughing while crossing the park to where Olivia was working. When I was close enough, I called out, "You about done?"

Olivia looked over her shoulder at me before reaching up to pull her goggles off. She tossed the hose to the ground but when the nozzle hit the concrete, it shot a burst of water straight up into her face.

Olivia squealed, dancing around.

I ran over and grabbed the hose, keeping the sprayer pointed down. I crossed to the building to turn off the water spigot, dragging the hose with me.

"It went up my nose," Olivia whined, waving her hands in front of her face.

I heard Mike laughing from across the park. Since I was pretty sure he was recording another video, I kept my back to him.

After detaching the hose, I took off the sprayer nozzle and started looping the hose over my arm, letting the other end of the hose drain into the grass. "The building looks pretty good," I said, seeing how white the blocks were. "How's the inside?"

"Okay, I guess. But man, so disgusting," Olivia said, gathering the soggy rags that were lying around.

"I bet. Did you get it all done? Or do you have to come back tomorrow?"

Olivia leaned sideways to wring out her hair. "It's done. This was the last wall."

Keeping the wrapped hose over one arm, I picked up two empty jugs of bleach, carrying them to the trash barrel. When I returned, Olivia had already picked up the last jug and the bucket that now held the smaller scrub brush and the rags. I grabbed the long-handled brush. "I stopped to say goodbye. I'm ready to take off."

"Already?" Olivia asked, walking beside me toward our vehicles.

"Yup. It's almost five." I looked down at the stuff we were carrying. Not wanting to soak everything in the back of my van, I veered toward the wagon, opening the back. When I stepped back to let Olivia move her stuff inside, I saw she was focused on her phone, tapping buttons.

"Dang it. My phone's not working. The battery must be dead."

"Dead or fried?" I asked, picking up the half gallon of bleach and the bucket, tucking them in the back of her wagon before swinging the back door closed. "Please tell me you didn't have your phone on you when you were working."

"I take my phone everywhere, you know that. Besides, it's waterproof."

I shook my head at her, moving toward my van. "Your phone is water *resistant*. Get a little water on it, and it might survive. Drench it for six hours while running a garden hose..." I shook my head.

"*Ugh*. Well at least I have spares at the office."

"You can't go to the office, remember? Big bad bikers might show up."

"But I have to," Olivia whined. "I packed a box for you to take with you. Burner phones and an untraceable laptop."

"That's sweet, but it's too late. It's not safe for *anyone* to go to Nightshade Treasures right now."

She pouted, looking away.

"Chin up. If all goes well, I'll be back in a few days."

"I know, but if it doesn't..."

"Let's not dwell on it, okay? Just promise me you'll watch your back and get out of Dodge if the bikers start sniffing around."

"Yeah, yeah," Olivia said, still pouting. "I already told my mom that we're staying at her house the rest of the week. She thanked me for the advance notice, so she had time to pack away her expensive breakables."

"Good. That's a start. But I know you. You tend to think you're invincible, and that's not the case with these guys."

"I know, I know. I'll play it safe and stay away from Nightshade Treasures."

I nodded, glancing down the street. "Then I guess this is it. It's time for me to leave." I felt a heaviness slam into me, and tears threatened to undo me. I didn't want to leave. I didn't want to say goodbye.

Olivia bounced up and down, grabbing my arm. "Wait, what day is it?"

"Monday. Why?"

"We've gotta go." She shoved me toward the passenger side of my van. "We're late."

"Olivia, I need to leave town."

"It won't take long. Get in." Before I could stop her, she ran to the driver's side and climbed into the seat.

I cringed, thinking how wet the seat would be. The drive to LoJack's secret house would take at least three hours. My butt would be soaking wet the whole way.

I climbed into the passenger side and passed her the keys. "Ten minutes, then I'm gone."

"Uh-huh," Olivia said, starting the van and peeling away from the curb.

Five minutes later she dragged me by the arm inside Mrs. Denning's inn, soaking the side of my shirt with her closeness.

I jerked my arm free at the entrance to the dining room, about to scold Olivia for dripping water on Mrs. Denning's floors when I noticed the room held a good twenty people.

Oh boy, I thought, reading the poster displayed on an A-frame stand. *Daybreak Falls' Sweet Treat Speed Dating.*

I turned to sneak out, but Mrs. Denning snagged me before I could escape. "There you are, dear. I was afraid you weren't coming." She steered me into the room, nudging me forcefully into a chair. I looked up to see Austin grinning at me from the other side.

"Why?" I asked, looking at him before looking around the room.

"We were bribed," Austin said, sliding a sample-sized piece of chocolate cake in front of me. "Mrs. Denning offered the bachelors a free meal for participating."

I looked around the room again, recognizing all the men. Most of them were the same bachelors who took part in the auction last month. Each bachelor had a platter of sample-sized desserts and a stack of small plates and forks.

"The better question is, how'd *you* get roped into this?" Austin asked, his dimple popping out. "I can't see you paying thirty bucks to put yourself through this."

"Thirty dollars?" I asked, glancing behind me toward the entryway where Mrs. Denning was passing Olivia a stack of towels. "Oh, Olivia's going to pay for this one."

Austin barked a laugh. "Relax. It's twenty bachelors, three minutes per bachelor, but only ten rounds. The women get to pick the ten tables they want to stop at."

I forked half the sample-sized cake, readying it to eat. "Ten rounds at three minutes each?"

"Yes, ma'am. This is a thirty-minute gig. Mrs. Denning wanted a full hour, but we refused to stay that long."

"Fine." I ate the cake, moaning at how good it tasted.

I could postpone my trip for another thirty minutes. Setting my fork down, I thumbed out a text message to Bernadette. Since it would take me twenty minutes to get to her place, I let her know to expect me around six, asking her to make sure Addy was ready to leave.

Picking my fork back up to eat the other half of my sample, I asked, "Who has Mrs. Denning's cheesecake?"

Austin's dimple popped out again. "She gave Jimmy-Bart the strawberry cheesecake and I think Jed has the chocolate fudge cheesecake."

"All right, ladies and gentlemen," Mrs. Denning said, getting everyone's attention, "It's time to begin. The timer starts.... *Now*."

Austin and I shared a grin, and he slid me a second sample of cake.

CHAPTER FORTY-NINE

"DON'T FREAK OUT," I TOLD Jimmy-Bart, sliding into the chair across from him. "I'm only here for the strawberry cheesecake."

"Oh, thank goodness," Jimmy-Bart said, patting his chest. "If word got around town that we were dating, it'd kill my business."

"Geesh. Thanks for the ego boost," I said sarcastically, sliding a dessert sample in front of me.

"Sorry, but you know how this town is," Jimmy-Bart said, having the decency to at least blush.

Deciding to change the subject, after I swallowed, I asked, "Anyone in particular you're hoping to talk to tonight?"

Jimmy-Barts' eyes darted across the room to Tara Gibbons, a shy and quiet woman I only knew in passing. When he looked back at me, he said, "No. I'm doing this for the free meal, like the other guys."

I glanced over at Tara. She caught me looking and her cheeks pinked. Her eyes darted to Jimmy-Bart before glancing down at her hands.

I ate the second half of my dessert and picked up my fork and plate, waiting for Mrs. Denning to walk over with the dish tub. "Why are you putting yourself through this?" I asked, placing my plate and fork in the tub. "Why hold a speed dating event?"

"I'm trying to find new income streams for the slower season." She looked around the room, frowning. "I think this will be the first *and last* speed dating event though."

"Makes sense," I said, nodding. "The desserts were a nice touch though."

"I thought so too." Mrs. Denning winked before moving to the next table to clear a plate.

I looked back at Jimmy-Bart. "If I can get Tara over here, are you going to puke on her shoes?"

"She won't sit at my table," Jimmy-Bart said, pouting. "She's the woman I went on the hayride with. I embarrassed her. She'll never go out with me again."

"She probably felt bad about your hay fever reaction. Besides, just because *you* were embarrassed when the kids teased you, doesn't mean *she* was."

Jimmy-Bart fidgeted with his napkin, not saying anything.

I leaned back in my chair, waiting for Mrs. Denning to call time. When she did, I launched to my feet, snared Tara's arm, and not so gently planted her at Jimmy-Bart's table, saying, "You'll thank me later. The strawberry cheesecake is superb."

Tara giggled and I sat in the chair across from Noah.

"I'm surprised you picked my table," Noah said, sliding a dessert plate to me. "I've only got cookies."

"I'm surprised to see you here, at a dating event." I bit off a chunk of cookie.

"Why not," Noah said, frowning. "I'm single again."

"About that," I said, sitting my cookie down. "I think you need to go track down Britt."

"Why? I thought you were happy we split up?"

"I didn't want you to break up, I just wanted you to act like you again. But none of that matters. I ran into Britt about twenty minutes ago."

Noah's shoulders stiffened and his face pinched in a scowl.

I held up my hand, gesturing for him to wait. "Before you yell at me, you need to hear this. Britt is suffering."

"Suffering?"

"Yes, suffering. She can't get over what happened with Raina. She needs help. Professional help, but she seems to feel that'll make her weak or something."

Noah's face shifted to concern. His head lifted, looking past me toward the door before glancing around the room, debating whether to stay or go.

"Get out of here," I said, waving toward the door. "Go find Britt."

Noah launched up and charged across the room and out the door.

As the door closed, Olivia raced to Noah's chair and sat. "I'll sub in for Noah." She plated several cookies and slid them in front of herself.

"No offense, Olivia," Jackie Jones said from the next table over, "but you're married, female, and you look like you walked through a car wash."

"I'm good with that. More dessert for me," Olivia said, shoving a mini cookie into her mouth.

"Time," Mrs. Denning called out.

Without hesitating, I jumped up and dove toward the open chair in front of Jed. In a cross between musical chairs and full-contact football, I rammed into Alexis Bennett, knocking her to the floor as I claimed the chair.

My eyes widened, staring down at her, realizing how aggressive I'd been. "Alexis, I'm so sorry. I don't know what came over me." I covered my mouth with my hands. "Are you okay?"

Alexis stood and stepped back, looking at me like I'd lost my mind before sitting in the open chair across from

Austin. Austin was laughing so hard his eyes were watering.

I looked around, noticing everyone was staring at me, laughing, including Stone who sat along the back wall.

"What?" I stared at everyone. "I like cheesecake!" I looked at Jed and grinned. "Gimme-gimme."

Jed, also laughing, slid my prize toward me.

I forked half the sample and stuffed it into my mouth, moaning and giving Mrs. Denning two thumbs up.

She shook her head at me and crossed the room toward Olivia's table.

I turned back to face Jed when my phone chirped. I picked it up, turning it over to read the text message. I jumped to my feet.

Bernadette's text started with a string of insults about Addy being young and stupid, followed by saying Addy had snuck off. She'd left a note that she'd gone to pick something up and would be back by seven. Bernadette didn't know where, but Bernadette's precious Nova was also gone.

I bolted toward the lobby while pressing the call button on my phone. Holding the phone with one hand, I pulled the door open and raced out onto the porch. When I heard the click of someone answering the call, I shouted into the phone, "What do you mean she's gone? You're psychic! Why didn't you sense her leave?" Sprinting down the steps, I angled across the yard toward my van.

"She tricked me," Bernadette snapped. "It's not my fault. She's a sneaky one. The girl is too smart and too stupid, all rolled into one. She used my phone to text Darrel, inviting him over. She waited until I had my hands full dealing with him and stole my car. My Nova! My baby! I should call the cops!"

"No! No cops!" Almost to my van, I glanced over my shoulder, sensing someone. Olivia was chasing after me. I slowed, focusing on the call. "Do you have any idea where she would've gone?"

"After you left, she was a nervous nelly about leaving town without her money, so I gave her one of my cash envelopes to hold onto. That seemed to calm her. I thought she was fine. The only other thing I can think of is that stupid moped she keeps mentioning. She loves that thing, though for the life of me I don't understand why. It's nothing but a bicycle with a puny motor attached."

"This is bad. Really bad," I said, opening my van door.

Olivia pulled me back, pointing to the other side.

I jogged around, not bothering to argue. "I'll call you back when I find her." I hung up and hopped into the passenger seat.

"Where to?" Olivia asked, pulling away from the curb.

I looked at the keys in the ignition, realizing she'd still had them. It was a good thing she'd followed me outside. "The cottage, but Olivia, the bikers might already be there. I think you should stay here."

"We stick together, like always. If the bikers are there, we'll figure out a way to help Addy, but it's still daylight. Aren't bikers a lot like vampires, only coming out at night?"

"I don't think so," I said, scrolling through my phone to call Bones.

"Yeah?" Bones answered, sounding annoyed.

"Are you at the cottage? Is Owen still there?"

"Owen, huh? Haven't heard him called Owen in years."

"*Bones!* Are you at the cottage or not?"

"No. I'm stuck on the side of the road with a flat tire. I changed the tire, but the spare was flat. What's wrong?"

"I think Addy went back to the cottage. I'm heading over there to look for her."

"Not good."

"I know."

"I'll call Headquarters to send someone out to look for her. You need to get out of town."

"I'm not leaving without her. Besides, if she's hiding, she won't show herself to anyone else. She doesn't know who she can trust."

Bones cursed his frustration. "Get in and get out. I'll call LoJack's burner phone to give him a heads up."

CHAPTER FIFTY

OLIVIA SPED THE WHOLE WAY, getting us to the cottage in record time. We both leaned forward in our seats, scanning the surrounding woods for nefarious bikers while she followed the drive back to the cottage, parking in front of the house. We glanced at each other, exchanging worried looks.

"Are you sure she'd come here?" Olivia asked.

"No, but she knows I have her laptop and Bernadette gave her cash, so the only other thing she'd want is her moped. She hid it in the woods out here somewhere."

"I don't see Bernadette's Nova," Olivia said, glancing at the side of the house.

"Me either, but Addy could've parked on one of the roads along the back of the property line and crossed by foot through the woods. Who knows, maybe she avoided the house altogether and is halfway back to Bernadette's already."

"Fingers crossed," Olivia said, nodding. "Since we're here, let's check inside real quick, then get the heck out of here."

"Fine, but leave the van running—*just in case*."

We both got out and jogged to the door. Turning the handle, I pushed the unlocked door open. Standing shoulder to shoulder in the doorway, we both leaned inside and looked around.

"*Hello?*" I called out. "LoJack? Addy?"

When no nefarious bikers jumped out, I entered, checking the front bedroom before moving to the bathroom, then the kitchen. Olivia trailed close behind me, bumping into me when I stopped just inside the kitchen entrance. The mudroom's back door was open.

"*Hello?*" I called out again, louder this time. "It's Davina! If you're here, call out!"

"Hey," a man's voice said behind us.

Olivia and I both jumped and screamed, spinning around, coming face to face with LoJack.

Olivia leapt to the side, snagging a hammer to raise above her head.

Standing behind her, I grabbed the hammer from her hand before she had time to swing it at LoJack's head.

"Are you crazy?" LoJack asked, ducking while holding an arm out to protect his head. "What's wrong with you?" LoJack was still wearing the sweatpants I'd seen him in earlier, but now he also wore a t-shirt and boots. Likely he'd gotten the call from Bones and had been out searching for Addy.

"What's wrong with *you*?" Olivia asked, jabbing a pointy finger at his chest. "Didn't anyone tell you it's rude to sneak up on people?"

"*Quiet!*" I shouted. "*Listen.*"

We all turned to face the front of the house. The low rumble of motorcycles could be heard from the road. *A lot of motorcycles*. And by the sound of it, they weren't far away.

"*We're gonna die, we're gonna die, we're gonna die,*" Olivia whined, clinging to my arm.

"We need to find the girl," LoJack said. "Where did she hide her moped?"

"I don't know. I thought for sure she'd be here." I crossed to the bottom of the stairs, looking up. "Addy, if you're here, we need to leave, *now*. It's not safe here!"

"I already searched the house, she's not—" LoJack started to say.

One of the cabinet doors under the stairway swung open and Addy crawled out. *"Davina, he's one of them!"* She pointed at LoJack. *"He's one of the bikers!"*

"I know, I know," I said, grabbing her by the hand and dragging her through the kitchen. "I'll explain later. We've gotta go." I tugged harder on her arm, racing out the back door.

"But they're in the woods." Addy pointed toward the south. "I was looking for my moped when I heard their bikes pull up near where I'd parked Bernadette's Nova."

"Then we'll run west." I dragged her by the hand across the back yard.

LoJack and Olivia ran behind us as we entered the woods along the back of the property.

"It's the girl!" one of the bikers yelled over the roar of the bikes.

I ran faster, keeping a tight grip on Addy as my heart raced. The woods were so dense only a sliver of fading sky reached the ground, just enough to light our path. I kept running, kept moving forward, hearing nothing more than the twigs under my feet crack and my own panting breath.

After crossing a narrow clearing, I slowed and turned, glancing back. Olivia and LoJack were falling behind, struggling to keep up. The front of LoJack's shirt had a growing wet patch, soaked in blood. He must've popped a staple.

I dropped Addy's hand, moving to LoJack's side. Lifting his arm over my shoulders, he leaned on me as I propelled him forward. Addy shifted to Olivia's side, locking arms with her before taking the lead.

We weren't going to make it. Olivia and LoJack were too slow. My brain raced to come up with a plan to get us out of this mess, but the noise of the bikers thrashing through the woods behind us kept getting closer and closer. It wouldn't be long before they caught up to us.

My eyes shifted to Addy's back. I had to protect her. I had to make sure she made it out alive.

I watched Addy and Olivia splash through a narrow creek. I tightened my hold on LoJack. He stumbled, nearly taking us both down.

"I can't keep going," he groaned.

"You don't have a choice. Think about Kami. Think how ticked off she'd be if you died. Not happening. Not on my watch. Don't rat me out, but I'm a little afraid of her."

LoJack grunted, but stepped up his game, moving faster.

~*~*~

"*STOP*," LoJack called out, panting heavily.

I stumbled to a stop, scanning the woods behind us for signs of the bikers. I could hear them, but I couldn't see them. By the sounds I heard, there were at least a dozen of them, maybe more.

I glanced at a red-faced Olivia. She was coated in sweat and trying to catch her breath. We'd run at least two miles already and she looked ready to drop.

I looked at Addy. Youth was on her side, but her face was full of fear.

"We need a plan," LoJack said, resting one hand on his knee, bent over. His other hand was against his side, coated in blood. "I can't keep running."

"We have to," I whispered. "There are too many of them."

"Exactly," Olivia said. "There are too many of them to outrun. If it was only you and Addy, you'd make it, but LoJack and I are slowing you down."

"I'm not leaving you," I told her. "Get that out of your head right now. Come on. Let's go."

"I'm staying," LoJack said, straightening. "I'll do what I can to lead them away."

"They'll kill you. You don't even have your gun."

"Yeah, I know," he said, panting. "I lost it in the woods earlier when I was searching for her," he said, nodding to Addy.

"See? You don't even have a weapon! You can't stay."

LoJack shrugged, leaning over to pick up a stick. "It's not a hammer, but it'll work," he said, nodding down at my hand.

I looked down and sure enough, I was still gripping the hammer I'd taken from Olivia earlier in the kitchen. *Huh.*

I held it out, offering it to LoJack, but he shook his head. "Keep it. Hopefully you won't need to use it." He pointed toward the west. "Keep going west but veer a few degrees south. Try to get around their net. If I see Bones, I'll send him your way."

The sound of the bikers yelling and thrashing through the woods drew closer.

I smacked a kiss on LoJack's cheek and forced the hammer into his hand. "The kiss is from Kami. No matter what happens, don't die. I don't want her mad at me."

"Aw," LoJack said, smiling through a grimace of pain. "You do care."

"You wish," I said, grinning. "Be safe."

LoJack nodded. "*Go. Run.*" LoJack scurried between a pair of trees, moving north.

Addy tugged on my arm, antsy to get going. I ran ahead, leading them to the west. Daylight was fading fast. Soon we'd be stumbling around in the dark.

"Odd time to ask," I whispered over my shoulder, "but did either of you happen to bring a phone? I left mine in the van."

"Mine's fried, remember?" Olivia said.

Addy's scared eyes shifted from Olivia to me. "Mine's at Bernadette's with the battery sitting next to it."

"Great," I mumbled. I tried recalling the layout of the acreage behind the cottage from the satellite images I'd looked up a few nights earlier. Most of the land was either farmland or hunting properties.

Farmers. I looked to the south, remembering old man Thompson's place. "We're going to shift to the south, but we'll need to run faster."

"I'm not sure I can," Olivia whined.

I slowed and waited until Olivia was beside me to lock my arm through hers. "We have to."

With Addy on one side of her and me on the other, we kept Olivia running forward, and when she stumbled, we kept her upright, half dragging her while veering to the south. If we could make it to old man Thompson's house, we had a chance.

CHAPTER FIFTY-ONE

IF IT WEREN'T FOR THE moonlight glowing over the field as we exited the woods, I would've missed it. "The maze," I whispered, pointing. "Head for the maze."

"Are you sure?" Addy asked, looking around. "Maybe we should keep running."

"I can't keep going and neither can Olivia. I won't leave her behind, but if you feel safer without us, run past the maze and hide inside old man Thompson's barn."

"No way," Addy whispered. "Are you nuts? In the horror movies, they always kill off the girl who leaves the group. We stick together."

Olivia, still struggling to catch her breath, pushed forward, stumbling over the uneven dirt.

Addy and I both tightened our grip, hauling her upright, and ran with her across the field toward the maze's back entrance. Just as we entered the stacks of hay, a shot rang out in the distance. The hay bale next to my head *poofed* a cloud of dust, tossing strands of hay into the air.

"*Run, run, run,*" I yelled, yanking Olivia by the arm as I led us deeper into the maze.

Racing down the rows, turning willy-nilly in whichever direction, I was soon lost, not knowing which way we were heading. When we reached the next intersection, needing to choose between left and right, I hesitated.

"Which way?" Olivia asked between gulps of air.

Hearing the bikers' voices getting closer, I took off to the right, moving away from them. At the next crossroad, I turned right again.

"I don't think this is the way out," Addy whispered.

"We're not trying to get out," I whispered, hurrying down another row, meeting a dead end.

"Now what?" Addy asked, resting her hands on her knees.

"Now we hide," I said, reaching up to tug one of the bales of hay down, moving it back toward the dead end and setting it vertically on its smallest end. I crossed back, pulling down the next bale. "We build a wall to create a cubby hole to hide in."

Addy, catching on to the plan, shifted Olivia to the back wall before helping me with the next bale, dragging it back with us.

After stacking two bales vertically next to Olivia, we stacked the other two bales on top of each other to start our new wall. Hopping over the bales, squeezing into the smaller space, the three of us worked together to shift the other two bales over our heads, setting them in place.

In the dark, I felt Olivia's hand grab mine, clenching it.

"I really hope this works," Addy whispered.

I reached past Olivia to grab Addy, tugging them both down into the small space we'd built. I felt Olivia's body expanding and contracting as she tried to slow her breathing. A cloud above us moved, and when the moonlight lit our cubby, I saw Olivia had her eyes closed as she nervously fiddled with her pendant, a calming habit she'd picked up years ago.

While she rubbed the pendant between her fingers, I caught the flicker of moonlight reflecting off the silver.

Silver. Silver Aces. I grabbed the pendant, staring at it. It was the security alert necklace the Silver Aces' team had forced her to wear back when my sister had escaped. Yanking it, I broke the chain and pulled the two sides of the pendant apart.

I glanced up at Olivia who stared down at the pendant. Her mouth formed an O-shape before she glanced up at me and gave me a weak smile. Silently, she mouthed the word, *sorry.*

Addy lifted a hand to get my attention. "What is that?" she whispered.

"An alert necklace. If it's still active, an army of men will be sent to rescue us."

"What if it's not active?"

I raised a finger to my lips, hearing footsteps somewhere on the other side of the wall outside the maze. We all waited, listening, barely breathing.

"This would be fun if Hurricane wasn't acting so damn crazy," a man said, not more than ten feet away.

"Just think of the fun we'll have when we find the women," another man said as their voices moved away from us.

I shuddered, sensing his dark intentions.

Holy sam-ol-ey, I thought. *I sensed them. My abilities were back.* Maybe Bernadette's theory was right. Maybe my abilities were linked to life-and-death situations, and my brief lull from danger caused them to stop working.

Either way, now wasn't the time to dwell on the why of it all.

I leaned forward, digging my fingers into the soft soil. Closing my eyes, I smiled as my energy roared to life, ready to be unleashed.

Centering it, I let it gather before pushing it outward, first tasting Addy and Olivia's spikes of fear before reaching further to pick up spikes of anger and frustration from the bikers who wandered in or around the maze, coming closer and closer.

My head snapped to my right, sensing a biker on the other side of the hay wall. I held my breath, hoping Olivia and Addy would remain silent. The energy shifted down the corridor, moving in the opposite direction.

I opened my eyes, glancing at Olivia. She opened her mouth, about to speak, but I frantically shook my head. Addy slapped a hand over Olivia's mouth.

They both locked their widened eyes on me.

I pointed to the stack of hay behind Olivia.

Olivia nodded, turning sideways to stare at the hay like she could see through it.

"This blows," a voice said. "I could be at the bar getting hammered." He hit the wall of hay, likely working out his frustration.

Olivia yelped, startled by the movement.

"Who's there?" the voice called out as the top bale was rolled off. A biker's head peered down at us with a slow smile spreading across his face. "*I got 'em*," he yelled.

Scrambling to think of an idea, I stood, but no ideas came.

Olivia popped upright and threw a handful of dirt into the biker's face.

Anger filled his expression as he wiped the dirt off. Reaching across the bale, he latched onto a wad of Olivia's hair.

Olivia screamed. The biker laughed, dragging her toward him. Olivia twisted, trying to get away, but the biker hauled her backward, stretching her over two bales of hay.

Addy wrapped both her arms around Olivia's legs, looking at me for answers. I just stood there, empty handed and without any idea of how to stop this, wishing I wouldn't have given LoJack my hammer.

My abilities. I still had my abilities.

I mentally reached out, sensing the bikers moving faster toward us. They were both inside and outside the maze, circling us.

The hay bales on all four sides were torn down and tossed away from us, leaving us exposed.

The biker who'd grabbed Olivia now held her a good foot off the ground with both his arms locked around her.

Someone grabbed me from behind, but rather than feeling a spike of fear, I was flooded with images. I choked and coughed, trying to fend off the visions while fighting his hold on me.

Unable to break free, I looked downward, seeing Addy huddled on the ground with her arms wrapped around her head. I couldn't let them hurt her.

Think, Davina.

Mentally scrambling, I tried to sense an opening we could use to escape, but there were too many of them. We'd never be able to fight our way out.

I whimpered as a switchblade snapped open next to my cheek. Closing my eyes, terrified, I almost missed the change in energy just beyond the maze.

It was only a flicker, but it was familiar. I stretched my energy, feeling a massive void move toward us. A void like that meant only one thing: *the men from Silver Aces.*

Military trained. Guns. Moving fast as they split apart, some circling the maze, others entering it.

We needed to stall. Give them time to rescue us.

I locked eyes with Olivia who was still struggling, trying to fight for her freedom. I shook my head ever so slightly. She held my stare, trying to read my face.

"*This is your fault,*" I screamed at her. "*If you weren't so slow, we would've escaped!*"

"*My fault?*" Olivia screeched. "You're the one who got us into this mess. You have the worst luck of anyone I know. Trouble has been following you since the day we met."

"*Oh, yeah?* Well did you ever think my life would've been less chaotic if I didn't have you as a friend? I mean really, Olivia? You let a client dupe you into finding the girl! How stupid can you be?" I cringed, feeling the bite of guilt as the words poured out unfiltered.

Olivia winced at the last line, my words striking a little too close to the truth. "Stupid? You're calling me stupid?" she shouted. "I'll show you stupid!" She tried to lunge away from the biker, trying to get at me with her hands curled into claws.

The biker holding her laughed, shifting his grip and lifting her higher off the ground.

"Bring it!" I yelled. "I've been waiting years to punch you in the face!"

"*Enough!*" the biker behind me yelled, startling us. "Say one more word and I'll kill you both." He flashed the knife in front of my face again, less than an inch from my eye.

We both stilled. *Okay, now what?*

"She's feisty," another biker said, moving closer to Olivia and running his grubby finger down her cheek. "I like it when they fight back."

I felt sick to my stomach.

Another biker stepped over a bale of hay and used his boot against Addy's thigh to keep her pinned to the ground. "This one's younger. I sure hope we get to play with her before we kill her."

Addy swung a fisted hand upward, nailing the biker in his privates.

The biker roared in pain, stumbling back.

Addy scrambled to her feet, launching herself over two bales of hay, trying to escape. Before she'd made it halfway over, another biker shoved her back. She landed in the dirt, rolling toward my feet.

"Stop it!" I yelled. "Don't hurt her! Don't you dare touch her!"

"Or what?" the biker behind me hissed in my ear. "What are you going to do about it?"

Hurricane. It was Hurricane who was holding me. He moved the switchblade to my neck, and I pushed backward, pressing into his shoulder to distance the blade from me.

"If you hurt her, if you hurt either one of them, I won't tell you what I know," I said, trying to sound unafraid.

"Oh, I'm sure we can get you to talk," Hurricane hissed.

"Your brother," I said, picking up on fragmented visions. I felt Hurricane's body stiffen.

"What do you know about my brother?"

I focused my energy on him, letting my extended net over the Silver Ace's team drop. "You're afraid of him. You should be. If he finds out what you've gotten the club mixed up in, he's going to be furious. It's *his* club."

"It's *my club*," Hurricane hissed.

I felt a sting on my neck and knew he'd nicked me with the knife. One wrong word and he'd slice my throat.

"Davina!" Olivia's voice called out.

I raised my eyes to meet her wet ones. Taking a deep breath, I continued talking to Hurricane. "If your brother finds out about the deal you made, if he finds out about—"

Hurricane jerked my shoulder, turning me to face him. "He won't find out." He shoved me, *hard*.

My butt hit the dirt next to Addy. I looked up.

Hurricane leaned forward, knife out. "My brother won't find out because none of you are going to live long enough to tell anyone."

"One more thing," I said while draping my arm across Addy and nudging her behind me.

"Last words?" Hurricane said, sneering down at me.

I shrugged, feeling less afraid.

"Say what you've gotta say," Hurricane ordered.

I glanced up and around the tops of the hay bales. "It's about time," I said, wearing a hint of a smile.

A confused look crossed Hurricane's face before he glanced up to the top of a hay bale, turning in a slow circle. He gasped.

The bikers around us staggered and cursed under their breaths.

A slew of red laser dots lit up, pinned to the bikers. Both cops and the men and women from Silver Aces, dressed in tactical gear, stood perched on top of the hay bales, pointing their guns at the bikers.

I pressed my weight backward and with my arms spread wide, I smushed Addy into the ground while trying to shield her the best I could.

Three red dots were sitting on Hurricane, two on his chest and one on his forehead—dead center between his eyes.

"Playtime's over," Bones said. "Back away from the women one step at a time. Anyone moves funny, they die."

I sensed Olivia being released before she crawled toward me, ducking into my shoulder. I could feel her body tremble against mine.

I kept my eyes on Hurricane, waiting to see what he'd do. When his energy shifted, I rolled over, pulling Olivia on top of Addy and draping myself over them. I squeezed my eyes shut.

Gunshots fired all around us, sounding like fireworks.

Chapter Fifty-Two

"Get him off me!" I shrieked.

"I got him," Wayne, one of the guys from Silver Aces, said, lowering himself off the haybale wall to the ground. He grabbed one of Hurricane's feet, dragging his corpse face first off me into the dirt.

I scrambled to stand, shuddering. Hurricane's blood and other bodily bits were in my hair and soaking through the back of my shirt. "Ew."

"Are we alive?" Addy asked, sounding unsure. "Did we seriously just live through that?"

"I think we did," Olivia said, climbing up before pulling Addy up off the ground. "That was exciting."

Addy and I both pinned Olivia with a look.

"Well, you know what I mean."

"Not really," Addy said, looking around. "These guys friends of yours?"

Cops were moving in to cuff the few bikers who were still alive. The four bikers closest to us were dead. I stepped around the hay bales, exiting the maze. More cops were in the field, checking bikers for heartbeats.

Bones jump off the haybale wall, landing beside me. He was full-out, ear-to-ear, smiling.

"LoJack?" I asked.

"He's fine. He managed to take down two bikers before he passed out from blood loss. One of our guys stayed behind to get him medical attention."

I nodded, glad to hear LoJack would be okay. "Thanks for rescuing us. I thought we were goners."

"No sweat. It was kind of fun." Bones gave Donovan, one of the owners of Silver Aces Security, a fist bump as he passed. "We were surrounding that house a few miles back when Olivia's alert necklace went off. Tech radioed us from Headquarters to give us the coordinates."

I glanced back at Olivia who was smirking, staring down at her feet.

Addy hooked her arm through mine, seeming giddy. "I can't believe you know all these hot guys." She grinned at Bones. "Hi, I'm Addy."

Bones scowled, glancing at me before glancing back at Addy. "You're a kid. Not interested." He turned and walked away.

"Geesh," Addy said, watching him walk away.

I tugged her along, moving away from the chaos and narrowing my eyes at her. "I swear, if you ever get yourself mixed up in something illegal again, you'll be grounded until you're thirty!"

Addy's face lit with a smile. "Grounded? I've never been grounded before."

"That's about to change," I said. "Don't think I'll leave one bit of information out when I tell your dad about all of this." I stopped, trying to decide which way to go.

My van was at the cottage, but I was too tired to walk that far. I started toward old man Thompson's house which was easy to see now that every light inside his house was on. The poor man was probably coming unglued with fear.

"My father won't care. Just so you know," Addy said, following behind me.

"If he doesn't step up, I will. It's time you learned the hard reality of consequences. If I need to ground you myself, make you a prisoner in my home, that's what I'll do."

"Really? Cool," Addy said, hurrying her steps until she was beside me. "Would I still have my own room?"

I stopped to look at her. The tough, smart-mouthed teenager was excited at the thought of someone caring enough to ground her. I shook my head. "You're not alone anymore. I mean it. If your dad can't get it together, we'll work it out so you can stay with me. But give him a chance. I think he might just surprise you."

Addy snorted again. "You're dreaming." She skipped ahead, heading for the farmhouse, unconcerned that she didn't even know who lived there.

"Is her dad really that bad?" Olivia asked as we started walking again.

"He's made some huge mistakes, but I think Addy taking off shook him back to reality. Let's hope he'll do better."

"And if he doesn't? Are you really going to take her in?"

Would I? I wondered.

Living across the street from the Donaldson family, I'd witnessed for myself how tough a job it was to raise teenagers. And the Donaldson boys were good kids, seldom misbehaving. A teenager like Addy would be a handful to manage full-time, but someone needed to step up before it was too late.

I shrugged. "We'll see."

CHAPTER FIFTY-THREE

I STEPPED OFF THE A-FRAME ladder and rolled my shoulders, trying to loosen the knots in my muscles from the hour I'd spent sanding the drywall mud along the ceiling seam. My skill level at mudding drywall was improving, but my back and shoulders were telling me that I'd done enough today. I scraped my putty knife clean and rechecked the bucket of mud to make sure it was sealed. It was.

Exiting the smaller upstairs bedroom, I peeked into the larger bedroom. Davey was stapling the insulation between the studs and Griffin was following him, running the new electrical wire through the already drilled holes. "Looking good, fellas, but it's almost time to go."

"Dang," Davey said. "We were hoping to get the drywall up in this room today."

"It can wait until next weekend," I said. "I'll be busy at the construction site during the week, so we'll put the drywall up next Saturday."

"Okay, just let me finish this wall. It's supposed to get cold this weekend."

"Davina?" Jared called up the stairs. "You've got company."

I crossed to the stairway and went downstairs, taking the mud pan and putty knife with me. "This place is still a dump," Addy said, pushing her red-framed glasses up her nose.

"Manners," her dad scolded, poking her in the arm.

Addy ducked her head to hide her smile.

"Give me a minute. I want to rinse the mud off my tools."

"I'll do it," Jared said, taking my mud pan and putty knife and moving into the bathroom.

"Is Davey upstairs?" Addy asked, blushing.

"Yes, he is, but he'll be down in a minute."

"I'll just be a second," Addy said, racing up the stairs.

Trent started to say something, but I raised my hand, stopping him. "It's not worth it. Let her be."

Jared chuckled, walking back out of the bathroom while drying my putty knife. "Besides, Addy likes Davey, but Davey has an eye on a girl from college. And Griffin likes Addy, but Addy won't give him the time of day. It's an anti-love triangle."

Trent glanced up the stairs, smiling. "Ahh... To be young again."

"No thanks," I said, crossing the room to where I'd left my purse.

In less than a week, Trent and Addy had gone from a decade spent ignoring each other to one of the biggest parent-child shouting matches I'd ever seen. Their verbal slinging only ended when I brokered a truce.

Trent agreed to let Addy transfer schools to Daybreak Falls and on nights he was working late, Addy was allowed to stay at my house. In exchange, Addy agreed to follow the terms of her grounding, which included no moped for the next three months and to spend every Saturday with Trent for some much needed father-daughter time.

I still wasn't sure if they liked each other, but at least they were both making an effort.

I dug out the pages I'd tucked inside my purse and separated them. "Here you go," I said, handing Trent his pages. "This is your half of the list for the city kids you need to track down. Jared and I will handle the kids in Daybreak Falls."

Trent pulled an envelope from his back pocket, exchanging it for the list. "Here's the money you'll need."

We'd agreed that demanding the fake IDs back from the city kids without paying them was acceptable, but since Addy was transferring schools, we were offering a refund to the kids in Daybreak Falls if they surrendered their IDs willingly. Starting at a new school mid-semester was hard enough. I didn't see a reason to make Addy enemy number one on her first day.

I'd also transferred all her blackmail files to my computer, erasing them from her laptop, just in case she got any bright ideas about restarting her business.

"How are things going between you two?" I asked, taking advantage of Addy being out of earshot.

"Better. She's still wary of me, but I don't blame her. I really screwed up."

"Yes, you did, but she wants to trust you. She wants to believe you'll be there for her. It'll take time though."

"Yeah, I guess. I hate to admit it, but you were right about the grounding thing." Trent rolled his eyes, grinning. "My daughter is over the moon about being grounded."

"I get why it makes her happy." I leaned against the living room wall, looking out the front windows. "I remember when my neighbor, Mrs. Paulson, grounded me, making me go to her house after school for two weeks straight instead of hanging out with Olivia. It felt good to be treated so normal, like the other kids."

"Your parents sucked too?"

"My mom died when I was young and my dad, well, he had some mental issues." I shrugged. "You could say everyone raised me." I looked across the room, seeing Lance and Jared had once again scattered tools and supplies everywhere. "I feel the urge to clean this mess up, but it's time to leave."

Trent crossed back to the stairway, leaning against the railing. "Addy, time to go! I'm holding a long list of names and addresses. It's going to take forever to track all these kids down."

"Coming..." Addy called out, jogging down the stairs.

Griffin, smiling wide, followed Addy. Davey trailed behind Griffin, rolling his eyes.

"Guess it's time for us to head to town too," Griffin said. "Are you going to be at Davina's house this weekend?" he asked Addy.

"Yeah," Addy said, peeking a glance at Davey. "Trent's dropping me off later tonight."

I caught Trent wince when she called him by name instead of saying dad, but I didn't feel sorry for him.

"Cool," Griffin said, scuffing his shoe against the floor. "Maybe we can hang out."

Before Addy could drop a smart-mouthed remark, I interrupted, "She's grounded, remember?"

"As are you," Jared said, talking to Griffin but winking at me.

"Sucks to be you guys," Davey said, chuckling. He crossed the living room to dig through a box of supplies. "Davina? You cool if I stay here and work while you guys do your thing?"

"Sure. Just—"

"—*don't do anything stupid*," Griffin, Davey, and Jared finished for me, all three grinning.

I laughed, slinging my purse over my shoulder.

CHAPTER FIFTY-FOUR

WE REGROUPED AT EDGAR PARK with Jared in charge of the money, Griffin checking names off our list, and me collecting the fake IDs. Being we lived in a small town, Griffin had been able to connect with all the kids on the Daybreak Falls' list via either text message or social media, ordering them to show up with their fake IDs *or else*. Anyone who didn't, would get a personal visit from me and Isaac, which was guaranteed to include a conversation with their parents.

I shook my head, looking down the long line. Addy had been busy. Nearly every teenager in town was waiting for their turn, ducking their heads, trying to hide their faces.

Thirty minutes later, I tossed the last ID card into the plastic bag.

"That's it," Griffin said, handing me the clipboard. "Only one kid didn't show, and he's a dumbass."

"Language," Jared scolded, swatting the back of Griffin's head.

Griffin grinned.

I took the clipboard, frowning at the circled name.

"What's wrong?" Jared asked.

"This kid's address. He lives in Felony Row."

"Felony Row?" Jared asked.

"Yeah, it's a stretch of housing just north of the city. The county cops named it that because the residents who live there tend to cycle through the prison system."

Jared took the clipboard from me. "I'll drive out to deal with it." He nudged Griffin. "You can walk home."

"Walk? It's like a mile away," Griffin said, looking across the park. "Can't I just call Mom for a ride?"

"No. She's working until two o'clock today. Get going. It'll be good for you."

Griffin pouted, dragging his feet but crossing the park.

"I can give him a ride," I whispered to Jared.

"Nah. He's fine. Besides, I'm not very good at this punishment thing. Noelle caught me playing video games with Griffin last night," he said, chuckling.

I laughed, nodding at the list. "Are you sure you want to take that over?"

"Yes. I owe you. In fact, every parent in town owes you." He picked up the sack of IDs, shaking his head. "What are you going to do with these?"

"Addy is coming over later to cut up ID cards. She'll have blisters by the time she's done. The list in the city was three pages long."

Jared shook his head, passing the bag back to me as we crossed back to our vehicles.

"How's Griffin doing with the counseling stuff?" I asked.

"Good. He likes his counselor. Having someone explain how Griff's anxiety issues factored into his binge drinking helped me to understand some of this."

"It's funny," I said, squinting. "I never saw Griffin as an anxious person."

"Compared to you, he's probably not," Jared teased, elbowing me. "You're the biggest worrier I know."

"Hey, I'm getting better," I said, nudging him back.

"You are," Jared said, nodding. "I don't know what changed, but you seem more relaxed lately. As for Griffin, he's always been comfortable around you, so I'm not surprised you never noticed how anxious he can get."

"Makes sense," I said, nodding. "I suppose it helps that he's always had Davey to lean on."

"Yeah, I got lucky with those two. My brother and I hated each other growing up. I'm glad my boys aren't like that. Davey's been great with Griffin, supporting him through all this."

Reaching our vehicles, we said our goodbyes, parting ways.

I was about to climb into my van when Isaac pulled his police cruiser along the curb to park. I moved to the front bumper, waiting for him to get out before saying, "Well, hello, Officer Hooper. Are you here to arrest me?"

Isaac chuckled. "Maybe. You did seem to be having some kind of event in the park without a permit."

"I wouldn't call it an event."

Isaac rocked back and forth on his feet. "What would you call it then?"

I grinned. "Let's just say that we gave the teenagers in Daybreak Falls a chance to come to their senses before we took further action."

Isaac's lips curved upward. "And what was this further action?"

"You, me, and their parents having a little chat about their recent behavior."

"Is that so," he said, chuckling. "Any of the kids stupid enough not to show up?"

"Just one. But Jared's driving out to the kid's house now. I suspect the kid either doesn't care if he gets in trouble or he couldn't find a ride to the park."

"What's his name?"

I checked the list. "Devin Schuller."

"Ah," Isaac said, nodding. "He's on my list too."

"Troublemaker?"

"Nah, not yet. But he could pivot that direction, you know? Not a lot of role models in his life."

I knew exactly what Isaac was saying. "You're a good man, Isaac Hooper."

"I do what I can, but some days... it just doesn't feel like enough."

"Well, since you know Devin, maybe you should call Jared and give him the scoop before he pounds on the kid's door."

Isaac chuckled. "I'll do that." He started back toward his cruiser. "Are we still invited for dinner tonight?"

"Yes, sir. Pretty much everyone said they were coming, including both Austin and Stone, but they promised me they wouldn't fight."

Isaac snorted. "I'll bring two pairs of handcuffs. What about Britt? Did she and Noah work things out?"

"Yeah, they're doing good. Britt stopped by my place last night, apologizing for the way she treated me. She's back to tagging along with Noah to mooch dinner off everyone, so warn Alice."

"I'll do that," Isaac said, chuckling. He lifted a hand, waving goodbye before dropping down into his seat and shutting the door.

Chapter Fifty-Five

Driving to Nightshade Treasures, I was about to open the storefront door when it was thrown open. It would've hit me in the face if I hadn't jumped back so fast.

Bernadette stormed out the door with Darrel trailing behind her wearing his happy-go-lucky smile. "What is wrong with you?" Bernadette screeched at him. "I'm not a teenager! Holding hands in public is unacceptable. Keep your hands to yourself!"

"Enjoying the day I see," I said, smiling.

Bernadette swiveled, directing her scowl at me. "I've been looking all over for you." She glanced back at Darrel and pointed to her Nova which was parked curbside. "This doesn't concern you. Wait for me in the car."

"Okay, snookums." Darrel blew her a kiss before walking away, unaffected by her tantrum.

"I thought you two broke up?" I asked when Darrel was out of earshot.

"We did, but then I called him." Bernadette's face mushed together in something between a look of frustration and a look of disappointment. "A woman has needs."

"Ew." I held up my hand to stop the conversation.

"Not like that. Flowers, chocolates, romance. The occasional dinner out."

"Oh."

"Of course, sex is nice too."

"Ew." My hand went back up.

"Oh, quit being such a prude."

"I'm not being a prude, but I'd prefer not to think of you and Darrel naked. Now, why were you looking for me?"

"We need to discuss the adjacent lots out at the cottage to decide how best to resell them."

"And you couldn't ask me later tonight when you came over for dinner?"

"That's a social event," Bernadette huffed. "We don't discuss business in front of strangers."

"They're not strangers, they're—" I stopped myself, shaking my head and steering the conversation back on course. "Okay, let's meet here Monday to discuss the lots. Does three o'clock work?"

"I have yoga at three, but I can meet you at two o'clock."

I raised an eyebrow at Bernadette, looking down at her broad body and trying to imagine her maneuvering into one of those impossible yoga poses. I couldn't see it. I could, however, imagine her toppling over to knock over a row of other yoga people.

I shook off the thought. "I'll make two o'clock work, but before you run off, explain this," I said, pointing to her outfit. "Why are you dressed like me?"

Bernadette was wearing denim overalls over a long-sleeve t-shirt, almost identical to the outfit I was wearing. The only difference was the color of our shirts.

"What?" she said, scowling. "I saw you in them and thought they looked comfortable."

"I guess they are, but I'm wearing them because they're cheap. I don't feel bad when I ruin a pair working at the cottage. What's your excuse?"

"I'm wearing them because they don't have a waistband that cuts into my full-figure body. Get over it." Bernadette stomped away.

Darrel was in the passenger seat of her Nova, waving like a maniac. I waved back before hurrying inside Nightshade Treasures. I really hoped Bernadette didn't bring Darrel with her to dinner tonight.

"Boys, stop running please," Mrs. Paulson said, snagging Tait by the arm to stop him.

I was about to ask why she was watching the boys when I felt a cold chill come over me. I looked up and across the suite. "Where's Olivia?"

"In the back office with a client," Mrs. Paulson said, snagging Trevor with her other hand, trying to get them to settle.

I crossed to Mrs. Paulson's desk, pulling her up from her chair. "Boys," I whispered, "go with Mrs. Paulson to Daddy's office next door. Be very quiet. We're playing a prank on Mommy."

I locked eyes with Mrs. Paulson, whispering while leading all three of them to the door, "Call 911."

"What?" Mrs. Paulson stared at me for a long second before glancing across the room. "Are you sure?"

"Ninety percent sure."

"Close enough," Mrs. Paulson said, herding the boys out the door and down the sidewalk.

While crossing the suite, I grabbed a tall vase off a display table. Sneaking into the back hallway, I stopped short of the conference room door. The door was open, but I didn't dare peek inside. Instead, I kept myself tucked against the wall while I listened.

"Please," Olivia said. "Do whatever you want with me, but when you're done, leave out the back door. Don't hurt my boys."

"The little rugrats out front?" a woman asked. "They're yours?"

Way to go, Olivia, I thought.

"Please, leave them alone. They're innocent," Olivia cried.

"In my line of work, the innocent are fair game. I think I'll let you watch while I put a bullet in their heads."

"You don't want to do that," Olivia said, her voice growing stronger. "You have no idea the number of people who'll come after you if you hurt them."

"Like who? Your sidekick carpenter girl? Or your nerdy husband? Ooh, I'm so scared." The woman tee-heed, enjoying herself. "I'm the daughter of a cartel boss, honey. You can't scare me."

Using my renewed abilities, I knew Olivia stood on the opposite side of the room, probably with a gun pointed at her. The woman was closer to the door, but if she saw me coming, she might shoot one of us before I had a chance to whack her with the vase.

I looked down at the vase I was holding. It didn't make for the greatest weapon—*but it might work as a distraction*.

Stepping back and around the corner into the main room, I tossed the vase a few feet away to the other side of the hallway entrance.

Silence.

I waited, pressing my back against the wall.

"No, don't go out there," Olivia pleaded. "It was just my boys. They're always breaking things."

"Stay here," the woman ordered.

Closing my eyes, I focused on her energy. She edged down the hallway, staying close to the conference room side of the hallway wall, just around the corner from me.

Inches away, I could hear her breathing. I stiffened, readying myself to spring out. The bells above the storefront door jingled.

Forcing myself not to look away, I saw the barrel of her gun rise. I pounced, latching both hands on her arm and shoving her gun hand down. The gun fired.

Headbutting her before ramming my shoulder into her chest, I knocked her off balance, causing her to stumble. I hooked my leg behind hers, sending us both tumbling to the floor, still wrestling for control of the gun.

Olivia came out of nowhere, pouncing on top of us, swinging wild fists. *"You will not hurt my boys!"*

I ducked, trying not to get hit in the face while I peeled the woman's fingers off the gun. Once free, I slid it away from us and crab walked a few feet back to keep from getting pummeled.

Olivia screamed, full of fury. *"Nobody messes with my boys. Nobody! I'll kill you, you filthy wench!"*

The woman was shifting her knees up, getting ready to toss Olivia off her. Tucking in behind Olivia, I threw myself over the woman's legs, pinning them back to the floor.

Looking behind me, I saw Isaac and Officer Napier moving across the suite, guns out. Isaac jerked his head to the side, silently ordering me to move away. I rolled off the woman, scurrying several feet clear before pressing my back against the wall.

"Mike, get Olivia off the other woman," Isaac ordered.

"Uh, sure. I'll try." Mike holstered his gun and maneuvered himself closer, trying to avoid Olivia's flying fists. Latching under her armpits, he dragged her kicking and screaming into the conference room. Isaac scrambled forward, holding his gun on the woman who was lying on the floor. "Don't know who you are, lady, but didn't anyone ever tell you not to piss off a mama bear?"

The woman eyed Isaac while swiping the back of her hand at the blood running from her nose. She tilted her head, looking down the hall. The back door opened, and Officer Robert Gable entered, gun out.

The woman's body relaxed and she raised her hands, surrendering. Rolling onto her stomach, she interlocked her fingers on the back of her head, familiar with the arrest process.

Isaac did another head jerk motion, this one directed at Robert.

Robert holstered his gun, pulling out his cuffs.

"Davina!" Mike called from inside the conference room. "Help!"

I crawled around the woman to the conference room doorway, seeing Olivia still kicking and thrashing about, trying to tear free from Mike's hold. Standing, I grabbed a nearby open bottle of water and splashed water into her face.

Olivia sputtered, blowing the water out of her mouth and nose. "What'd you do that for?"

"Because you were acting like a lunatic." I waved my hand toward Mike. "Stop fighting. It's over."

Olivia settled, glancing back to see Mike was the one holding her. "Sorry... I just..."

"Yeah, yeah," Mike said, releasing her. "You just lost it."

Olivia locked eyes with me, tearing up.

"Don't you dare cry," I said, pointing a warning finger at her. "The boys are next door. They're safe."

Olivia deflated, sinking to sit on the floor.

I sat beside her, putting my arm around her. "Better?"

She nodded. "I thought she'd hurt them. I thought…"

"I know." I tugged her against me, and she leaned her head against my shoulder.

Mike stepped over us, entering the hallway.

Isaac popped his head inside the room. "What's this all about?"

"That's the woman associated with the bikers who hired Olivia to find Addy," I explained. "Apparently, she's associated with a cartel. Call Owen Sable with the narcotics division in the city. I'm sure he has a warrant with her name on it."

Isaac shook his head, glancing back in the hallway. "I don't know how you two get mixed up in so much trouble." He disappeared down the hallway.

Olivia giggled against my shoulder before sitting up. "We make a pretty awesome team you know."

I leaned my back against the row of filing cabinets and tilted my head, looking at her. "It's not going to work."

"What's not going to work?" Olivia asked, a sly grin appearing.

"Buttering me up so I'll go with you on the stakeout tonight."

"*But it's a cheating spouse case*," Olivia whined. "You know I hate going on those alone. It makes me feel all icky, waiting to take a picture of some bald, overweight dude while he's doing the nasty."

"The answer's still no."

"Fine, but you owe me."

I laughed, pointing toward the hallway. "I just saved your life. How do you figure I owe you?"

"That?" Olivia asked, rolling her eyes. "That doesn't count. I had it under control."

I raised an eyebrow at her.

"Okay, fine. I owe you. Happy?"

I looked down at my sneakers, one of which had a layer of blue paint across the toes. I lifted my hands, seeing more than one scrape and the beginnings of a callous. My thoughts jumped to the three pot roasts I had cooking in the crockpots at home. I knew by the time the dinner hour rolled around, there'd be at least a dozen people at my place to feed, most of whom would bring a side dish to serve.

"You know what," I looked over at Olivia, "I *am* happy. Life is finally getting good."

"It'd be better if we spent some quality time together tonight."

"Don't push it," I said, laughing. I pushed myself up to stand. "Now come on. You know the drill. It'll be an hour at least to give our witness statements." I held out my hand, offering her help up from the floor.

Olivia slapped her hand in mine, pulling herself up. "Let's do this." She marched out into the hallway, back to her normal self.

I smiled, following her.

What's next for Davina and her family of friends?
Seven Crimes – Follow the Signs

BooksByKaylie.com

KELSEY'S BURDEN SERIES
Living a life of lies, ex-cop Kelsey Harrison is hunting her enemies—the people responsible for taking her son.

DAVINA RAVINE SERIES
Small-town amateur psychic Davina Ravine is in over her head, stumbling from one mystery to the next while unraveling her dark family secrets.

SLIGHTLY OFF BALANCE
When small-town baker Deanna Sullivan finds herself in danger, Reel Thurman returns home, vowing to protect her.

DIAMOND'S EDGE
Raised on the wrong side of the law, Diamond Cambell knows how to navigate within the criminal world. And when someone targets her in a deadly game, they'll get what's coming to them.

Printed in Great Britain
by Amazon

CW00455417

The Field Guide to Supergraphics

The Field Guide to Supergraphics

Graphics in the Urban Environment

Sean Adams

WITH 375 ILLUSTRATIONS

 Thames & Hudson

First published in the United Kingdom in 2018 by
Thames & Hudson Ltd, 181A High Holborn, London
WC1V 7QX

© 2018 Quarto Publishing plc

This book was designed and produced by
Quid Publishing, an imprint of the Quarto Group
The Old Brewery
6 Blundell Street
London N7 9BH

Book design and text:
Sean Adams
www.seanadams.design

British Library Cataloguing-in-Publication Data
A catalogue record for this book is available from
the British Library

ISBN: 978-0-500-02134-7

Printed and bound in China

To find out about all our publications, please
visit **www.thamesandhudson.com**. There you
can subscribe to our e-newsletter, browse or
download our current catalogue, and buy any
titles that are in print.

Previous, top left
HERE AFTER
London, England
Craig & Karl
2017

Previous, top right
Rapport: Experimental Spatial
Structures
Berlin, Germany
J.Mayer.H
2011

Previous, bottom left
Magic Box, State Grid Pavilion
Location: Shanghai, China
ATELIER BRÜCKNER GmbH
2010

Previous, bottom right
Adidas Gym, Germany
Herzogenaurach, Germany
Büro Uebele
2011

Contents

Interviews

Introduction

As a species, we have added language and imagery to our structures for thousands of years. The Egyptians adorned their temples with hieroglyphs and paintings to tell stories and explain how to live and die. The Olmec and Aztecs built large cities and huge pyramids, and then filled the interiors with words and images. Western cultures built great cathedrals and used stained glass and Biblical stories to create narratives for a mostly illiterate population.

Opposite
Ceiling, Gallery of Maps
Vatican Museum, Vatican City
Cesare Nebbia and
Girolamo Muziano
1580

S·MICHAEL·IN·MONTE·GARGANO·APPARET

Below, left
Heliopolis, Egypt: The Obelisk
Detroit Publishing Co.,
1905

Below, right
Wall at Dendera, photograph
detail
Francis Frith
1850–1880

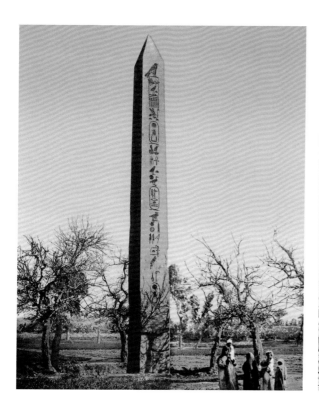

Today, we continue to use words, symbols, images, and forms as part of our built environment. We may not be telling the story of Hathor, Quetzalcóatl, or Moses, but we use design to bind communities, create branded spaces, help a visitor find the way, and create delight with colour and typography.

Supergraphics were long considered an inferior form of communication, used on dull architecture to hide flaws, and in many instances, this is exactly what happened. Large bands of coloured stripes adorned bland waiting rooms and municipal government offices in the 1970s.

However, the definition of supergraphics has changed over the last twenty years. Once, only a large geometric design on a wall or building was a supergraphic. Today, the term encompasses architectural delineation, wayfinding and identifying signage, illustrative murals, and branding elements. Digital technology now allows for interaction and screen-based media on a large scale. The audience can now actually communicate with an architectural space in a unique and personal manner.

The difference between a large overwrought design on the wall and a successful supergraphic is typically based on three points: a strong concept, interaction with the architecture, light, and space, and relationship to the viewer. Many people can paint stripes on a wall, whereas a designer can use the entire volume, sense of place, and context, and change the environment to create a story with words, colour, and shapes. This book includes examples of the best supergraphics internationally. These are evidence of the sense of delight evoked when a beautifully crafted graphic solution, smart concept, and awareness of the community are combined.

1

Types of
Supergraphics

Opposite
Rapport: Experimental Spatial
Structures
Berlin, Germany
J.Mayer.H
2011

Typographic

Opposite, top left
Lisbon Bikeway
Lisbon, Portugal
P-06 Atelier
2009

Opposite, top right
Public Theater Lobby
New York, New York, USA
Pentagram
2013

Opposite, bottom left
Adidas Gym, Germany
Herzogenaurach, Germany
Büro Uebele
2011

Opposite, bottom right
QV Car Park
Melbourne, Australia
Latitude
2011

These forms use words, logos, and phrases typeset in one or a range of typefaces. Typographic graphics serve as decoration or as identifying signage to demarcate a particular space. A designer will apply brand messages, information, and wayfinding content to walls, panels, and other surfaces. Typographic graphics succeed when they are integrated with or react to the architecture or the space of an environment.

Colour

Opposite, top left
Commonwealth Bank
Sydney, New South Wales, Australia
*Frost
2012

Opposite, top right
Google Japan
Tokyo, Japan
Ian Lynam Design
2015

Opposite, bottom left
Project Colour Corp.
Cambridge Elementary
Concord, California, USA
Gensler
2015

Opposite, bottom right
Art es Part
Barcelona, Spain
Anna Taratiel
2012

These supergraphics utilize colour as the primary means of reinforcing a brand message, introducing a decorative element, or guiding the viewer as wayfinding signage. The graphics may also enhance the architecture and structure of a dull interior or exterior.

Typically, the colours are rich and vibrant, and can withstand varying light and weather conditions. Production techniques include handpainting on a wall or digital output: on vinyl material that is applied to the wall, as a projection, or using screen-based media.

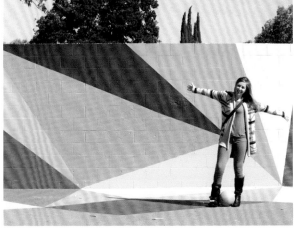

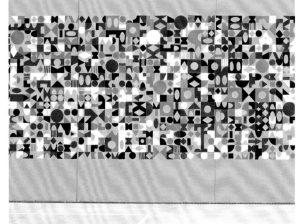

Graphic

Opposite, top left
3M Australia Headquarters
Sydney, Australia
THERE
2011

Opposite, top right
Sweet as One
Hong Kong, China
Craig & Karl
2015

Opposite, bottom left
100 California Signage Programme
San Francisco, California, USA
Volume, Inc.
2016

Opposite, bottom right
Open Your Space
Siping, Shanghai, China
Tongji University College of
Design & Innovation
2015

Purely graphic- or image-based forms can create meaning and add interest to an environment. The most successful examples work with the architecture and challenge the viewer to see a structure differently. The forms may be patterns, solid shapes, illustrations, or photographic images. A designer may simulate three dimensions, apply graphic forms that reinforce a brand message, or assist in wayfinding.

Vernacular

Opposite, top left
Somos Luz
El Chorrillo, Panama
Boa Mistura
2013

Opposite, top right
LinkedIn Australia Headquarters
Sydney, New South Wales, Australia
THERE
2015

Opposite, bottom left
Salumeria G. Albertini shopfront
Verona, Italy
Artist unknown
Photograph: 2013

Opposite, bottom right
Planned Parenthood offices
New York, New York, USA
Pentagram
2016

The term 'vernacular' refers to language. In design, it is a culture's specific visual language. This can take the form of colours related to the local community, typography based on historical references, or materials that are indigenous to, or synonymous with, a region, such as flip-flops and Sydney.

Vernacular design can be created by a trained designer. As integral to a unique culture, it can also be made by non-designers, such as a sign painted by a shop owner. The primary factor of vernacular supergraphics is a visual solution based on a specific set of cultural connections.

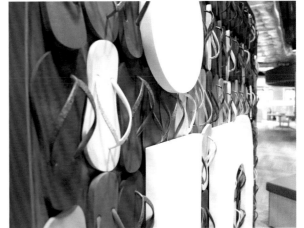

Typographic

Opposite
Vai com Deus (Go with God)
Lisbon, Portugal
R2 Design
2008

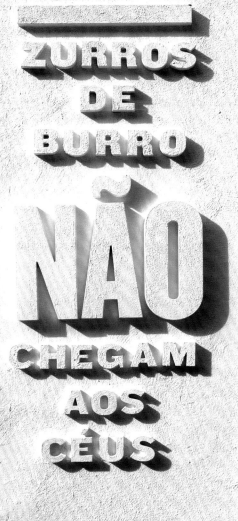

13–17 East 54th

Pentagram

Location: New York, New York, USA
Usage: Wayfinding
Date: 2010

A car park is typically dull. One might find the occasional coloured column or wall, but they are rarely worth noticing as places for innovative design. Pentagram partner, Paula Scher, reimagined the experience and produced a typographic symphony in black and white.

As shoppers exit shopping centres, heading out into vast multi-storey car parks, the most important thing on their minds is not the items they purchased, but rather, 'Where the @#$% did we park the car?!' Scher's solution addressed this issue directly with bold and simple graphics and typography.

The seven-storey car park, owned by Cohen Brothers Realty and managed by Ampco System Parking, is located at 13–17 East 54th Street, between Fifth and Madison Avenues, and adjacent to an office building at 3 East 54th Street, also owned by Cohen Brothers.

Scher's first concept was to fill the windows of the non-descript structure with the question, 'Did You Remember Where We Parked the Car?' Codes in New York City, however, required more traditional signage on the facade, now in elegant neon. These supergraphics identify parking levels and elevators. The interior signage also acts as a backseat driver. Set in Verlag, the large scale typography includes instructions for drivers: 'Slow and steady wins the race', 'Do not stop here', and 'Continue'.

Opposite
Typically, signage dedicated to costs, rules, and codes is ignored and treated in the same fashion as an 'Exit' sign. Here, however, the designer Paula Scher enlarges the information to create compelling and refined typographical compositions.

O 1 HOUR
6.19
2 HOURS 37.17
10 HOURS 41.39
24 HOURS 49.00
'SIZE ADD'L 9.29
LY RATE 608.24
'SIZE ADD'L 84.48
.375%
NG TAX EXTRA

AMPCO
SYSTEM PARKING
13-17 EAST 54TH ST.
LICENSE NO
1288781
CAPACITY 225
OPEN
24 HOURS
7 DAYS A WEEK

THE DEPARTMENT OF CONSUMER AFFAIRS OF THE CITY OF
NEW YORK HAS ISSUED THE FOLLOWING
LICENSE TO THIS BUSINESS:
LICENSEE: AMPCO SYSTEM PARKING
LICENSE NO
1288781
THE DEPARTMENT OF CONSUMER AFFAIRS
42 BROADWAY NEW YORK, NY 10004 (212) NEW YORK
ATTENTION MANHATTAN RESIDENTS:
BE ELIGIBLE FOR AN EXEMPTION FROM THE 8% PARKING TAX
CONTACT: NYC DEPARTMENT OF FINANCE PARKING TAX
NOTICE
UNLESS
VEHICLE BY FIRE, THEFT OR EXPLOSION LIMITED TO $25,000
ADDITIONAL FEE PAID WHEN VEHICLE FIRST PARKED
AND RECEIPT ISSUED FOR SAME.

ATTENDANT PARK
WAIT FOR PARKING TICKET. READ YOUR PARKING TICKET.
LEAVE IGNITION KEY ONLY.
ONLY ATTENDANTS WILL PARK AND DELIVER CARS
CARS MUST BE LEFT WITH ATTENDANT
NOT RESPONSIBLE FOR ANY ARTICLES LEFT IN CAR.
ATTENDANTS ARE PROHIBITED FROM REPAIRING ANY VEHICLE
UNAUTHORIZED VEHICLES
WILL BE TOWED AWAY AT OWNER'S EXPENSE.
CHECK CLOSING HOURS.
MONTHLY ACCOUNTS MUST BE
PAID ON THE 1ST
OF EACH MONTH
OR DAILY RATES WILL BE CHARGED.
CARS
SUBJECT TO BEING HELD AFTER THE 5TH.
CARS SUBJECT TO ROOF PARKING WHEN APPROPRIATE

STAND STILL BRAK
CLAIM
FOR DAMAGES W
NOT BE ACCEPT
UNLES
VEHICLE IS CHECK
UPON ENTERING A
LEAVING GARA
WE ARE NOT RESPONS
FOR REMOVA
RADIOS, STER
EQUIPMENT, RA
DETECTORS, TELEPHONES, IPOD

Below and opposite
Black-and-white supergraphics are installed on the elevator doors used to transport cars to other levels.

Following
The language provides more than simple directions. The signs suggest better ways of living and puns based on the traditional directional signs.

Adidas Gym, Germany
Büro Uebele

Location: Herzogenaurach, Germany
Usage: Branded environment
Date: 2014

The Adidas Gym alters the traditional gym environment of grey concrete by introducing colourful and vibrant graphics. Büro Uebele added dynamic numbers and letters to enhance the environment, conveying energy. Reaching up to 10 metres (33 feet) high, the graphic elements are more than background wallpaper. They communicate actively with the gym's users. The numbers and letters contain coded messages. The viewer either deciphers these or dismisses them as random forms.

The numbers and forms are typical of the typographic language of various sports. The palette, borrowed from the athletic world, combines colours in unexpected ways. A viewer may spot the number '13', worn by German football player Gerd Müller. He or she may then notice the '10' and '23', and decode these numbers. A visit to the bar reveals the meaning of the large letterforms 'Om', 'Bliss', and 'Relax'.

Opposite
An illuminated large numeral in the meditation room relates to the eight jhanas, the states of meditation in Buddhism.

Below
Typography and colours appropriated from the language of sport create the dynamic and energetic atmosphere of the gym.

Following
Huge illuminated numbers on the ceiling of the space communicate the concept of a bright idea. Fittingly, the number '54' refers to the year of Germany's miraculous 1954 FIFA World Cup Final victory. Large black-and-white letters contrast with the extreme colour of other graphics in the gym.

Right
The numerals invite the viewer to
create meaning and determine
what each number references. The
graphic '49', for example, may be
boxer Rocky Marciano's perfect
record of forty-nine wins.

Opposite
The typographic and colour
treatment of sporting language
continues in the locker room,
identifying individual lockers.

Following
The graphic system continues in the
café area of the gym. The designer
adopted a simplified colour palette
in single rooms.

Bloomberg
San Francisco Tech Hub
Volume, Inc.

Location: San Francisco, California, USA
Usage: Identifying and wayfinding
Date: 2015

For their tech hub in San Francisco, Bloomberg wanted to create a space that embodied their status as an established and innovative technology company and leader. Bloomberg is famous for data mining and innovative applications. Volume used the ancient motif of the five Platonic solids that represent the base materials of the physical world. These symbols 'unfold' in tessellating horizontal bands that speak to both the physical world with white vinyl and the creative world with translucent plastic.

Historical vignettes are silk-screened in metallic gold on steel panels and attached to the existing concrete columns. These include a diagram of a viewer's eye motion when viewing the Nefertiti bust, Darwin's *Origin of Species* chart, and an infographic that compares the size of an organism against its life span. Interactive elements are also incorporated into the space.

Opposite
A system of clips on the wall facing the reception desks allows the employees to post information about events ('Today' and 'Soon') and more inspirational content ('Always').

Below
The Platonic solids motif grows more complex in the larger communal spaces, such as the 'Void' library.

Following
The same motif also plays out in a spatial way on the stairwell doors, where the 'view' of the five foundational solids on the stair exit doors 'rotates' as one ascends from floor 22 to floor 23.

Since data are at the heart of Bloomberg's work, meeting rooms are identified not only by their names but also by an exact GPS location.

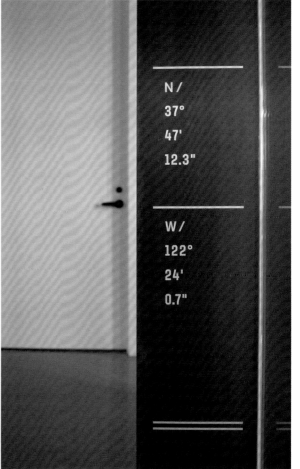

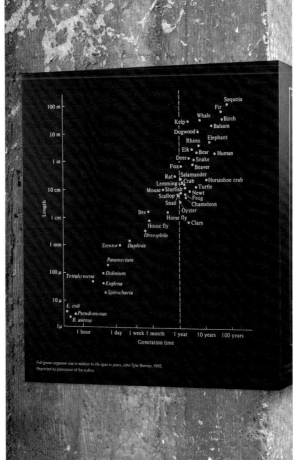

Full grown organism size in relation to life span in years, John Tyler Bonner, 1965.
Reprinted by permission of the author.

The Field Guide to Supergraphics

BRIC
Poulin and Morris

Location: Brooklyn, New York, USA
Usage: Wayfinding
Date: 2015

BRIC produces and promotes arts and media programmes throughout Brooklyn, including live music and performing arts, contemporary art exhibitions, and community media broadcasts. Newly named BRIC House, the 3,700-square-metre (40,000-square-foot) site boasts an urban foyer featuring contiguous panes of glass on the ground-level facade, which integrates the interior main floor with the street outside.

Poulin and Morris deconstructed the parallelogram of BRIC's existing logotype into various planes, perspectives, and dimensions for a series of directory, identification, and wayfinding signs that wrap around corners and doorframes at dramatic angles.

Graphics overlap with nearby doors, so that information is always visible, whether the doors are opened or closed.

Right and opposite
Wayfinding and identifying signage engage the viewer with parallax graphics; the words change appearance based on the position of the viewer.

Below and opposite
For the foyer's amphitheatre,
the name 'Stoop' is fully legible
when viewed at certain angles
and appears as a decorative
pattern when seen at others.

Brighton Dome
Johnson Banks Design Ltd

Location: Brighton, England
Usage: Branded environment
Date: 2013

To those in the know, the Brighton Dome was a key cog in the city's vibrant arts sector. Unfortunately, even when standing just yards away, visitors often didn't know where it actually was due to chronically low visibility. The Dome is on the opposite edge of the world famous Royal Pavilion estate and had struggled to clearly identify and differentiate itself from its famous royal cousin.

Johnson Banks used the building's extraordinary architecture as the starting point for an environmental graphics programme. From the entrances to the main building, and the concert hall's ceiling itself, extravagant Regency-era 'scalloped' shapes are a major feature throughout the building.

The 'big D' is created with architect William Porden's careful curves echoed in the serifs. The 'D' is then used in all digital, printed, and architectural applications throughout the site. The palette is restrained – black, gold, and white – setting a restrained design 'stage' to allow performers and productions to shine and dominate.

Suspending banners with simple layers of information helps the visitor in the complex setting. Johnson Banks also used the site's rich history on the walls. Key facts, figures, and phrases about its history are used at huge scale to evoke some of its past and more recent successes.

Opposite
The Brighton Dome identity echoes the building's architecture. The heroic large scale of the logo serves as an identifier for the entrance of the structure.

Concert Hall Stalls Right ∨|

Left and opposite
Large banners serve as
wayfinding and identifying signage.
The typeface, Mrs Eaves, is limited
to one weight, style, and colour.

Following
Phrases, facts, and other
information are painted around the
walls, recalling traditional gold leaf
applications of ornament on the
walls and ceiling of the building.

Brighton Dome, built by William

rden in 1804–1808   to house the Prince Regent's horses, was celebrate

GLG Global Headquarters
EGG Office

Location: New York, New York, USA
Usage: Branded environment
Date: 2014

GLG is the world's largest network for one-to-one professional learning. Their global headquarters in Manhattan, designed by Clive Wilkinson Architects, is the first activity-based working office space in the United States, reflecting GLG's desire to support interdisciplinary collaboration and interaction.

Instead of a desk, workers store personal items in one of the lockers located around the building. Each locker's locale is known as a 'neighbourhood'. GLG provides a laptop and a licence to work across a variety of office landscapes, ranging from conference rooms and sofas to the company's coffee bar.

EGG Office used the text from GLG's mission statement to create the logo mural in the reception area. Similarly, EGG designed murals using text related to various practice areas and featuring images appropriate to those disciplines.

Below
The lift foyer welcomes visitors
with the bold black-and-white
palette and high-contrast logo on
a simple black background.

Opposite
A cluster of lockers is used to house
employees' items. The numbers
refer to each 'neighbourhood'.

Below

Letterforms on wall panels communicate GLG's brand promises and mission, and reinforce the internal message of GLG's values.

Opposite

Nikola Tesla is best known for his contributions to the design of the modern alternating current electricity supply system. The graphics in the Tesla room pay homage to his work.

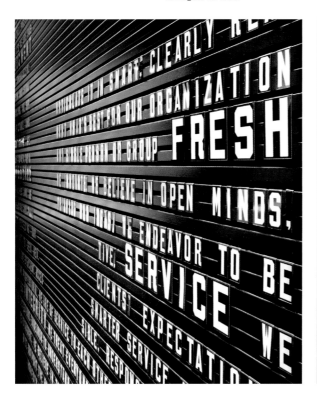

Lisbon Bikeway
P-o6 Atelier

Location: Lisbon, Portugal
Usage: Public space
Date: 2009

The Lisbon Bikeway runs along the Tagus River. It is 7.4 kilometres (4.5 miles) long and crosses different urban spaces, each one demanding a different solution. The goal was to define a new urban environment beyond the bikeway, to improve the area along the river.

The graphics tell the rider a story, guide him or her, and seduce the rider to continue along the route. Signage directs the viewer towards tourist, cultural, and natural points of interest. Symbols indicate points to stop and rest or break from the path. P-o6 Atelier exceeded the parameters of the project beyond the bright, clear, and utilitarian aspects, by using a verse about the Tagus River from Portuguese poet Alberto Caeiro (Fernando Pessoa). Using the verbiage as an intervention emphasizes the poetry of the structure.

Opposite
Using large stencils, words and symbols were spray-painted directly onto the bikeway pavement.

Below
A poem about the Tagus by Portuguese poet Alberto Caeiro (Fernando Pessoa) is stencilled onto the pavement of a pier providing an unfolding narrative along the route.

Below, opposite, and following
The letterforms create words, such
as those in Caeiro's poem, and are
also used to create sounds such
as 'zzzuumm', and guide the viewer
along the bikeway. The bike stencil
was also used to adorn old buildings.

Mad Campus
Studio Matthews

Location: Seattle, Washington, USA
Usage: Wayfinding, information
Date: 2014

For MadArt Seattle, Studio Matthews designed an identity and graphic system that would visually connect twelve disparate art installations spread across the University of Washington's Seattle campus, creating a visually coherent experience.

Twelve emerging artists created site-specific works inspired by the landscape of the university campus. The twelve individual art works were a range of different sizes and located across the university's 700-acre campus. Studio Matthews designed a strong and clear numbering system that included captions for each piece. The large-scale numerals were also beacons to guide visitors to each artwork.

The numbers also communicate that there are other installations. While the viewer stands next to the number '3', he/she is aware that elsewhere there is a '2'. Each numeral graphic had a map of the entire campus installation.

Below
The location map is repeated on
a massive scale as a floor graphic
in Red Square, a large plaza at the
heart of campus. This lively layout
references the game Twister.

Sentinel
Kevin McCarthy

Wood, Cardboard, Holographic Vinyl,
Lenticular Prints

madartseattle.com

Lone Stranger
(inflated)
Piper O'Neill

Vinyl-Coated Nylon, Fan

madartseattle.com

Left and opposite
The design incorporated three
different sizes of number
discs, with a range of mounting
hardware: they were hung with
cables, attached to steel posts,
and strapped to tree trunks.

Moderna Museet
Stockholm Design Lab

Location: Stockholm, Sweden
Usage: Branded environment
Date: 2004

Moderna Museet, Sweden's national museum of contemporary art, opened on Skeppsholmen, an island in the centre of Stockholm, in 1958. Within a few years, it had developed an international reputation, with acclaimed exhibitions of works by Picasso, Duchamp, and American Pop Art. In 2002, the museum closed for repair and refurbishment. For the reopening, Stockholm Design Lab (SDL) created a visual system that would attract new visitors and be accessible to multiple audiences.

Early in the process, SDL focused on the idea of a logo that could animate the museum's long, linear facade and stand out to the cultural audience of Skeppsholmen. Together with staff from Moderna Museet (MM), they experimented with many concepts.

The solution eventually came via the cover of the 1983 25th Anniversary catalogue, designed by Robert Rauschenberg, an artist with a long association with MM.

Rauschenberg's 'Moderna Museet' signature was arresting, compelling, and expressive of both the artistic process and art world notions of authenticity. It resonated with MM's past, too, and its leading role in promoting Rauschenberg and the Pop Art movement in the 1960s. More than a decade later, MM's signature has helped put the museum back on the modern art map. The new visual system, with a special version of Wim Crouwel's Gridnik typeface, also serves as a navigation tool to guide visitors around the museum building.

Opposite and following
On a cold day, the museum building stands out boldly as an enormous red box. The identity is woven into the perforated structure. A special version of Wim Crouwel's Gridnik typeface is used for identification and wayfinding.

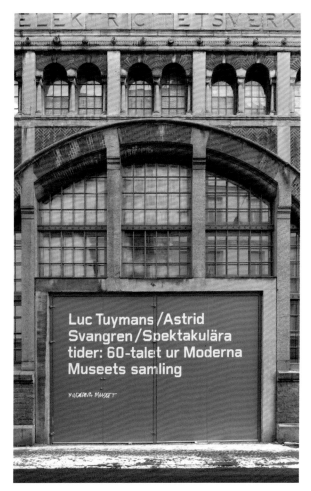

Opposite and below
Simple primary colours and
minimal typography are used at
various sizes, from an artist's name
printed on a locker to the large
letterforms on the pavement.

The Public Theater

Pentagram

Location: New York, New York, USA
Usage: Branded environment, identifying
Date: 2013

As part of a major renovation by Ennead Architects, the foyer of the Public Theater was transformed into one of New York's most vibrant and welcoming spaces for theatregoers. Pentagram's Paula Scher created a programme of environmental graphics for the space that integrates her iconic identity for the Public into the architecture of the theatre itself.

The environmental graphics inventively marry type and architecture to make the Public identity feel like an integral part of the building. Scher's graphics for the Public are recognized for their expressive use of typography (set in Hoefler & Frere-Jones's Knockout, the font of the identity), and here the type performs in the space, guiding theatregoers and setting a friendly tone that invites audiences to linger.

The various theatres in the building are identified with dimensional typography that has been etched into the foyer's distinctive arches. Plaster archways feature typography carved into the surface and painted with textured paint; steel archways use laser-cut steel sheets. The reconfigured foyer centres on a circular front desk that features a dimensional, large-scale version of the Public logo.

Scher helped commission a chandelier-like multimedia sculpture designed by the artist Ben Rubin that hangs over the desk. Called the Shakespeare Machine, the piece randomly generates phrases from Shakespeare's works and is flanked by projections that provide information of current productions.

Opposite

The marquee canopy dramatically renders the Public logo in glass over the steps of the entrance. To win approval by the city's Landmarks Commission, the awning is only connected to the building at two points. The letters of the logo are clear and transparent, reversed out of the pattern of the glass.

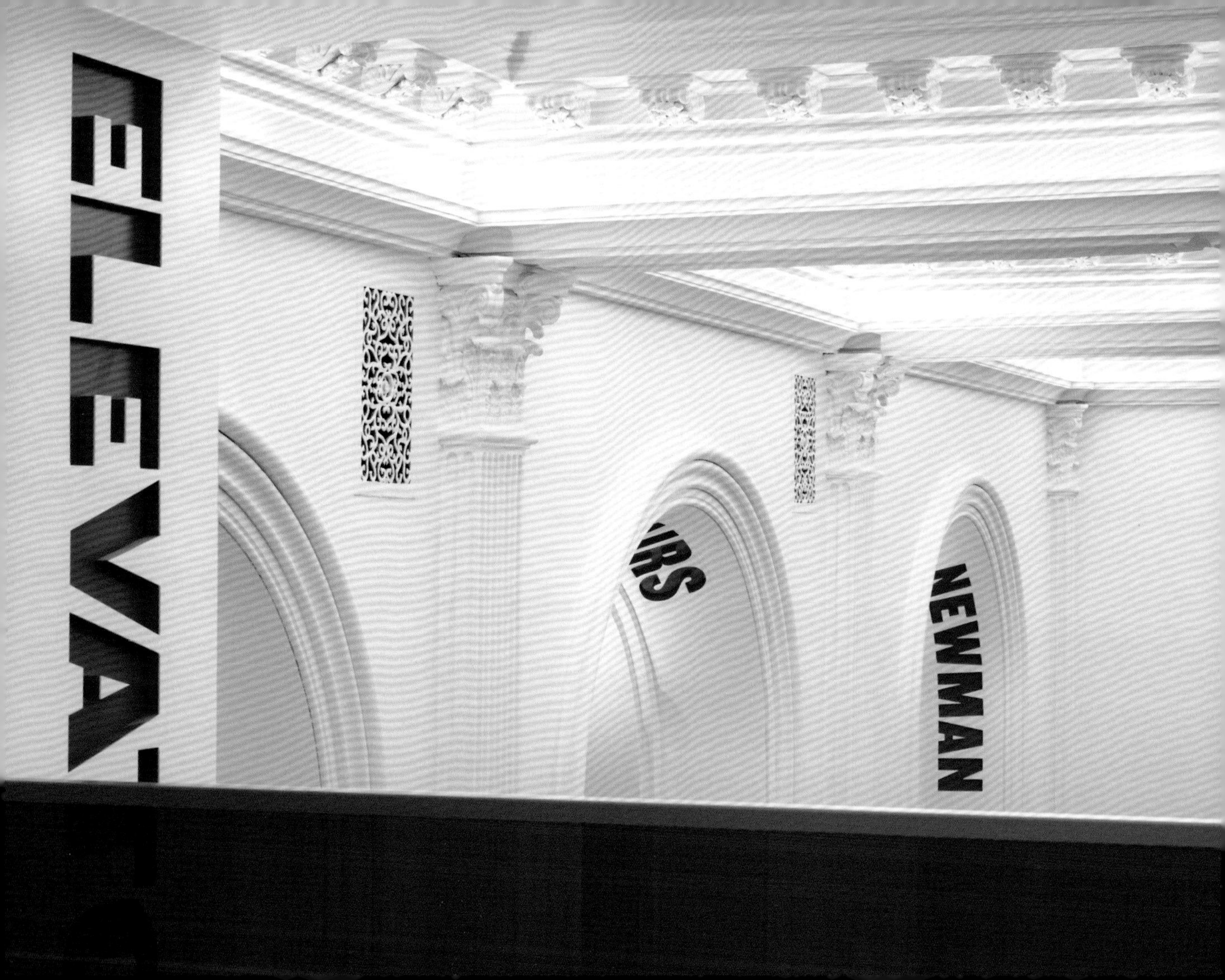
ELEVA
NEWMAN

Below and opposite

The colour echoes the red and black typography of the first identity Scher designed for the institution in 1994. A red railing also runs around the balcony lounge on the foyer's second level; this line was referenced in the 'Open the Public' campaign that accompanied the official reopening of the space.

Opposite
The box office at the back of
the foyer features a colourful
collage of Public posters from
the last two decades.

Below
Large-scale typography is carved into the building, or uses variations of matt and gloss to identify individual theatres and theatre functions.

Opposite
The front desk features a large-scale, dimensional version of the Public logo and the Shakespeare Machine.

QV Car Park
Latitude

Location: Melbourne, Australia
Usage: Environmental, wayfinding
Date: 2011

Latitude added life to the QV Melbourne Car Park by implementing a series of large-scale environmental graphics.

The design took inspiration from early modernist graphic design, and acts both as environmental graphics and wayfinding. Each typographic piece was individually hand-painted on-site, overlaying the painted forms and producing a multiplied effect onto the existing brickwork. The location of each word was carefully considered to ensure high visibility, with the design also providing a welcome use of colour and brightness to the underground levels.

Below, opposite, and following
Oversized and overlapping
letterforms based on Futura create
a vibrant and playful solution for an
otherwise dark and dull car park.

Rapport: Experimental Spatial Structures

J.Mayer.H

Location: Berlin, Germany
Usage: Exhibition
Date: 2012

Rapport: Experimental Spatial Structures is an exhibition at the Berlinische Galerie that offered insights into the interdisciplinary approach of the architectural office J.Mayer.H. The installation was housed in the museum's 10-metre-high (33-foot-high) entrance area. Walls and floors were clad in carpeting with data security patterns, printed in black and grey. The macro, repeating patterns transformed the white cube into a playful scenario of interacting forms and structures. Supplementary three-dimensional models translated the two-dimensional patterns into concrete forms.

The use of 'rapport' in the title was intended to be ambiguous. As a German term from textile manufacturing, it refers to the repeating pattern of the installation. Alternatively, in a military context, it is synonymous with 'dispatch', while in psychology, it describes a human relationship in which those involved convey something to the others. In this sense, the title also referred to the starting material of the installation: data security patterns, which were used, for example, on the inside of envelopes. In this case, they stood for confidential communication between two parties.

Opposite
The oversized typography interlocked to create the abstract pattern. The scale of the graphics created an immersive motif that surrounded the viewer.

Right, opposite, and following
The pattern was reproduced in two dimensions. From a distance, numerals began to be apparent. Three-dimensional typographical forms were cast in concrete.

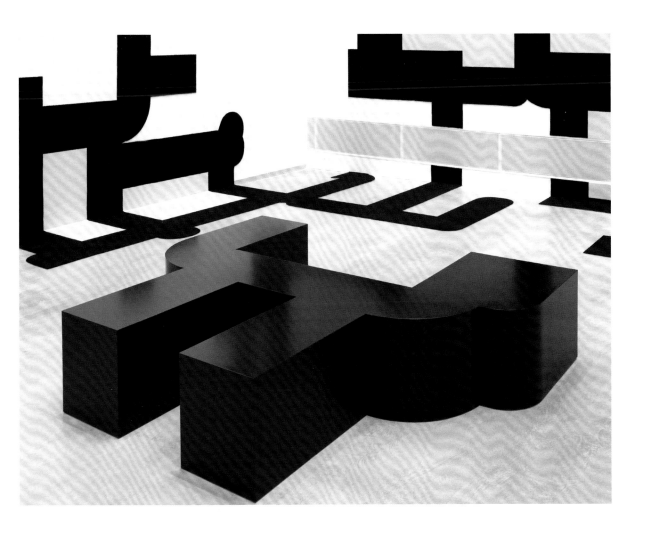

SKIN –
Pavilion of Knowledge
P-06 Atelier

Location: Lisbon, Portugal
Usage: Branded environment
Date: 2010

SKIN – Pavilion of Knowledge was developed in partnership with the architect João Luís Carrilho da Graça for the foyer of the Pavilion of Knowledge, a science museum in Lisbon. The client's directive to P-06 was to create an environmental skin that is functional, acoustical, and inspirational.

P-06 Atelier designed a texture based on the universal computer language American Standard Code for Information Interchange (ASCII). The language is an analogy of the museum's mission of sharing information. The 'acoustic skin' of perforated patterns allows sound and light to enter the space at different densities. White LED lighting between the wall and the SKIN maintains consistent light distribution. The panels are made with rigid MDF board and faced on both sides with reflective aluminium surfacing.

Nuno Gusmão explains the project: 'ASCII is a code for information exchange, and a museum is also a place for information exchange. The overall aesthetic, colours, and light were intended to be calm enough to frame the "embroidered wall", yet robust enough to stand up to other elements that are competing with it.'

Opposite
Fastening the wall into place required several rounds of prototypes before reaching a workable solution. To allow easy panel placement and removal, the panels were attached to the wood structure with screws.

Opposite

White LED lighting between the SKIN and wall allows for illumination control throughout the day and evening. Other rooms are visible through the variously sized ASCII characters.

Below

The ASCII characters were computer-generated, then cut from the MDF panels with a Computer Numerical Control router.

Opposite and below
The typeface, OCR-A, echoes the
ASCII code language and is applied
to walls and repeated on the floor

Sotheby's
Franklyn and Sotheby's Creative

Location: Philadelphia, Pennsylvania, USA
Usage: Exhibition
Date: 2015

With over $500 million on the line, Sotheby's had the dauntingly enviable task of hosting the world's most valuable private art auction. Billionaire real estate mogul and former Sotheby's chairman A. Alfred Taubman was a true art connoisseur. Sotheby's was the only choice for selling off this formidable collection.

With an eye towards showcasing the legendary artists represented in the sale, Franklyn created an identity system based on flexible custom typography inspired by the mid-century modern aesthetic Mr Taubman loved. The designers used the stretchy type and mosaics of Picassos, Rothkos, and Kandinskys to design a wide range of materials from a four-volume, 400-page catalogue to the two-storey vinyl banner wrapping the exterior of Sotheby's HQ.

Previous and below
The custom letterforms that
wrapped around the entire building
spelt out the names of artists in the
A. Alfred Taubman collection.

Opposite
The pattern is continued on interior
walls and publications.

St. Louis Public Library
Kuhlmann-Leavitt, Inc.

Location: Saint Louis, Missouri, USA
Usage: Branded environment
Date: 2012

The St. Louis Public Library renovated its historic 1912 Cass Gilbert-designed building and reopened it to the public in late 2012. Kuhlmann-Leavitt, Inc. worked closely with the library and project architects Cannon Design to establish a signage system and environmental graphics that integrated seamlessly with the grandeur of the existing architecture and the streamlined sophistication of the reimagined spaces. The carefully created patterns were inspired by the buildings' original adornment and repurposed as a wayfinding method through each of the four levels of the building.

Scale and colour created multiple variations of typography to be subtle or bold, as needed. A variety of materials were used to create visual interest, while also guiding the viewers throughout the Library.

Opposite
Kuhlmann-Leavitt used large- and small-scale typography in subtle and bold ways to inform the viewer and reinforce the joy of reading.

Below
Elements from the building's iconic and historic architecture inspired shapes, colours and iconography translated into large-scale forms.

Following
Typography is found throughout the building , including the ceiling, with text added to the Reading Center. Colour and transparency weave the elements together.

The Field Guide to Supergraphics

Vai com Deus (Go with God)
R2 Design

Location: Lisbon, Portugal
Usage: Public space
Date: 2008

When an eighteenth-century Portuguese chapel 'Ermida Nossa Senhora da Conceição' in Belém, a district of Lisbon, Portugal, reopened as an art gallery, the owners and R2 Design used its facade as the canvas for an artful typographic composition that recalls the building's former use but creates a new cultural venue.

With a tight budget and only two months to bring the project to fruition, R2 Design needed to draw visitors' attention to the gallery, located down a small alleyway adjacent to several important historical buildings in Lisbon. They started by painting the yellow facade white and using it as the slate for idiomatic expressions that refer to God and that by force of repetition have become commonplace in the Portuguese language. The design team chose the Knockout typeface and rendered the words at various depths and sizes. A thick paint made it possible to simulate the texture of the facade.

Opposite

After designing the composition in InDesign, the letterforms were cut from MDF and fastened to the wall using glue and screws, finishing off with sand paint to complete the white-on-white setting.

Below

R2 played with the scale of the three-dimensional type to bring out different rhythms and shades of meaning within each familiar phrase.

Below and opposite
For a project the following year, the wall was illuminated at night by a projector that turned off periodically. The wall was painted in two kinds of photo-luminescent ink, keeping the words lit for a few moments. Vistors could create the same effect with a flash light or a mobile phone.

Following
For the Lisbon alleyway, the designers, fascinated by the venue's eighteenth-century origins, decided to bring God back into the conversation, making use of everyday expressions that include the word. The designers' intention is that, as the passerby reads the text, 'little by little, it will be progressively discovered'.

DN, 05/09

SACO DE PAPE
SUSPEITO
FECHA METRO DURANT
DUAS HORAS

TO RE
BUSIN
SCHOO

Waltham Forest Council
Vic Lee

Location: London, England
Usage: Public space
Date: 2012

Walthamstow has been undergoing a radical transformation, with the aim of enhancing the local area by working with local artists to improve shop fronts, continuing the E17 Art Trail, and promoting the Blackhorse Studio areas as a creative space for artists. Waltham Forest Council gave Vic Lee absolute freedom to decorate a wall in Wood Street in the London borough.

The final design incorporated stories Lee collected from locals and schools in the area, including urban myths and tall tales. Lee mixed local stories of horse thieves, wandering cows on motorways, and baby Superman with some fabrications of his own to create the illustrated mural. Initially, the mural was to be temporary, lasting three to six months, but the locals have since kept it maintained for over a year and a half so it stands untouched and immaculate.

Below and following
The final piece of artwork stands
2.5 metres high and 18 metres long.

Professor Joachim Sauter
ART+COM Studios
Interview

What was the first project you did that involved large environmental graphics? How did you approach the problem and solve it?

It was stage design for the opera the *Jew of Malta* by Andre Werner (1999–2002) at the Munich Opera Biennale. The challenge was to create a large-scale dynamic stage that supports the story. Machiavelli, the main character of the play, has power over the other actors. We allowed him to change the whole space with gestures. With the ability to modify the environment, we used interactivity as a metaphor for power.

How has your process for creating environmental graphics changed since then?

After many interactive, immersive environments we moved from interactivity (intentional dialogue with an installation) to its little sister, reactivity (unintentional dialogue with an installation). Through this responsiveness, our environmental installations communicate on an intuitive level with pedestrians, change their everyday experience, and make them identify with a space.

Opposite
BMW Museum
ART+COM Studios
2008
Installation and testing of
interactive panels

Below
Obsessions Make My Life Worse
And My Work Better
Stefan Sagmeister
2008

What was the most challenging environmental design project you've done?

It was the first project, the *Jew of Malta* by Andre Werner. The necessary technology didn't exist at that time, and we had to develop it. Today you can get the same technology off the shelf. Also, if you are working with the theatre or opera, you always have to deal with a director who is usually harder to handle than any client from other industries.

What is your favourite project you've done?

Chronologically:

1990: *Zerseher*

1990: *Invisible Shape of Things Past*

2000: *Jew of Malta*

2000: Kinetic Sculpture for the BMW Museum

2010: *Symphonie Cinétique*

If you had the chance to redo a project now, what would you do differently?

In general, I would accept fewer projects.

What is your dream environmental graphics project?

I'd love to design the interior of a church (although I am a pagan).

Where do you find inspiration for this type of work?

By getting into a natural flow, like practising a sport with repetitive movements.

What is your favourite example of environmental graphics by someone other than yourself, and why?

Stefan Sagmeister's *Obsessions Make My Life Worse And My Work Better*. It was a piece of typography with thousands of coins arranged to form a sentence. It also had the potential of being destroyed.

From Stefan Sagmeister:

'The coin mural spelt out the sentence "Obsessions make my life worse and my work better." After completion, the coins were left free and unguarded for the public interaction. Less than twenty hours after the grand opening, a resident noticed a person bagging the coins and taking them away. Protective of the design piece, they called the police. After stopping the "criminal", the police – to 'preserve the artwork' – swept up every remaining cent and carted the money away.'

What's the best piece of advice for a young designer interested in pursuing environmental graphics as a career?

Develop a clear attitude towards what you are doing and stick to it.

Nuno Gusmão

P-06 Atelier
Interview

What was the first project you did that involved large environmental graphics? How did you approach the problem and solve it?
Our professional path was 'crescendo/moderato', meaning it was a gradual process that made our team and us able to be responsible for bigger and more complex projects.

How have your process and ideas about environmental graphics changed since then?
New technical solutions and new ways of communicating, like multimedia, are ever-changing issues that oblige us professionals to stay up-to-date in terms of solutions and conceptual processes. I do think that our processes and ideas have to change to fit with the changes around us.

What was the most challenging environmental design project you've done and why was it challenging?
From the heart, it is always the last one . . . but I would choose one project in particular, the P7 bridge experience, that combines graphics, an exhibition, a multimedia experience/installation, and wayfinding, which makes this project very 'rich' in terms of our intervention. It is now under construction, nearly finished.

What is your dream environmental graphics project?
Like I said before, the more complex, the better, because it brings more responsibility, more challenge, and more opportunities to experiment with new things and new ways to communicate.

Where do you find inspiration for this type of work?
Art, architecture, and all kind of artistic manifestations, including the works of our colleagues in the profession from around the world.

What is your favourite example of environmental graphics (supergraphics) by someone other than yourself, and why?
I find the 1940 Exposição do Mundo Português (Portuguese World Exhibition) a very complete work in terms of environmental graphics. It has really outstanding examples of art, architecture, design, supergraphics, etc., and I find it innovative for that time.

Below
Guidebook for the Exposição do Mundo
Português (23 June to 2 December 1940). The
festival commemorated the date of the foundation
of the Portuguese State (1140) and the Restoration
of Independence (1640).

**What's the best piece of advice for a
young designer interested in pursuing
environmental graphics as a career?**
Observation is really important in this line of
work, plus a lot of interest in all art (natural
or man-made). We have a lot to learn from it.

The Field Guide to Supergraphics

3

Colour

Opposite
Fresh Eyes Cuba
Havana, Cuba
ArtCenter Designmatters and
Instituto de Diseño
2017

Art es Part
Anna Taratiel

Location: Barcelona, Spain
Usage: Public space
Date: 2012

Anna Taratiel (aka OVNI) is a Spanish artist based in Amsterdam. For Art es Part, Taratiel collaborated with students from two schools to develop a big mural at a basketball court and playground. Participants were given a grid and a set of tangram forms to create any pattern they liked. Each sixteen-square design, created by the students, was then painted on the wall to create a huge pattern.

Taratiel explained the project and the impact it had on her work: 'Art es Part is a collective project I worked on with two schools and CIS gallery. I created a formula where each kid used the same nine shapes and five colours inside a small portion of a huge grid. This collective project changes the way I understand art and expression. The union of 400 kids, ranging from three to eighteen years old, working together and taking part in a bigger work but feeling individually challenged . . . it was amazing and very powerful.'

Opposite and following

As many as 400 students used the same nine shapes and five colours inside a small portion of a huge grid. Each section was joined to the others, and the children worked together to complete the work. This gave them the experience of taking part in a bigger artwork but feeling challenged on a personal level.

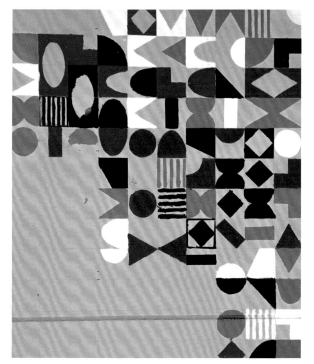

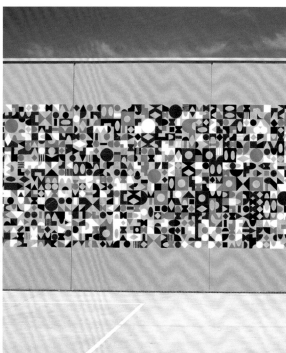

The Field Guide to Supergraphics

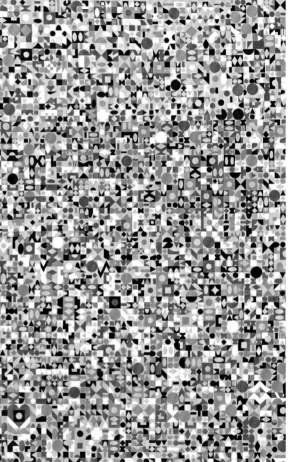

Commonwealth Bank Offices, Melbourne Call Centre

Urbanite, a part of Frost*collective

Location: Melbourne, Victoria, Australia
Usage: Branded environment
Date: 2013

Urbanite was asked to animate CBA Melbourne's activity-based workplace in line with corporate workplace well-being policies.

First and foremost, Urbanite wanted to spark enthusiasm and inspire staff, who are often working on intensive and arduous tasks. The design team divided the building's floor plans into a series of visual 'work', 'rest', and 'play' zones, and used references from Melbourne's urban-laneway culture (the pedestrian alley between buildings) for the 'work' zones, injecting the city's parklands and nature into the 'rest' and 'play' spaces.

New York-based artist James Gulliver Hancock used the theme of a Melbourne summer's day to tell stories of the city's inhabitants with a fantastical twist. The illustrations incorporate quirky details at a micro-scale as a nod to the city's iconic laneways, uncovering the new, and relishing the sense of discovery.

Opposite
Iconic Melbourne architecture creates the visual language. This embedded the environmental graphics programme firmly into its location.

Below
The collaborative project with interior architects Davenport Campbell spanned signage, wayfinding, and environmental graphics across seven floors. It used illustration to surprise and shift outdated productivity and workspace paradigms.

Below
The graphics provide a strong sense of belonging and an overall environment that is an uplifting and unique portrait of Melbourne.

Opposite
The colour and illustrations focus on the psychological benefits of positive workplace environments. This improves productivity and workplace attitudes in the centre.

Opposite and left 131

By imbuing the interior
environment with personal
associations, individuals relate
differently to their workplace,
and the city of Melbourne tells
its stories.

The Field Guide to Supergraphics

Fresh Eyes Cuba

**ArtCenter Designmatters and
Instituto de Diseño**

Location: Havana, Cuba
Usage: Exhibition
Date: 2017

This studio's objective was to allow faculty and students to experience the exceptional ecosystem of innovation and creativity that Cuba represents as the diplomatic ties between Cuba and the United States are reestablished. A key part of the project was a cross-cultural collaboration with the communication design students of the Instituto de Diseño (ISDi), Cuba's only design school, and ArtCenter in Pasadena, California.

A four-day workshop brought together both student groups to learn through sharing their different experiences and perspectives. The workshop was highly experimental and a multisensorial, cross-cultural exploration.

The exhibition for the release of the book documenting the project was limited to one day. With little to no resources available, ArtCenter shipped 1,800 metres (6,000 feet) of coloured tape to Havana. The participants from both ArtCenter and Instituto de Diseño used the tape to create a low-fi, supergraphic environment that was installed in hours and dismantled that evening. The tape was applied to the floors, ceiling, and stairwells leading to the gallery, and from the gallery to the neighbourhood below.

The project tapped into the expertise of the leaders of the Incúbate initiative that is connecting American and Cuban entrepreneurs and creatives to exchange knowledge and insight. Prior to the trip to Cuba, students conducted in-depth research on the history and current state of Cuba, guided by lectures from guest experts.

Opposite and following

Students from ArtCenter and Instituto de Diseño created an immersive visual experience with rolls of tape. There was no pre-planned design. The designers improvised and collaborated over an eight-hour span of time.

The installation existed for one day only. After the reception, the tape was removed.

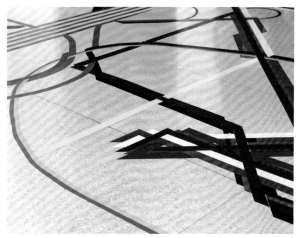

Google Japan
Ian Lynam Design

Location: Tokyo, Japan
Usage: Branded environment
Date: 2013

Ian Lynam Design's solution for a visual system for one of the largest buildings in Tokyo is immersive and transcendental. It is also diverse, and allows Google workers to navigate expansive spaces with ease.

Lynam watched how the humans who inhabit the area were interacting with their environment. He discovered the average time an employee spent trying to decipher the previous wayfinding was thirty seconds. The new graphics incorporate repeating patterns, hyper-illustrative wallpapers, and varied interior environments that span thousands of metres of some of the most expensive office space in the world. Hundreds of metres of custom wallpapers create six complementary graphic themes. The environmental graphics provide graphic complexity and a reductive, multilingual approach to creating functional spaces.

Opposite
The door signage of frosted glass incorporates the shape of the building. The typography recalls 1960s Japanese science-fiction films.

Below
Wall graphics and dual interactive projections create a stylized koi pond at the office entrance.

Below
The Tokyo of the future,
with a psychedelic take on
science-fiction book jackets,
expands a meeting room and
adds energy.

Opposite
An abstract, hyper-pop alternate
Tokyo is used in the dining area,
bringing together the intensity
of Tokyo street culture and the
beauty of a Japanese garden or
woodblock print.

Google Singapore
THERE

Location: Singapore
Usage: Branded environment
Date: 2016

Google asked THERE to help resolve navigation and orientation confusion for staff and visitors at their Singapore headquarters. Google also tasked the firm with injecting some fun and energy to an additional floor of the offices. The solution worked with a variety of different interior graphics and themes, across four floors totalling 13,000 square metres (140,000 square feet).

For wayfinding, THERE drew inspiration from one of the largest container terminals in the world, which neighbours the Singapore offices. The directional signage system is made with randomly 'stacked' shipping container-like forms in Google brand colours. Location totems and zonal activation graphics further aid orientation and add interest while continuing the shipping container theme.

The new workplace also combines references to eight-bit arcade classics, such as Super Mario and Space Invaders, and traditional games played in Southeast Asia, including tangrams, wooden puzzles, and kite flying. Google visual motifs are woven into the graphics in subtle ways to reinforce the brand experience.

Opposite
The concepts and graphics of gaming culture capture the Google culture and communicate the brand's values. Google brand items, such as the Android, are integrated into the eight-bit arcade game graphics, such as Pac-Man and Space Invaders.

Opposite and below
The graphics in the Ping-Pong room simulate the path of the ball during a powerful volley between two players.

Opposite

The wayfinding system refers to stacked shipping containers, seen from the Google offices.

Below

Google brand colours subtly shift on each floor. The entire graphic programme incorporates the South Asia trade theme.

Grafton Car Park
ECE Architecture and Creative Forager

Location: Worthing, England
Usage: Public space
Date: 2017

ECE Architecture collaborated with Creative Forager on a project to decorate a brutalist car park in Worthing, West Sussex. The inspiration behind the dazzling riot of bright colour and bold pattern is the stripy deckchairs and colourful items that can be bought along the seafront promenade. The plan was to produce a graffiti wall, inspired by life at the seaside and reproducing the colours of ice cream, inflatable toys, pastel-coloured clothes, and sweets. The writing displays the slogan 'Right Now', which refers to the creative rebirth occurring in this region. Artist Ricky Also assisted and completed the work in a week, making use of 600 spray cans.

This new beach front installation has taken a grey car park in Worthing, a site that Adur and Worthing Councils would like to promote for future regencration, and painted it with an Incredible large-scale pattern, graphics, and the words 'Right Now' to transform it and the public's perception of it. The phrase 'Right Now' focuses on the current nature of the installation, but, in a creative twist, it is also an anagram of Worthing.

Opposite and following
Stuart Eatock, ECE Architecture's managing director, explains, 'We have been working on ideas to engage people with architecture and creativity for three years. Right Now is about reimagining a car park as a canvas, creating a new landmark for Worthing.'

Lyon–Saint Exupéry Airport
Graphéine

Location: Lyon, France
Usage: Branded environment, wayfinding
Date: 2010

Anticipating increased passenger travel, Lyon–Saint Exupéry Airport began a construction project to accommodate expanded traffic. During the construction phase, travellers entered one of the terminals through a long tunnel. Graphéine designed a solution that transformed the long journey through an otherwise bland tunnel into an experience.

They incorporated concepts of optical art: visual parallax, vibrant colour, and unexpected scale. This, combined with typography, information, shapes, and images, created an entertaining narrative for the viewer as he or she travelled along an escalator. Changes in light and point of view alter the forms along the journey, deconstructing the meaning of the visual language.

Below and opposite
Distances and a timeline
accompany the traveller as
they progress through the
various tunnels.

Following
Vibrant colours, parallax, large
typography, and iconography
provide entertainment for an
otherwise uneventful journey, and
create a branded experience.

Life
Boa Mistura

Location: Bogotá, Colombia
Usage: Public space
Date: 2016

Plaza de la Hoja is a complex of twelve buildings built to house 475 families displaced by violence and conflict in Colombia. These families share little in common. They are from various regions: the Pacific, Caribbean, Amazon, and mountains. The only thing they share is having lived the drama of fleeing without looking back, abandoning their land, customs, and most of their family, as a result of armed conflict. Their new home, the Plaza de la Hoja, was deemed ugly and prisonlike by the press.

At the centre of the Plaza, Boa Mistura added a giant leaf, created from hundreds of smaller leaves that are arranged to form the word 'life'. Each of these smaller leaves belongs to a significant species from the ecosystems of Colombia, symbolically representing the places of origin for the inhabitants of the building. It brings a piece of their land to them. This is a reminder to the 457 families who have been relocated in this urban housing development that they must rebuild their future together.

The mural was painted in collaboration with the residents, creating a sense of community. The painting on the ground is perceived very differently by a pedestrian at ground level than by a resident viewing it from above. At ground level, the viewer perceives enormous geometric coloured forms, but when seen from above it takes on a greater meaning, representing the hope of a new beginning.

Opposite
The revitalized Plaza de la Hoja is now a space for meeting and recreation, and provides a symbol of hope.

Below
The Plaza prior to the addition of the graphic was underused, grey, and unwelcoming to residents.

Opposite and following
The finished graphic on the Plaza was painted by the designers and occupants of the development.

New BMW Museum
ART+COM Studios

Location: Munich, Germany
Usage: Branded environment
Date: 2008

The BMW Museum in Munich embodies a new approach to combining architecture and exhibition design, placing particular emphasis on new media. BMW commissioned ART+COM Studios to develop and produce the museum's spatial media design and interactive installations, and asked Atelier Brückner to produce the architecture and exhibition design. The concept was determined by two underlying themes: mobility and dynamism.

ART+COM Studios based the media concept on interactive, reactive, and cinematic elements. Spatial choreographies of projections, light, and sound create a dynamic backdrop for the seven 'exhibition houses' and twenty-five rooms, appearing to animate the architecture and 125 exhibits. Interactive installations and so-called 'auxiliary' formats help convey the museum's content by providing in-depth information.

One of the highlights of the museum is 'Spheres', a 700-square-metre (7,500-square-foot) media facade surrounding a central indoor square, which is illuminated with purely abstract and abstract-figurative moving images.

Opposite
Immersed in a flow of images, visitors experience the space in a new way each time they pass through it, thus expanding its perceived dimensions even further.

Opposite
White monochrome LEDs and
opaque architectural glass cover
the 700 square metres of wall space
surrounding the piazza. In this way,
the LEDs are no longer identifiable
as a technical system or classic
video screen but simply become
part of a dynamic facade.

Following
The atmospheric imagery
and powerful words in German
and English continue to the base
of the piazza and a collection of
BMW vehicles.

Panasonic North America Headquarters Building

Graham Hanson Design

Location: Newark, New Jersey, USA
Usage: Wayfinding
Date: 2014

For the Panasonic North America Headquarters Building, GHD created a system of signage and environmental graphics that reflects the innovative heritage and defining brand attributes of Panasonic. The system highlights the concept of innovation in a tangible way that is understandable to employees and visitors.

The twelve-storey building has interiors that provide an open, bright canvas for environmental graphics. GHD chose seven great innovators, balanced with representation by gender, race, and culture, to be the 'stars' of the building's main floors: Alexander Graham Bell, Thomas Edison, Albert Einstein, Grace Hopper, Marie Curie, and Granville Woods.

On each of these floors, the environmental graphics celebrate the chosen innovators by portraying his or her world-changing work. They include large-scale photographic portraits of the innovators, as well as wall coverings featuring their actual patent drawings and notations, overlaid with innovative typographic treatments inspired by the line work drawings.

The executive floor highlights the innovations of Panasonic founder Konosuke Matsushita and other company innovators. Each level is also assigned a saturated colour and one of Mr Matsushita's basic business principles (honesty and fairness, or cooperation and team spirit, for example). The graphics incorporate current president Kazuhiro Tsuga's patents. When the new office opened, he signed the wall that features his innovations.

On the ground floor, GHD provided a colour-coded overview of the innovators featured throughout the building. Clear acrylic panels appear to float in the space.

Opposite
Each floor has colour-coded diagrams throughout, which relate to that level's name and are based on an inventor. Scottish inventor Alexander Graham Bell is credited as the inventor of the first practical telephone. His portrait and name, along with the details of his inventions, delineate the sixth floor.

Below

Wall-sized graphics celebrate Marie Curie's research on radioactivity. The wallpaper provides visual interest and a connection to Panasonic's brand values, and it identifies the location.

Opposite

Granville Tailer Woods was the first American of African ancestry to be a mechanical and electrical engineer after the Civil War. His diagrams for the Multiplex Telegraph create dynamic mural images.

Following, left
Rear Admiral Grace M. Hopper was
an American computer scientist
and United States Navy rear
admiral. She developed COBOL,
an early high-level programming
language that is still in use today.

Following, right
Thomas Alva Edison was an American
inventor. He developed many devices
that changed the world, including
the phonograph, the motion picture
camera, and the long-lasting,
practical electric light bulb.

Novo Nordisk
North American Headquarters
Poulin + Morris

Location. Princeton, New Jersey, USA
Usage: Branded environment, wayfinding
Date: 2013

Novo Nordisk is a world leader in diabetes care. Poulin and Morris developed a full-building graphic programme that provides a consistent visual language. The designers introduced a colour-coding system that designates each of the large facility's five zones with a different colour. Bold patterns representing molecular compositions of insulin accentuate the colour system. This pattern further differentiates each zone by scale, colour, and application.

The solution celebrates Novo Nordisk's remarkable innovation and history in diabetes care. Murals, glass entrances, and glass partitions prominently integrate the insulin-inspired patterns throughout the project. A modular sign panel system featuring a design based on elements from the periodic table displays an intuitive room numbering system to guide people through the building. Graphic murals show large-scale floor numbers and wayfinding information for additional navigation throughout the LEED Silver-certified facility. LEED, or Leadership in Energy and Environmental Design, buildings use less water and energy, and reduce greenhouse gas emissions.

Opposite
Shared and collaborative spaces, including private offices, open offices, and conference rooms, incorporate the molecular structure of insulin. The colours and patterns of the graphic system adhere to Novo Nordisk's design values and provide visual cornerstones in a new and dynamic way.

2A101 – 2A149
2A301 – 2A315

2A201 – 2A271
2A320 – 2A322

Below
The Princeton facility occupies
46,500 square metres (500,000
square feet) of a 3.6 hectare (9-acre)
campus. The colour-coded patterns
identify individual zones.

Opposite
Poulin and Morris designed the
branding of the headquarters' dining
facilities – Lakeview, a cafeteria
featuring a two-storey wall of
windows overlooking views of the
adjacent lake, and The Market,
a self-service 'grab and go'. The
designers created a graphic identity
programme for these two venues,
for all printed materials, menu items,
and visual sign elements.

Project Colour Corp, Cambridge Elementary

Gensler

Location: Concord, California, USA
Usage: Public space
Date: 2016

The project focused on The Cambridge Elementary School, located in a disadvantaged and underserved neighbourhood in Concord, California. Project Colour Corps's research team engaged all 700 young pupils to find out which words came to mind when they were asked how they wanted to feel at school every day. Students expressed needing to feel excited, happy, natural, calm, and safe.

This project engaged the students and the larger community throughout the design process to help them feel ownership, empowering the participants to become agents of change in their community. The students operated as a democracy to pick a winning design and helped to paint their space. The geometry of the design evokes the movement and depth associated with a brilliant gem or a gleam of light that glitters.

Opposite

One of the descriptors that the students came up with was 'sparkle', which inspired the design team to develop the geometric forms.

Below

The students explained their colour preferences with responses such as, 'Orange makes me feel like I ate breakfast in the morning'.

Opposite
The students possessed the
power to influence the outcome
by sharing what inspires them,
operating as a democracy to pick a
winning design, and finally, helping
to paint their space.

Below
The winning theme of energetic,
kaleidoscope shades forms a
geometric arrangement of triangular
patterns, using equilateral,
isosceles, and scalene
shapes along various walking paths.

Stuttgart Region Chamber of Commerce

Büro Uebele

Location: Stuttgart, Germany
Usage: Wayfinding, identifying
Date: 2015

The Stuttgart Region Chamber of Commerce, designed by Wulf Architekten, is located next to a vineyard. The even rows of the vines are an ever-present element within the building. Büro Uebele used these rhythmic rows to create a series of graphics that form a wayfinding and identifying system. The diversity of the Stuttgart region is expressed by fifteen different colours. These colours create a clear set of rules that help visitors and staff to quickly find and navigate the structure.

Cheerful bands of colour direct the guests to their destination at the entrance. If the visitor's route leads up a hidden staircase, he or she will know the destination – from the two-storey foyer, he or she can already see the colourful signs on the floor above. The layered stripes blend naturally with the architecture. At each new wayfinding point, the pattern of bright colours changes to a different tone.

Opposite
The building is situated in an urban area in the immediate vicinity of the central station, as well as the sloping topography of the adjacent vineyard.

Below
From the two-storey foyer, a visitor is guided to the next destination and can already see the colourful signs on the floor above.

Opposite, below, and following
The stripes of the system reinforce
the visitor's location and serve as
stations for wayfinding information.
They also provide a colourful and
vibrant interior against the minimal
materials palette.

University of Kansas Design Week
University of Kansas Design Programme

Location: Lawrence, Kansas, USA
Usage: Educational installation
Date: 2016

University of Kansas (KU) Design Week is an annual series of events aimed at promoting interdisciplinary design thinking at the University of Kansas and within the Lawrence community. Each year, the design team creates and installs a series of poster walls in the art and design and architecture buildings to create a visual identity and build excitement. In 2016, each poster featured mini design challenges, inspirational quotes from influential design masters, or design jokes.

Neon colours transformed the clean, underutilized surfaces in the buildings to create environments that were vibrant and energizing. The posters also acknowledged and combatted feelings of mental exhaustion that design students often experience. With a limited budget, the team looked for cheap materials and ways to activate the space with resources that were already available but underutilized.

Neon sheets of letter-sized paper provided a cheap way to fill the walls with invigorating colour. Black-and-white prints kept costs low and simplified printing. In the time leading up to Design Week, students were encouraged to take down the posters and put them in private places to remind themselves to keep racking up hours of practice. Within a short amount of time, over half of the posters were removed, creating an interactive experience that caused the environment to transform over time.

Awareness created by the poster installations was a contributing factor to one of the most successful KU Design Weeks. Feedback from the University of Kansas community was overwhelmingly positive, with many people commenting on how the added colour made them happier to be in the building.

Opposite

A suite of designs based on quotes from students and designers, facts, typography, and patterns was printed in black and white on inexpensive off-the-shelf paper.

Below and opposite
With a limited budget, the team looked for cheap materials and ways to activate the space with resources that were already available but underutilized. Most studio classrooms have tackable wall surfaces, which presented an opportunity to the students.

Below
Students stapled each poster to the walls of the building with the intention of easy removal at the end of the Design Week.

Opposite
Each neon poster was printed with an event calendar on the back, giving participants a takeaway that was both informative and inspirational.

ACTUALLY MADE SOMETHING WORTH KEEPING (I THINK)

AT LEAST it's only MIDNIGHT

The only windows in A & D are on the computer.

SPENT ALL NIGHT BOXCUTTER ONLY CUT MYSELF ONCE

WE'RE ALL JUST KINDA MAKING IT UP AS WE GO

is it too obvious that i'm not following the grid?

10,000

00368 Switched color palettes for the seventeenth time this project.

skip class to finish homework for the class you're skipping.

go give 'em hell.

TEN THOUSAND HOURS

FEBRUARY 06 through FEBRUARY 12

I think time is a constraint to destroy and then reinvent. If you give me a constraint, I'll accept it. But I always try to move it around, or to readapt it. If you lock me in a room, well, I'll go out through the window!

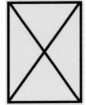

Wonderlab

LucienneRoberts+

Location: Bradford, England
Usage: Exhibition
Date: 2017

LucienneRoberts+ designed an interactive colour-based graphic installation for or the Wonderlab Gallery at the National Science and Media Museum in Bradford, to communicate the science of light and sound. The gallery features twenty-two interactive exhibits, including a musical laser tunnel and a three-dimensional printed zoetrope. Visitors can hear their voice echo through a fifteen-metre-long tube.

The large-scale installations use interactivity to engage the audience, typically children. David Shaw from LucienneRoberts+ worked with illustrator Saroj Patel to create a display that comes to life under RGB light (parrots printed on a wall appear to fly when lights change from red to green to blue). Another display created for a section on UV light allows visitors to mix and match fluorescent faces. LucienneRoberts+ explains that the space is designed to appeal to both adults and children, and be as visually enticing as it is informative.

Opposite
Large-scale images of local children appear on four-metre-high lenticular sheets: one shows a boy blinking in astonishment, and another shows a girl gasping.

Below and following
Interactive panels engage the viewer using scale and colour. The title of the gallery appears in brightly coloured letters above the entrance.

Move the pieces and create a face

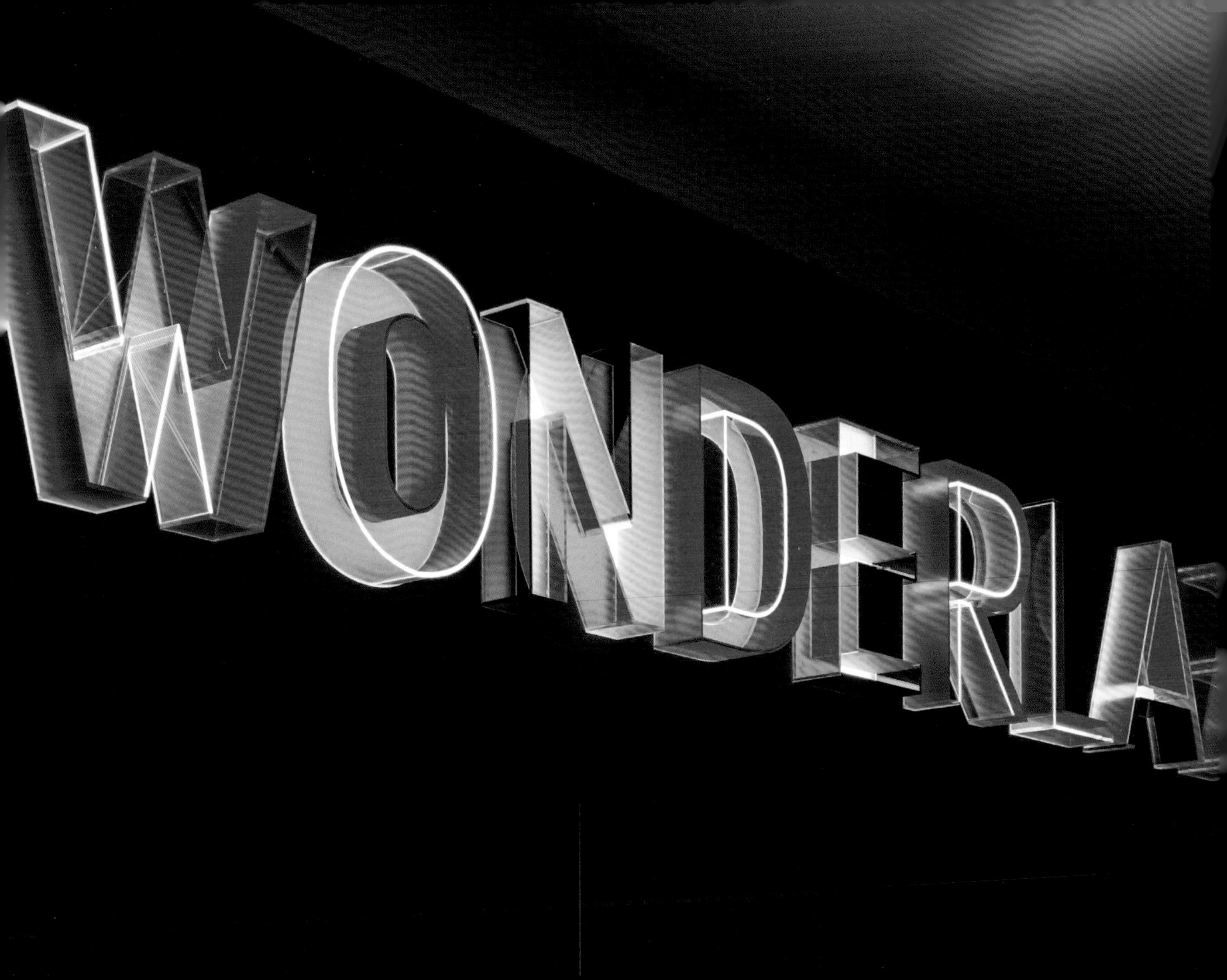
WONDERLA

Carlo Giannasca

Partner/Head of Environments, Urbanite
Interview

Did you study architecture or graphic design in school?
I did a degree in Visual Communications. I majored in Graphic Design, photography, and film and video production.

What was the first project you did that involved large environmental graphics?
The first large environmental project I worked on was to develop the signage and wayfinding system for the Downing Centre law courts in 1988.

How have your process and ideas about environmental graphics changed since then?
Our process has evolved significantly in that time. When I started working, we did everything manually (there were no computers), and we had a lot more time to work on projects than we do now. We undertake a lot more customer/user research now, before we move onto the creative execution. There is less of an emphasis on aesthetics, and more on designing practical solutions.

What was the most challenging environmental design project you've done and why was it challenging?
Every project we undertake is challenging in some way. The larger, more complex projects, such as hospitals and shopping centres, tend to be the most challenging, as they usually involve collaboration with multiple stakeholders over a long period (sometimes two to three years). One of the most challenging projects that stands out in my mind was the development of a signage and wayfinding system for Qantas's Domestic airport in Sydney. This project was challenging because we had to design the system and have it built and installed in a nine-week period.

What is your favourite project you have done?
One of my favourite projects was the design of the signage and wayfinding system for the new commercial towers in Barangaroo, Sydney. We worked with a collaborative and design-literate client who shared our design vision for the project. What resulted was a fruitful and efficient system that harmonizes with the architecture and enhances the user experience throughout the precinct. It's easier to do great work when you have a great client.

If you had the chance to redo a project now, what would you do differently?
I prefer not to think like that. We undertake every project with the focused intention of doing the very best job possible.

What is your dream environmental graphics project?
I look at every opportunity as a dream environmental graphics project, from a simple one-level commercial fit out to a fifteen-level hospital.

Where do you find inspiration for this type of work?
Inspiration comes from everywhere. I travel widely, both nationally and internationally, and gain a lot of inspiration from all that I see and experience.

What is your favourite example of environmental graphics (supergraphics) by someone other than yourself, and why?
One of my favourite environmental graphics projects is the design of the Mexico Olympics by Lance Wyman. The groundbreaking work is immensely inspirational. It influenced a generation of environmental graphic designers.

What's the best piece of advice for a young designer interested in pursuing environmental graphics as a career?
Be prepared to work hard and absorb knowledge like a sponge. Always ask questions and have a relentless desire to learn and improve.

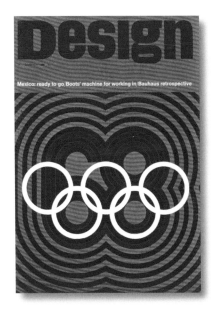

Ian Lynam

Interview

What was the first project you did that involved large environmental graphics? How did you approach the problem and solve it?

I worked at a studio in Portland Oregon called Plazm in 2001, and I got to work on a few projects for Nike revolving around the World Cup. We designed some immersive environments for children and teenagers to play, train, and develop their skills as players. The team made these settings kind of dark and insidious, playing up the antihero nature of a number of the world's best football players at that time.

We designed interior graphics, interactive football skill-building obstacles, and other bizarre shit. Imagine a mini-golf course, but dark and evil-feeling, as we were promoting football as an alternative to dominant United States sports.

How have your process and ideas about environmental graphics changed since then?

After that time, I was able to work on a few small projects, but my career was mostly devoid of environmental graphics for a decade. It was the kind of thing I always wanted to do, but finding appropriate clients was difficult in Los Angeles and Tokyo as a small studio. Over the past six years, I have been lucky enough to work with some businesses that saw the potential in the identity work I was doing previously (and now) and would let me go to town.

What was the most challenging environmental design project you've done and why was it challenging?

The most challenging project was the design of Google's Tokyo offices. Their office spaces are massive, and to be able to execute my idea – mixing different conceptual graphic themes and making everything bespoke, not just patterns – was extraordinarily time-consuming. The plans for the layout of the space kept shifting, as well. All in all, it was half of a year well spent.

What is your favourite project you've done?

It's always the one that you are currently working on, right? Now, I am working on a new interiors project for an architectural firm in rural Kansai, Japan, where I am making the holistic branding – working at every touch point for the company. I am writing the copy, designing the corporate identity, and designing the interiors. The project involves designing the typography, colour palettes, patterns, imagery, and abstract form. The result is a building made with a kit of parts presenting the firm's brand. It is incredibly exciting.

If you had the chance to redo a project now, what would you do differently?

There's this famous saying by Lord Alfred Tennyson: 'Tis better to have loved and lost than never to have loved at all.' I take that approach to life – be it design or romantic pursuits or trying weird food. (Randomly, I heard that saying early in life, but up until a few years ago thought that Elton John had said it – somehow I thought it fitted into the 'Rocket Man' ethos of things . . .)

Collectively, contemporary culture is caught up in this twin conceptual hang-up around nostalgia and time machines – we don't get to redo things, though we'd like to. I just try and do everything to the best of my ability, but also don't have a large enough portfolio of this kind of work to consider redos – I am just grateful to get the projects I do.

What is your dream environmental graphics project?

I am excited by the idea of projects that hark back to old school supergraphics à la Munich or Mexico City Olympics. The graphic identity of a business or event was expressed in the interior and exterior of a project, as well as expressed in a totalizing plan that extends into other areas, as well. I'm currently working on a plan for a graphic skin to wrap the UBER headquarters in Pittsburgh, Pennsylvania, with a local community arts group there – if this scheme could extend into the company's interiors, I'd be excited.

Where do you find inspiration for this type of work?

The work of Otl Aicher is inspiring regarding his holistic planning, often alongside Norman Foster, for many of his past initiatives. The Los Angeles designer Jens Gehlhaar is one of my favourites for his modular approaches to design.

The late British designer Barney Bubbles is extraordinarily inspirational for his conflation of exposing the processes of graphic design in his projects, his referencing of art/design history, and his exceedingly high craft and graphic expression. Contemporary San Francisco designer Eli Carrico is my muse – no one does work like him globally.

What's the best piece of advice for a young designer interested in pursuing environmental graphics as a career?

Be entrepreneurial. Get your hustle pants on. Find a company that does work that you admire and work with them for a while. Don't get bogged down in the minutiae – sure, there are always specifications to fuss over, but take the long view. One will always find sustainability in working for others, but dream projects are usually won outside of the parameters of being employed by others. Oswald Cooper, the designer of the typeface Cooper Black, said that a robust piece of work has 'heft, gravy, and swing' – projects should have depth, breadth, detail, and seductive form. Also, be nice to people.

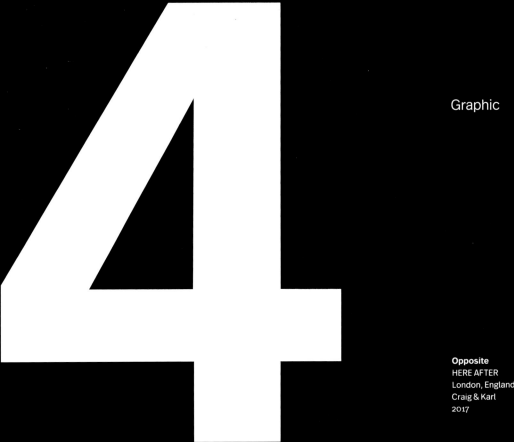

4

Graphic

Opposite
HERE AFTER
London, England
Craig & Karl
2017

100 California
Volume, Inc.

Location: San Francisco, California, USA
Usage: Branded environment, wayfinding
Date: 2017

The challenge for Volume: reposition a building created for a former American industrial giant in the mid-twentieth century to appeal to the creative information workers of the twenty-first century. Volume answered the challenge by designing graphics for 100 California, originally Bethlehem Steel's stark west coast headquarters (built in 1960), into a place more welcoming, human-focused and sensitive to the San Francisco worker of today.

Volume created a brand and marketing strategy that celebrates Bethlehem Steel's history and connects the ambition of the mid-century industrial age to the innovations of today's technology-fuelled era.

The creative process took cues from the building's industrial origins and human-focused mid-century modernism. The graphics draw upon the interplay between history and the present day – for example, the elevator cabs. They also relate to the building's architecture and location, with orange bike lanes on the end-of-trip San Francisco map mural and the steel building directory, which matches the steel of the building.

Opposite
The graphics utilize replicated cross marks and lines to create a cohesive experience. The cross symbol represents a steel support seen from the top.

Opposite
The designers placed an aerial view of the location of the building in the reception foyer. The mural of crosses and lines connects to the other graphic elements in the building.

Below
The orange bike lanes on the San Francisco map mural provide information for the twenty-first-century worker and reflect the city's changing demographic.

Left and opposite
The graphics in the lifts each
tell a different story relating to
the history of the building and
its Bethlehem Steel origins. The
overprinted images and collage
aesthetic ensured that the effect
was contemporary, not antique.

3M Australia Headquarters
THERE

Location: Sydney, Australia
Usage: Branded environment
Date: 2012

THERE Sydney designed a branded environment that celebrated the history of 3M's brand: 'harnessing the chain reaction of new ideas'.

Using the concept of collaboration, THERE developed a unique pattern for each of the six floors. The creative team used 3M's extensive image library of macro-photography of micro replication technology as the foundation of the geometric forms.

Simon Hancock, the project's creative director, explains, 'We created more than fifteen large illustrative and graphically treated portraits that pay homage to innovators and scientists from 3M's history.' THERE celebrated the company's rich heritage with the timeline. The wall graphic welcomes visitors to the Australian headquarters, showcasing the company's brand evolution over the last one hundred years.

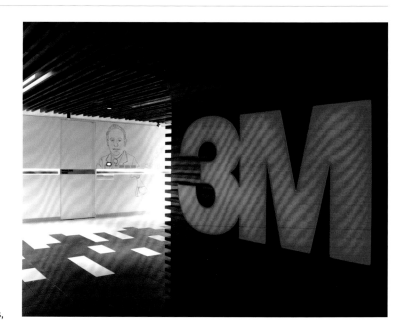

Opposite

The illuminated 3M logo and a portrait of one of the company's innovators brand the foyer.

Below

The 100-square-metre (1,000-square-foot) wall at the ground-floor entrance is a dimensional timeline made from horizontal slats routed at different depths to form 3M's logo history.

Following, left

A detail shows the routed forms and dimension of the timeline. An illuminated inset strip contains the pattern for each floor. Panels of information are placed on each illustration.

Following, right

The 1.5-metre (5-foot) high-gloss red 3M logo standing boldly in the entrance foyer states, unmistakably, 'This is 3M'.

1957 The Sydney office moves to the Leuben Brasch building on Wentworth Avenue, Sydney NSW – Australia

1958 The Melbourne office relocates to 17/23 Queensbridge Street, Melbourne VIC – Australia

The Tasmanian branch opens at 201 Elizabeth Street, Hobart TAS – Australia

The South Australian branch opens at 9 North Terrace, Adelaide SA – Australia

959 The Brisbane branch opens at the Plumbridge Building at 166 Barry Parade, Brisbane QLD – Australia

Worldwide results are consolidated and sales exceed $500 million

The Field Guide to Supergraphics

Below
In the workspace, large-scale illustrative and graphic portraits highlight talented innovators and scientists from 3M's history.

Opposite
Bold directional graphics in the parking garage use simple icons and a minimal colour palette.

LIFTS TO RECEPTION

Beijing Design Week
Johnson Banks

Location: Beijing, China
Usage: Installation
Date: 2011

Johnson Banks designed banners and a set of images for Beijing Design Week, titled 'What Design Can Do', to celebrate the power of design through Chinese and British collaborations. The graphics appeared on postcards and posters in both the UK and China, but the most visible application was the set of six huge banners that hung on a former power generator plant in the 751 district of Beijing, one of the hubs for the city's Design Week.

The UK and Chinese project teams developed a series of slogans headlining global design ideas and theories, which intended to echo the passion for sloganeering that has played a unique role in Chinese culture and society. These headlines included 'New from Old', 'Shared Design History', 'Collaborative Practice', and 'The Power of Making'.

Two final themes focus on 'Design Process' and 'The Next Generation'. The studio worked with animators Realise to create the imagery for the posters, rendered using three-dimensional software. The images created a bizarre world of real and imagined images, which were then rendered out in pieces and reconstructed to provide images large enough for the banners.

The banner 'New from Old' is inspired by the development of the keyboard and typewriter, and illustrates the impact of the past on our future. The 'Shared Design History' banner contrasts Chinese and British porcelain to show how our shared influences date back centuries.

Opposite
The banners are a counterpoint to the industrial setting of the power generator plant. Contrasting colours and complex imagery create a modern, clear, and bold statement.

Left and opposite
The six banners are on display in
751 D-Park's Power Square, on the
towers of an old power station. The
area, now regarded as the city's
design hub, is close to Beijing's 798
Art District.

The Field Guide to Supergraphics

HBF
Vanderbyl Design

Location: Washington DC, USA
Usage: Branded environment
Date: 2015

Michael Vanderbyl's initial break into the commercial design industry came in the early 1980s when the North Carolina-based contract furniture company HBF contacted him to design a simple postcard advertising a trade show booth. At the time, HBF was called Hickory Business Furniture and made very traditional pieces, including wingback chairs. 'I saw the potential of the company', Vanderbyl recalls. 'Even though they only asked me for a postcard, I presented them with an entire programme: a new logo, tagline, catalogue, advertising campaign, and ideas for new products. HBF hired me on the spot.'

HBF's Washington DC showroom features floor-to-ceiling windows on one side, creating an abundance of natural light. Vanderbyl creates a dramatic backdrop with minimal construction: walls are removed to open up space, and the walls are painted white to enhance the natural light reflection. Six double-sided 2.5-metre (8-foot) monoliths feature portraits of designers. These twelve pictures represent a selection of the many furniture designers that have created products for HBF over the years. The large scale photographs also act to provide a visual separation between the company's products. The overall palette of light-coloured finishes creates a neutral stage to exhibit HBF's products while at the same time avoiding visual clutter.

Opposite
The large-scale portraits enhance the space, add a human element, and celebrate the brand's commitment to design.

Following
Silver typography on a white wall comunicates HBF's values and mission, serving as a backdrop to the company's products.

HBF OFFERS A DIVERSE PORTF[...] [...] OF PRODUCTS B[...]
TOGETHER BY AN ETHOS OF DESIGN THAT DEFINES
REFINES THE CONCEPT OF NEW MODERN ELEGA[...]
OUR COMMITMENT TO DESIGN EXCELLENCE IS W[...]
INTO AND THROUGHOUT OUR CULTURE. HBF HAS S[...]
BENCHMARK FOR THE ART AND CRA[...] OF FURNI[...]
MAKING WHILE CREATING PRODUCT[...] [...] ARE US[...]
AND SIMPLE, FUNCTIONAL AND ELEGA[...]

HERE AFTER
Craig & Karl

Location: London, England
Usage: Installation
Date: 2017

Designers Craig & Karl have playfully revived a derelict petrol station on Wood Lane in London's White City to create HERE AFTER, a public and visually arresting art installation that riffs on the area's importance to British broadcasting history.

Adapting the bright hues of a television test card, the colourful design is a nod towards the petrol station's location, set directly between Television Centre, the BBC's former headquarters, and White City Place, the former BBC Media Village, both of which reopened in 2017 following extensive redevelopment.

HERE AFTER gives the site a new life by twisting the appearance of commonplace petrol stations and patching together the mishmash of striped forms and colours found in the branding of major petrol companies. In an almost chaotic fashion, the site reinvents itself from the fragments of its past.

Opposite, below, and following
Vibrant, striped sections of painted
colour wind and bend around
the petrol station site, leading all

passersby and visitors to discover
the space's 'here after', a reference
to heaven or utopia, suggesting a
place or something yet to come.

233

Hyundai City Outlet
Thonik

Location: Seoul, South Korea
Usage: Public space, wayfinding
Date: 2017

Hyundai City Outlet is a new branch in an existing building. Thonik designed the facade that integrates the visual identity and the architecture. Dongdaemun Gate is a beautiful piece of the heritage of Seoul. Large department stores with neon lights on their facades line the main street. The building of Hyundai City Outlet has a public square in front of the building. A glass lift shaft dominates the facade of the building.

Thonik designed the identity for the City Outlet with the identity of The Hyundai Department Store in mind. The logo refers to the symbol of a gate, referencing the location. The colours connect to the abundant neon signs in the area and traditional painted decorations on buildings in Korea. A repetition of the 'H' symbol adorns the lift shaft, like a colourful ladder going up to the sky.

Opposite
The identity system and logo for
Hyundai City Outlet reframe the
symbol of a gate and neon signage.

Below
The large-scale logo adds colour,
energy, and an iconic element to the
public square at Dongdaemun Gate.

The facade design adds energy
to the building and the square. It
connects to the architecture and
provides an iconic image.

Below
Wayfinding signage incorporates the identity's forms and connects to the neon in the neighbourhood and the black exterior of the building.

Opposite
The 'H' logo on the lift shaft uses a colour scheme that reflects both the heritage and the present-day spectacle of Seoul's Dongdaemun area.

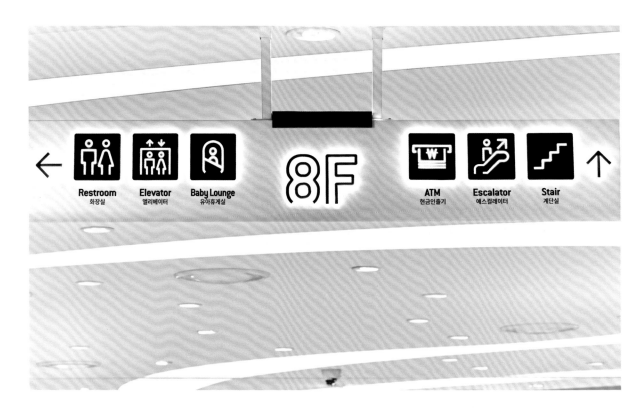

Innsbruck Exhibition Centre
Büro Uebele

Location: Innsbruck, Austria
Usage: Wayfinding
Date: 2013

Büro Uebele provided a new identity and environmental programme for the characterless Innsbruck Exhibition Centre. This changed the old-style cacophony by overlaying a new and harmonious vibe. National flags – intrinsic to the exhibition centre's business – form the basis of the graphic design. They have been divested of their heraldic elements – the shields and animals, the swords, sabres, and stars – and of their national colour schemes, and allocated a single colour shade along with the text. Particular halls employ the individual text-patterns as a wayfinding function.

When the text-patterns are lined up together in the orientation overviews, the unique design become part of a different, larger system. The result is a systematic chaos, an orderly disorder that responds to the venue's intrinsic disorderly qualities.

The brightly coloured stripes make a bold statement, standing out against the non-uniformity of the setting. In the neatly dimensioned and relatively monochrome new building, they add contrast and variation, providing a rhythmic element that naturally expands to cover whole walls in particular locations, such as staircases, a restaurant, and the underground car park.

The system's distinctive features include its treatment of umlauts and the structural simplicity of the basic two-tone composition (colour and contrast colour), which responds to the variety of surfaces, materials, and colours in the halls.

Opposite
The centre's massive volume and rectangular shape contrast with the surrounding architecture and landscape.

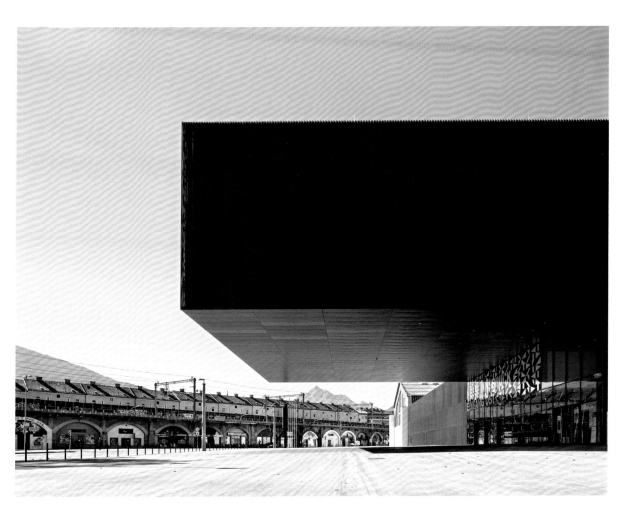

Below
The patterns at the entrance are
the visitor's first view of the ordered
disorder of patterns on the interior.

Opposite and following
Bright and colourful patterns add
contrast and variation, providing
a rhythmic element that naturally
expands to cover whole walls in the
monochromatic building.

The individual elements of the
geometric pattern are enlarged to
encompass the entire wall in the
underground car park.

Magic Box, State Grid Pavilion
ATELIER BRÜCKNER GmbH

Location: Shanghai, China
Usage: Exhibition
Date: 2010

The Magic Box is the pulsating heart of the State Grid Pavilion, a Chinese state-owned power company. Standing on a glass bridge, visitors are immersed in a spatial installation that becomes an emotionally charged experience.

A tight grid of LEDs on the inner walls of the Magic Box enclose the visitors on six sides. They become part of a film, which transports them on a journey through time and space: from the origins of energy, by way of the transfer of energy across all of China, down to the consumption of energy in the cities of the future.

In striking images, the film (directed by Marc Tamschick, Berlin) conveys the company's responsibilities and visions: the responsible supply of a solid national power grid, which leads to improvements in living conditions in cities.

The all-embracing power grid, the prerequisite for a targeted supply of energy, is represented in the prologue and epilogue to the film as an animated grid, revealing three-dimensionality and depth. The exterior facades of the Magic Box also utilize the large-scale motion graphics. The building appears to float above the surface and is engulfed in energy-related images.

Opposite
The Magic Box, State Grid Pavilion is designed to represent a metallic square with a crystal cube embedded inside. Covered by LED screens, the box appears as a silver cube and transforms into a motion experience.

Following
High-resolution LED screens and twenty-three-track audio create an immersive media-enhanced space for 250 visitors that communicates the way energy enhances life.

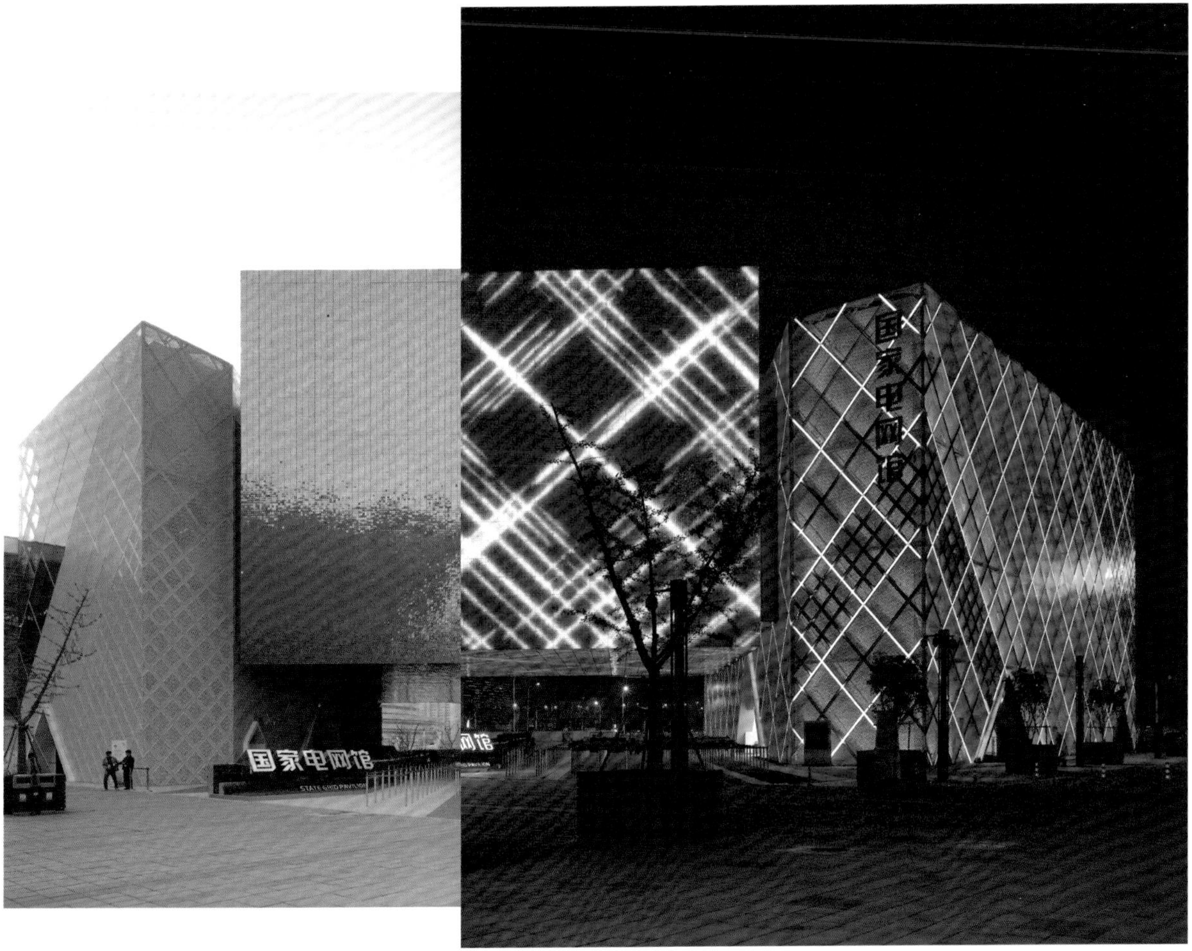
国家电网馆
国家电网馆

Macquarie Bank Ltd Headquarters
EGG Office

Location: Sydney, Australia
Usage: Identifying, wayfinding
Date: 2011

Macquarie Group, Australia's largest investment bank, needed a comprehensive signage and graphics programme for its new headquarters in Sydney. This forward-thinking bank values transparency, a global outlook, and collaborative work behaviour, and sought to express those brand attributes in its physical space.

EGG Office developed an overarching graphic device derived from the building exterior's open diagonal grid pattern over the glass facade and used the grid as the inspiration for a custom font and pictograms. The grid and the open texture of other patterns and materials convey the idea of transparency. Gridlike patterns laser-cut through opaque panels create rhythm and continuity, and the surprising scale of pictograms and the playfulness of the supergraphics support an open attitude and a collaborative work environment.

The exterior main identification graphics are tall, vertical totems with LED screens that project patterns, colours, and type, and hint at the building interiors, as well as animating the entry courtyard and drawing visitors inside.

Opposite
EGG Office developed a custom typeface based on the structure of the building's exterior and the concept of transparency.

Below
Supergraphics executed on large glass panels allow for meeting and conference room activities to be revealed in whole or in part.

Opposite
Themed plazas on each level underscore the notion of collaboration by referring to various collaborative environments and meeting places.

Below and opposite
The EGG team developed unique graphic design elements and colour palettes for each plaza area to communicate function. This creates distinct environments in which employees meet and collaborate.

Open Your Space
Tongji University

Location: Shanghai, China
Usage: Public space
Date: 2015

Open Your Space (OYS) is a research and design project for regional innovation strategy exploring an urban community that contains physical spaces with social and cultural significance. It draws on the relationship between design factors and socially motivated ideas in a Chinese urban context, as well as exploring and practising how design intervention shapes the public realm to maximize shared value in the built environment.

OYS adapted a design approach based on principles of acupuncture: a series of small but connected design projects generate systemic changes. The design team created ten site-specific projects and more than thirty micro design interventions, spread across outdoor public space within the centre of Siping community. The process involved residents, artists, and students, making a formerly plain wall into a colourful expression and establishing a connection between the participants.

Right and opposite
The Wide Life public art project uses plants as the primary images, responding to the increasingly man-made living environment, and promoting the balance between urban life and nature.

Below and opposite
The OYS Wall project used
graphics as a response to the
urban environment. The project
applied graphics and colour using
the elements of the 'open your
space' logo.

Following
The OYS project follows three
main design strategies: empower
multiple stakeholders to drive

local change; encourage creativity
and new appropriation; and
enhance the diversity of the
community environment.

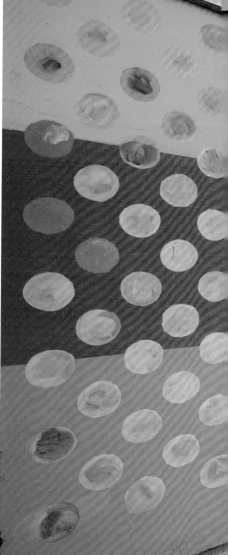

Parts 'n Pieces
Anna Taratiel

Location: Amsterdam, Netherlands
Usage: Public space
Date: 2014

R.U.A., Reflexo on Urban Art – is an organization that works with artists to create public space exhibitions. In 2014, the group challenged Anna Taratiel to design a graphic treatment for twenty-six murals on a large apartment building in the Amsterdam neighbourhood of Hoptille. Taratiel tackled the project by creating an online and analogue version of a game that would involve as many people in the neighbourhood as possible.

Taratiel created twenty different shapes with a complementary colour palette. Users could combine the different shapes in any way they chose. Taratiel then collected the 'parts 'n pieces' and chose the final compositions for implementation on the building. Many of the residents were pleased with the murals. Taratiel explains the larger concept: 'I live in a city – which is total chaos – so I am always looking for ways to bring balance and harmony into that space, or to give "sense" to it.'

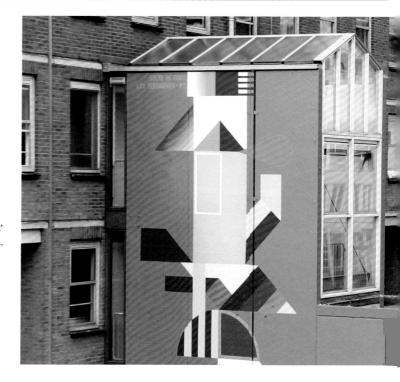

Opposite and below

Taratiel describes her work as being the creation of layers and structures of a fantasy world that is almost tangential. The abstract shapes on the structure come together as a composition, interacting and referencing one another.

Following

People from the neighbourhood or anywhere in the world could influence Taratiel's creative process by sending in their own compositions.

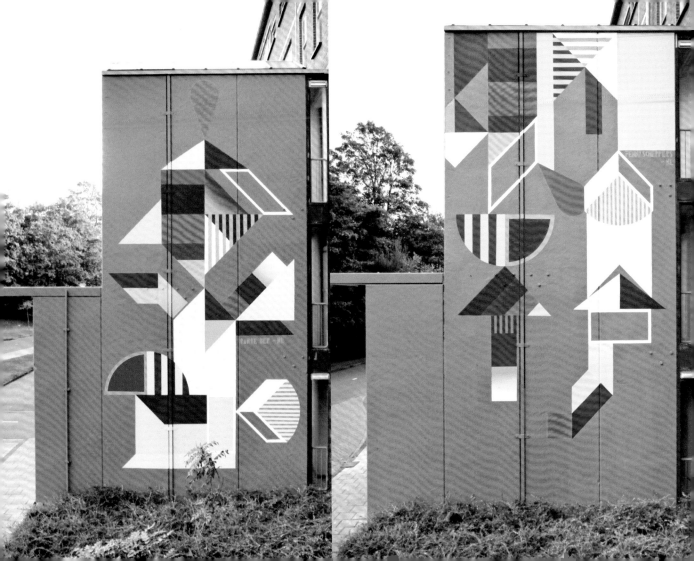

Rabobank
THERE

Location: Sydney, New South Wales, Australia
Usage: Wayfinding
Date: 2017

Rabobank is the world's leading food and agribusiness bank. THERE was asked to help develop its internal branding and signage across five levels of a new regional hub for its Australia and New Zealand markets.

Drawing inspiration from the business's core agricultural offer, THERE developed a series of textural patterns associated with farming, and in particular the clear graphic language of cartography and land-mapping. They then applied this distinct design language across a variety of touch points throughout.

A primary driver for the branding was to ensure seamless integration with the interior design, which utilized a warm 'domestic' materiality throughout the fit out. A bold monochromatic style, paired with a simple wayfinding system and simple iconography, was created, resulting in an understated and elegant spatial experience that harmonizes different floors and spaces.

Opposite

Graphics are applied to the lift areas and locker banks, helping to activate otherwise forgotten operational spaces.

Below and following

Three-dimensional level identification signage is integrated with the design to further aid the vertical navigation.

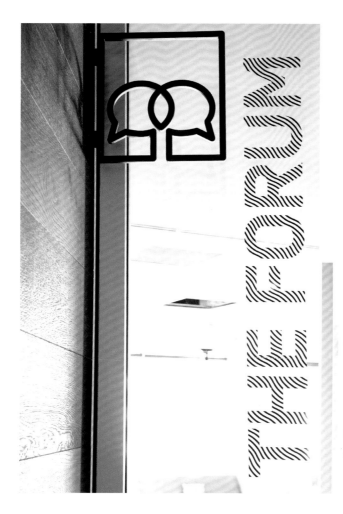

WE FOCUS
ON
GLOBAL
FOOD
SECURITY
AND
EMPOWERING
COMMUNITIES.

RESPECT,
INTEGRITY,
PROFESSIONALISM
AND
SUSTAINABILITY—
OUR CORE
VALUES
ARE THE
FOUNDATIONS
FOR OUR
ACTIONS.

THE
STRAIGHT
TALKING
SAVINGS
BANK.

FIRE HOSE REEL
FIRE EXTINGUISHER

Ravensbourne

Johnson Banks Design Ltd

Location: London, England
Usage: Branded environment, wayfinding
Date: 2009

Ravensbourne University, in Greenwich, London, inhabits a building meticulously clad with 30,000 interlinked tiles in a tessellating pattern. The visual statement of the tiles – three shapes with multiple permutations possible – metaphorically echoes the education process as a multi-layered and evolving experience.

Johnson Banks rotated the tiles, which creates a sense of movement. The signage and wayfinding are critical to the building's success as a viable work-and-play place. Because of the complex interior architecture, with staggered floors, similar to an underground car park, Johnson Banks opted to use supergraphics in the form of vast painted and stencilled shapes derived from the tiling pattern. These incorporated large floor numerals to make it clear to visitors exactly where they were at any stage of their visit.

Opposite

Following a tiling pattern established by Roger Penrose, tens of thousands of anodized aluminium tiles tessellate across the building's skin and dominate the design

Below

The tile shapes inform the large directional forms with essential information. These direct the viewer, as traditional small directional arrows would otherwise do.

Following

Corridors and walkways link two discrete sections of the building. Level numbers 1 to 10 replace the original level names (1a, 1b, 2a, 2b, and so on). Now, one side has odd numbers, and the opposite side has even numbers. In some cases the shapes 'bleed' over onto walls and ceilings, or around corners

701 to 703
704 prototyping

705 prototyping
706

301 open media
302 online edit 1
303 online edit 2
304 audio post production
305 colour grading
306 audio recording studio
307 audio recording control
308 media studio
309
310 to 313

lift serving levels
0 M 2 4 6 7 8 9

Below
The new logo and tiling pattern were the starting point for Johnson Banks to develop a series of shapes stencilled onto walls for navigation and identification.

Opposite
Three tiles create the logo forms. These incorporate the Ravensbourne name, which is added to the tiles at different angles. There are multiple combinations for the logo.

Sweet As One
Craig & Karl

Location: Hong Kong, China
Usage: Public space
Date: 2015

Incorporating nearly 12,000 kg (26,500 lbs) of candy and covering nearly 4,300 square metres (46,000 square feet), the installation for the Sweet As One exhibition in Chengdu aimed to celebrate the Chinese New Year in a festive and celebratory way. The curators – Hong Kong creative studio AllRightsReserved – aimed to bring awareness to the plight of underprivileged children in rural areas. The artwork within the candy carpet includes a variety of symbolism, from blooming flowers that symbolize good luck to stylized pandas (Chengdu being their 'hometown').

The candy carpet measured 185 metres long by 7 metres wide (605 feet by 23 feet). Small squares were filled with single-coloured sweets and these squares were arranged to form a grid that became the basis of the artwork. Over 2,000 volunteers meticulously assembled the entire piece by hand over just five days. Organizers donated meals and the sweets from the installation to the under-privileged in the city.

Opposite
Thousands of individual pieces of candy are grouped to create images, symbols and graphic shapes along a roadway in Hong Kong.

Below and opposite
Volunteers meticulously laid out the
pieces of candy following a grid to
create the temporary, enormous
sweet installation.

Teknion

Vanderbyl Design

Location: Chicago, Illinois, USA;
and Montreal, Canada
Usage: Branded environment
Date: 2016

Michael Vanderbyl has worked with the furniture maker Teknion on solutions for environments, collateral, identity, and furniture design. The showrooms and trade show spaces demonstrate the restrained elegance and minimal palette of Vanderbyl's approach. The Montreal showroom reflects the city's French heritage. A high-tech modern dot pattern reinterprets a traditional French brocade effect applied to the showroom's feature walls. The effect is a transparent wall that runs down the central spine of the display space and allows natural light to penetrate into the interior of the showroom.

Walls in the Teknion Chicago showroom are clad with custom-designed FSC-certified panels. The opaque white sculptural graphic form creates a backdrop visible from all points in the showroom. The effect is opaque and yet provides the translucency to allow the natural daylight to pervade the full depth of the showroom. For a trade show exhibit, the power of words saturates the entire exhibit floor, with their sustainability statement articulating Teknion's environmental philosophy. The text is interactive, displayed under furniture for viewers to find.

Opposite
The patterned walls are reverse stencils cut out of 0.5-centimetre-thick (a quarter inch-thick) aluminium panels and finished in gloss white. The floor is also high-gloss white, creating a range of shades within one colour.

Below and opposite
The 90-centimetre-tall (36-inch-tall) Garamond letters, inkjet-printed onto the recycled-fibre carpet, read: 'At Teknion we believe that every leap forward is the sum of many steps. Small moves can create a significant shift, leading us toward our larger goal of shaping a genuinely sustainable future.'

Below and opposite
An organic-patterned wall treatment cut from panels made of milk jugs and other recycled post-industrial plastic encloses this 315-square-metre (3,400-square-foot) booth. Fully recyclable, the treatment is opaque but provides translucency, creating a new allusion to nature.

Wired Store
Mother Design

Location: New York, New York, USA
Usage: Retail
Date: 2012

For *Wired* magazine's annual New York retail experience, *Wired* asked Mother Design for an environmental design concept that helped to showcase the most innovative products and technologies of the past year.

Mother's team added a physical dimension to the magazine's existing 'What's Inside' monthly feature. Mother Design added architecture to space, designed custom furniture and fixtures, and created a visual system that spoke to both the editorial and experiential inner workings of the publication. Large-scale interactive installations investigate a variety of products, from mobile phones to cars.

Mother created a digital shopping platform to purchase any product featured within the space. A mixture of commissioned and selected works were displayed, featuring older technologies, aesthetically exploded.

Opposite

Every possible element, including staff T-shirts, incorporated the minimal typography and monochromatic colour palette.

Below

The weaving of language created a wall that explained the content of the retail experience as a collage, rather than a traditional text wall.

Below
Objects are combined with flat graphic forms to reference the language of instruction diagrams, manuals, and on-screen icons.

Opposite
Typographic collage incorporating the vocabulary of entertainment with multicoloured objects and a series of *Star Wars* posters.

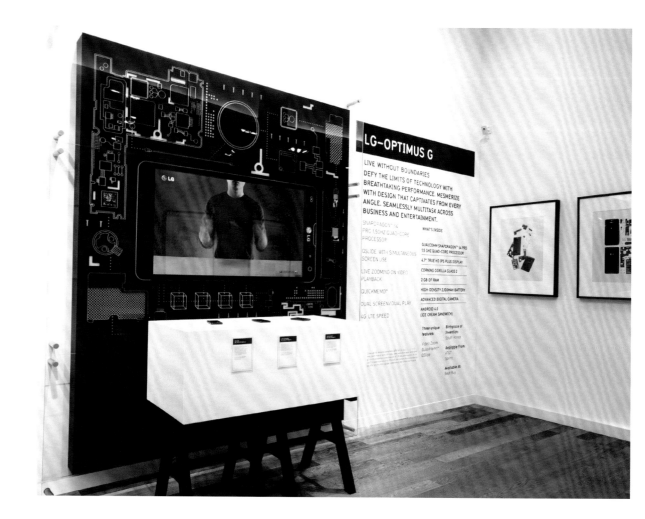

Opposite

A wall-sized capabilities list, diagram, and video deconstruct the LG-Optimus G smartphone. The video screen's dimensions match the phone's screen.

Below, left

A series of black-and-white steps holds icons, instructions, and contents for a selection of Incase products.

Below, right

The Citi® Price Rewind programme is presented with a laptop, 'check out box', and oversized instructions.

Adam Brodsley and Eric Heiman
Volume, Inc.
Interview

What was the first project you did that involved large environmental graphics?

AB: The California Academy of Sciences Islands of Evolution main floor exhibit programme was probably the first project of this sort we were intimately involved in. We were thrust into the nexus of the CAS's new brand (designed by Kit Hinrichs / Pentagram), the new CAS building (designed by Renzo Piano), and a deluge of content about the Galápagos and Madagascar. The main floor of Piano's new building had this poetic, almost ancient temple-like quality, so we wanted to create something that was as visceral as it was educational. The lush, macro-scale imagery does the former by pulling people into the individual exhibit modules, which, upon close inspection, deliver the latter.

EH: We have this 'three-twos' rule (cribbed from our pal Jean Orlebeke) we like to follow: all good design needs to work in two seconds, two minutes, and two hours, and it's especially important for content-heavy, large-scale environment projects.

How have your process and ideas about environmental graphics changed?

AB: Not too much, actually. Our rigorous, bang-our-heads-against-the-wall-for-the-first-few-weeks ideation process is the same as it is for a book, a website, or a brand – though there's a lot more consideration of scale and materials, obviously. And full-size mockups are a must.

EH: As a former architect-in-training, I have immense respect for the architects who design the spaces in which we do our work. We always want to create impactful design, but design that also fits into the project's

holistic vision, that is a natural extension of the space – as opposed to a simply cosmetic layer that fights it.

AB: Not that it's about always deferring to the architects, since it's the client and audience needs that are paramount. But an impactful solution doesn't always manifest as large type and bold colours, though we certainly use such strategies when they are called for.

EH: What's always stuck with me from architecture school is this idea of 'site-specific' design. In other words, taking the context – landscape, location, use, people, local culture, etc. – into consideration when making design decisions. Graphic design and especially branding are often positioned as one-size-fits-all systems – consistency above all else. But that can get boring (if not oppressive) pretty quickly. This is where things like the architecture, the site and surroundings, the people that work there – the overall existing context – can inform and enrich the design. Coherence of communication doesn't necessarily mean everything must look the same in every location. It's at this intersection of consistency and variety that is interesting, especially in the environment space.

What was the most challenging environmental design project you've done?

EH: The difficulties come less with the design and more the execution. I tend to take the approach that these days anything we design can be fabricated, so we shouldn't get too hung up on execution too early in the process. But sometimes our imaginations go beyond what's possible – or at least possible, budget-wise. And sometimes Adam (who is much more versed in materials and fabrication processes) will

just tell us naïfs, 'There's no way that will possibly work, folks.' Not that I don't like to challenge him, but he's usually right.

AB: The Boy Scouts Sustainability Treehouse was probably the most difficult in this respect because of its size and complexity. The design was pretty much approved in the first presentation. But making it was a whole other animal. Painting big type on a wall? Pretty easy. Creating a huge Rube Goldberg ball machine? Not so much.

EH: Adam shouldered a lot of the burden for making sure this project was completed with the usual eye for detail we demand. Don't get between him and quality execution. He's tenacious.

What is your favourite project you've done?

AB: The California Academy of Sciences exhibits for the great subject matter, working with great people (including Renzo Piano), the incredible location, and the results. And how often does one get to request that the entomologist interns pin up thousands of ladybirds for your display?

EH: I will always love the aforementioned Boy Scouts Treehouse – for the design, and because it was for an audience and area of the country that rarely get the 'good' design we sophisticated urbanites celebrate. But my favourite lately has been the First Amendment 'moat' that was part of the workplace branding system we created for Bloomberg's DC News Media office. I just loved the idea of carving that US Constitution text (which includes freedom of the press) in marble around the entire perimeter of the office to create this symbolic barrier that 'protects' the journalists within. It's not flashy or formally innovative (and impossible to photograph well), but in the aftermath of Trump's election and his attacks on the press, it's become this galvanizing symbol for the Bloomberg employees who work there.

If you had the chance to redo a project now, what would you do differently?
EH: There are probably some select tiny details I'd change, but overall our projects in this space have all turned out better than I could have ever imagined.

AB: Way back before Volume, on a job for Apple (just before Apple was cool again), I remember silk-screening portraits of employee faces on 10,000 square feet of wall panels for a huge exhibit. Unfortunately, the pearlescent ink colour inverted the images, and they all looked like X-rays, and it was too late to redo them. Fortunately, no one noticed. (Again, remember this is pre-Jobs.) It's good to remember that no one is perfect, and not every project will turn out well, despite trying our damndest.

What is your dream environmental graphics project?
EH: I would love to design a memorial or monument of some kind. Something that would be around for a while and has some real emotional freight to it. I saw Maya Lin's Vietnam Veterans Memorial in Washington DC as a child not long after it first opened, and the experience has never left me.

AB: I agree with Heiman on that one, especially since so much of what we do as designers is usually pretty ephemeral. We work on a brand for a year, and in five years the company is gone or acquired. We spend six months building a website, and six months after that the technology changes. Too bad the San Francisco Presidio Gateway competition team we were on didn't land the project. That would have been a good opportunity to realize this dream.

What is your favourite example of environmental graphics by someone other than yourself, or historically, and why?
EH: Certainly the Vietnam Veterans Memorial I mentioned before (all the more impressive to me because it uses the Optima typeface, which I despise). I always loved that EVERYBODY installation Tibor Kalman and Scott Stowell did in New York in the 1990s. The wooden doors with the carved dimensional type at Sagrada Familia in Barcelona. The 1993 Shimon Attie projections of pre-war Jewish storefronts on their present-day sites in Berlin. Rigo 23's *One Tree* mural in San Francisco.

Ben Rubin's *Moveable Type* installation in the lobby of the *New York Times* building. Again, I tend to gravitate towards work that goes past just the graphic and is more site-specific, tactile, and/or experiential. Or even something that is just needed more. My friend and colleague Ryan Clifford took a group of MICA students to Greensboro, Alabama for a week-long design blitz. They ended up designing and installing this great 'Welcome to Greensboro' mural. It was the only piece of art like that for miles around.

AB: Who can choose just one? That's why Eric listed half a dozen. The first thing that popped into my mind is the work by Barbara Stauffacher Solomon at Sea Ranch. It doesn't communicate in a direct way, but I love the colour, the graphic quality, and how it lives in a unique environment. The roots of supergraphics all go back to that project.

What's the best piece of advice for a young designer interested in pursuing environmental graphics as a career?
EH: Do it! We're always looking for designers with this expertise to help us! It's not the easiest path to pursue initially, since the expertise needed falls between graphic design and architecture, and neither field seems to really want to own it (at least in the education space). I started teaching a class at CCA recently to fill this gap, but there's only so much one can teach in a single semester.

AB: Environmental graphics, signage programmes, and site-specific installations all require an added sensitivity to scale and context that isn't as simple as it looks. And this work will most likely be around longer than the typical ephemeral graphic design project, so that sensitivity is doubly important.

Vernacular

Opposite
Planned Parenthood
New York, New York, USA
Pentagram
2017

Boudin Bread
Studio Hinrichs

Location: San Francisco, California, USA
Usage: Branded environment, exhibition
Date: 2006

Established in 1849, at the start of the California gold rush, the Boudin Sourdough Bakery is the oldest retail establishment in San Francisco. Its authentic historical connection to the gold rush of 1849, the founding of the city, and real sourdough bread make the bakery a natural tourist attraction.

Studio Hinrichs was commissioned to design and implement a comprehensive identity for the compound, including curating a Boudin museum and bakery tour, and creating internal and external signage for a new café and retail environment, graphics for Bistro Boudin, and assorted collateral in connection with this new location.

Using the company's history as a theme, the supergraphics and large-scale information signage reinforce Boudin's authentic ties to the Bay Area, while creating a retail attraction as a destination in itself for the thousands of tourists who visit Fisherman's Wharf each year.

Opposite

Fisherman's Wharf gets its name from the mid- to late 1800s, when Italian immigrant fishermen moved to San Francisco. The city was in the midst of a population explosion due to the 1849 gold rush, and seafood was in high demand.

Below

Hinrichs applied an industrial and varied aesthetic with neon signage and a large-scale identity to the flagship of the Boudin brand at

Fisherman's Wharf. Here, visitors see the bakers at work and learn the history of the sourdough bread and San Francisco.

Opposite and below
Graphics with different colours
and typography recalling Boudin's
heritage identify locations such as the
marketplace, café, and espresso bar.

Das Neue Österreich
ART+COM Studios

Location: Vienna, Austria
Usage: Exhibition
Date: 2005

In 2005, Austria celebrated fifty years of postwar independence. To mark the occasion, Vienna's Belvedere Palace housed an exhibition covering one hundred years of Austrian history. At its centre: the original Treaty of Independence. The focus of the presentation was a 250-metre (820-foot) Austrian flag, which ran through all the exhibition rooms and acted as a 'narrator'. Seventeen multimedia installations were woven into the flag, making Austrian history an interactive experience.

A visitor could listen to the flag with an audio installation consisting of original recordings from politicians from the first decade of the twentieth century, such as Emperor Franz Joseph I. Another installation explored 1938, when Austria became a part of Germany and lost its flag. The exhibition flag was grey in this section, with a bird's-eye view of marching Wehrmacht soldiers projected onto it. The projector is over a doorway, so people were forced to march with and over the soldiers. Loudspeakers in the door frame play the sound of marching boots.

In the Bow to the Flag exhibit, the volume of the speakers embedded in this section of the flag is so soft that visitors must lean very close to hear the audio. They look as though they are bowing to the flag and so become an active part of the exhibition design. In the Bowl of Clichés space, the flag becomes virtual in a giant 'bowl'. Visitors can stir it like noodles in soup and bring to the surface words that represent Austrian stereotypes.

Opposite
The fluid forms represent changes in Austrian social dynamics. The idea of family has shifted over time. Today, life and work are not necessarily separate. Mobility and new technologies are part of every aspect of a house. The weaving, rising and falling, dynamic ribbon conveys these ideas.

Below
Typewriter keys were projected
onto this section of the flag's
path. Touching the keys
triggered audio explanations
of 'key words' dealing with the
post-war occupation of Austria.

Opposite
A section of the flag intersected
with flags of the Allied Powers
in the Second World War: the
UK, France, the United States of
America, and the Soviet Union.

DAZZLE: San Diego International Airport
Ueberall International

Location: San Diego, California, USA
Usage: Public space
Date: 2017

DAZZLE is an artwork that transforms the 490-metre (1,600-foot) façade from the newly developed Rental Car Center (RCC) at the San Diego International Airport into a public art installation. Dazzle camouflage was a type of ship concealment developed by Norman Wilkinson and used in the First and Second World Wars. The bold graphic elements are animated by colour-changing film. The work can be seen daily by many thousands of motorists on the adjacent Interstate 5 Freeway.

Ueberall teamed up with fellow artists Dan Goods and David Delgado from NASA's Jet Propulsion Labs to create DAZZLE, which features thousands of custom-developed autonomous dynamic tiles engineered and produced by E Ink Corporation. The DAZZLE pattern evolved in countless variations to create a balance between visual impact and an optimal distribution of the dynamic elements.

Opposite
A photo of the *FFS Gloire* in New York in 1944. The warship is painted in Dazzle camouflage.

Below
The Ueberall team animated sequences using natural shapes, such as clouds and patterns, similar to the Dazzle camouflage used in the First and Second World Wars.

Following
The individual panels animate in sequence across the building, creating a kinetic and ever-changing supergraphic experience.

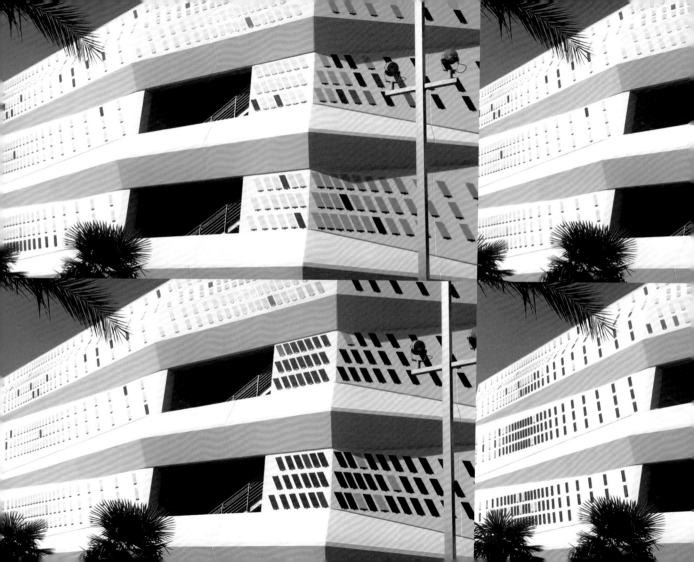

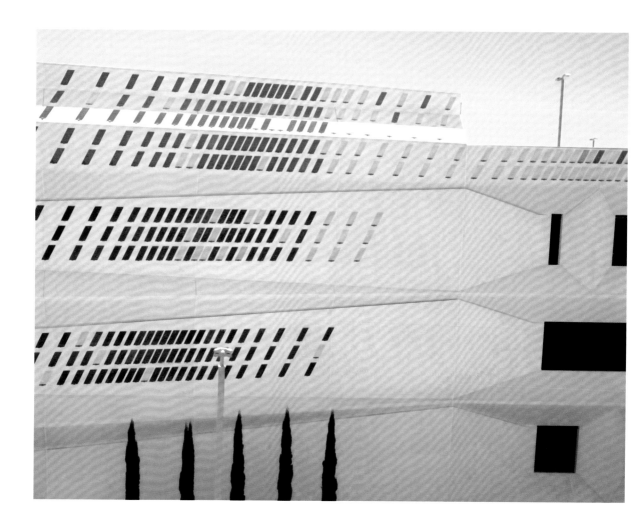

LinkedIn Australia Headquarters
THERE

Location: Sydney, New South Wales, Australia
Usage: Branded environment
Date: 2015

THERE's solution for LinkedIn's Australian headquarters was to create a series of branded experiential graphic features that would be uniquely Australian. The programme has a Sydney-centric feel and presents LinkedIn's global values and culture to an international audience of visitors.

The key to the solution was to localize LinkedIn's well-established brand assets, providing both regional and international recognition. Starting with the LinkedIn symbol, the designers created a three-dimensional, super-sized free-standing logo covered in blue-toned flip flops. The LinkedIn sign is now often used as a social photo opportunity for visitors and employees.

The beach theme led to 'paddle pop' sticks for wayfinding signage, custom beach-inspired amenities iconography, and coastal staff engagement feature walls.

Opposite
A detail of the flip-flop version of the LinkedIn logo

Below
The flip-flop sign references Sydney's beach culture and transforms the LinkedIn logo into a uniquely Australian icon.

Following
The dynamic typographic map depicts Sydney's coastline with LinkedIn branded colours and visual cues. A surfboard and longboard shorts indicate a toilet sign.

319

The Field Guide to Supergraphics

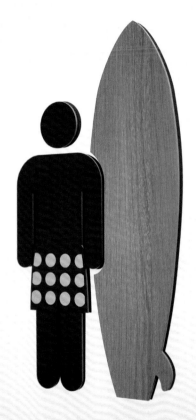

The Field Guide to Supergraphics

Luz Nas Vielas
Boa Mistura

Location: São Paulo, Brazil
Usage: Public space
Date: 2014

Boa Mistura is a multidisciplinary team of artists whose work all began with graffiti. The group formed in late 2001 in Madrid, Spain. They work mainly in public spaces on projects in South Africa, USA, UK, Mexico, Norway, Cuba, Colombia, or Panama. Boa Mistura's project Luz Nas Vielas (Light in the Alleyways) in Vila Brasilândia, São Paulo, is part of Boa Mistura's Crossroads series: a number of participatory urban art interventions devised to modify disadvantaged communities using art as a tool for change and inspiration.

For two weeks, the Boa Mistura team lived in Vila Brasilândia, hosted by the Gonçalves family, which gave the group direct contact with the community. After preliminary studies and analysis, they identified the project space as the narrow and winding streets that connected two neighbourhoods. The residents actively participated, painting words in parallax that translate as: 'Beauty', 'Stability', 'Love', 'Sweetness', and 'Pride'.

Below and opposite
The residents and Boa Mistura chose
the concepts for the murals. After
completing the first phase of the project,
Boa Mistura returned to Brasilândia and
added two new words to the project,
'Poetry' and 'Magic'.

323

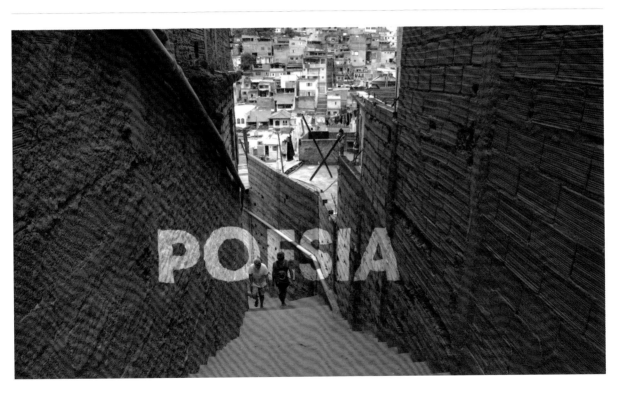

Opposite, below, and following
The residents of the
neighbourhood worked with Boa
Mistura to complete the painting.

Manchester School of Art
Anthony Burrill Typographic Workshop

Location: Manchester, England
Usage: Public space
Date: 2015

For a typographic workshop entitled 'Picture fun makes me happy ok' at the Manchester School of Art, Anthony Burrill focused on typography in an urban landscape. Using a construction wall as the canvas, Burrill assigned each student one letter. The students then used that letterform and worked with a simple grid to produce a semi-abstract form. Burrill encouraged the students to be as expressive and free as possible, exploring the abstract nature of typography and pushing the letterforms as much as possible.

One morning was spent designing the letterforms on paper. In the afternoon, students worked collaboratively to paint the letterforms by hand onto the wooden panels of the neighbouring building site. The focus was a hands-on analogue workshop. The intention was to encourage the students to create work by hand, explore letterforms, leave their laptops behind, and integrate experimental work into the physical urban landscape.

Opposite
The students worked with analogue tools (hands and paint) and worked collaboratively to create the composition in their own community.

Below and following
The project created an energetic and expressive dynamic in a monochromatic space.

Mattel Store

Collins

Location: Shanghai, China
Usage: Retail
Date: 2009

Ruth Handler created the Barbie doll in 1958 to help young girls believe they could become anything. In China, where female empowerment is growing in urban centres, women fell in love with the iconic toy with no overt marketing. Barbie represented the most desirable ideas in Western culture: self-determination and self-creation. Based on the strategy 'Inspire Aspiration', Collins created The House of Barbie.

On each floor, visitors could interact with the brand, customize dolls, design outfits, and dream. Every visitor received a Barbie Passport and earned stamps for engaging in different activities throughout the store. Collecting stamps unlocked passes to 'Barbie Nights' at the city's museums, ballet, and cultural institutions. In the first ten days, 50,000 people visited the flagship store, while two million people visited annually, until the store's closure in 2011.

Below
Ascending a large spiral staircase, visitors could view Barbie's varied careers through history.

Opposite and following
The House of Barbie was a colourful, six-storey pageant dedicated to Barbie and the mission of the brand: girl empowerment.

Below

At the Barbie spa, visitors could have hair styled and nails done while sampling the line of Barbie beauty products.

Opposite

Materials and graphic forms covered most surfaces of the store, including the glossy flower patterns, which were unapologetically feminine.

Planned Parenthood
Pentagram

Location: New York, New York, USA
Usage: Branded environment
Date: 2017

For over a hundred years, Planned Parenthood has fought for reproductive health and rights, championing the idea that women should have the information and care they need to live strong, healthy lives and to manage their fertility. Pentagram's Paula Scher and her team designed a large-scale installation that spotlights the dynamic history of this remarkable organization. The mural at Planned Parenthood's new national headquarters remixes graphics from a century of ephemera created by Planned Parenthood, capturing its dedication to caring, education, and activism.

The designers collaborated with the project architect, Juan Matiz of Matiz Architecture and Design, to integrate the graphics in a high-profile location in the offices. In addition to the installation, Scher placed smaller murals on walls throughout large conference rooms and other meeting spaces. The mural is a colourful collage composed of artefacts from a century of various initiatives – a mix of newspaper ads, instructional posters from clinics, protest posters, pins, photos of protests, and other historical material from the Planned Parenthood archive. The installation acknowledges the important role that activism and posters, placards, symbols, and other graphics have played in garnering support.

Opposite
The main mural is about 9 metres (30 feet) high and ascends through a three-storey staircase at the centre of the headquarters.

Opposite

Grassroots activists created many of the designs, and the mural is a tribute to their impact on the movement for reproductive rights.

Below

To create the mural, Scher and her designers researched historical images. The original images were of varying age and quality, so the team digitized the pieces to assemble the collage.

Following

The mural is made up of layers of vinyl wall covering, creating a three-dimensional effect, with acrylic forms cut out and mounted on the surface.

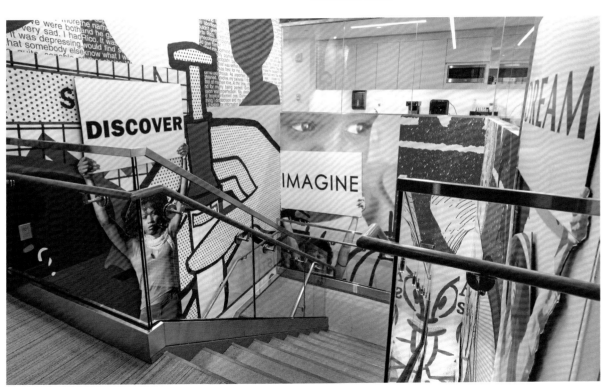

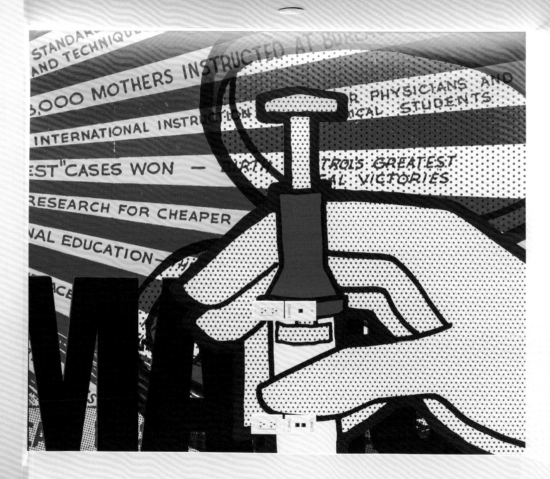

Qinhu Wetland National Park
TRIAD Berlin

Location: Qinhu, China
Usage: Exhibition
Date: 2011

China has begun to realize that environmental pollution due to rapid urban and industrial growth constitutes a major problem. The visitor experience centre of Qinhu Wetland National Park represents new directions in communicating the idea of sustainability. It makes ecology a topic relevant to the future of China and contributes to a change of thinking in Chinese society.

The Qinhu Wetland National Park is located in the Yangtze River Delta in the Chinese province of Jiangsu. The park is a 30-hectare (74-acre) wetland area being restored to its natural state. TRIAD Berlin developed the experience-orientated visitor centre that particularly aims at stimulating the younger generation's understanding and appreciation of sustainability and ecological issues.

On three levels and with a total floor space of 4,500 square metres (48,000 square feet), the visitor centre allows guests to visualize the biological and ecological characteristics of the wetland area. The narrative of the graphics moves from small to big. Large-scale images and text present the animals and plants of the Qinhu region and expand to cover global ecological issues. During the tour, visitors are virtually accompanied by a magpie, a bird that represents luck in China and is also featured in the emblem of Qinhu.

Opposite
Aimed at a younger audience, the interactive elements and encompassing images create a transition between the urban civilization and the national park, with its inhabitants and wonders. Projections and videos show the seasons reflected through several perspectives.

Below
Fireflies are simulated in a room
with black light and large-scale
projections of the night in the
wetland environment.

Opposite
Fixed imagery and projections
create the environment for a flock
of birds in flight.

Royal Shakespeare Company
Vic Lee

Location: Stratford-Upon-Avon, England
Usage: Branded environment
Date: 2016

The Rialto Bridge is a significant structure serving as a thoroughfare for the Swan Theatre and main building of the Royal Shakespeare Company. The Company engaged Vic Lee and asked for a design to celebrate the development of the architecture of the Royal Shakespeare Company, and reference Shakespeare's works.

Lee created a deep red-and-black mural, painted on the walls and ceiling, with text, visual references, insider humour, and iconography specific to the Shakespeare audience. A window and individual peep holes interrupted the intricate forms and revealed historical references. Both of these devices reinforce the concept of a proscenium, making the world a theatre stage.

Below, opposite, and following
The mural weaves together multiple historical, artistic, cultural, and architectural elements. The intricate forms invite the viewer to slow down and examine each part.

349

Somos Luz
Boa Mistura

Location: El Chorrillo, Panama City, Panama
Usage: Public space
Date: 2013

In the early twentieth century, El Chorrillo was a neighbourhood of fishermen and wooden houses. This changed on 20 December 1989, when the neighbourhood was razed during the bombings of the US invasion. In 1991, the current concrete tenement buildings of the neighbourhood were built, creating overcrowded conditions.

Today, El Chorrillo is associated with juvenile delinquency, gangs, and crime, giving it the reputation as one of Panama City's most dangerous neighbourhoods. However, the team of artists at Boa Mistura found friendly and wonderful people here who opened their houses to them and engaged with their project.

Somos Luz ('We are Light') is the message Boa Mistura painted across fifty of the apartments at the Begonia I building in El Chorrillo. The spirit and identity of the neighbourhood inspired the design of the graphics. The starting point was a colour grid, from which each occupant painted an area that he/she defined as his/her exterior space. The residents also painted the facade, corridors, and stairwells. This created abstract colour compositions that come alive when residents hang out laundry, or when someone looks out from the balcony.

The grid of colour blocks combine to create a typographic message. The collaborative process made apparent the connections between neighbours. The message, 'We Are Light' reminds each occupant and visitor that every person is invaluable, regardless of his or her economic status or geographic location.

Opposite and following
Boa Mistura's goal with the project complements part of their overall mission: to create urban art as a tool for encouraging the local residents of disadvantaged communities.

Sony Music Timeline

Alex Fowkes

Location: London, England
Usage: Branded environment
Date: 2012

Emma Pike (Vice President, Industry Relations for Sony Music) commissioned Alex Fowkes to design a graphic installation documenting Sony Music's 125-year history. The brief was to bring the inspiration of Sony's music into the heart of the building and make the office space live and breathe the company's incredible musical legacy.

Fowkes's solution was to design the Sony Music Timeline that runs throughout the central atrium of Sony's open plan offices. The timeline features nearly 1,000 artists signed to Sony Music, from 1887 to the present day. It covers over 150 square metres (1,600 square feet) of wall space, comprising fifty-four columns of typography, each over 2 metres (6.5 feet) tall. Organized by decade, the wall features artists' names and key developments in technology, musical formats, and corporate history. Fowkes's illustrative and expressive typography creates a sophisticated and definite solution, repeatedly inviting the viewer to discover something new.

Opposite

Multiple typefaces, primarily monochromatic, and on a rigid grid, create the multilayered murals. The materials are vinyl cut with a Computer Numerical Control router, a computer-controlled tool used to route and cut a range of materials, from vinyl to metal.

Below

Each column presents information from one decade. There are fifty-four columns. The secondary red colour is used sparingly to maintain harmony.

Following

The density of information serves as a branding element that reinforces Sony Music's position in the history of music and its commitment to artists and new technologies.

Terranova
Alex Fowkes

Location: Barcelona, Spain
Usage: Retail, wayfinding
Date: 2017

Terranova invited Fowkes to design the signage and environmental graphics for their flagship shop in Spain, located in the heart of Barcelona's Gothic Quarter. The goal was to create a welcoming and approachable persona with the analogue graphics, and to incorporate the same aesthetic on the oversized LCD panels throughout the ground floor. Fowkes designed a series of colourful murals and heartfelt greetings alongside the functional wayfinding system to 'express the whole of the Terranova world as well as possible'. The shop interior features restored exposed walls, period paintings and floors, wood coverings, and golden stuccos spread across three floors.

Fowkes hand-painted seventeen murals and the navigational signage on the walls and ceilings of the shop. The result is a necessary and expressive typographic language that rejuvenates the space and provides a clear branded experience. He incorporates a *trompe l'œil* effect with flat graphic forms and typography on acrylic panels. While the overall effect is a 'mash-up' of colour and typography, the system retains a simple and consistent palette, creating harmony.

Opposite and following
Upbeat statements reinforce the shop's optimistic and energetic spirit. Multiple sections of the store merge *trompe l'œil* and two-dimensional graphics.

Opposite
Black-and-white type on clear acrylic panels displays the wayfinding signage. These float off the wall, creating shadows and three-dimensional effects. Fowkes painted directions to the denim area on the walls and ceiling of the escalators.

Left
The furniture, materials and surface colors integrate with the graphic colour palette.

Paul Taboure
ECD THERE
Interview

Did you study architecture or graphic design in school?
I studied graphic design, but was fascinated by the permanence and longevity of graphic and signage in the built environment.

What was the first project you did that involved large environmental graphics?
We worked on a new community leisure centre in Sydney that needed a design concept to appeal to a largely non-English speaking audience. Our approach was based on 'images speak a thousand words', so we developed a pictogram inspired design solution. This was our first exposure to large supergraphics and ignited our passion for creating engaging branded experiences for the built environment.

How have your process and ideas about environmental graphics changed since then?
Over the last ten years, we have developed inch-wide, mile-deep expertise in environmental graphics and signage. This means we have developed methodologies and processes to unearth opportunities and mitigate project risk. Materiality, legibility, compliance, durability are all considered for each and every project opportunity.

What was the most challenging environmental design project you've done?
Almost every project we work on is 'the most' challenging. We foster a curiosity to know more, do more. Most recently, we were commissioned to design an eighty-by-nine-metre building facade . This louvre-style graphic placemaking design adopted a nautical theme and required collaboration with industrial designers and facade engineers to realize our design.

What is your favourite project you have done?
My favourite project is an interpretive building facade design we completed for a Swiss bankers' private art gallery in ACT in Australia, along with Fender Katsalidis Architects. We designed an interpretive timber facade inspired by the riverways, where the timber had been sourced (from a disassembled local bridge.)

If you had the chance to redo a project now, what would you do differently?

We never look back at projects, because we are always too busy working on the next project. We love a challenge and, along with it, the constraint that 'time and budget' puts on a project and how it influences its outcome.

What is your dream environmental graphics project?

An airport wayfinding, a new city wayfinding, a new mega-campus workplace.

Where do you find inspiration for this type of work?

Our inspiration comes from many places ... art, architecture, film, and social channels. Over the years of deepening my expertise, we have developed a creative rigour and methodology to ensure a great creative outcome every time. A fine combination of discovery workshops, visual references, sketches, and working renders all helps create a visual representation that enables our clients to understand the vision.

What is your favourite example of environmental graphics (supergraphics) by someone other than yourself, or historically, and why?

I personally love the works of Otl Aicher and the signage system he implemented for the 1972 Munich Olympics.

What's the best piece of advice for a young designer interested in pursuing environmental graphics as a career?

The best piece of advice I would give a young designer is not to be constrained by your current ability – think beyond, and then work with collaborators who help bring your vision to life.

Alex Fowkes
Interview

What was the first project you did that involved large environmental graphics? How did you approach the problem and solve it?

My first environmental graphics project was my first ever project as a freelancer and also the largest and best-known project to date: the Sony Music Timeline, the project that catapulted my career forward and put me where I am today. I approached it with a simple concept and repeated the idea throughout the whole project; it proved pretty successful. I approached the problem like any other design problem, in stages. Initially, it meant looking at the content and then also looking at the building itself and trying to work out how best to combine the two.

I took the information about how the employees used the building to influence the flow of the artwork. With something as big as the Sony Timeline – at over 150 square metres (1,600 square feet) – I knew the production and installation needed to be as simple as possible, too.

How has your process with environmental graphics changed since then?

I tend to use lots of mixed media now. Whereas before I was only confident with vinyl or markers, now I use a mixture and increasingly hand-paint my murals with sign-painting brushes and paint. This only helps to give my work a more professional finish. The size of my murals has decreased because of this approach, but now I'm trying to combine painting, vinyl, and illustration in my installations.

What was the most challenging environmental design project you've done?

There are challenges to every project, and usually they are different. The biggest problem in the Sony Timeline was the sheer amount of digital type design I needed to do, which ended up being over eight weeks straight. The challenge with Terranova was trying to create murals while working in a building that was still in construction stages. At the end of construction, we had to work around the visual merchandisers to design. Other challenges can be like trying to master a certain technique with a brush, or trying to work out how to access the walls you want to use. Every project has a challenge, and staying calm and thinking logically often benefits me.

What is your favourite project you've done?

My favourite is usually my most recent. That tends to be because I've tried to use a new technique or approach to help push my work. My latest large-scale project was for Terranova, a three-storey retail store in the heart of Barcelona. I was lucky enough to be invited to paint the whole store in three weeks. We ended up with seventeen separate murals and an entire signage system designed in that time.

If you had the chance to redo a project now, what would you do differently?

Every project is a learning curve. Some I would do entirely differently; some I would add or change certain aspects. I think that's true for anyone. If you are trying to progress your work and practice, then being progressive is the best way to be. I wouldn't choose to do anything differently in my design. There are a hundred things I'd like to do, but I try not to look at previous projects and wish I had done something differently. It's all part of a journey; the biggest thing is to recognize the things you would change and then try to apply those in future projects.

What is your dream environmental graphics project?

I'd love to collaborate with a bunch of mural artists to create one huge mural; perhaps we split it into five-metre sections. A different designer would design each section, but the whole piece would remain coherent, with one message. That would be kind of cool. For me, it's not about new or big clients; it's about progressing myself and my work more than it is about working for huge companies. Collaborating with others is high on my list of things to accomplish at the moment. I would quite like to paint at some skate- or snowboard-related festivals or events though.

Below
Alex Fowkes painting the
Urban Outfitters Nottingham
exterior mural.

Where do you find inspiration for this type of work?

I tend to be inspired by the environment or space. I like the work to be as customized to the space as possible. The best way to achieve this is to use the room's or building's features to dictate and influence your design.

What is your favourite example of environmental graphics (supergraphics) by someone other than yourself, and why?

I love Gemma O'Brien's work. She does some awesome typographic and illustrative murals. Her recent murals have an enormous amount of detail flowing in and out of them. They make me want to put more illustration in my work. Other huge environmental graphic examples would be the comedy carpet in Blackpool, designed by Gordon Young and Why Not Associates. I love the scale and interaction with this installation. Allowing the public to get involved and enjoy the project is a significant aspect.

What's the best piece of advice for a young designer interested in pursuing environmental graphics as a career?

Don't be afraid to trust your gut instinct; it can be quite daunting to enter a blank space and try to work out how to put an installation together. The best thing, as always, is to break it down into stages, get your ideas gathered, and mock things up to try and get a feel for how things work.

Credits

Alex Fowkes
Sony Music Timeline
Designer: Alex Fowkes
Client: Sony Music
Photography: Rob Antill
Terranova
Designer: Alex Fowkes
Client: Terranova
Photography: Joe Wheatley

Anna Taratiel
Art es Part
Designer: Anna Taratiel (OVNI)
Client: Nova Electra School
Parts 'n Pieces
Designer: Anna Taratiel (OVNI)
Client: Reflexo on Urban Art

Anthony Burrill
Manchester University,
Anthony Burrill typography workshop
Designers: Holly Bennett, Joe Britch, Brad
Dickinson, Mark DeMuth, Jake Halsam and
Josh Williams.

ART+COM Studios AG
Das Neue Österreich
Architect: Martin Kohlbauer
Creative Consultant: Wolfgang Luser
Location: Vienna, Austria
New BMW Museum
Design: ART+COM Studios, ATELIER BRÜCKNER
GmbH,
Idee und Klang, Integral Ruedi Baur, G-LEC Europe
GmbH, ICT AG, MKT AG
Architect: ATELIER BRÜCKNER GmbH, Idee und
Klang, Integral Ruedi Baur, G-LEC Europe GmbH,
ICT AG, MKT AG, Graphics I
Client: BMW Group

ArtCenter Designmatters and
Instituto de Diseño
Fresh Eyes Cuba: Workshop
Designers: ArtCenter Designmatters and Instituto
Superior de Diseño (ISDI), Havana, Cuba
Fresh Eyes Cuba Publication Book Design:
Tracey Shiffman with Ricardo Imperial and
Simona Szabados, Shiffman & Kohnke

ATELIER BRÜCKNER GmbH
Magic Box, State Grid Pavilion
Media Planning: Medienprojekt p2
Spatial Media Design: TAMSCHICK MEDIA+SPACE
Sound Composition: Idee und Klang
Architecture: CCDI, Shanghai
Photography: Roland Halbe

Boa Mistura
Life
Design: Boa Mistura: Javier Serrano Guerra,
Juan Jaume Fernández, Pablo Ferreiro Mederos,
Pablo Purón Carrillo, Rubén Martín de Lucas
Photography: Adrián Suárez aka Mr Lausiv,
Good Mix.
Luz Nas Vielas
Design: Boa Mistura: Javier Serrano Guerra,
Juan Jaume Fernández, Pablo Ferreiro Mederos,
Pablo Purón Carrillo, Rubén Martín de Lucas
Photography: Boa Mistura
Somos Luz
Design: Boa Mistura: Javier Serrano Guerra,
Juan Jaume Fernández, Pablo Ferreiro Mederos,
Pablo Purón Carrillo, Rubén Martín de Lucas
Client: Bienal Del Sur
Photography: Boa Mistura

Büro Uebele
Adidas Gym, Germany
Designers: Carolin Himmel
Andreas Uebele
Interior Design: ZieglerBürg, Büro für Gestaltung,
Prof. Diane Ziegler
Architect: AGPS Architecture
Client: Adidas AG
Photography: Brigida González
Stuttgart Region Chamber of Commerce
Project Team: Angela Klasar, Andreas Uebele
Colour: Harald F. Müller
Architect: Wulf Architekten
Client: Stuttgart Region Chamber of Commerce
Photography: Brigida Gonzalez

Collins
Mattel Store
Designers: Brian Collins, Charles Rudy, Richard
Bates, Shannon Mullen, Kapono Chung, and Ogilvy
& Mather
Architect: Slade Architects

Craig and Karl
HERE AFTER
Designers; Craig & Karl
Client: White City
Photography: Jamie M Smith
Sweet as One
Designers; Craig & Karl
Client: AllRightsReserved
Photography: AllRightsReserved

ECE Architecture
Grafton Car Park
Design: ECE Architecture, Creative Forager,
Ricky Also

EGG Office
GLG Global Headquarters
Architect: Clive Wilkinson Architects
Photography: David Wakely Photography
Macquarie Bank Ltd Headquarters
Designers: Christian Daniels, Jonathan Mark
Copywriter: Jane Bogart
Project Manager and Copywriter: Kate Tews
Architect: Clive Wilkinson Architects
Fabricators: Wizardry Imaging & Signs,
Cunneen Signs
Photography: Shannon McGrath

Franklyn
Sotheby's
Designers: Michael Freimuth, Patrick Richardson,
Kenneth Lian; Sandra Burch,
Ola Kapusto, and Jeanette Diaz
Clients: Taubman Family
and Sotheby's
Photography: Kendall Mills

Gensler
Project Colour Corp, Cambridge Elementary
Designers: Fabiola Catalan, Sergio Mondragon,
Alison Haynes, Paul Choi, Litha Zuber, Kathryn
Moore, Emily Hall, Robert Shurell, Doug Wittnebel,
Prasert Wiwatyukhan
Client: Project Colour Corps
Photography: Jennifer Chaney

Graham Hanson Design
**Panasonic North America Headquarters
Building**
Designers: Graham Hanson, Adam Tanski,
Mayuko Soga, Pilar Freire, Beatriz Castro,
Allison Christensen
Client: Panasonic
Photography: Deborah Kushma

Graphéine
Lyon–Saint Exupéry Airport
Design: Graphéine

Ian Lynam Design
Google Japan
Ian Lynam Designer: Ian Lynam
Architect: Klein Dytham Architecture
Photography: Koichi Torimura and Toshiki Senoue

J.Mayer.H. und Partner, Architekten
Rapport: Experimental Spatial Structures
Design firm: J.Mayer.H and Juergen Mayer H.
Project architect: Jesko Malkolm Johnsson-Zahn
Project team: Wilko Hoffmann
Courtesy: Magnus Müller
Photographers: J.Mayer.H., Jesko Malkolm
Johnsson-Zahn, and Ludger Paffrath

Johnson Banks Design Ltd
Brighton Dome
Designers: Michael Johnson, Julia Woollams
Signage consultant: Whybrow Signing Consultants
Location: Brighton, England
Ravensbourne
Architect: Foreign Office Architects
Tile Pattern: Roger Penrose
Signage implementation: Whybrow
Interior photography: Jan Masny

Kuhlmann Leavitt, Inc.
Saint Louis Public Library
Designers: Deanna Kuhlmann-Leavitt,
Jill Berkbuegler-Lembke, and Krista Lawson
Architect: Cannon Design
Photography: Gregg Goldman

Latitude Group
QV Melbourne
Design: Latitude Group

LucienneRoberts+
Wonderlab
Designers: Lucienne Roberts, David Shaw,
John McGill
Architect: Ab Rogers Design
Photography: Luke Hayes

Mother
Client: Wired Magazine

P-06 Atelier
Lisbon Bikeway
Design directors: Nuno Gusmão and Pedro Anjos
Designers: Giuseppe Greco, Miguel Matos,
Pedro Schreck
Landscape Design: GLOBAL and
Arquitectura Paisagista
Clients: APL (Lisbon Seaport), EDP
(Energy of Portugal), and Lisbon City Hall
Photography: João Silveira Ramos and P-06 Atelier
SKIN – Pavilion of Knowledge
Design Director: Nuno Gusmão
Designers: Giuseppe Greco, Vera Sacchetti,
and Miguel Matos
Photography: Ricardo Gonçalves

Pentagram
13-17 East 54th Street
Partner/Art Director/Designer: Paula Scher
Associates/Designers: Drew Freeman
Designer: Nikola Gottschick
Photography: James Shanks
The Public Theater
Partner/Art Director/Designer: Paula Scher
Associates/Designers: Drew Freeman and
Courtney Gooch
Designer: Rafael Medina
Architect: Ennead Architects
Photography: Peter Mauss/Esto
Planned Parenthood
Partner/Art Director/Designer: Paula Scher
Associates/Designer: Courtney Gooch

Poulin + Morris Inc.
Novo Nordisk North American Headquarters
Designer: Richard Poulin
Client: Novo Nordisk
Architect: Granum A/I
Photography: Jeff Totaro
BRIC
Designer: Richard Poulin
Photography: Deborah Kushma

R2 Design
Vai com Deus (Go with God)
Designers: Lizá Ramalho and Artur Rebelo
Photography: Fernando Guerra and Sérgio Guerra

Stockholm Design Lab
Modern Museet
Client: Moderna Museet

Studio Hinrichs
Boudin Bread
Designers: Kit Hinrichs, Laura Scott,
Myrna Newcomb
Architect: EHDD
Photography: Cesar Rubio

Studio Matthews
Mad Campus
Designers: Kristine Matthews, Katherine Wong
Photographer: Boyd Hart, Cassie Kingler,
Kristine Matthews

THERE
LinkedIn Australia
Executive Creative Director: Paul Taboure
Head Of Environments: Charlie Bromley
Designers: Justine Lesmana and Christina Maricic
Project Manager: Danielle Senecky
Architect: Woods Bagot
Photography: Steve Brown
Rabobank
Executive Creative Director: Paul Taboure
Head Of Environments: Charlie Bromley
Designers: Scott McNamara, Christina Maricic
Project Manager: Danielle Senecky
Industrial Design: Vert Design
Architect: Geyer Sydney
Fabricators: Wizardry Imaging & Signs
Photography: Steve Brown

3M Australia Headquarters
Designers: Paul Taboure, Simon Hancock,
Jon Zhu, and Sinead McDevitt
Architect: Colliers Project Services
Client: 3M Australian
Fabrication: Spike Design and Infracraft
Photography: Simon Hancock
Google Singapore
Interior Design: HASSELL
Project Manager: Cushman & Wakefield

Thonik
Hyundai City Outlet
Photography: Nicole Marnati and Kim Jaewoo

Tongji DESIS Lab
Open Your Space
Design: Tongji DESIS (Design for Social Innovation
and Sustainability) Lab

TRIAD Berlin
Qinhu Wetland National Park
Desigers: Gabriele Karau, Volker Klingenburg,
Ulli Koller, Pingting Wang, Anja Osswald,
Heike Czygan, Hajo Gawins, Daniel Scheidgen,
Ole Bahrmann, and Eva-Marie Heinrich
Photography: TRIAD Berlin

Ueberall
DAZZLE: San Diego International Airport
Artists: Nik Hafermaas, Dan Goods,
David Delgado, Jeano Erforth
Animation and Programming: Ivan Cruz
Engineering and Fabrication: E Ink Corporation
Project Management: Jeano Erforth,
Ueberall International
Images: Rick Williams, Nik Hafermaas

University of Kansas Department of Design
University of Kansas Design Week
Lead Designers: Patrick Blanchard, Lucas Nelson,
Triana Thompson
Poster Design and Installation Assistants:
Chloe Hubler, Grace Cantril, and Mary Sniezek
Installation Assistants: Nick Manoogian,
Kevin Bower, Evan Tarry, and Zaira Torres
Photography: Triana Thompson, Patrick
Blanchard, and Lucas Nelson
Fabricators: Dimensional Innovations

Urbanite, a part of Frost*collective
CBA Darling Quarter
Designers: Carlo Giannasca, Henry Ellis-Paul,
Charlie Bromley, and Katie Bevin
Client: Commonwealth Bank of Australia (CBA)
Commonwealth Bank Offices,
Melbourne Call Centre
Designers: Charlie Bromley, Katie Bevin
Client: Commonwealth Bank of Australia (CBA)
Interior Architects: Davenport Campbell
Illustration: James Gulliver Hancock

Vanderbyl Design
HBF
Designers: Michael Vanderbyl, David Hard,
Peter Fishel
Teknion
Designers: Michael Vanderbyl, Peter Fishel

Vic Lee
Royal Shakespeare Company
Designer: Vic Lee
Client: Royal Shakespeare Company
Waltham Forest Council
Designer: Vic Lee
Client: Waltham Forest Council

Volume, Inc.
100 California
Designers: Adam Brodsley, Eric Heiman,
Bryan Bindloss, and Jon Hioki
Architect: Blitz
Photography: Mariko Reed
Bloomberg
San Francisco Tech Hub
Designers: Adam Brodsley, Eric Heiman,
Bryan Bindloss, Aine Coughlan, Paola Meraz
Bloomberg Design Lead:
Emanuela Frattini Magnusson
Client: Bloomberg
Architect: IwamotoScott
Photography: Bruce Damonte and Gabe Branbury

Index

About the Author

Sean Adams is the Executive Director of the Graphic Design Graduate Programme at ArtCenter. He is the founder of The Office of Sean Adams, a design studio. In 2007, Adams founded the online publication, Burning Settlers Cabin. He is an on-screen author for LinkedIn Learning/lynda.com.

Adams is the only two term AIGA national president in organization's 100 year history. In 2014, Adams was awarded the AIGA Medal, the highest honour in the profession. He currently is on the editorial board and writes for Design Observer. Previously, Adams was a founding partner of AdamsMorioka. He lives in Los Angeles, California.

Back Cover

Top left
Vai com Deus (Go with God)
Lisbon, Portugal
R2 Design
2017

Top right
Somos Luz
El Chorrillo, Panama City, Panama
Boa Mistura
2013

Centre left
Adidas Gym, Germany
Herzogenaurach, Germany
Büro Uebele
2011

Centre right
HERE AFTER
London, England
Craig & Karl
2017

Bottom left
Planned Parenthood
New York, New York, USA
Pentagram
2017

Bottom right
Moderna Museet
Stockholm, Sweden
Stockholm Design Lab
2013